I0526192

BATTLE SCARS

By Kevin O'Hagan

Grosvenor House
Publishing Limited

All rights reserved
Copyright © Kevin O'Hagan, 2018

The right of Kevin O'Hagan to be identified as the author of this
work has been asserted in accordance with Section 78
of the Copyright, Designs and Patents Act 1988

The book cover picture is copyright to Inmagine Corp LLC

This book is published by
Grosvenor House Publishing Ltd
Link House
140 The Broadway, Tolworth, Surrey, KT6 7HT.
www.grosvenorhousepublishing.co.uk

This book is sold subject to the conditions that it shall not, by way of
trade or otherwise, be lent, resold, hired out or otherwise circulated
without the author's or publisher's prior consent in any form of binding or
cover other than that in which it is published and
without a similar condition including this condition being imposed
on the subsequent purchaser.

This book is a work of fiction. Any resemblance to
people or events, past or present, is purely coincidental.

A CIP record for this book
is available from the British Library

ISBN 978-1-78623-179-6

About the Author

Kevin has been a well-known and highly respected Martial Artist worldwide for 40 years. At present, he runs his own training premises in his home town of Bristol named 'Impact Gym'. He also manages his own website www.kevinohagan.com

Kevin is now semi-retired and spends most of his spare time writing and travelling. He still teaches privately and on the seminar circuit.

He is a husband, father and Grandfather.

This is his first fictional novel.

Dedication

For my beloved Tina. Thank you for your unfailing support, belief and love.

Acknowledgements

I would like to firstly thank my wonderful daughter Lauren for proof reading my original manuscript and lending her advice and suggestions. Love you always.

My wife Tina for giving me the time and space to write when needed.

I would also like to thank my friend Sandy Geddes for his knowledge, advice and insight to the paratroop regiment. Your help was invaluable.

Also Radio 2 for being my constant background companion when some days were long and tough to get my thoughts and ideas down in a readable order.

I would also like to mention my spiritual writing home of Lanzarote in the Canary Islands were much of this books ideas and rough manuscript was first written by hand over the course of our yearly visits to the sun, sea and tranquillity have been an inspiration.

My 40 plus year journey in the world of the Martial arts as student, coach, competitor and Instructor provided me with ideal insight into the psychology and physical skills of the fight sequences in this book.

This story, its characters, names, businesses, organisations, places and events are either used fictitiously or a product of my imagination although many of my life experiences and people I have crossed paths with over the years have provided me with inspiration and source for my plot. Any resemblance to actual people living or dead, events or locales is entirely coincidental.

Thank you to all my family and friends for giving me the spark to write this book.

The Present

Tony Slade flinched as the car backfired. He instinctively reached inside his jacket for the gun, cursing under his breath as he slopped some of his coffee onto the table. He reached for a serviette to wipe it up and glanced furtively around the coffee shop to see if anybody had noticed him nearly jump out of his skin.

He was edgy. She said she would be here at 7.30am. She was late. They had no time to waste. They would have to get moving soon. The clock was ticking against them and it was only a matter of time until they would be found.

Tony sat in the *Alpha* coffee house in the city of Bristol in the South West of England. It was a lovely part of the country, but he wasn't here for pleasure.

He had been in Bristol for over nearly three weeks. *It had been far too long. Much longer than he had intended. He should have been out of the country by now. Away from immediate danger.*

He had been coming into the *Alpha* most mornings for breakfast. He liked it here. It felt safe and unobtrusive. Yet, this morning, he was nervy because she was coming. He sipped his coffee. Americano, black, with no sugar. It was good. He liked his coffee.

The *Alpha* coffee house chain had sprung up in recent times and was trying to compete with the 'big boys' such as Starbucks and Costa. They were holding their own. Tony thought they served the best Americano. He also liked the staff. They were polite and friendly, and had got to know him and his order. If they were overly busy, they would tell him to take a seat and they would bring it over to him. *A nice touch*. But Tony was also getting worried that this made him a little predictable. *Too easy to be identified if somebody came asking questions.*

He had to stay focused. It had been a long journey to this point. He was almost there. *Where was she?*

He had come to Bristol to meet a friend and a useful contact. He hadn't planned to be here for so long, but there had been problems.

In the brief time he had been here, he had grown fond of the city. He was staying in his friend's small flat, a stone's throw away from Brunel's famous Suspension Bridge and a short walk to the zoological gardens. He loved the historic harbour side that housed another of Brunel's ingenious creations, the mighty SS Great Britain. Launched in 1843, she was at that time the largest iron steam ship in the world, and in 1845, she became the first ship of her kind to cross the Atlantic Ocean to New York in a record time of fourteen days. The harbourside was different to his home docklands in Tyneside. Bristol was a pleasant change and a million miles away from his troubled Northern roots. But that was in the past. It was time to think of the future. He glanced at his watch. *She said she would be here.*

As he took another sip of his coffee, his eyes surveyed the room. The shop was reasonably busy for a dull and damp November morning. A few older school children sat drinking hot chocolate and nibbling on muffins whilst noisily chatting about a programme they had watched on the television the previous evening. A businessman in a smart black suit sat at a table by the door sipping on a cup of tea as he tapped away on his laptop, and a couple of young women dressed in sports gear spoke in whispers over their lattes.

Tony turned his gaze to look out of the window next to where he was sat and watched the city slowly yawning into life. The traffic was beginning to build. Buses squelched to a halt by the many bus stops across the road, their tyres kicking up spray from the rain soaked tarmac. Groups of people trudged gloomily onto them, either taking a seat or jammed up together standing like sardines. They looked miserable, staring sullenly out of the steamed-up windows. All of them trapped in their own space bubbles. *Thinking about the week ahead of them and all the shit that would go with it, no doubt.*

Tony shook his head and smiled ruefully. How he longed for their boring and mundane lives. Part of him yearned to be one of those people out there rushing along, umbrellas held high against the driving rain heading for another day at the office.

If only his life was as simple and uncomplicated. A wife, 2.4 children and a mortgage. A nice semi-detached house with a flower garden and a barbecue. A Ford Focus in the garage. Down the pub on Saturday evening, a leg over Sunday morning and a roast dinner later. Magic. Now how ironic was that for a man like him.

No, Tony Slade never did anything the straightforward way in his life. His existence to date had been anything but conventional. As it stood, it wasn't going to get any better just yet. *Especially if Kenny Robbins and his cronies caught up with him.*

He took another sip of coffee. Damn, it was good. He then became aware of somebody watching him and turned to see the manageress Kim wiping down the tables nearby. He liked Kim. She was a grafter and ran the *Alpha* like clockwork. Tony estimated she was around forty. She had short blonde hair, stunning blue eyes and an eye-catching figure, even in her work attire.

As she approached his table, he noticed the little cut above her left eye was healing nicely. She smiled and said, "Good morning. You're an early bird again. Can't keep you away from the place, eh? Trouble sleeping, I bet?"

Tony laughed. "Oh, I sleep like a baby. The sleep of the innocent, you know."

"Oh really?" she laughed, "You are a bit of a mystery man, aren't you? I was only saying so to the rest of the staff yesterday."

Tony raised his eyebrows. "Didn't know I would be the topic of hot gossip around here. I am honoured." There was a brief awkward pause. "No mystery, pet. Just between jobs, that's all."

"What sort of work do you do then, if you don't mind me asking."

"Social worker," replied Tony, holding a deadpan face.

Kim's face broke into a radiant smile. "Yeah, okay. I believe you."

As she went to move away, Tony asked her how she was feeling after the recent incident.

"I am okay, I guess. It did shake me up at the time, but I have tried to forget about it and get on with things."

There had been an incident a few weeks ago.

Kim had been forced to sack a member of her staff. A guy whose name was Colin Crane. She had caught him red-handed stealing from the till. She had suspected for a while that he may have been doing this, but she couldn't prove it. That was until the end of an evening shift when she had come out from the stockroom to witness first hand Crane stuffing notes from the till into his coat pocket.

She had confronted him, and he had seemed mortified and apologetic. He begged her not to involve the police and against her better judgement, she had agreed, but only if he would leave the premises and not return.

Crane had pleaded with her not to dismiss him from the job and that he would never steal again, but Kim told him that he had to go.

He had meekly left and that seemed to be the end of things. But then, over the next few days, whenever she had answered the phone on the premises, on more than one occasion, she had been greeted with silence, but she sensed somebody was there on the other end of the line.

Then one evening, totally out of the blue, Colin Crane had come back into the *Alpha* and asked Kim for his job back. He told her he was desperate for money and needed to work. He told her he owed money to some people that weren't particularly nice.

Kim sympathised with him but refused him his job back. He then got angry and started hauling abuse at her. It had got heated until Kim had told him that she was going to call the police if he didn't go.

This seemed to do the trick and he walked off, but not before picking up an empty coffee mug from a table near the door and throwing it in Kim's direction. It had hit the wall next to her head and exploded into pieces. One of the pieces had cut Kim above the left eye. It hadn't been a serious wound, but it could have been a whole lot different if a piece of the broken china had gone into her eye.

Her co-workers urged her to tell the police, but she refused. She felt the sacking had probably hurt Crane enough without police involvement.

Since then, she hadn't seen Crane, but sometimes after locking up and leaving work, she had the sensation that she was being watched. It was all a little unnerving, but she was a grown woman. She could handle herself. She was also a blue belt in Brazilian Jujutsu. If Crane tried anything, she would choke his skinny ass out. That said, she hoped that he would not be around again.

Tony regarded her. "I can't say I can picture this Crane character. I know Tom and Melanie at the counter and the Polish girl, small, dark, attractive. Don't know her name."

"Janina," Kim replied, "You think she's attractive then?"

"Only in a fatherly sort of way, nothing more I assure you. Anyway, what about this Colin Crane?" Tony asked.

"You must have seen him working in here. You know, tall, geeky, wears glasses."

Tony looked puzzled. "Can't say I had the pleasure."

"I thought he was alright. How wrong can you be about a person?" Kim said.

Tony's face darkened. "He seems like an asshole to me. He could have put your eye out. Did you report him?"

Kim forced a smile. "Well, I told head office, but I don't know what will happen. After he threw the mug, he just walked out mumbling that he needed the job. I don't know if the mug was meant for me. He threw it in anger, I suppose. But I stuck to my guns. This is a busy and successful branch of *Alpha*. I have worked hard to build it up and I need the right people working for me with the same goals. At the end of the day, I get paid to make the big decisions as tough as they may be."

"Good for you, Kim. But if you take my advice, just be careful and keep an eye out. Like you said, it might be something and nothing, but in my experience, it's best to keep your guard up," Tony replied.

Kim threw up a mock salute. "Will do, Mr 'Social Worker'. I suppose you wouldn't want to tell me where you got all this good advice from?"

"When you're twenty-one."

Kim flashed Tony a stunning smile as she walked away.

He returned to his coffee. Women, he mused. Beautiful but complicated.

Tony returned to looking out of the window. It was still raining. It was a woman which had brought him to this point in his life. The woman he was now waiting for. She was his one bright light in an existence of darkness. *Where was she though?*

Today he felt too old for all this. He was jaded. His body ached, and his mind was tired. When most men of his age would be winding down, he was still out there walking where angels feared to tread. This was now his last chance to grab some happiness and peace of mind. But sometimes he did question at what cost.

Since meeting this woman, he had done a lot of soul-searching and looking back introspectively at his life.

As he continued to gaze out of the window, he let his mind drift back to another place in time to remember how his life started, and the pain, violence and darkness that had accompanied him on his journey to the present, sitting here waiting for the one woman he ever truly loved and waiting for the man who wanted to kill him...

CHAPTER ONE

The Past

Anthony James Slade came into this world on a bitterly cold January night in the Royal Victoria Infirmary, Newcastle on Tyne. He was a healthy 8 pounds 10 ounces.

He was the son of Frank and Jean Slade. His father had worked in the shipyards of Tyneside and his mother in a dressmaker's shop. They had lived a simple but contented life until around the time that Tony was five and his father lost his job.

Shipbuilding in the North went through a crisis in the 1960s due to an economic slump and jobs had to be cut. Frank Slade had worked for the mighty Swan Hunter shipyard that, from 1860 to their final closure in 1993, built 2,700 vessels. Swan Hunter was responsible for building many well-known ships, including the HMS Mauretania, HMS Edinburgh and HMS Ark Royal. Shipbuilding in the North East had been the life-blood of the community and Frank Slade took it hard when his job was gone.

He was a welder and a riveter. He was a proud man. But with no work and no longer the chief breadwinner, he tried to find solace in the bottle. This led to drunken

1

and violent mood swings that ended up with Jean Slade becoming a battered wife and eventually, the violence filtered down to young Tony.

They both lived in constant fear of Frank Slade. He was a big bear of a man with a barrel chest and hands like digger buckets. The slightest thing could trigger his mood swings. Jean Slade did her best to protect her son and usually ended up taking the brunt of her husband's anger.

Tony could recall countless times where his beautiful mother sported a black eye or had one of her arms in plaster. His stomach tightened as he vividly remembered a time his father had pushed her down the stairs. She broke her left arm and fractured two ribs. His father had bundled her into the car and drove to hospital. How he got there in his drunken state was anyone's guess. He dropped her at the door of the A&E department and told her to say she had fallen along the road over a curb stone. He threatened her that if she ever breathed a word of the truth, he would kill her. It wasn't the first or last time she would be visiting casualty.

Tony hated the life around him. He hated his father. He felt so helpless. Tony was too young and too small to do anything about it. Many a night he would cower under the blankets in his bed crying as he heard his father return from the pub and start a blazing row that would end up with his mother screaming in pain as she took another beating.

Tony hated the man with a passion.

If Tony had done something wrong, he would be dragged from his bed shivering in the cold and his father would take his heavy leather belt to his backside until he either drew blood or he ran out of breath through the exhaustion.

Tony would be left in a heap on the threadbare carpet of his bedroom whilst his father stumbled off in search of another drink.

When sleep finally claimed Frank Slade, his mother would appear sobbing quietly as she helped tend to her son's wounds and tucked him back up in bed. She never spoke a word. Even when Tony knew she was in terrible pain. She would kiss him gently on the cheek and leave the room.

Lying in the dark listening to his father's snoring echoing around the house, he vowed one day that he would get even with this man.

The hell of living with her violent husband was too much for Jean Slade to bear in the end. She began developing blinding migraines which finally resulted in a brain haemorrhage. She died in hospital when Tony was just 14 years old.

At last, she was at peace, but Tony's world had been torn apart. He had loved his mother so much. As he had got older, he had asked her on many occasions why she hadn't left his father. She always answered that underneath it all, he was a good man. He had just lost his way. He needs me. This, Tony could never understand. To put her life and his in danger for this monster was unforgivable. Whoever Frank Slade once had been was now well and truly gone. All Tony could see for as long as he could recall was a drunken and dangerous bully.

He went to his mother's funeral two weeks later. He remembered standing by the graveside with the rain pouring down on that dismal November morning two days before Tony's birthday. He knew there would be no celebrations.

The rain fell out of the grey sky continually like a big veil of tears. Tony just wanted to get away.

He remembered his father standing next to him shedding his crocodile tears for the assembled mourners. The callous bastard had been responsible for this. It sickened Tony to hear people giving him their condolences and Frank Slade snivelling what a wonderful wife and mother she had been and how could God have been so cruel to take her away from him.

On that grey and wet November morning, something changed inside young Tony Slade. He knew deep down that now that his mother was gone, he was going to become the main punching bag for his father's angry, drunken outbursts. He made up his mind that this wasn't going to happen.

Whilst everybody after the funeral traipsed into the small community centre built onto the church for the wake, Tony slipped away. His father wouldn't even notice that he was gone after he sank his first few shots of whiskey. He knew in his mind what he had to do.

Tony ran back home and quickly packed a bag of clothes. He then went to the tea caddie in the kitchen cupboard where he knew his mother had hidden money away. There was no way that drunken bastard was going to get his hands on it. He took the bundle of notes out of the tin and guessed that there must be a couple of hundred pounds or more. In his pocket, he had an address and a letter. The letter was yellowed and faded with age.

His mother had given them to Tony when she was first experiencing the migraines. She told him to hide them well away and make sure not to tell his father. He was told that if anything happened to her and he needed to get away, then he should go and find the man whose name and address were on the scrap of paper. As far as she knew, he still loved in Durham, which was about fifteen miles outside of Newcastle.

She told him that this man had been a good friend to her many years ago before she was married and moved to Newcastle. Jean Slade, or as she was then known, Jean McDermott had been born and grew up in Durham. She had met his father at a party that she had been invited to in Newcastle. From then on, they started seeing each other and finally, they got engaged to be married and she moved up to Newcastle to live permanently.

Her parents had tragically died in a car crash when she was eighteen. Jean had learnt to fend for herself. She was earning money as a dressmaker, so she found a little flat to live in over a gym called the *Top Dog*. The landlord and the owner of the gym, Terry Norris, had known her parents. He was ten years older than her. He was a handsome lad but a bit of a fighter. He had been sweet on Jean. They had met many a Saturday evening in the pub next door to the gym but just remained good friends.

When Jean had moved into the flat and told Terry of the death of her parents, he had kept a protective eye out for her and their close friendship remained.

She told Tony that she hoped he would still be there now. If so, he would know what to do. She also told him to give this man the letter. Tony promised her he would do what she asked. He knew it was important to her. It was to become her dying wish.

Tony left by the backdoor and made his way to the bus station and bought a ticket to Durham.

He sat at the back of the bus as it started on its journey. He saw the familiar sights of Newcastle begin to fade away. He knew it was the right thing to do. He had no home life or future there.

He had left school that summer and had worked for a month on a building site as a labourer, receiving his wages cash in hand at the end of the week. But work was still scarce in Newcastle, so he was laid off.

He was smart enough and had finished his education at Carpenter Road Grammar School with four O-levels. He just couldn't see the point of schooling.

Working on the buildings was just a means to an end. He wanted more from his life.

He liked sport and being outdoors. He could read and write fine; he just found it all boring. He knew that there was a big wide world out there. A world, he hoped, with more happiness than he had experienced up to now, and he was off to find it. But he also knew that he would be back one day for some unfinished business.

CHAPTER TWO

Tony found the gym tucked away off the main high street. It was an old red brick building, two storeys tall. A hanging weather-beaten metal sign swung and creaked in the breeze on the outside wall. It read *Top Dog Gym* and there was a logo of a bulldog pressing a barbell above its head and another sporting boxing gloves below the faded lettering. Next door to the gym was the pub that his mother had talked about, the *Red Lion*.

Tony walked up to the door of the gym and noticed a small sign about it which read, *Owner: Terry Norris. Thank God, he must still be here.* Tony now felt nervous. He had been in such a hurry to get away from Newcastle that he hadn't really thought about what he was going to say when he got in here, and was this man, Terry Norris, going to want to listen?

Just then, the door was yanked open and Tony flinched back as two very large men exited carrying gym bags. "Hey, steady on, kid, I nearly knocked you over." The man who spoke had a mop of blonde hair and a friendly, ruddy face. His mate was a black man sporting a vivid scar on his left cheek. His face broke into a huge grin revealing a mouthful of gold teeth. "Thinking of pumping some iron, eh. Looks like you could use it, boy. Well, you have come to the right place. Go on in there, my son. They won't bite."

Tony pushed open the front door and walked into a reception area. Well, really it was a shabby space with an old work counter in one corner and a battered red leather sofa and a few matching armchairs in the other. The foam stuffing was hanging out of them in various places. On the floor was a threadbare carpet whose original colour had faded to a dull brown many years ago.

There was nobody around except a black and white cat curled up asleep on one of the chairs. The place smelt of stale sweat and liniment. Tony was drawn to the walls. Not the peeling grey paint, but the many fight posters that adorned them. Some yellowed with age. He studied them, looking at faces of hard men from down the years. He felt a tingle of excitement in his belly. He didn't know why, but he was drawn to these images.

He had grown up watching boxing legends, such as Sonny Liston, Archie Moore and the brash young World Champion, Cassius Clay/Muhammad Ali.

He supposed that he had always harboured a keen interest in boxing that hadn't really been explored. Stood here now, he felt a strange affinity with these tough men that stared out at him from the walls.

In the far corner of the room by the counter was a large glass cabinet which contained an array of trophies, cups and medals. On closer inspection, he noticed that many were engraved with the name Terry Norris, the man he was here to see. Tony read the newspaper clippings that went with all the trophies. Terry Norris had been a successful boxer in his day, a good welterweight fighter who had fought for the British title back in the fifties. This man had suddenly become very interesting.

"Admiring my trophies, are you?" The voice made Tony jump. He turned around to see a middle-aged man with thinning grey hair. He sported a crooked nose, broken many a time, Tony suspected, and there was plenty of scar tissue around his eyes as well. He wore a white t-shirt which was stained with sweat. On the front of the shirt was the logo of the bulldogs that he had seen on the sign outside.

The man still looked in decent shape and Tony estimated he must be in his sixties.

"What can I do for you then, young man? My name is Terry Norris. I own this place. Do you want to sign up?"

"Well, not exactly," Tony mumbled.

Terry eyed him warily. "Well, what is it I can do for you? I am a busy man, you know."

Tony walked closer. "Mr Norris, my mum sent me."

"Your mum sent you? This isn't the boy scouts, you know," Terry growled.

"You knew her. Her name was Jean Slade."

He saw puzzlement on Terry's face. He then realised why. "Sorry. You will have known her as Jean McDermott."

Terry's face then broke into realisation. "Little Jeanie McDermott. Now there is a name from the past."

He studied Tony more closely.

"You are Jean's boy, you say? What's your name, son?"

"Tony."

Tony hesitated and then handed over the letter. "My mother asked me to give you this. She said that it was important."

Terry took the letter. The envelope was faded, yellow with age. He examined the writing on the front of it, then gently slipped it into his pocket. "Thank you. I will have to read it later. I have mislaid my damn reading glasses somewhere."

"Well Tony... Slade, was it? How about I put the kettle on and we have a good old chat, eh? Jean was a good friend. How is she?"

Before Tony could answer, Terry Norris went over to the door leading back into the gym and shouted out to a couple of guys in the ring. "Harry, give him three more rounds on the pads, then he can hit the showers. I am going to be busy for a while. And if you see my glasses out there anywhere, bring them to me."

The man called Harry raised a gloved hand in acknowledgement.

Terry ushered Tony into a small untidy office space. "Take a seat, son, and I will fill the kettle up. Is tea okay or do you want something else? A can of coke maybe or some orange juice? I think I have got some in the gym somewhere."

"Tea is fine, Mr. Norris." Tony sat down into an old leather chair which also had the stuffing hanging out of it.

"Call me Terry. The only people that call me Mr. Norris these days are the tax office or the bank. So, how is Jean? Is she still married to that useless bastard Frank?"

He suddenly realised that he was speaking about the boy's father and coughed to hide his embarrassment. "Do you take sugar in your tea?"

Tony nodded. He thought to himself that this man certainly knew his father alright.

Finally, Terry handed Tony a mug of tea and then, he sat down behind his cluttered desk with a mug himself. He looked Tony in the eye. "Okay, lad. What brings you here?"

"My mum is dead, Mr, Norris, I mean, Terry."

The older man looked shocked and put his mug of tea absentmindedly down on his cluttered desk on top of a lot of paperwork.

"Jean? Dead? How? She was still young. Jesus."

Over the next hour, Tony told Terry everything. About his mother and her passing away. About his father and the abuse and beatings inflicted on them. Basically, he told him everything about his miserable life to date and how his mum had given him Terry's address.

Terry listened. His face was sombre. When Tony had finished, there was a tear in the older man's eye. "I am sorry to hear about Jean and the terrible things that you have endured. You see, we were close friends, very close. We went out for a brief time. But I was into my boxing, see, and just didn't have the time for a proper relationship."

Terry took a sip of tea which was now cold. Tony noticed a couple of what looked like bills stuck to the bottom of the mug. Terry didn't seem to notice.

He opened a drawer in the desk and produced a half empty bottle of scotch and poured some into his mug and took a large swallow. He was quiet for a moment, obviously thinking back in time. Finally, he carried on talking.

"Then, she met your dad and that was it. They had a whirlwind romance and got married quickly. Shortly after that, she left the flat to move to Newcastle with him. She did call me once not long after she got married and said that she may have made a mistake. She told me that Frank had hit her on a few occasions after getting drunk. She said that he was always remorseful afterwards, but it scared her. I asked her to come and see me, which she did, and I told her to leave Frank and come back here. I told her that I would marry her. Give up the boxing if she wanted. But she wouldn't hear of it. She was a stubborn and proud woman and said that she shouldn't have come here and involved me. She had to make the marriage work and things would turn out okay. It was probably just a blip."

He smiled ruefully shaking his head. "I told her that if she ever needed anything, she only had to call me. No matter where I was, I would have come for her. I truly loved her Tony. Maybe she would still be around if she had only told me the hell she was living in."

He paused again staring into space for a second. "I did hear a brief time later through the grapevine that she was expecting a child." Terry regarded Tony. "And here you are."

Tony didn't know what to say. This was a part of his mother's life that he had no idea about. He didn't know how to react. The one thing he did know was that he was drawn to Terry Norris. Somehow, Tony sensed that this man could put things right for him.

"So, you left Newcastle and that bastard Frank?"

Tony just nodded.

"I take it you don't want to go back?"

Tears welled up in Tony's eyes. He couldn't stop them.

"Have you left school? Maybe I can find a job around here for you? What do you think?"

"I would like that very much, Terry, but I don't want you giving me it through some sort of guilt or because you feel sorry for me. Whatever happens to me, I am never going back to that man. I hate him."

Terry smiled. "You get to keep the job on merit. Let's have a month's trial and see how we do. Alright?"

"Thank you, Terry. I really appreciate it. I didn't come here looking for any hand out. I was just follow-ing my mum's dying wish."

Tears began to roll down Tony's cheeks. He couldn't control his emotions.

Terry Norris threw a comforting arm around the boy.

"It's okay, kid. I understand. You will be safe here. It's not the Ritz but we do alright. The flat where your mum used to live above the gym is empty. You can sleep up there for now and we will see if it works out."

Terry told him that no one would know where he was, especially Frank Slade. He could earn his keep by working around the gym cleaning and running errands. In return, he got his board, keep and a few quid in his pocket. He could also start training. Terry told him that he would never be bullied again in his life.

He said that his gym housed some of the toughest and best fighters, powerlifters and bodybuilders but no bullies. This environment soon sorted the 'would be' tough guys from the real deals. Boxing had shaped Terry's life. It had taken him off the streets and had given him a purpose. With the money he earned, he had eventually bought his own gym to give others an opportunity such as he had.

He warned Tony though that as much as he thought of Jean, if he didn't toe the line and do what he was told, then he was out and would have to make his own way in the world.

"I haven't got the time for passengers," Terry said.

Tony nodded in understanding and assured him that he would knuckle down. He couldn't thank Terry enough. He had come here not knowing what to expect. Up to now, his life had been pretty much hell. This was a fresh start for him and a chance to break away from the past.

That evening, in the quiet of his room, Terry opened the letter he had been given. He sat in his favourite armchair with a glass of single malt whiskey and read it. When he had finished, he folded it slowly and sat for an age staring into space and then gently wept. He couldn't remember the last time he had cried.

The room was dark when he eventually climbed into bed.

* * *

Tony immediately loved the environment and fell straight in with its way of life. He relished getting up early every morning and working in the gym and meeting all the great characters that came there to train. They all accepted him without question.

When Tony wasn't working, Terry began to school him on his fitness work. Every day, he would do a different routine. Running on the treadmill, skipping and body weight exercises or weight work. Barbells and dumbbells. He also started him boxing. Tony took to it like a duck to water.

He loved hitting the bags and pads. Sparring in the ring was his biggest buzz. He knew he could take a punch. He had experienced plenty from his father. But now, he knew he could also throw one.

He was training twice a day seven day a week and showed immediate promise. When he wasn't working out, he was hanging out with all the guys in the gym, soaking up their knowledge like a sponge. It was a whole new life for him and he felt reborn.

Tony began to grow and fill out. He felt so fit, it was amazing. It boosted his confidence and a lot of his old fears and insecurities began to melt away.

Terry entered him into a few amateur boxing shows and Tony did incredibly well. After a while, he boasted a 10-0 fight record with seven stoppages and three knockouts. He was unstoppable. For Tony, all the years of pent-up frustration seemed to come out of him when he was in the ring. He had no fear. Terry told him that if he wanted, he could possibly go all the way to pro level one day.

One night in the gym, Tony was passing a back room which could be hired out for training. He looked in and saw a small group of men all in white uniforms, barefooted practising throws, takedowns, joint locks and strangles. He was fascinated by this training. He later asked Terry what was going on in there. He told him that they were practising the art of Japanese Jujutsu. It was very efficient training for self-defence.

Tony asked who taught the class and was told that it was a man by the name of Ray Steele. Ray was a third Dan black belt, who had trained in Japan. He also travelled down to Liverpool regularly to train with some of the UK's premier Jujutsu masters. Liverpool was a Jujutsu stronghold.

Ray also worked on the door of the *Blue Lagoon*, one of the biggest and busiest nightclubs in the city. He was a fearsome fighter but also a very humble man.

Tony knew that he just had to train with him.

Martial arts weren't particularly well-established in the Western world back then.

In the American comic books that he had read growing up, he had seen little bits of Karate being executed by Batman and Captain America, and they ran some adverts on how to learn deadly Asian fighting arts. He also recalled watching an old black and white film on television when he was younger entitled *Bad Day at Black Rock*, featuring Spencer Tracey as a one-armed army veteran who was also an accomplished exponent of Martial Arts.

These moves had always interested him and many a night, he lay in his bed thinking about how great it would be to use them on his abusive father.

The next week, he turned up at the mat side in the back room and asked to speak to Ray Steele. He was informed by one of the class members to refer to and address him as Sensei, which was the Japanese term for teacher. This was part of the etiquette of Jujutsu.

He waited for Sensei Steele to come over to him. Ray certainly looked the part. He was, Tony estimated, around 30 years of age. Stocky build with close cropped sandy hair. He had a matching pair of cauliflower ears. He also had a vivid red scar running down the left side of his face from eye to mouth. Tony later found out that he had survived a gang attack with knives on a late-night bus ride home when he was younger. He said that his Jujutsu training had saved his life. He had been training since he was a kid, as his dad had been a close quarter combat instructor in the army.

"So, you want to try some Jujutsu, eh? Well, it's tough, lad, and I have no time for wasters or cry-babies. Are you up for it?"

Tony assured him that he was.

He took to the mats a boy amongst men but, as with his boxing skills, he soon proved very adept in his new pursuit.

Ray was tough, but his technique had a flow and power to it that only an expert in his trade could possess. Tony learnt so much from this man, just as he had with Terry. He was privileged that both these guys had given him their time and experience.

Tony now trained in boxing and Jujutsu daily. He lived and breathed the fighting arts.

By the time that Tony was seventeen, he was a brown belt in Jujutsu and now had a boxing record of 20-2-0. He had filled out in to a six-foot thirteen stone specimen. His reputation in the gym had grown hugely. He was not a lad to mess with. For all his hard training, he was also a handsome guy.

With his thick dark hair and engaging smile, he turned the girl's heads whenever he went into town. But Tony only had eyes for training, much to their disappointment.

Tony looked a lot older than he was, so Ray got him a cash-in-hand job working the door of the *Blue Lagoon* under his guidance. Back then, you didn't need any formal S.I.A qualifications; you just needed to be able to handle yourself, keep your mouth shut and sometimes turn a blind eye. If you did, no questions were asked, and you weren't hassled. He soon found that at this club, he had to put his fighting skills into use on a regular basis.

Being so young and baby-faced, people thought that he was an easy touch. They were to learn differently. Tony had natural talent and a fire blazing inside him like an inferno.

The techniques he had been taught held up well against the local troublemakers and thugs. He was soon beginning to make a name for himself. He had power and control. It felt good when he scored that knockout or choke-out on somebody. Maybe he was getting to like it too much. He was beginning to become a bit of a handful and Ray, on a few occasions, had to rein him in, especially if the police came sniffing around.

Tony was slowly but surely starting to become his own man. He had come a long way in a short space of time.

In the four years since he had left home, the boy was gone and had been replaced by a confident young man. He was big, strong and fit. He was popular at the gym and around the city. Tony was riding a crest of a wave and was feeling good about himself and life for the very first time.

CHAPTER THREE

Working on the door of the *Blue Lagoon* not only brought Tony his share of trouble; it also brought him his share of ever-growing female attention. He would share the banter, but that was as far as it went. That was until he spotted a girl waiting in the queue to get into the club one night.

He couldn't understand why he was suddenly drawn to her, but it was like being struck by lightning. He had never felt like this before.

She was small and slim with strawberry blonde hair and icy blue eyes. He was captivated. He had never seen such a beautiful girl. As she drew closer in the line, he studied her even more. She caught his eye and smiled shyly. That was Tony gone, hook, line and sinker. He had to find out her name. He wanted to know if she was going out with anybody.

Throughout the evening, he watched her. She liked to dance and could really move. This drew the attention of many males who asked her for a dance, but she declined, much to Tony's relief.

At the end of the evening, as things were quietening down, Tony approached her and asked her name. She said it was Katy Connor. He commented that he hadn't seen her in the club before and she told him that it was her first visit. She added that she worked in an ice cream parlour nearby and it was her first night off in ages and she had wanted to go dancing. She normally went to the *Mango Grove*. It didn't get so much trouble there. But her friend had persuaded her to try here. Tony stated that he was glad she had and hoped she would come back again. As she left, she told him that if he was passing anytime, he should pop in for an ice cream.

The next evening, Tony stood outside *Snowball*, the ice cream parlour where Katy worked, and nervously gazed through the window. He had been standing there for five minutes. He watched Katy serving behind the counter, but he had not yet made a move to go in. He felt foolish. Why was he nervous? He had stepped into a boxing ring on hundreds of occasions and here he was, hesitant to go in and meet this beautiful girl.

Eventually, Katy came to the door and asked him if he planned on staying out there all night or was he coming in. They both laughed.

That was the start of their relationship. Tony never ate as much ice cream in his life, and the boys at the gym kidded him that he would be boxing at heavyweight if he carried on like this. Tony took their good-humoured banter in his stride. He was officially in love and enjoying life.

When they weren't working, Tony and Katy saw as much of each other as they could. Terry was privately concerned that the 'ice cream maiden', as he had nick-named Katy, would turn Tony's head. He spoke to Ray about this and he said that he would keep an eye on him. He reminded Terry that they were all young once and not to worry. Terry wasn't convinced. He had been in Tony's position once upon a time.

Tony tried to keep the violent side of his life separate to his private life with Katy but evidently, somewhere along the line, it would cross. He was getting well-known 'on the door' and had made a few enemies.

One evening, they were coming out of the cinema after watching the big film of that year, _The Exorcist. Katy had wanted to see it for weeks and Tony had surprised her by taking a Saturday evening off the club and secretly buying tickets. They were like gold dust. But he had a mate who worked at the *Odeon* cinema that got him a pair for half price.

The film had scared the living daylights out of Katy and she had spent most of the time hiding her face or clutching Tony's arm tightly in a vice like grip.

Tony had to admit that he wasn't too keen on the film. He had really wanted to see *Enter the Dragon*, starring Bruce Lee.

After the film, they walked through the city centre arm-in-arm. Every now and then, Katy would glance furtively over her shoulder and once nearly jumped out of her skin as a car nearby backfired.

She clutched Tony tightly and conceded that maybe they should have watched *Enter the Dragon* after all.

Tony put his arm around her and drew her close to him. He felt good inside.

As they cut across a car park at the back of a nightclub called *Oceans*, three guys were loitering around in the semi-darkness. One was pissing against the wall whilst the other two puffed on cigarettes.

They glanced up and saw the couple walking happily side by side. One of them, through beer blurry eyes, recognised Tony from the door of the *Blue Lagoon*.

He had been refused entry to the club by Tony the previous weekend for wearing trainers on his feet. An argument had ensued, and Tony had been forced to wrap a choke hold on this guy and eject him from the doorway. He hadn't liked it much and threatened a comeback.

Tony hadn't taken too much notice, as he heard this kind of talk all the time in his line of work. But now, the guy saw his chance to get even. He pulled his two mates together and whispered his plan.

Although Tony was chilled out in Katy's company, his survival antenna went up as he saw the three men approaching. He quietly told Katy to get behind him. His awareness had now fully clicked on.

The guy who recognised Tony spoke. "Well, well, well, if it isn't the boy wonder, Tony 'fucking' Slade. Remember me, cunt?"

Tony played it cool. "No, I don't think so. Are you that important?"

The man's face broke into an angry sneer. "Well, you should. You chucked me out of the *Lagoon* last Saturday, boy. Went all fucking caveman on me for no reason. Didn't he, lads?" He looked in their direction. The men nodded.

Tony did recognise him, but he wasn't going to register it. He knew this situation had gone beyond talking. He subtly planted his feet and sucked in some air before saying. "If I remembered every wanker I threw out of a club, I'd be on fucking Mastermind. It would be my specialist subject."

He knew this would light the fuse, but he was ready.

"You bastard," the man shouted. He stepped forward to swing a punch, but Tony was ahead of him. He landed a crunching right hook onto his jaw and he crumpled to the floor like a marionette with it strings suddenly cut.

Katy let out a cry of shock. Tony was now in full fighting mode. The switch had been flipped. These young guys were out of their depth, but he was pissed off that they had dared to confront him when he was with Katy.

"Come on then, wankers. Who fucking wants it?"

Tony grabbed the next man. He was a lanky fucker. But Tony had his head firmly trapped by grabbing two handfuls of his hair. He drove two powerful knees into 'Lanky's' body and one up into his face. The man's nose exploded in a spectacular spray of crimson.

The third guy was short and stocky. He had a face like a bulldog's arse. He was frightened. He turned to run and Tony should have let him go, but he didn't. His anger had consumed him.

Tony grabbed him by the coat collar and slammed an uppercut into his kidneys, then wrapped his arm around his throat in a vice like grip, shutting the blood flow to his brain. He squeezed so hard as the man slipped into unconsciousness that he had a wet patch spreading across the front of his jeans. Tony let his limp body hit the ground to join his other two sleeping mates.

Tony breathed deeply and only then did he become aware of Katy's sobs. The red mist that had descended on him was now clearing. He moved to comfort her, but she pulled away. "Are you okay, Katy? What is it?"

He saw fear in her eyes but also, something else like disgust. Suddenly, she turned and ran away. Tony shouted after her, but she kept running. He followed, but she flagged down a passing taxi and was gone before he could reach her.

The next day he rang her, but she wouldn't come to the phone. Her mother told Tony that she wasn't feeling well. When he suggested that he come around to the house to visit, Katy's mother told him no and that Katy wanted some time to be alone. She promised that Katy would ring him soon.

Tony waited a week for that call, but it never came. He was gutted, but knew that he would have to give Katy time. In his heart, he understood that she shouldn't have seen the violence he had administered. He had only done what he had because he cared so deeply for her and was frightened that she could have been hurt. This was the flip side of him. She had chosen to go out with him knowing what he did for a living.

The following Saturday night, Katy turned up at the *Blue Lagoon* club and told him it was over. She explained that she couldn't go out with him anymore and that she hadn't recognised him when he turned on those guys. She couldn't live in that world.

Tony pleaded with her to reconsider and that he would try to change his ways, but she wasn't having any of it. Tony knew deep down that his words were only hollow, as he enjoyed his way of life. Still, Katy had meant the world to him and he was saddened to lose her.

In the next few weeks, Tony began to realise how much he missed Katy and he went into a depression. He didn't train and Terry and Ray didn't see him around the gym. One night, Tony went out and got heavily drunk. He wasn't really a drinker, but he just wanted to ease the pain he was feeling. This led him into trouble.

Terry got a phone call early Sunday morning from the police informing him that Tony had been arrested for being drunk and disorderly and was locked up in the local police station cells.

Terry went down to the station. A lot of the local police trained at his gym, so he managed to persuade the desk sergeant, John Norton, a good friend, to release

Tony into his care and assured him that it wouldn't happen again.

Later in the day when Tony had sobered up, he received a massive talking down from Terry. He pointed out to him that he had a promising career ahead and he couldn't let one relationship ruin it. No matter how he felt, he would heal in time and things would get better.

Tony asked him how he knew this and Terry told him that he had been there himself.

Then, he dropped a bombshell on Tony.

"Remember the letter you gave me when you found me, son?"

Tony nodded.

Terry continued. "In that letter, your mother revealed something that I suspected for years."

"What was it?" asked Tony.

Terry reached out and his gnarled and calloused hand gripped Tony's.

"I am your real dad. Not Frank Slade."

Tony sat silently trying to take this revelation onboard.

After what seemed like an age, he spoke. "You didn't know until I brought you the letter?"

The older man sadly shook his head.

"No, son. Part of me maybe hoped. You see, that night your mother came to see me when Frank had been beating her, we slept together. It just happened. Two people looking for comfort. The result of that night would be a baby. Your mother hadn't known at the time and she went back to Frank. Some weeks later, she discovered that she was pregnant, but knew she would never have the courage to reveal the truth about who the real father was. So, she passed you off as Frank Slade's boy. The secret was supposedly hidden forever.

That was until you turned up at the gym and gave me the letter that your mother had asked you to deliver. That was the first I knew about it. It was just as much of a shock to me as it must be to you now, lad."

Both men sat in silence for a while. Tony mulled over another unexpected twist of fate in his life. He began to realise why he had felt so drawn to Terry. He wondered how his young life would have been if his mother had decided to stay with him. What would her life have been like?

"Why tell me now?" asked Tony.

Terry sighed. "I wanted to tell you as soon as I read that letter, but I couldn't. I didn't know what you might feel or even what you might think of me. But now, I see you hurting and as a father, I wanted you to know that no matter what you face in life, I will be here for you. I am not Frank Slade. I love you, son."

Tony looked at Terry's face and saw the concern and knew that this man was telling the truth. He had been there for him since day one when he walked into his gym. In the time he had been at the gym, Tony had felt loved.

He embraced Terry and tears stained both men's cheeks as they realised that they must have both been thinking the same thing. But what was done was done. You can't bring back lost time.

Through his tears, Tony said, "I am proud to call you Dad. I am glad that you are. I love you and I won't let you down again."

The two men talked long into the night.

Tony promised to get his act together and get his life back on track.

* * *

A few weeks later, Tony was in the town centre. Walking past an Army careers office, he stopped and looked in the window at the advertisements and felt something stir inside him. On impulse, he walked through the door.

The following week, it was his turn to drop a bombshell on Terry. He told him that he had just signed up to start training to join the Parachute regiment. He was three weeks shy of his eighteenth birthday.

Tony told Terry that it was nothing to do with the recent events; it was just something that he felt he had to do. He needed to get out of town and put the memories of Katy behind him and see a bit of the world.

After the initial shock and surprise, Terry gave him his blessing.

Terry told him that he was always welcome back at the gym. It was his home now and no matter where he went in the world, he knew that he could come back here. He also said that he understood as a young man that he needed to find his own goals in life.

Three days later, he said his goodbyes to Terry, Ray and all the boys at *Top Dog* gym. He would miss them dearly. They had become his family in more ways than he could have ever imagined. In the time he had been there, he owed them much.

Terry watched Tony get into a waiting taxi and thought, how ironic. He had found a son he never knew about after so long and now he felt he had lost him again.

A week later, Tony was travelling to Aldershot in Hampshire for his training. He was hellbent on becoming a soldier. He was on a mission.

CHAPTER FOUR

It was September 1975 when Tony started his training for the Parachute regiment. He sailed through twenty-six weeks of training with P. company. He relished the tough and uncompromising environment and thrived on it.

Many 'would be' tough guys fell by the wayside, but not Tony. At week twelve, he earned the coveted maroon beret.

After the twenty-six weeks, he had three more in the Brecon Beacons mountain range in South Wales for survival training and then off to Brize Norton in Oxfordshire for parachute jumps.

Many of his colleagues were so nervous of the jumps, but Tony felt strangely calm, just as he did inside a boxing ring. He realised that he had been born for this moment.

Drifting down through the clouds on a parachute had a peaceful and serene feeling for Tony, which he had never experienced anywhere before. He felt at one with the world.

After eight jumps, he had gained the famous wings from the 2nd Battalion or 2 parachute regiment as they were known. It was the proudest moment of his life.

Terry Norris and Ray Steele travelled to attend his passing out ceremony, which made the day even more special for Tony.

Terry Norris was a proud father that day, although he kept this secret to himself, not even Ray knew.

Trouble in Northern Ireland was now at crisis point. The bombings and violence were escalating.

Two paras had been stationed there since 1970. They were to spend 114 months and sixteen tours in Northern Ireland stretching from 1970 to 2002, the longest of any parachute regiment in history.

As anticipated, it wasn't long before Tony was sent to Belfast. His first tour was in late 1976. The troubles there were at their peak and it was a fast learning curve for a young soldier. Having an amateur throw a punch at you or try to smash you over the head with a bottle was a far cry from a professional attempting to shoot you or blow you up.

During his time in Belfast, he saw more than enough action. He was constantly on red alert. The British army wasn't welcome there and they didn't have many friends or allies. You could trust nobody but yourself and your fellow soldiers.

The worst time for Tony was in 1979 and the shocking death of eighteen paras at Warrenpoint, County Down. They were all blown up and killed by a cluster of remote controlled bombs. Three of his best mates lost their lives that day. It was a tragic moment, but it hammered home the point to Tony: rightly or wrongly, they were certainly in the middle of a war.

Things got worse and violence increased. On August 27th 1979 at Mullayhmore, County Slago, Lord Mountbatten, the uncle of Prince Philip, was killed when a bomb was planted on his boat.

This all happened just before Tony was due some leave. But security was upped, and any leave was cancelled. It was another six months before Tony came back to England. Thankfully, he was all in one piece, but in the few years that he had been stationed in Ireland, he had grown up rapidly. He knew that he was a different man to the 18-year-old that had joined up to the forces in search of adventure. Although still a young man in his early twenties, he already carried a few mental and physical scars of combat.

He decided to return to his home city. He wanted to visit his mother's grave.

Tony knew that with the ongoing conflict in Northern Ireland, he could be thrown back into action at any given time. He felt that now was the right time to say goodbye properly to his mother and his past forever.

Ironically, it rained once again as he stood at her graveside. Exactly like the day she had been buried. Tony spoke softly and told her all about what he had done and where he was going. He also told her that Terry had explained everything and that he didn't blame her in anyway. He loved her, and he understood her reasons for what she had done.

He shed a tear as he laid a bunch of flowers on her grave. The first to be placed there, he noticed, for some while.

He stood and pulled his coat collar up high around his neck. The wind had picked up and it was bitterly cold. The grey sky seemed full of rain as he trudged away from the graveside.

Tony jumped in behind the wheel of a blue Ford Capri that he had borrowed from a mate. He drove into Newcastle city centre and decided to nip in for some lunch at a pub called the *Ship Inn*. He remembered it way back from his childhood. Frank Slade had brought him in there before a Newcastle United home game. You could see the floodlights of St. James' Park from there. It used to be a sea of black and white inside on a Saturday lunchtime.

Tony walked inside and immediately smelt the aroma of beer and hot meat pies. His stomach growled as he remembered that he hadn't eaten any breakfast. He ordered a pie and a bottle of Newcastle brown ale. He took his drink to a quiet corner. The pub wasn't particularly busy today. It was Tuesday lunchtime. Most people were at work.

On the table he sat at, he found a disregarded copy of The Sun newspaper. He glanced at the headlines. More power cuts and coal mine closures on the way. They lived in troubled times. He flipped over to the sport on the back page and noticed that Liverpool were still topping the league. Newcastle as usual seemed to be treading water in mid table.

The barman brought him his pie and Tony tucked in hungrily. It was good. He planned to head on out of the city after and journey up to Durham. He was looking forward to calling in at the gym and seeing Terry and all the boys. He had missed them.

It seemed so long ago that he had been there. He also longed to get in a bit of training.

He had managed to keep up his boxing and Jujutsu training whilst in the Paras. But nothing beat the familiar sights, smells and sounds of the *Top Dog*.

Tony was just finishing up his beer when *he* walked into the pub. In a blink of an eye, he was transported back to his childhood.

He was sitting in the corner of the pub with a glass of coke and a packet of ready salted crisps, the ones with the little blue salt bag in them. He would sit in silence listening to the men speak about footballers, such as Bobby Moncur and Wyn Davies. Newcastle legends. He could remember Frank Slade getting louder and more raucous with every pint he sank. He loved to hold court there with his cronies.

Tony now felt a surge of adrenaline hit his stomach so strongly that he thought that he might be seeing his dinner again sooner than anticipated.

It was Dad. Or now, should he say his stepdad? Anyway, it was Frank fucking Slade himself. A little older and a little fatter, but there was no mistaking him.

To Tony, it looked like he had already had a few beers inside him as he plonked himself heavily down onto a barstool. He noticed the daily newspaper hanging out of his coat pocket turned to the racing pages.

"Danny, my old mate," he shouted to the barman, "Let's have a pint of your finest bitter and a single whiskey chaser. I come up a little flush on the horses."

Danny grabbed a glass and started pulling a pint of beer. "You're a jammy beggar, Frank. How much did you win this time?"

Frank Slade tapped the side of his nose knowingly. "My business, that. But it was a nice little tickle. Lucky fucker, I am. Well, I've got to do something constructive with my dole money." He broke into a loud laugh.

Tony watched him with hate sieving out of his every pore. The feelings of dread were still there. He just wanted to leave. Go and drive away. But part of him was transfixed and glued to his chair.

The pub door swung open with a bang. This pulled Tony's attention away from the bar. Two men had staggered in both worst for wear. "Get those beers in, Frank, and spend some of your winnings, you tight fucker." Both laughed and headed for the bar. The larger of the two clapped a friendly hand on Frank's shoulder. "Nice little treble there, my friend. That last horse virtually flew home."

Danny the barman busied himself with some drinks for Frank Slade's companions as they all sat at the bar chatting.

Tony breathed deeply to keep a lid on the adrenaline that was beginning to run riot in his body. He had often dreamt of this moment. A moment in time where he would bump into his 'dad' and no longer would he be that small, skinny and frightened kid.

The box that he had locked and hidden away in his head reading *'do not open'* now just had. The memories of the beatings and abuse that his mother and he had taken from this violent man came storming back to him in fucking technicolour.

He regarded the slight tremor in his hands. An adrenaline surge. No worries. He knew it well.

As he rose from his table, he remembered something that Ray Steele had said to him once not long after his encounter with the bunch of lads when he was walking Katy home.

He told him, "Sometimes, son, it takes a bigger man to walk away from a fight." Tony had listened to that advice. He also pondered it over now as he headed to the bar.

His rational instincts said walk out. You don't need this. But it wasn't the day for rational. After visiting his mother's grave and the opening of a lot of old wounds, Tony's emotions were raw. Fuck rational.

Yes, he could walk out. Nobody would be the wiser. But Tony had run from this violent fucker all his young life. Always wary that he may come looking for him one day and drag him back to a life of misery. He just couldn't run anymore.

An image of him as a 7-year-old lad suddenly came into his head, of being locked in the backyard coal shed because he was frightened of the dark and spiders.

Frank Slade had told him that it would help overcome his fears and that he would let him out in ten minutes. The only problem was that a mate of Frank's came calling and they both hit the whiskey bottle and forgot about Tony.

Jean Slade eventually found him two hours later when she returned from work, as she needed to get coal for the fire. Young Tony was traumatised.

He ran out of the shed screaming and clawing at imaginary spiders that he thought were on him.

His mother immediately got him into a warm bath and helped calm him down.

When her husband woke up from his drunken stupor and she told him what had happened, he just laughed and called Tony 'a little pansy'.

Later, he stopped Tony on the stairs and whispered to him that next time he would lock him in there all night. He got some sadistic pleasure from seeing the look of fear on the young boy's face.

Tony swallowed hard as he tried to put the images from his mind.

He walked right up next to Frank Slade and put his glass on the bar. He gestured to Danny the barman. He knew that his next words would only head this situation one way or the other. It was his call. He made it.

"Give me another bottle please and get a whisky for this fat, cowardly cunt sitting here."

The barman's eyes grew wide with surprise, then fear. Obviously, Frank Slade still had a big reputation around here.

Frank Slade and his pals couldn't believe what they had just heard. A sudden looming silence enveloped the place. If there had been a piano playing, it would have stopped.

Frank Slade turned around to face Tony. At first, recognition didn't come to him. Too many beers clouded the sub conscious. "Do you know who the fuck you are talking to, laddie?"

Tony calmly regarded him. "Yes, Dad, I know who I am talking to. How could I ever forget?"

Frank Slade's eyes focused and then he registered just who it was he was talking to. His face broke into a sour grin and he partially turned to his cronies. "Lads, I would like you to meet my prodigal son."

The two men stared dumbly at Tony. Frank Slade turned back. "Well, the little fucker returns home, eh? This shit fucked off and left me in the lurch while his mam and my dear old wife was still warm in her grave. Ungrateful bugger..." His words were cut off in midsentence as Tony dropped a solid back elbow into his face.

Frank Slade fell backwards off his stool and crashed heavily to the sticky beer soaked carpet. For a moment, his two mates were frozen. Then, the bigger one reacted lunging towards Tony. He didn't get too far as a bottle of Newcastle brown ale connected with his skull and he went the same way as Frank Slade. The third man made the dreadful mistake of pulling a knife from his pocket. Like a pouncing tiger, Tony sidekicked the man's kneecap which shattered on impact. He then stepped up close, grabbed the knife hand and viciously twisted the wrist, taking the man to the floor with a snap of his tendons. A well-timed stomp to the face finished him.

Tony turned to see Frank Slade gamely struggling to his feet. He had to partially admire the old bastard for that. He quickly grabbed him by the hair and slammed his head into the bar top, pulled him up, drove a knee into his testicles and headbutted him fully in the nose. Frank Slade slid to the carpet once more like a giant slug slippery with his own blood and this time, he stayed there.

The carnage had taken only seconds. The few people in the pub had already got up and fled. Tony saw Danny the barman with the telephone in his hand ready to dial. "Don't make that fucking call," he shouted. "You know as well as I do that he was a bullying prick and deserved it."

Danny hesitated, then replaced the phone in the cradle. "Okay, son. Just go. I don't want any trouble. You may be right about what you just said, but this is still my pub. Now, get out."

Tony nodded and regarded the three men on the floor. He recalled the words once more of Ray Steele. He shook his head. He guessed he wasn't that big enough to walk away just yet.

As he turned to go, he heard a mumbled call from Frank Slade's bloodied lips. He stopped and regarded him lying on the floor battered and beaten. How the roles had been reversed.

Frank Slade grimaced through his pain and nodded in acknowledgement. As Tony turned once more to leave, he heard him call, "Hey, son, I fucking deserved this and more. I was a prick. I knew some day it would come."

Tony paused momentarily, then kept on walking. His hands were now shaking badly as the adrenaline in his body began to subside.

He quickly entered the toilets keeping a watchful eye out as he cleaned himself up. He regarded himself in the cracked mirror above the sink. The damaged glass made his features distorted and ghostly.

Was he any better than the man he had left soaking blood into the carpet in the bar? He splashed some more water on his face and grabbed a paper towel to dry it off.

The violence that rose in him was frightening and it was getting harder to control it.

As he left the toilets and headed to the pub exit, he noted the three men were just coming around.

He walked around the corner and got into his car. He headed out of the city. He now felt a strange calm suddenly flood over him. Maybe some ghosts had been buried today. Maybe?

CHAPTER FIVE

Tony drove the 15 or so miles to Durham straight down the A1 and visited Terry's gym. His day was about to get worse.

He arrived at the *Top Dog* and was shocked and saddened to learn that Terry had passed away. He had died from a massive heart attack three weeks ago.

Ray Steele told him that Terry had been in the ring working the pads with a young boxer when it happened. No warning. It was all over so quick. Terry had died before the ambulance had arrived.

Everybody at the gym was totally shocked and couldn't believe it. The gym would never be the same again.

They had tried to notify Tony, but the powers-to-be had told them that security alerts were so tight at present and that Tony was heavily involved in the ongoing war in Northern Ireland. Unless it was a member of the family, they wouldn't tell him or issue leave.

Nobody but Tony and Terry had known about their secret that Tony truly was a family member.

Tony felt cheated that he hadn't had time to speak with Terry, but nobody had seen it coming. There had been no signs that he hadn't been well. He had mentioned to Ray how he was looking forward to Tony coming home on leave soon. Of course, it had been cancelled and put back; otherwise, Tony would have been here earlier and seen his father alive.

Ray was running the business at present, but it was only a temporary measure. Nobody knew what would happen to the gym. He was also thinking of moving on. Things weren't quite the same without Terry being there at the helm barking out his orders.

Tony spent some time with Ray and the other lads at the gym and got in a little Jujutsu training, but his heart wasn't in it. His time there was tinged with sadness. He kept expecting Terry to walk in at any moment. This hadn't been the cheerful homecoming that he had expected. Every time Tony thought that he had turned a corner, something else came out of the woodwork and slapped him in the face.

Terry hadn't made out a will, but in his belongings, he had left an envelope marked to Tony. In it, he found the letter from his mother and a small faded black and white photograph of a younger Terry stood outside the gym with his arm around Tony's mother. They were both smiling happily at the camera.

It was time to go and pay his last respects to the man who turned out to be not just a mentor and a friend, but also a father, his real father. More than this, he had truly been his saviour in his desperate hour of need when he had run away from home. It was a pity that the time they had shared together had only been short, but Tony had only good memories of their brief reunion.

The next day, Tony took a drive out to where Terry was laid to rise. It was at the *Sunset Crematorium*, just outside of the town off the A167.

Tony found a small plaque marking where his ashes were buried in the Winter Garden. It was one of the four season-themed gardens of rest.

He lay some flowers down by the plaque and stood in silence for a while and then told Terry about what he had been doing since they last talked. Tony noticed a lot of boxing memorabilia around the plaque and he reached into his own coat pocket and placed next to the flowers his first ever boxing medal that he had won as a boy, when Terry had guided him through the entire process of fighting with a wise old head, settling his nerves and helping him to win.

Tony had always carried the medal as a good luck charm and a reminder of Terry. He now felt it fitting to leave it with the man who gave him so much.

Tony then walked to the ornate pond in the walled gardens and sat on a bench. The day was bright and surprisingly warm for this late time of the year.

He regarded the four gentle flowing fountains and the bronzed cranes. It really was a tranquil setting. He sat in reflection for some time until the sun disappeared behind the clouds and it became chilly. Warily, he rose and headed back to the car park.

At the weekend, he went down town and for old time's sake, he made his way to the *Blue Lagoon* night club. Ray still worked on the doors there and had asked him to drop in.

Nothing much had changed about the place, except the fashion sense and music. Tony felt a little out of place.

As he headed to the bar for a drink, he instantly spotted a face he knew. It was Katy. All the memories flooded back to him in an instant. He looked at her. She was still beautiful. More mature and stylish, but still the girl he had once loved.

This really had been a few days of bittersweet memories. He watched her as he waited to be served. She was talking with a group of friends. He noticed a large blonde-haired guy paying her close attention. *A boy-friend perhaps or maybe more?*

As he was deciding that maybe it was better he left, Katy suddenly broke away from the group to head for the bar and her eyes found his. For a moment, both seemed to freeze in time. The instant recognition was there. Her face suddenly broke into a smile and she walked over to him. Tony stood there smiling back and then she hugged him tightly.

For a fleeting second, he felt the softness of her hair on his cheek and the fragrance of her perfume. Then, she broke away and spoke. "Tony Slade, well, this is a surprise. I heard you were in Belfast or somewhere."

Tony was surprised, but also secretly pleased, that obviously, she had been asking about him after all this time.

"Back home now, on leave for a bit. I thought I would head back to my roots and see what's changed."

Katy laughed. "Not much as you can see. I am still here occasionally on a Saturday night, but I no longer serve ice creams. I work in the advertising department for a local paper."

Tony nodded and regarded her empty glass. "Can I get you a refill? That's if you have time." He gestured towards her group of friends and the blonde guy who were now taking interest in the stranger that Katy was talking to.

"They are just work colleagues. We meet up here occasionally."

"What about Blondie there? Will he mind me buying you a drink?"

Katy laughed. "I shouldn't worry about him. I think Toby there would prefer you to buy him a drink, if you know what I mean."

It was Tony's turn to laugh now.

"Right. I get where you're coming from. Still gin and tonic, is it?"

"Well remembered, Mr. Slade. I'm impressed."

Tony laughed again and gestured to the barman.

They found a quiet spot in the club and sat down at a table and began to talk. A lot of water had gone under the bridge since those early days, and both admitted that maybe in hindsight they had both been too young for a meaningful relationship.

Talking was easier than Tony had thought, and it was just as if they had been together all their life. He needed this pleasant distraction after the sadness of the last few days.

Later, they danced. They both laughed as Tony told her that for all the drill marching he had done, he still had two left feet. She teased him and said that he was no John Travolta. At the end of the evening, Tony offered to walk Katy back to her flat. She accepted and told her friends that she was going home with him.

As they walked, Tony asked her if there was anyone special in her life and she replied that she had been going out with an American guy named Clint for a while. He was also in the newspaper business. She went on to tell him that there may be a career opportunity in the offering in the States and she was considering it.

Katy asked Tony in for a night cap. They talked late into the night. All the old feelings of closeness bubbled up after they shared half a bottle of brandy together. Inevitably, as if it was meant to be, they ended up in bed together.

Next morning, to avoid any awkward situations, Tony left early without waking her. He didn't want her to wake up with regret. He knew that there was no future for them. It had just been a moment of weakness.

Their lives were now on totally different paths. It had been lovely to see Katy again and he knew if he stayed, it would be harder to leave. The night they had shared just seemed fitting, but now he had to move on. His life was not here, nor was his destiny. He wished Katy all the best in her life and hoped she would be happy.

As for himself, he had the gypsy in his soul and he couldn't settle down. Being back in Newcastle and seeing Katy again only reinforced that he still had feelings for her, but it was better to cut them off now. It would save them both any more grief in the long run. There wasn't room in his life at this stage for a relationship.

He returned to Northern Ireland. The early 80s continued with bombings and shootings instigated by PIRA and the IRA. As the world went into a new decade, nothing much had changed for the people of Northern Ireland.

A year later, he was surprised to receive a letter from Katy. She told him that she was married to Clint and she was now residing and working in New York. She had got the dream job. She also told him that she had just recently given birth to a baby daughter named Ruby.

She had wanted him to know first-hand from her and not find out sometime later.

He didn't reply. Part of him was strangely jealous, although he knew that he didn't want that type of life, or did he? Maybe he was running away from commitment. Katy had been the only girl in his life that he had been serious about. In fact, it was his one and only meaningful relationship. Since then, he had had a few one-night stands, but that was it. Nothing heavy. The army was his only serious commitment.

No, he was pleased for her, but he couldn't shake off the feelings of what might have been. Also, a fleeting thought crossed his mind that the baby had been born a year after they had slept together. But Katy had told him that it was her husband's, didn't she?

Tony put the thoughts from his mind and went back to soldiering. He began to crave more action. It was his way of forgetting Katy. But he was getting reckless. It was only by chance that an incident pulled him back from the brink of self-destruction.

One evening, his patrol stopped a van at a checkpoint between Belfast and Londonderry. The occupants were asked to step out of the vehicle. On doing so, Tony noted two men. One was in his sixties; the other was maybe mid-twenties. A young woman also got out. She was carrying a small baby. From its size, Tony deduced that it could be no older than a few months.

A routine search of the van was made, and nothing seemed untoward. But Tony and his team couldn't shake off a feeling of unease.

Only a brief time back at a place called Glasdrumman, a PIRA ambush at a British Army checkpoint had resulted in the death of one soldier and another was badly injured. They were on red alert.

Finally, they told the people that they could get back into the van.

The girl had somehow reminded Tony of Katy. The baby had also triggered thoughts that he hoped he had buried.

As the girl headed to the van, Tony instinctively asked her if the baby was a boy or a girl. She seemed taken aback by the question and then answered a boy. Tony nodded and was going to let her go when he suddenly caught sight of a pink blanket wrapped around the sleeping form and he felt a tingle of adrenaline in the pit of his stomach.

"Excuse me asking, but wouldn't a boy have a blue blanket?"

The girl stared dumbly at him.

"Do you mind showing me the child?"

He saw fear and panic not only in her eyes but also the men's.

Tony raised his gun. "Show me the child now, slowly."

The woman glanced towards the men.

"Now, please. Show me." Tony raised his voice.

The girl opened the blanket and the baby fell to the tarmac. It was a doll. Also, under the blanket was a 9mm Browning pistol.

Tony and the rest of the team moved in. "Drop the weapon now. Right fucking now," he shouted.

The girl gripped the pistol. For a moment, Tony saw defiance in her eyes.

He stared her down. "Don't be stupid. Drop the gun now."

The older man's voice sounded, "Put it down, Deirdre. The game's up."

The girl looked towards the man that Tony presumed must be her father. Her eyes stared into his and he nodded at her.

With shaking hands, she dropped the pistol to the ground. The incident was over.

Somehow, the whole scenario had brought Tony out of the darkness and back to reality. The ghosts of his past once again exorcised.

1982 saw Britain go to war with Argentina over the Falkland Islands situated in the South Atlantic. Over the course of history these islands had changed rule, but now they belonged to Great Britain.

The Falkland's war started on the 5th April that year and ended on the 14th June of the same.

Nine hundred men lost their lives.

Tony was involved in one very significant moment of the war when the British 2nd battalion Paratroopers captured the Argentinian stronghold garrison at Goose Green on 27th May. It was a major turning point in the war, which Britain eventually won.

Tony returned from the Falklands feeling disillusioned. So many young men had lost their lives for a barren piece of land over 7,500 miles away, mainly inhabited by sheep. Fighting for Queen and country was one thing, but for Tony, this had been a sheer waste of time, energy and human life. But, as he knew, if you were in the forces, you didn't question motive; you just did as you were told.

Tony believed, as it was alleged by many others, that Britain went to war as a political gamble by the then-prime minister, Margaret Thatcher. She was in her first term and well down in the opinion polls. Going to war and winning was a way to boost her popularity and hopefully retain office at 10 Downing Street.

That was a fucking hell of a price to pay, if this was true. Gambling with people's lives was a tall order and one you would have to sleep with for the rest of your time on the planet.

Tony had never really been into the politics of war. This was probably because he had been too gung ho and never really paused to think about it. But in this conflict, he had lost some very close friends and it had made him stop and contemplate.

Part of him longed to leave the army, but he knew nothing else. What the hell would he do in 'Civvy' street?

Then, an old buddy of his told him about a private security company recruiting mercenaries. They were looking for elite forces soldiers for some dangerous assignments. They wanted experienced men who were looking for good pay and willing to travel and not ask too many questions.

After the disillusionment of the Falklands, Tony decided if he was going to use his fighting skills, he might as well get well-paid for them. *Fuck it,* he thought. *I'm in.*

He had no one in his life waiting for him at home and nobody worrying where he was or what he was doing. He had nothing to lose.

So, when his time was up in the Paras, he signed up for mercenary work. Tony was just the type of soldier they were looking for.

Over the next six years, Tony found himself in some far-off corners of the planet. He soldiered in many different countries. Most were internal wars, such as in the Sudan, Libya and Uganda.

He witnessed much bloodshed, horror and atrocities. He also wasn't proud of some of the things he had done. But he was now a fully-fledged and paid up 'Dog of War'.

Ironic really that he had been so principled about the Falklands and now he was fighting in places in Africa that he hadn't even heard of or much less cared about.

He began to question if the forces were really his family or was he still running away from the real world?

Tony eventually returned to England once more physically, if not mentally, unscathed. He had more lives than a cat. He had some money now tucked away, but the good times had dried up. He had to admit though that part of him was glad to be back on home soil. It had been a long road since he had left these shores as an 18-year-old young man.

It felt strange to be back in ordinary civilian clothes. He was renting a small bedsit for the time being. He really wasn't sure what he was going to do with his life. He was now 31 years of age.

In these times, when you left the forces, you didn't get much in the way of help or support. You were basically on your own with maybe a network of a few army buddies. After being in a regimented environment where you didn't have to think too much for yourself, suddenly, you found yourself unleashed in society.

Tony thought he would travel to Durham and visit Ray at *Top Dog* gym. Maybe he could get some work there coaching or help with the running of the place. He felt more positive as he drove along the A1.

When he pulled up outside the place in his second-hand Cavalier, he was shocked to find it wasn't there any longer.

He got out of his car and walked up to the entrance of a freshly painted new looking establishment. The large sign above the door read *Zodiac Gym and Health Club*.

Tony wandered in and was confronted by a large reception counter.

He was greeted by a bubbly blonde by the name of Angie. All hair, teeth and lycra. When he enquired about the whereabouts of Ray, she informed him that Mr. Steele had sold the former property to *Zodiac Fitness Ltd* and had moved, she believed, to Lanzarote.

Tony was gutted. He did recall Ray often mention about moving abroad, as this country had gone to the dogs, but he never thought that the old bastard would do it.

Angie carried on explaining how the *Zodiac* was the new face of the fitness industry in the nineties and gyms like *Top Dog* were rapidly dying out.

"We have job vacancies if you are interested? We like to have an older age presence in the gym. Equal opportunities and all that. We are not ageist, you know."

Tony thought Angie was a lovely girl and he was sure she knew her job, but at that moment, he wished she would shut the fuck up.

"Have you got a level 2 or level 3 qualification?"

Tony didn't understand what she was waffling on about. "Level 2 or 3 of what?" he asked.

Angie rolled her eyes as if he had just crawled out of the ocean. "Why, fitness qualifications of course, silly."

By now, Tony had lost the will to live.

He thanked her for her time and declined the offer of a free gym induction and made it outside and back to his car.

He drove away shaking his head in disbelief. Things had changed drastically. In the army, you were insulated from change. You were in control of your own little world. Now, Tony felt lost and a little inadequate.

He went back to working the doors, but found that even this had changed. Bouncers were now door supervisors and they needed special training and a license to work. What the fuck was going on?

He managed to find work at a few pubs and clubs that were not overly concerned about the new laws coming in. He was paid cash in hand. Not big bucks, but it paid the rent.

Tony kept the little nest egg he had from his foreign adventures safely hidden for that rainy day. At this moment in time, he felt that day wasn't far away.

The problem for Tony was that he couldn't see himself doing a 9 to 5 job. He just wasn't cut out for it, plus these computers that were suddenly appearing on the scene scared the shit out of him.

For a short while, he did get a job as a delivery van driver. It was okay and it got him out and about, but the only problem was his supervisor. He was a sanctimonious prick. He abused his position and he thought that his job status gave him the right to treat people like shit and talk down to them. The guy's name was Ernie Ledbetter. He had been doing the job for years and thought he was bulletproof. He strolled around the depot as if he owned it.

To Tony, he was just another bully and Tony hated bullies. Things weren't going to end well.

He had no problem with authority. He had dealt with that all his army life. He just didn't like bastards that abused it, and Ledbetter was one of those people that did.

The law of the jungle outside the confines and restrictions of a working environment was a totally different animal. Out on the streets, your boardroom status or job title won't save you a punch in the mouth if you overstep the mark against a seasoned professional in violence or criminal activity. They live in a different world where respect is a matter of life or death in some quarters.

Men like Ledbetter were used to intimidation and threats because most people are shit scared of losing their jobs and worried about how they will pay their mortgages if they are sacked.

The Ledbetters of this world knew this and thrived on their little power plays.

Men like Tony Slade, who lived outside of these parameters, didn't give a shit about position or status. You fuck with them and it is like stirring up a hornet's nest.

One Friday afternoon, things came to a head. Tony had returned to the depot with a parcel still in his van. It needed to be signed for, but when Tony had reached the delivery address, the place was shut and everybody had gone off for the weekend.

He was in the canteen pouring himself a cup of tea and chatting to a few of the other drivers when Ernie Ledbetter stormed in.

"Ah, there you are. What's going on with the undelivered parcel then, Slade?"

Tony carried on pouring his tea, ignoring the rude outburst. He took a deep breath and explained the circumstances of why the parcel hadn't been delivered.

Ledbetter wasn't having any of it and went off on a rant. "You get paid to deliver parcels, not to sit here on your lazy ass and drink tea."

Tony regarded his supervisor. "As I said, there was nobody there. What did you want me to do? It needed a signature. I couldn't just leave it there, could I?"

Ledbetter got right up in Tony's face. "Maybe you should have got there fucking earlier. You might have been a big shot in the forces, Slade, but your jack shit here. Next time, fucking deliver it properly, Rambo."

Tony now saw red. He didn't need this. In the Paras, he had overseen men and never treated them like this. Also, he had overseen millions of pounds of hi tech equipment. This joker was treating him like a ten-year kid.

Ledbetter turned to go when Tony called him. "Excuse me, Ernie. Can I just say something please?"

Ledbetter turned around. "I have nothing more to say. Next time you will get the... Bang!

Tony headbutted him straight in the face. Ledbetter staggered back holding his nose as a fountain of crimson seeped through his fingers.

Tony followed this up with an uppercut into Ledbetter's flabby guts and the man went down to the ground. Tony grabbed him by his hair and pulled his face upwards to his own. "Don't worry about threatening me with the sack, you fat bastard. You can stick your job up your ass! If I ever come across you outside, you better run for fucking cover because I will destroy you. Do you understand me you prick? Well, do you?"

Ernie Ledbetter just nodded his head, as he had no breath left in his body to speak.

With that, Tony left to rousing applauses from his workmates. Another job down the plughole.

Over the coming years, Tony drifted around the country. Now and again, through an old army contact, he managed to get some decent chauffeuring and body-guarding work. Down in London, he 'minded' a few Arab Sheiks. They paid well, and Tony carried on living simply and putting money aside. He knew in this game that the bubble could burst at any time.

It often did, and he would find himself back on a pub door or doing shop floor security in a supermarket.

Age was against him as he hit his 40's and it was becoming increasingly more difficult to find any sort of half decent job.

He held down another job for a few years which he enjoyed. He became a jump instructor at a skydiving centre open to the public. It was great to put some of his army skills back into practice.

All went well until the company went into bankruptcy due to a couple of the directors giving themselves overinflated wages and perks. First came the redundancies, of which Tony was one of the casualties, and then it all shut down and went to the wall.

Tony knew though that he wasn't getting any younger and he desperately needed a change of lifestyle and a purpose for the future.10 years or more had just disappeared without any fanfare. It was all a far cry from his army days.

Tony had an old army buddy called Graham Wilde who had emigrated to Australia after leaving the forces and for a little while, he went out there to visit him. It was a beautiful country, but soon, he was missing the British shores and returned once again. Restless and unfulfilled.

He still liked to keep up his fitness and his Martial arts training. He gained his black belt in Jujutsu whilst in Australia. On his return to the UK, he also had half a dozen unlicensed white-collar boxing matches on a few small shows. The pay was nothing more than pocket money, but he enjoyed the competition again but being in the ring in your late-forties was not ideal.

Then a local promoter Joe Henderson of the White-collar boxing shows *Square arena* asked Tony if he might like to come onboard and train the would-be fighters who entered the events. Tony jumped at the chance to do something that would give him a buzz again.

The events were an enormous success, and Tony began to earn a steady wage as he travelled around the country working on these shows.

All went well for quite a few years until Henderson got convicted of underage sex with a minor and that was the end of the shows and the franchise it had brought with it.

Tony was back on the doors of the local pubs. Now well into his fifties life just seemed to love kicking him in the teeth every time he thought he had found a settled job.

Being a loner outside the army for most of his life Tony also now missed female companionship. Sure, he had met a few ladies, but none that he really considered having a long-lasting relationship with. He found it difficult to share and be intimate. Too many years of being on his own, he supposed.

That was until recently. Suddenly, his life had been turned on its head again. Unbelievably, Tony Slade was in love.

CHAPTER SIX

The Present

The door of the *Alpha* coffee shop suddenly opened, and a woman hidden behind an umbrella struggling to close it rushed in from the rain.

Tony's heart momentarily lifted. Could this be her? But joy turned to disappointment when she closed the umbrella and he realised it wasn't her.

He went back to his coffee, the remains of which had now gone cold.

He gazed out of the window once more and saw that the rain had got heavier.

Everything always appeared worse when it rained. The dark skies seemed to breed dark thoughts.

He suddenly had a moment of panic. What was he doing? He was at the wrong end of fifty and up to his neck in trouble.

He could get up now and walk away. Fly to another country and put her out of his mind, but he knew he couldn't. He had to see this through.

Annette had come into his life in the last year and changed it totally. Never in his wildest dreams would he have thought that he could love somebody the way he loved her, but it was true.

His life up to this point had literally and metaphorically been a battlefield.

Over the years, his heart had hardened. It had to do with some of the things he had seen and done.

Now, just maybe he could see a light in the black. He calmed his mind again, the anxiety easing as he took a sip of his coffee.

He gathered his thoughts once more and remembered back to how he had met her...

Past

Tony was working on the door of *The Engineer* pub, not far from Newcastle's only railway station known as Central.

It was a late September's evening and the still warm remnants of the sun rays seemed to have a soothing effect on the clientele. Everything was peaceful for a Saturday night and he was feeling quite mellow.

He watched a sleek blue Mercedes pull up across the road. A man jumped out of the driver's side. He heard the electronic bleep of the doors locking and saw the man start to walk across the road towards the pub. As he got nearer, he shouted, "Stand by your bed, soldier!"

Tony looked closer and realised it was an old mate of his from Northern Ireland and the Falklands. Rob Green.

Rob had been a young soldier when he was assigned to the team that Tony was in. Tony had taken him under his wing and watched his back as he was a fellow Geordie. During the Falklands conflict, he watched as this young lad became a man and a good soldier.

When the conflict was over, they went their separate ways and lost touch. Then, one Saturday afternoon in a sea full of faces at St. James Park watching Newcastle United play, they bumped into each other when they both were buying a half-time coffee.

They watched the second half of the match together and enjoyed witnessing Alan Shearer smash home a hat trick as Newcastle beat Everton 3-0.

After the match, they had gone for a beer and caught up on old times. They promised to keep in touch, but once again they hadn't. Now, here was Rob turning up out of the blue.

Both men shook hands. "I've been trying to track you down. You're a hard man to find," Rob said.

"You have been looking in the wrong places then, my friend." Both men broke into laughter.

"Look, I can see you're working. I'm going to get a couple of beers and unleash myself on any willing females inside. Can we talk after your shift? I might have a job for you if you are interested?"

Tony was intrigued. "Yeah, sure we can. But only on one condition."

"What's that then?" asked Rob.

"That you're buying the drinks."

Rob threw up a mock salute. "You got it, buddy."

As he walked into the pub, he called back over his shoulder. "What are the women like in here anyway?"

"Not bad." replied Tony, "Some have even got their own teeth."

Rob broke into laughter once more and then disappeared towards the bar.

Later that evening when Tony had finished work, both men sat in the back bar. Cyril the landlord was happy to let them have a late drink. He was in the main bar with a few of his mates playing some after hour's poker.

Tony nursed a single malt whiskey while Rob sipped on double vodka on the rocks.

"I've been back in Newcastle a while now and asked around to see if you were back in the area," Rob said, "I was down in London for a few years doing security work, but it's a competitive business down there. Too many security companies jostling for business. Anyway, I lost my job and went through a bad patch. So, I thought I would come back up here. I managed to secure a nice little job. A lifeline really. The man I work for asked me recently if I knew anybody suitable for a job vacancy in the firm. I thought of you straight away. This guy likes ex-military working for him."

Tony took a swallow of his drink and felt the warmth of the amber liquid heat through his body. The whiskey was good. He had grown partial to this drink over his years in the forces.

"I'm intrigued. Who is this guy you're working for?" He felt that he wasn't going to like the answer.

Rob swallowed a huge gulp of vodka. "Kenny Robbins."

"What? *The* Kenny Robbins?" Rob looked sheepish.

"Kenny Robbins, local villain. Tyneside's Mr Fucking Big?" asked Tony.

'Yes, it is, and can you keep your voice down a bit, a guy in the front bar didn't quite hear you."

"Fucking hell. What are you doing working for that man? He's unwelcome news. He's a fucking lunatic. What the hell are you thinking of?"

"Look, Tony. In case you haven't noticed, although I am sure you do seeing you are working on a pub door, jobs aren't exactly stacking up for blokes like you and me. Ex-army that either don't fit in anywhere or feel like dinosaurs, or we just aren't cut out to work in fucking TGI Fridays or B&Q or sat on our asses tapping on a keyboard."

Tony said nothing and took another sip of his drink. He knew what Rob had just said was true. Even still, working for a man like Robbins just didn't sit right.

"I was down on my ass, Tony. Rock bottom."

Rob finished off his drink in one gulp.

"I even thought about suicide and then, this opportunity came along. I know Robbins isn't a saint, but he has looked after me. He has given me a flat, nice motor and money in my pocket."

"Yeah, but at what price? Did you have to sell your soul?"

"Don't fucking rubbish me, Tony. You weren't so choosey when you were gunning some poor bastard down in Africa somewhere, were you?"

Tony reached across in a flash and grabbed Rob by his expensive looking tie. "Don't fucking judge me."

Rob stared him down. "Well, don't judge me either. We have come a long way since the Falklands. We have both done things we are probably not proud about. But I can't do a 'civvy' job. I've got some money behind me now and I want to make a better life for myself. Yes, Robbins is a crook, but his money is as good as anybody's. When I make enough, I walk. It's as simple as that, okay?"

Tony released the grip on his friend's tie and sat back. "Alright, Rob. I understand what you are saying, but I don't know if I can do it."

Rob regarded him. "It's your call, my friend, but what else have you got going for you now? What future have you got to look forward to?"

Rob got up from the table ready to leave. "This job gives me purpose, a reason to get up in the morning and it gives me a fucking buzz. When is the last time you felt like that?"

Tony sat quietly regarding his empty glass.

"Here's my card. It's got my number on it. Think about it. But don't leave it too long."

Tony watched Rob leave. His friend's words had wounded him, but there had been a lot of truth in what he said.

He was tired and needed to sleep. It was all too much to take in.

As he walked into the main bar, Cyril saw him. "Wait up, Tony."

Cyril came up to him. "Almost forgot, here's your money for tonight." He pressed some notes into Tony's hand. "Same time tomorrow night, mate?"

Tony nodded and left the pub.

Outside he counted the money. £50. He sighed as he counted it again. Fifty fucking lousy quid for putting my ass in the firing line of some drunken moron.

He recalled what Rob had said earlier about job offers not exactly stacking up for him and how he was at last earning decent money.

He thrust the money into his pocket and walked towards his car.

Tony couldn't sleep that night. He tossed and turned. By 5.00am, he had given up. He got up and put on his tracksuit and went out for a run.

The crisp morning air cleared his head as he ran along the streets. It was still quiet and there was very little traffic on the roads. Tony did his best thinking whilst he ran.

He headed out past the Metro station along Northumberland Street and eventually ran along Barrack Road and into Leazes Park. It was a lovely open space to run in away from the noise and pollution of the traffic.

He ran on towards the bandstand and then to the lake that lay beyond the trees. Tony began to feel better. The exercise was giving him clarity.

He decided maybe he had been a little hard on Rob. After all, the man could have offered the job to some-body else, but he had specifically hunted down Tony.

Tony had no right to be so sanctimonious and judge-mental. He had killed people for money when he was a mercenary and not lost any sleep over it, so doing a bit of 'minding' for a local villain wasn't exactly the end of the world, was it?

There weren't many other options left for him. There was no imminent prospect of him becoming a brain surgeon or rocket scientist soon, and standing on the doors of shitty little pubs and being paid peanuts was not the best of futures.

He was getting older. His best days of playing Action Man and Rambo were in the past.

If he swallowed his pride and did this job, he could accumulate enough cash for a better life. Then maybe, just maybe, this was the answer.

He circled the park and exited the beautiful Jubilee gates that had been erected in 1887 to celebrate Queen Victoria's Diamond Jubilee.

By the time he returned to his bedsit, showered and had breakfast, he had decided that he would phone Rob.

Rob was over the moon that he had changed his mind. "It will just be like old times," he told Tony.

He said he would call Robbins now and see if he could arrange a meet as soon as possible and get the ball rolling. His last words before he hung up were, "You won't regret it."

Tony hoped that would be the case, but he somehow doubted it.

CHAPTER SEVEN

10.00am the following morning saw Tony and Rob sitting in Kenny Robbins's outer office. His business premises were situated in a large tower block overlooking the dockside. It was a prime site and obviously didn't come cheap.

Tony had heard about Robbins back in his younger days. Kenny had inherited his empire from his father, Joe 'The Rhino' Robbins. Joe had been a decent middleweight boxer in the 1940s, but his career had ended abruptly when he was glassed in a bar fight and lost the sight in his left eye.

He then moved into boxing promotion and that led into some more shady business practices, and it had grown from there.

Joe had a frightening reputation and as his empire grew, he employed the toughest of men to help make sure it ran smoothly.

Tony could remember his old man mentioning Joe Robbins and later, he began to hear about his son coming on board and beginning to take the reins from him.

When Joe passed on, Kenny took full control of the business and ruled it with an iron fist just like his father had.

Kenny had done service in the Navy in his early years and some time behind bars for GBH.

As he took over the business, he became smarter and kept one step ahead of the law, transforming into a very clever operator.

You didn't get business premises like the one Tony and Rob were in now by being a third-rate thief.

Both men sat on a plush purple sofa. The room's decor was all creams and purples with deep pile carpeting on the floor and expensive looking prints on the walls.

Across the room from them sitting behind her desk was Rosie, Robbins' personal secretary.

Rob and Tony eyed her casually. She was in her early 30s, they estimated. She had long black hair tied back in a ponytail. Her make-up was immaculate, as was the black suit she was wearing. She was a very classy lady and, according to Rob, a bit of a cold cow. This deduction had been made on the fact that he had asked her out three times without any success.

She tapped away on her computer, glasses perched seductively on the end of her nose.

"So, how are things, Rosie? Keeping busy, are we?" spoke Rob, trying to make some light conversation.

Rosie continued tapping away on her keyboard, not looking up as she answered him. "Yes, all is well Rob, and yes, I am very busy." She emphasised the word 'busy' in hope that Rob would get the message.

Rob glanced at Tony and gave him a wink. "Any new men in your life at present?"

Tony shook his head. It was a pathetic throw of the dice from his old mate.

Rosie stopped her work and regarded Rob. "Not that it is any of your business, Rob Green, but no, there isn't and no, I am not looking for one, especially not you, I might add."

"Aww, that hurt, Rosie. It really did." Rob mimicked clutching his heart. "You really know how to make a man feel special."

Rosie was just about to answer him when the phone on her desk buzzed. She picked it up and answered the call.

When she had put the phone down, she said, "Much as I would love to keep this stimulating conversation going, Mr. Robbins is now ready to see you. Go on through, gentlemen." She gestured towards a large oak panelled door to her left.

Both men rose from the sofa, straightened their jackets and headed towards the door.

Tony felt a tingle of anticipation in his stomach. He recognised it as pre-confrontation adrenaline. He had felt it many times before in his life. He breathed deeply and composed himself.

As Rob passed Rosie's desk, he leant in close to her and said, "I am so glad I stimulated you, Rosie. The pleasure was all mine, I can assure you."

She didn't reply.

Rob moved to the door and knocked on it. They heard a voice from beyond telling them to come in.

Both men walked into Kenny Robbins' office. It was expensively and tastefully decorated, as you would expect for this upmarket part of the city. The main feature of the room was a large glass window that ran the length of the wall to their left. It afforded magnificent views across the Tyne towards Gateshead.

Tony could see part of the Tyne bridge and across the river, The Sage, a world class concert and music centre, funded by lottery money and opened in 2004 as

Gateshead's answer to the 'Angel of the North', some might say. Tony thought it resembled a miniature Sydney Opera House.

In front of the window was an expensive looking leather sofa and sat on it were two of the biggest men Tony had ever seen. One was white, the other black. Both sipped coffee and were watching Sky Sports News on a huge flat screen television mounted on the wall that wouldn't have looked out of place in a cinema.

Both these guys would have given Mr. Universe a run for his money. Tony deduced that you didn't get that big by just pumping iron and eating chicken and tuna.

They both momentarily tore their gaze away from the screen and regarded Tony and Ross with mild interest and then, both went back to watching the television.

Robbins himself was sat behind a large oak desk directly in front of them. He was finishing off a phone call and motioned for both men to sit down on the two chairs this side of the desk.

They both sat down, and Tony took time to appraise Robbins. He estimated that he was probably in his early sixties. He was built like a pit bull, had grey hair closely cropped to his skull and a deep suntan. Not a sun bed job either, Tony surmised.

He wore a blue fitted Armani suit and a white Armani shirt, opened at the neck. Tony spied what looked like a Cartier diver watch on his left wrist. Probably eight or nine grands' worth. He looked every inch the successful businessman.

But if you took a closer look, you could see scar tissue around his eyes and his hands were the hands of a man who hadn't shuffled paper clips for a living. The knuckles were gnawed. Old faded tattoos adorned them.

Obviously, this man had the money to get them laser removed, but he had chosen to leave them as a reminder. But for whom had he left them? For himself or maybe it was for others?

Behind him on the walls, there were many framed photographs. There was one of a younger Robbins holding a trophy aloft in a boxing ring. Another of him in a white karate gi with a black belt around his waist standing next to an imposing looking Japanese man.

Another image had Robbins stood with the cast of 'Auf Wiedersehen Pet', the popular 80s show about three Geordie bricklayers working aboard in Germany that had gone on to be a long running cult series.

Tony also spied another photo of Robbins at some official looking function pictured with the 'late, great' Sir Bobby Robson when he had managed Newcastle United in the late 90s and early 2000s.

Robbins finally brought his call to an end and put down the phone. He regarded both men with sharp blue eyes. His face then broke into a smile. "Sorry about that. Had a bit of business needing my delicate touch."

Tony was surprised that Robbins' voice was softly spoken and articulate.

'So, Rob. This is Tony Slade then?"

"Yes, Kenny. This is your man."

Robbins reached across the desk and firmly shook Tony by the hand.

"I'm pleased to meet you, Tony. You come in high regard from Rob." His eyes appraised Tony.

"Would you both like some coffee?"

"Yes, that would be good. Thank you, Mr. Robbins," replied Tony.

Robbins smiled again. "Kenny. Call me Kenny. How do you like it?"

"Black, no sugar please."

"What about you, Rob?"

"Same please, but one sugar. Thanks, Kenny."

Kenny looked across at the two men on the sofa. "Errol, Rudi. Would one of you guys kindly bring a couple of coffees over here for us? Both black, one with sugar."

Both men regarded each other. "It's your turn, Errol," said the white man.

"Fuck you, Rudi. I did it last time around."

The man called Rudi laughed. "No fucking way, brother. I did it because you said you had a big bet on the horseracing we were watching on the TV, so I did it as a favour, remember?"

Robbins interrupted the conversation.

"Enough of the lover's tiff and one of you get the fucking coffee now."

Errol rose from the sofa. He must have stood 6ft 6 inches in height or more.

"Okay, Kenny. I hear you." He still regarded the television as he moved across to a coffee percolator on a Japanese lacquered coffee table.

Errol brought the drinks across to them. "You need anything, Kenny?"

"No, I'm good. Thanks, Errol. I am glad you could spare the time."

The man made his way back to the sofa with a grin on his face.

Tony took a sip of his coffee. It was top quality stuff. Columbian, he thought.

Kenny lit up a large cigar and sat back in his chair.

"Well then, Tony. Rob tells me you are looking for some work."

"Yes, that's right."

"Well, from what he tells me, you come well-qualified. Experienced ex-para. You can box. A Jujutsu expert and you have done your fair share of door and security work. Quite an impressive CV you have. I don't know how I haven't picked up on you before."

Tony remained silent.

Robbins continued. "I like working with ex-military men. Do you know why?"

Tony took another sip of coffee and shook his head.

Robbins smiled once more. "I'll tell you why. Because they are willing to take and follow orders. They like structure. They are disciplined. They are not like these two cent wankers out there pretending to be gangsters."

As he said this, he gestured vaguely with his cigar towards the window.

"The type of clowns that walk around the streets with their baseball caps on back to front and their trousers half way down their arse listening to too much fucking rap music. Arseholes."

He paused momentarily for thought. "You know, that trouser thing originally came from the American penal system. If you walked around like that in prison, you were giving out the signal to others that your ass was for sale. What the fuck's all that shit about, eh? Today's gangsters. They are not worth a toss. Soft as shit little mummy's boys."

Robbins shook his head. "Anyway, I digress. Let me ask you Tony, can I trust you?"

As he asked the question, he leant forward in his seat to emphasise its importance.

"Obviously, you know who I am and what I am about. I have power in this city, but with power also comes a price. That price is people are always trying to find a way of fucking me over. They want a piece of the pie without putting any work into the ingredients. You understand?"

Tony nodded. "I think I understand where you're coming from."

Robbins took a pull on his cigar and blew out a cloud of smoke into the air. "Good man."

He then gestured across to the two men on the sofa. His voice suddenly hardened.

"That is Errol and Rudi. When they are not bickering between themselves, they are my personal minders. They are furiously loyal. If anybody remotely thinks they can fuck me over, those two will hunt that person or persons down to the ends of the earth and make them suffer unbelievable pain. Make no mistake."

Robbins paused for effect.

Errol and Rudi, as if on cue, both looked over and grinned. The smiles were not of a friendly nature. They reminded Tony of a couple of lolling Rottweilers.

Robbins' voice softened again. "So, can I trust you, Tony?"

Tony looked Robbins in the eye. "Yes, you can. May I ask what the job entails?"

"Sure, you can. It's a bit of everything really. Some chauffeuring, deliveries, debt collecting. Use a bit of muscle now and again. I will pay good money. I expect no questions asked. Loyalty is the key. You show me you are a man who can be a vital part of my team and I can make you a rich man. Have we a deal?"

Tony hated what he was going to do. But he had run out of options. There was good money on offer. He only hoped he didn't have to sell the remaining morsels of his self-esteem for it.

He reached across the desk and shook Robbins hand. "We have a deal."

"Good man," replied Robbins as he got up from his chair.

"Where are you living at present, Tony?"

"I have a bedsit over Northumberland Road way."

"Right, well, I have a little letting agency. I will sort you out a flat a little nearer to the city centre, so you are close to the business. First month's rent is on me. Also, you will need some wheels. Down in the parking garage is a blue Rover, it belonged to the man who's job you took he won't be needing it.'

The statement hung in the air uncomfortably.

Kenny Robbins carried on. 'You can borrow it for your work. Petrol is your call."

He then reached in his inside pocket and produced a bundle of £50 notes. He peeled off a dozen or more and handed them over to Tony. "Here. Take that as an advance on your wages and get Rob here to take you shopping for a few nice suits. Something a bit classy. I have a reputation to uphold and I except my men to be smart. Okay?'

Tony pocketed the money. "Thank you, Kenny."

'Also, if you need to contact me or any of the firm use this pay as you go phone and not your own.

He passed a small cheap mobile across the desk.

'That means nothing comes back to me if you get in the shit. You understand. If you do get in trouble destroy it.

Robbins nodded. "Rob will show you the ropes for a week or so and then you will work directly through me." He extended his hand once more. "Good to have you on board."

Tony and Rob headed towards the door. Robbins called out. "Oh, Rob. Can I have a quick word in private a moment, if you will?"

Rob's hand froze on the door handle. "Yes, no problem." He looked at Tony. "See you in the outer office in a minute or two."

Tony thought he saw fear in his friend's eyes. "Everything okay here?"

Rob smiled nervously. "Yeah, it's cool. I'll see you in a minute."

Tony nodded and left.

When Rob turned around, Robbins was right in his face and Errol and Rudi stood behind him, both blocking out much of the natural light.

"So, Rob what about this other problem we have? Running up a few quid debt at my casino is one thing, but now you owe me some big bucks. I like to think of myself as a fair man. You told me you would have the money by the end of last week. It's now Monday."

Rob raised his hands in a pleading gesture. "I will have it in the next few days, Kenny, honest. I just had a few cash flow problems. But I will sort it."

"Cash flow problems, eh? How come a couple of my lads saw you out partying in the *White Noise* and the *Midnight Lounge* on Saturday night to the wee small hours. Also, you and Fat Frank down at *Ace in the Hole* have been getting mighty friendly. Do I need to have a word with him, Rob?"

"Hey, Kenny. You know I am a bit of local celebrity and namedropping gets you into those places for free. No money was being spent. As for Frank, we have just been playing a bit of snooker together for the odd wager. Nothing heavy. Honest."

Kenny grabbed Rob by the shirt front. "You better be telling me the truth because I am hearing some alarming things about you, my son. I let you into my inner circle. I trusted you. If I find out you have been fucking me over, you are going to wish you were never born. Anything you experienced in the army won't even come close to what these two will do to you. You better not be holding out on me."

"Okay, I understand, Kenny. I will have the money in a few days. A few people owe me. They are due to pay up and all will be fine."

Robbins stared Rob in the eyes, seemingly looking for an answer that he was happy with. Finally, he released his grip.

"Alright then, Rob. You have got until Friday. Now go and help your mate and stay out of the fucking clubs and the casino until we are straight."

Rob nodded. He straightened his shirt and left the office.

Robbins turned towards Errol and Rudi. "Keep an eye on him, will you? The money he owes me from his gambling debts is one thing, but he has been spending money around the city that I know he hasn't got and I need to know where he's getting it from."

Rudi and Errol nodded.

"Will do, Boss," both men answered at the same time.

When Rob entered the reception, he was still straightening his tie. Tony noticed his friend looked a little pale in the face and somewhat shook up. "You okay?" he asked.

Rob painted a grin back on his face. "Yes, I'm fine. Let's go and do some shopping, shall we?"

Both men began to leave the office. Rob suddenly stopped, regathering his swagger again, and turned back to Rosie. "Anything I can do for you darling before I go?" His composure was now seemingly back in place.

Without even looking up from her computer, Rosie replied, "Yes, there is actually."

Rob waited expectantly.

"You can shut the door on the way out."

As both men entered the lift that would bring them down to the parking garage, Tony regarded Rob. He still looked a little shaken even though he was trying to put a brave face on.

"So, what did Robbins want you for?" he asked.

Rob regarded his friend. "Nothing really. Just checking up on a job I did for him, that's all. No big deal."

"Are you sure, Rob?"

Rob patted Tony on the back and smiled.

"I am sure, my friend. Now, let's go shopping for those suits. I hear Asda have some cracking offers on!"

"Yeah, very funny," replied Tony.

He knew that Rob was hiding something, but he didn't push it. He would find out in time.

After the little shopping spree, Tony dropped Rob back at the parking garage. The Rover was a smooth drive, so he decided he would take it for a spin out of the city. It was a lovely day and he thought he would make the most of it.

He asked Rob if he wanted to come, but he declined telling him that he had some business to sort out but he would pick him up tomorrow at 11.00am and bring him around some of the properties and businesses that Kenny Robbins owned. Tony said that was fine and bid his friend goodbye.

Once Tony had gone, Rob sat in his car. Many thoughts were racing through his mind and none of them were good. Did Robbins suspect him? Who would have told him? He pondered those questions and came up with one possible name, Frank Rawlings, aka Fat Frank.

Frank Rawlings managed the snooker hall and casino that Kenny Robbins owned called *The Ace in the Hole*. It was situated in the Grainger Town area of the city and was a popular haunt for those with some money to gamble. If you didn't have the money, you could always go into the more downmarket snooker hall. The place catered for people from most walks of life. Kenny Robbins had no class issues when it came to taking money off people.

Rob had got himself into a bit of a jam a year or so ago due to his ever-growing gambling habit. He went to Frank to see if he could lend some money. What had transpired was Frank and Rob began to cream a little of the casino and snooker halls profits. A lot of ready cash changed hands in this busy establishment and it was hard to keep a trace on it.

Frank kept the books and Rob used to pick up any of the cash profits at the end of the week to bring to Kenny, so it was relatively easy to skim some off with the help of manager Frank.

All had been good. Rob had stashed away some good profit, but last week, Frank had told him that he wanted out. That they had been lucky up to now and as he was coming up to retirement age, he wanted to ease out in one piece.

Rob told him no. He needed Frank's business brain to 'cook the books', so to speak, for another while longer. He needed more money to not only pay off this debt, but also to plan his disappearance when ready.

He told Frank another six months should do it, but Frank warned him that it was too dangerous. Frank said that he had heard rumours of maybe a takeover of Robbins' business and a visit by a mystery buyer. If that was the case, all the accounts would be scrutinised with a fine-tooth comb and if Robbins found they had been fiddling him, they both would be dead men.

Rob had argued why would Robbins find out. He asked Frank if he had covered his tracks properly and he answered that as far as he knew, yes, but you could never be 100% sure. Maybe something would be found. If this happened, they could be discovered and the game would be up.

Rob had asked Frank when this so-called visit was going to happen, but he told him that he didn't know. Rob informed him to hold his nerve and his tongue until they found out more. Frank had reluctantly agreed, but he didn't look very happy about it.

As Rob started up his car, he thought that he might give Frank a little visit and see if all was well. He hadn't seen him since the conversation last week, so a visit was probably due.

He headed out of the parking garage and onto the Tyne Bridge and the A167.The traffic was reasonably light for late afternoon.

He joined Mosley Street and then onto Collingwood Street cutting into Grainger Street. He drove pass the market towards the Metro station where he could see the imposing statue of the Grey's monument built in 1838 in honour of the 2nd Earl Charles Grey for passing the 1832 Great Reform Act. The figure of Lord Grey at the top of an impressive 130 feet column was surrounded by tourists taking photos, but Rob was far too preoccupied to really take any notice of the normal everyday activities going on. He was anxious to get to Fat Frank's place.

He eventually arrived outside the *Ace in the Hole and* walked up the steps into the snooker hall. It was early evening and mostly empty. He briefly scanned the place. There was no sign of Frank. A few tables were occupied, but apart from that, it was quiet as a grave. He headed to the bar and asked the young girl working behind it where Frank was. She spoke with a thick Scottish accent and informed him much to his annoyance that Frank had gone home feeling under the weather.

Rob left again and tried Frank's number, but it went straight to answer phone. He sensed that something was up. The fucker wasn't stupid enough to spill his guts to Robbins, was he?

Panic gripped Rob for a second, but then he got a grip and rationalised that if he had told Robbins, then Rob would have been summoned immediately. He pulled his phone from his jacket pocket and checked it. He saw no missed calls from Robbin's number.

He got back in his car, checked his hair in the driving mirror and smiled to himself. *You're getting paranoid Robbie, my boy. Take it easy and go get a drink. You can come back in the morning and catch the bastard cold.* He would bring Tony with him to watch his back. He could spin him a little tale just to make him believe that they were doing a job for Robbins. He would be none the wiser. Yeah, it was going to be alright. Rob Green didn't survive many a fire fight in foreign parts to go down to some two-bit gangster.

He pulled out into the traffic and headed towards Collingwood Street. He was going to hit a few of the up-market bars there this evening and maybe get lucky with the ladies.

CHAPTER EIGHT

The next morning, a grey sky and light rain welcomed Newcastle and Tony to a new day.

Rob picked Tony up in his white BMW at 11.30am half an hour later than promised.

As Tony sat into the plush leather passenger seat, Rob mumbled an apology blaming the traffic for his lateness.

Tony regarded Rob. His eyes were hidden behind an expensive pair of *Ray Ban* sunglasses. His *Boss* aftershave didn't quite hide a lingering aroma of alcohol. Presumably, he deduced, from partying the previous night. This was more than likely the reason for his lateness.

He decided to let it go and instead asked, "So, where are we off to then?"

"We are going down to Grainger Town to surprise a fat scumbag who manages the *Ace in the Hole* casino and snooker hall."

"So, what has this fat scumbag done?"

Rob negotiated the heavy downtown traffic. "I am not totally sure as yet, so I need to have a word with him. Put him straight."

"So, that's what you do for Robbins, is it? Put people straight?"

Rob pulled up at a red light and regarded his friend. "Yes, Tony. Sometimes that is what I do. Have you got a problem with that? Because if you have, you can tell Robbins you're fucking out, okay?"

Tony was surprised by his friend's agitated state.

"Take it easy, Rob. I'm just asking. No problem, my friend."

The lights changed, and Rob pulled away. He breathed a heavy sigh. "Sorry to jump down your throat, Tony. It was a late night last night. I must have got out of the wrong side of the bed."

Tony smiled. "Was it your bed or somebody else's?"

Rob broke into a laugh and the tension between them eased. "Now that would be telling."

Tony looked out of the side window as Rob drove further into the heart of the city. He couldn't shake the feeling that his life was heading for trouble yet again. Working for Robbins was killing him, but he knew that he would have to bite the bullet and go with it for now.

He regarded the city as they journeyed on. The place had changed dramatically since he had been a kid and it was hard to recall what some of the streets looked like way back then.

Newcastle had certainly come a long way from its industrial past. The Quayside where Robbins had his offices had seen the biggest facelift. It was now one of the UK's top night spots. In fact, a recent poll of top European nightlife destinations had positioned Newcastle in third place behind London and Berlin. The city had also come seventh in the world category. A far cry from when it was known for its coal and its shipyards.

Rob pulled up outside the *Ace in the Hole.* He stopped the car's engine and turned to Tony. "I'll handle things once we're inside. I just need you to watch my back. Fat Frank is well liked in here and there might be a few of his mates inside, know what I mean?"

Tony nodded. He zipped up his jacket. "Understood," he said, as both men got out of the car and made their way inside.

The casino was shut up and wouldn't be open until the evening, but the snooker hall had its door ajar and lights on.

Both men walked in and let their eyes get accustomed to the dim lighting. There were twelve tables laid out ahead of them. The green baize gleamed in the overhead lights and they heard the clack of balls. Two tables were already occupied.

Behind the bar, Rob noticed it was Harry on duty today. He liked old Harry. He was an old school barman and he knew when to turn a blind eye or keep his mouth shut.

"Morning, Harry," said Rob as he walked up to the bar.

Harry turned around from polishing some glasses. "Hello, Rob, my son. How are you?"

Rob shook the old man's hand. "All good, thanks." He gestured at Tony. "This is my good friend, Tony Slade. Tony, this is Harry Anderson."

"Good to meet you, Harry." Both men also shook hands.

"So, how are things?" Rob asked.

"They'll be a lot better when that owner of our football team starts spending some money, so that we stay in the premiership this time. Tight fucker. We need another *Supermac*. That's what I think."

Both Tony and Rob acknowledged the old man's reference to one of Newcastle United's most famous and revered strikers of the 70s, Malcolm MacDonald.

"It's going to be a long time before those days come back to St. James, Harry," Ross remarked.

"Yeah, you're right there, lad."

"So, what can I do for you gentlemen?"

"Frank about, is he? I need a word," Rob asked.

Harry nodded towards the office at the back. "He's in there. He was in early. I didn't expect to see him. I heard he went home ill yesterday."

"Yeah, so I heard. Fighting fit now, I hope," replied Rob.

Just then, the office door opened and out walked Frank. He was a big man, but out of shape. Tony placed him in his early sixties. He was balding, but he was one of those men that maintained a flimsy combover. His stomach noticeably hung over the waistband of his trousers. He was chomping merrily on a sausage roll. Fear filled the man's eyes when he saw Rob, and he nearly choked on the mouthful of food he was eating.

"Morning, Frank. I see your appetite hasn't been affected by your mystery illness."

Frank regained his composure.

"Hello, Rob. What can I do for you?"

"I need a word in private."

Frank's face looked worried again. "What about? I was just going out."

Rob walked towards him and grabbed the man by the arm.

"That wasn't a very friendly welcome, Frank. Where are you going in such a rush anyway? I came all the way down here to have a little chat. It would be rude not to see me."

The big man's face had broken out into a sweat. "Alright, Rob. Take it easy."

Rob held onto Frank's jacket. Although it didn't look like he was going anywhere fast. "In the fucking office now, Frank, and don't fuck me about anymore."

Rob pushed Frank in through the open door. He glanced back at Tony. "I won't be long. Keep an eye out, will you?" With that, he closed the door.

Harry had returned to polishing glasses. He knew better than to ask what was going on. He was too old for drama and he liked his job.

But the skirmish had aroused interest from the snooker tables and the four men that had been playing now wandered over. They looked from Tony to the office door and back again.

Tony felt the familiar tingle of adrenaline in his belly. He had been here many times and knew what was coming. He quickly appraised the men as they came closer.

The lead man was a big fucker. 6 feet 2 inches or more with dark hair cropped short. He wore a tight-fitting t-shirt that showed off his pumped chest and biceps. The next guy was a carbon copy in build, only he was blonde and sported one of these trendy beards that a lot of the young guys liked to wear currently. The other two were younger lads, feral looking little punks. They stayed in the background like a pair of skulking hyenas and let the lions go in for the kill first. When it was safe, they would make their move.

The dark-haired guy spoke aggressively. "What the fuck is going on in there with Frank?"

Tony kept him at arm's length, noticing that he had a half empty bottle of Corona beer in his hand.

"Nothing for you guys to be concerned with. There is just some business going down. Now, go back to your game. We'll be out of here in a minute." His voice was polite but firm.

The big guy wasn't having any of it. "Frankie's our mate and I for one ain't gonna stand here whilst some scumbag roughs him up." He made to walk past Tony and towards the office.

Tony spoke again. "Just leave it, pal and back off, okay?"

The man observed Tony. He looked him up and down, taking his measure.

Tony knew that this guy was now making the decision whether to pursue his actions, and if he decided to continue, he was going to have to come through Tony first.

Tony widened his stance a little and grounded his weight. The adrenaline was bubbling like a pressure cooker inside him. He knew it would soon have to be released.

The man curled his lips in a sneer and pumped out his chest. "Fuck off, asshole. Get out of my way."

* * *

Fat Frank stood by his desk, his face flushed.

"What the fuck is it, Rob? I thought we were cool."

Rob stood in front of him. "So did I. I'm just checking that you haven't had a change of mind and are thinking of giving it all up to Robbins."

Frank laughed nervously. "Why would I do that? I shop you, I also shop myself. It would be suicide. Why do you ask?"

"Robbins had a word with me yesterday and it was just something he said that made me think. You wouldn't be lying to me now, Franky boy, would you?"

The older man looked worried again. "No, Rob. I've said nothing, nor will I. You can count on me."

Rob closed the gap on Frank.

"Okay, Frank. I believe you, but just in case you think of changing your mind, here is a little reminder from me."

Rob's knee came up fast into Frank's balls. The big man instantly dropped to his knees clutching his groin in agony. Rob pulled him up straight by his tie and smashed three short punches into his face. Frank cried out in pain and collapsed to the carpet. Two well-aimed kicks from Rob sunk into his flabby belly for good measure.

* * *

The big man facing Tony heard a cry of pain from behind the office door. He moved forward and grabbed Tony by the jacket lapel and brandished the bottle of beer. In a blink of an eye, Tony applied a vicious wrist and elbow lock from Japanese Jujutsu known as *Nikkyo*. The big man crashed to his knees in pain as his wrist snapped. The follow-up knee under his chin dropped him to the floor.

His mate with the beard lunged forward swinging a snooker cue, but Tony front thrust kicked him squarely in the breastbone, sending him staggering back into a snooker table. "Fucking stay there, you bastard," shouted Tony.

The man was still game, and he reached back for a snooker ball to use as a weapon. Tony was on him like a panther. He still moved fast for his age. He kicked his aggressor in the balls and double palm slapped his eardrums. The following left hook probably wasn't needed, but Tony wasn't taking any chances. 'Beardy' ended up on the floor with his mate.

The two young lads were wide-eyed in terror. Tony faced them now. "Fuck off while you both can still walk, or I will squeeze your spots for you."

Both lads, without hesitation, gingerly made for the exit. Tony watched them go and then turned his attention back to the two men. The big fucker with the dark hair was getting up from the carpet. With his good hand, he drew a concealed hunting knife from a sheath attached to the back of the waistband of his jeans.

Tony saw it instantly. Well, he couldn't miss it. It was big enough to skin a fucking buffalo. Crocodile Dundee would have been proud of it.

Tony quickly picked up a snooker cue and gripped it by the heavy end. A professional doesn't hit somebody with the thick end first as you see in the movies; otherwise, it breaks off and leaves you with nothing of substance if you need a follow-up.

Tony jabbed the cue point into the big man's throat. He instantly dropped the knife and clutched his neck fighting for breath. Tony then brought the heavy end up like a paddle and slammed it into his jaw. His adversary dropped to his knees and Tony finished by bringing the heavy end down across his skull. It was over.

He glanced around, but there was no more danger. He then caught Harry's eye. The old fellow was still polishing glasses. "Sorry about that, Harry. Hope there was no damage to the premises." Harry said nothing and just carried on polishing.

The office door then opened, and Rob came out. He was wiping his bloodied hands on a hanky. There was no sign of Frank.

He surveyed the scene in the snooker hall and his face broke into a wide grin. "Fuck me, Tony. Can't I leave you alone for five minutes?"

Rob looked towards Harry as he and Tony went to leave the building. "Frank has come over a bit sick again and is having a little lie down on the sofa. I shouldn't bother disturbing him for a while."

Harry wiped down the bar surface and nodded.

As Rob passed him, he threw a £50 note down on the bar. "Take care of yourself, Harry. See you later."

Once they were back in the car, Rob told Tony that he had given Frank a bit of a spanking, but he would live. He continued to say that Robbins suspected Frank of maybe taking a dip into the snooker hall's profit.

Tony didn't question it, but went on to relate what had happened with the snooker players.

Rob grinned. "I'm glad I brought you along, my friend. It's good to have an old buddy I trust watching my back. God knows I could do with it. Remember the time in the Falklands when I got trapped in barbed wire when we were crossing that field under fire? I was fucked, but you came back and untangled me. You risked your bloody life that day. Everybody else had gone ahead and hadn't noticed me. But you did."

Tony nodded. "As you said, just watching your back. It was part of the job. Old habits die hard, I guess."

"Guess you're right, my friend." Rob started up the car and turned on the radio. They both turned and regarded each other and broke into laughter as the song playing was Queen's *Another One Bites the Dust*.

The rest of the day was a little more mundane. They travelled around the city centre and Quayside collecting money from various people that owed Robbins.

Rob was privately satisfied that Fat Frank would be staying put and carrying on with their little business arrangement. For now, he was in the clear, but he still owed Robbins.

He would pay off what he owed him come Friday and ironically, it would be with the bastard's own money. He knew that he was walking a tightrope, but he was willing to take the chance. He had never had so much money before, but he also knew that the cocaine habit he had begun to develop was often making him reckless. Being seen in those clubs the other night was a silly thing to let happen, but his addiction was becoming a hard habit to break.

Therefore, he had got Tony on board. Just like in his army days, he would watch his back and hopefully, be a second pair of eyes for him. He had to ease Tony in gently. He realised it went against the grain for his old friend to be working for Robbins, but he needed him around and had to keep him sweet.

He would just have to be more careful and frequent some venues beyond Robbins' reach where he wouldn't be spied upon. With that thought in mind, he turned to Tony who was absentmindedly playing with his mobile phone as they drove back towards his bedsit.

"Fancy a night out tonight to celebrate a successful first day on the job? I know a great club down at the Quayside. The *Omega.* I've got a couple of VIP passes."

"It's not one of Robbins' places, is it?" Tony asked.

"Actually, it isn't. It's all legit, my friend. So, what about it then?"

It had been a long while since Tony had been out for a night on the town when he wasn't standing on a pub door. Far too many microwave meals for one in front of the television as well. For fuck's sake, he had even started watching the early evening soap operas. That was the slippery slope.

"Yeah, you're on. It sounds good."

"Right, I'll order a taxi to be at your door 8.00pm. Get your best 'bib and tucker' on and make sure you have clean undies. You might just get lucky."

"Just a few beers and a bite to eat are fine," replied Tony.

The night out went well. Tony felt relaxed for the first time in a while. He had some money in his pocket and for a change, he was inside a club and not stood on the outside.

He had forgotten what a spectacular sight the Quayside was at night. Full of bars, pubs, clubs and restaurants, it was a premiere spot for a good night out, vibrant and alive with many different noises, smells and colours. The iconic Millennium Bridge stood large and proud, the world's first and only tilting bridge. It really was a magnificent feat of modern engineering. Built in 2001 to link the south bank of Gateshead with the North bank of Newcastle, it was affectionately known by locals as the blinking or winking eye due to its shape.

Tony and Rob had both had a nice steak dinner in *Kelly's Bar and Grill* and then moved on to the *Omega*. The place was full. Tony felt very old. The music wasn't his cup of tea and it was too loud. Rob, being the younger man, mocked him and called him Dad.

The VIP tickets afforded them their own private booth and free champagne. Rob was in his element and loved the attention of the ladies that gathered around for free drinks.

When it was time to leave, Rob had got two stunning ladies in tow with him. He persuaded Tony to come back to his flat with them.

Tony had to admit that he was tired and would rather go home to bed, but Rob and his silver tongue suggested just one more drink for his old buddy. Tony complied to his wish.

Once they were back at the flat, Rob poured out generous measures of Jack Daniels for them all and then proceeded to cut up a small pile of cocaine on his kitchen worktop.

Tony eyed it. "When did you start taking that shit?" he asked.

Rob stared at him through drunken eyes. "For a while now. It helps me relax. It's just recreational."

"Booze is one thing, my friend, but that shit can fry your brain."

"Thanks for the lecture, Tony. You need to lighten up a bit. Everybody is doing a little 'Charlie' these days. It's no big deal. Why not try a bit?"

"No, thanks, I'll stick to the bourbon."

"Suit yourself. Girls, come and get it." Rob stooped down and snorted up a line using a rolled up £10 note.

He stood back up and breathed deeply. "Fuck me, that is good stuff."

He glanced into the lounge and saw both women dancing seductively together to Marvin Gaye's *Sexual Healing*, which they had put on the stereo system.

Rob came in and joined them. He soon had his tongue down both of their throats.

Tony had seen enough. He drained his glass and told his friend he was off home.

By now, Rob was wild-eyed and animated. He cut Tony off by the door. "Hey, come on, pal. The night is young and these two are up for it. Don't tell me you aren't in need of some horizontal aerobics?"

"Not tonight. I want to get up for the gym in the morning and have a clear head."

"Come on, Tony, loosen up. It isn't going to kill you, man. It's on a plate here for you. They are begging for it."

Tony reached for the door handle. "Maybe that's why I'm not interested. Like I said, no thanks. And go easy on the Columbian marching powder, will you."

Rob knew it was no good pursuing the matter. When Tony Slade made his mind up, that was that. He could be a stubborn bastard.

"Okay, Tony. You're old before your time, my friend. Take it steady and I'll see you soon. Looks like I'm going to have a double whammy." He gestured over his shoulder towards the two women who were now snorting a line of coke each.

Tony opened the door and gave his friend a sly wink as he left. "I'm sure they will be gentle with you."

CHAPTER NINE

Tony walked out into the crisp night air. Rob lived near the Quayside, so he was right back in the hustle and bustle of the thriving crowd.

The city really was a magical place at night, its seven bridges spread out across a spectacular riverscape.

He strolled across the Millennium Bridge mesmerised by the reflection of the lights that shone and shimmered on the river. It was an amazing sight.

He remembered years ago standing on Westminster Bridge about 2.00am in the morning watching the lights of the Houses of Parliament and the accompanying landmarks dance off the river Thames. This was as equally impressive.

The streets were still heavily crowded. Local music legend *Sting* had been playing at the O2 Academy. The concert venue had spilled out earlier and a large section of the two thousand odd crowd were now occupying all the bars on the waterfront.

Tony stood gazing into the water and his thoughts went back to Rob. He sensed that he was up to his neck in trouble with Robbins. He was at his beck and call. The cocaine habit also wasn't a good thing. He would have to keep a close eye on him.

He was suddenly roused from his thoughts by a voice close by calling his name. "It is Tony Slade, isn't it?"

Tony turned and regarded a man around his own age. He wore a black beanie hat, had piercing green eyes and was sporting a neatly trimmed grey beard. His face did seem strangely familiar.

The man came closer. "It is you, Tony. Well I'll be fucked. Remember me? Phil Glover. I was your training partner for a while at Ray Steele's Jujutsu classes way back in *Top Dog*."

"Christ, yeah. I remember. Phil Glover. How are you, man?" Tony extended his hand, which the other man shook warmly. "Fucking hell, Phil. You've got a good memory."

"Never forget the face of a person who knocked my front two teeth out with an elbow strike." grinned Phil.

"Shit. I forgot about that, man. We were so young back then."

"That we were. You were heading for your black belt and then you up and left for the army. I heard you've been all over, the Falkland Islands and everywhere. What finds you back here?"

"I've been out of the army for ages now. I've just been moving around taking work wherever I can. I've been here in Newcastle for a while. What about yourself?"

"I just drove over from Gateshead for the concert this evening at the O2. I live there now. Have done for ten years or more. I'm married with three grown-up children and two grandchildren. I work in the market trade selling fruit and veg," replied Phil.

"Did you keep up your training?" Tony asked.

"Yes, I did. Finally earned my black belt, but now my knees are knackered. Too much rolling around on the mats back in the day. Thought I was fucking invincible. Now I realise your toughest opponent is time. No matter how skilled you are, you can't keep that bastard away. What about yourself?"

Tony smiled. "Yeah, I keep my hand in and still like to do a bit now and then. I normally get to the gym two or three times a week. It's just in the blood, I guess. Until recently, I was still working on the doors."

"Fair play to you, man. Is that what you were doing tonight?"

"No, I was just visiting a mate."

"Look, I'm on my way to get a drink. Do you fancy one?"

It was late and Tony was tired. All he wanted to do now was grab a taxi and get home and sleep. "Maybe I'll another time, Phil. Let me have your mobile number and I'll give you a call when I feel more up to it. It's been a bit of a long day."

"Okay, no problem," said Phil.

Both men exchanged phone numbers.

"Hey, Phil. Before you go, do you know where Ray is these days. I heard that he moved abroad."

Phil laughed. "He lives in Lanzarote. He's been there about three years or so. He owns a little beach front bar. He loves it over there. I went over there about a year ago to visit. Old Ray is still a hard fucker. He must be about 75 now and still runs on the beach daily."

Tony shook his head. "That man is a machine, I swear. Do you have a contact number for him?"

Phil produced his phone again from his pocket and gave Tony Ray's number and address. They shook hands once more and then Phil wandered off into the crowd to find that drink. Tony hailed a taxi and headed for home.

* * *

Next morning, Tony was up at 7.00 am sharp. In the last few months, he had found a good little gym over by Newcastle Central rail station. The *Sweatzone*. It was privately owned and not one of the big commercial chains. He also didn't fancy at the moment using on of Kenny Robbin's gym such as the *Powergym*. He liked it there. You could slip in and out and keep yourself to yourself.

He strolled into the gym reception and said good morning to Chloe, who worked there. He liked Chloe. She was in her early 30s. She had long black hair that today was tied back in a ponytail. Her complexion was flawless, and she had a toned body that most females would die for. She was a real beauty. She always had a smile for him, even this early in the morning.

"You're early today, Tony. Couldn't sleep, eh?" she remarked.

"No, I couldn't, and it was only because I was thinking of you, my love," Tony quipped.

"Is that right?"

They both laughed.

"Can I buy a bottle of water, please?"

"Sure, you can. It will cost you a pound."

She went over to the chiller cabinet and opened it and bent down to the bottom shelf to retrieve one.

Tony couldn't help but admire her shapely backside clad in ultra-tight leggings. It really was a wonderful way to start the day.

He looked away quickly as she rose and turned towards him.

"There you go. Enjoy your workout."

Tony handed her the money and wondered if she had caught him looking. As he walked off, he smiled to himself when he noticed that the chiller cabinet had plenty of water on the top shelves. *Naughty girl*, he thought.

He trained for about an hour or so, working out on the heavy bag and lifting a few weights. After, he grabbed a hot shower and then decided to go get some breakfast. Bidding Chloe goodbye, he said that he would be back in tomorrow. She flashed him a gorgeous smile.

Tony popped in for breakfast at a little cafe called *Tom's*. It was situated in Eldon Square shopping centre. The shopping centre was one of the largest in the UK, covering a staggering 1.4 million square feet.

Even at this early hour, the place was beginning to thrive. Big retail shops, specialist stores, cafes and coffee shops were up and open for business.

Tony slid into a quiet booth and ordered his breakfast. Scrambled eggs, bacon and toast with an orange juice and a large Americano coffee.

He remembered times when coffee houses and fast food joints didn't exist in the UK. He recalled reading about the first McDonald's opening in the UK in 1974 in Woolwich, South East London.

It wasn't until the 80s that fast food places sprung up in their hundreds and then, the 90s brought the coffee shop craze.

Being in the forces, Tony had drunk tea most of the time. Fucking gallons of the stuff. Frequenting coffee shops wasn't on the menu, so to speak. Now, he loved it. It was a sanctuary for him, where he would read the newspaper or maybe a book and chill out away from the world.

His breakfast arrived, and he tucked into it ravenously. His gym workout had certainly built up his appetite.

When finished, he sipped his coffee. It was good. Black and strong. Real coffee, not this latte shit. You might as well have a mug of warm milk. Coffee was meant to be tasted.

He saw a disregarded copy of the *Journal* on another table and reached over and took it. His eyes glazed at the sport on the back page. Newcastle United was at the present contemplating life back in the premiership. Manager Rafa Benitez was talking about strengthening the defence. He would probably need to buy Hadrian's Wall to keep out the likes of players, such as Kane, Sánchez, Agüero and God knows who else that would be starting the season with the 'big boys'.

He turned to the front page to scan the headlines. More talk about the continuing war on terror and speculation about when and where the next strike may happen.

He flicked to the inside of the paper and he suddenly felt like his breakfast was going to re-appear as his stomach lurched.

The headline read: *Local man stabbed outside pub and lies in a critical condition in the Royal Victoria hospital.*

Not unusual news for a big city, but it was the victim's name that hit Tony like a sledgehammer. It was Frank Slade.

He read on and discovered that he had been the victim of a mugging gone wrong. It occurred outside the *Royal Oak* pub in the city centre after closing time. Apparently, a witness saw two young men stab him with knives and run off in the direction of Mosley Street. The police were still looking for any leads.

It also said that the next forty-eight hours would be crucial to see if the victim would pull through.

Tony put the newspaper down. So, the old bastard finally got his comeuppance. It was karma, no doubt. What goes around comes around.

Tony sipped his coffee and wondered how old Frank Slade was. He could be 80 or maybe older. Who knows? It wasn't a bad innings for a nasty piece of shit.

He randomly recalled a time when he was a young boy and Frank had taken him to see his first Newcastle United football match. It was 1969, the year that Newcastle had won the Inter Cities Fairs cup. They beat their Hungarian opponents Újpesti 6-2 over two legs. It was the only piece of silverware they had won from then until now. It had been a team of Tyneside legends. Names such as Bobby Moncur, Ian McFaul, Wyn Davies, Frank Clark and Bobby 'Pop' Robson.

On the day Frank had taken Tony to see Newcastle United, they were up against the mighty Manchester United with a few legends of their own in their line-up. The likes of Best, Charlton, Law and Stiles.

Manchester United ran out as 2-0 winners. Newcastle had been well beaten.

At half time, Tony remembered going to the toilets with Frank. Back then, the toilets were just a concrete communal block. He recalled a semi-drunken man bumping into him and knocking him off his feet. The man turned to apologise. Although this man wasn't wearing Manchester United colours, Frank Slade recognised the accent.

As the man offered his hand to Frank to say sorry, Tony saw his father headbutt him straight in the face. The man staggered back clutching his nose. Blood seeped through his hands.

Tony watched in fear and horror as Frank followed this up with a heavy kick in his balls.

As the man dropped to the urine soaked floor, some other men joined Frank, kicking and stomping on the hapless fallen figure.

When they eventually stopped, they were all breathing heavy from the exertion. Frank grabbed Tony by the arm and said, "That's how we deal with Manchester filth up here."

They made their way back to the match after Frank had made a stop for a meat pie and a cup of tea. He carried on watching the game, eating and drinking as if nothing had happened.

Tony stood in shock for the rest of the match. The level and ferocity of the violence had shaken his young body and mind to the core.

Tony had nightmares about this incident for months and he wondered what had become of the man so cruelly beaten.

Tony folded the newspaper and put it back on the table. He drained his cup.

He didn't really know why, but he decided he would go to the hospital and visit him. Tony didn't know what he would do or say. The last time he had seen Frank Slade was lying on the floor of the pub in which he had given him a beating.

One thing he was sure of was that he wouldn't be visiting the old fucker's bedside with a bunch of flowers and some grapes.

* * *

Later that day, Tony stood outside the Leazes Wing entrance of the Royal Victoria Infirmary off Richardson

Road. The hospital was an impressive place and it had been serving the city of Newcastle for 250 years, dealing with all kinds of medical issues and illnesses.

He could remember back on many occasions when he had come here with his mother to A&E or outpatients after one of her many 'accidents'.

He felt a cold shiver run up his spine. He put it down to the chilly wind blowing and made his way in up to Level 5.

He went to the reception desk and asked if he could see Frank Slade, telling them that he was his son. He was informed that he was critical but stable and that he could only have ten minutes with him. That suited Tony just fine.

Tony stood by the bedside and looked down on Frank Slade's sleeping form. He had various tubes and wires coming out of him connected to drips and other equipment that made a lot of bleeping noises. He looked old and somehow small. He didn't resemble the big bear of a man that he had been back in the day.

Frank's eyes suddenly opened and focused on Tony. Realisation dawned on his face. He pulled at the plastic oxygen mask covering his nose and mouth and removed it. "You're the last person I expected to see." He breathed heavily between the words. "Come to gloat, have you? See the old man draw his last breath, eh?"

Tony regarded him. His mind was a mass of emotions. "Yeah, something like that."

Frank Slade laughed, then broke into a fit of coughing.

Finally, it subsided. "There were two of the little fuckers waiting outside the pub. Can you believe they asked me for my wallet? They asked Frank 'fucking' Slade of all people, cheeky cunts. I told them where they could go and then, they both pulled blades and asked me again. I had sunk a few beers, mind you, but I was still sober enough to tell them I would stick the knives up their arses if they didn't fuck off. Then, one of the little bastards just grabbed me by my coat and started sticking me. I just wasn't fast enough. Then, the other one joined in and I was down. I can't remember anything more until I woke up in this place."

Tony moved closer to the bed. "Are you looking for my sympathy? It's fucking karma. What goes around comes around. You were due it."

Frank's face broke into a grin. "I'm not looking for anything from you, my son. You owe me nothing. Why did you fucking come here, boy?"

"Maybe, it was to see you die. Just so I know you are finally fucking gone. The world will be a better place and there will be many a person raising a glass to your passing. Not in your memory either, but because they will be glad to see the back of you."

The older man's eyes narrowed. "Who the fuck are you to judge me? Never forget what they say; the apple doesn't fall too far from the tree. I heard through the grapevine that you are no saint. Like father like son, I would say." Frank Slade laughed again.

Tony leaned in closer until he was inches from the older man's face. "Well, that's where you are fucking wrong. Here is the clincher, old man. I am not your son and never have been. I am Terry Norris's son. Remember him?"

He saw Frank Slade's mind turning over the information.

"Mum had a relationship with him, didn't she? She went back to him one night after you beat her. She slept with him and that's how I came about. It was nothing to fucking do with you, thank God. It was like a great weight of my back to know that I wasn't the son of a vicious waste of space like you."

Frank Slade attempted to reach out and grab at Tony's jacket, but wasn't fast enough. Tony pulled away.

"You're fucking lying," Frank Slade spluttered, "Do you think that's going to hurt me when I am lying here at fucking death's door?"

"Yes, I do. It hurts you more than any of those knife wounds to know that Big Frank Slade couldn't father a child and had been firing blanks all his life. It was all in the letter that mum gave me. You had tried for a child many times without success. But you refused to see a doctor, content to blame it on your wife instead. Then, a fucking miracle occurred, didn't it, Frank? Or so you thought. But all along, I was Terry's son."

Frank Slade again tried to move, but the pain was too much. He bellowed out in discomfort, so loudly that it brought a nurse running in.

She regarded both men. "I think that Mr. Slade has had enough excitement for one day. I suggest you leave now, sir."

Both men glared at each other. Then, Frank Slade turned his face away.

"Yes, you are right, Nurse. He is getting a little emotional. He hasn't seen me for so long. I'll let him rest now," said Tony.

The nurse began fussing around the bed tucking the sheets back in.

"Maybe you could come back tomorrow, if you wish?"

Tony walked to the door. "I don't think so," he replied.

With that, he turned and was gone.

* * *

When Tony had gone, Frank Slade quietly weep. Deep down, he had suspected that Tony might not be his son, but his ego had chosen to ignore it. There was a time when he loved the boy dearly, but when he lost his job, he lost his way and eventually, his mind.

Alcohol dulled the pain for a while, but then it turned him into a monster who was capable of terrible things. He knew it was wrong, but couldn't stop himself. The self-destruct button had been pressed and there was no turning back. He lost everything that had been precious to him.

The pain he was feeling at present from the knife wounds inflicted on his body were nowhere near as painful as the mental scars of guilt and hatred that he felt for himself and what he had done to the people he loved.

He had been a good man once. A hard-grafting family man. Happy. But it was so long ago, he had a job to remember.

He eventually cried himself to sleep.

Outside the hospital, Tony breathed in the fresh air. It was good to be outside again. He began to walk back to his car. He felt the familiar tingle of adrenaline begin to subside. He reached into his coat pocket and produced a stick of chewing gum. He unwrapped it and popped it into his mouth and began chewing. That felt better. His mouth had been dry. That was a by-product of adrenaline that he knew well from going into combat. Some men smoked to deal with this; Tony preferred his chewing gum.

He was calmer now and glad that he had gone into the hospital. He would be a liar if he said that he hadn't got a great deal of pleasure from dropping that bombshell on the old bastard. He felt unfinished business was now completed. It was time to move on.

Frank Slade had looked old and helpless lying in that hospital bed. The brutal and heartless monster from Tony's childhood was all but gone. The years had eroded him. The wounds that had been inflicted on him from the knives of those two youths were the results of him believing that he was still a force to be reckoned with, but he wasn't anymore. He was just a sad, old man.

Tony drove away from the hospital and a piece of his life that he no longer needed to drag around with him.

As if to confirm this, two days later, he read in the newspaper that Frank Slade had died in his sleep. It had not been from the knife wounds inflicted on him, but from what was believed to be a heart attack. Tony didn't shed any tears. He felt nothing. He would not be crying at his graveside and he doubted that neither would many others.

CHAPTER TEN

Present

A loud crash shook Tony from his thoughts. His hand once again instinctively shot up to the inside of his jacket. The reassuring weight of the Glock 17 model 117 nestling in his jacket pocket gave him a degree of comfort.

The source of the noise had been some plates dropping behind the counter by one of the staff. He relaxed once more.

He scanned the coffee shop to see if anybody was observing him, but the few people that were in there seemed wrapped up in their own thoughts. He glanced at his watch. She had told him that she would ring when she was on her way. She hadn't, and it was far too risky for him to ring her.

He was worried. She should have been here by now. This was crazy. He could just get up and walk out of here and disappear. But he loved her. The first woman he had really loved from his early days with Katy. That was so long ago.

He picked up his empty cup and walked up to the counter to get another coffee shop. Kim saw him coming. "Same again?"

Tony smiled. "Yes please."

"I'll bring it over in a minute." Kim hesitated a moment, then added. "Do you mind me asking? Who is it you're waiting for?"

"Who said that I'm waiting for anyone?"

Tony winked, turned to walk away and stopped. "This Crane character you mentioned earlier. You sure it's not worth telling the police about?"

"I think the creep is well gone by now. I don't want to push it if it isn't necessary."

"Fair enough. Nevertheless, just keep an eye out."

Kim sensed Tony's unease. Her face became serious, "Is everything okay?"

Tony picked up a newspaper from the counter.

"Yeah. Everything is fine," he replied walking back to his table.

Kim watched him go. She liked Tony, but he was a bit of a mystery. She was truly curious to know who he was waiting for and why.

The day after the incident.

Colin Crane lay on the bed in his grotty little bedsit and stared at the ceiling. He listened to the rain beating on the window. He reached out, picked up his mobile phone from the bedside cabinet and looked at the time. It read 10.30am. He should get up, but he had nothing to get up for. He had no fucking job to go to. That was all down to the bitch at the *Alpha* coffee house. Who the fuck did she think she was firing him just like that?

Okay, he made one fucking mistake. He had even offered to put the money back. It had been the same at that burger joint and the pizza delivery place when he was late on a few occasions or had the odd day off. It was no big deal, was it?

Every fucking manager had it in for him. The bastards. They hated him, especially that stuck up whore Kim.

I should have given her a good slap instead of throwing that mug at her. In fact, I bet that's exactly what she needs. A good slap and then bend her over a table in that fucking coffee shop and stick it up her good and proper. She would love it. She would respond to me and beg me for more.

Colin felt himself getting aroused under the sheets. He touched himself. It felt good.

I would clamp my hand over her mouth and grip her hair as I pumped into her. Then, when I had finished, I would smash her face into the table top over and over.

The image was vivid in his head as he grunted to a climax.

He lay there now breathing heavily, a thin sheen of sweat covering his milk white skin. He was spent. The images he had conjured up now began to fade away, along with his hardness.

Nobody respected or took Colin Crane seriously. This had been going on all his life.

He hadn't known his real parents. Later in life he found out that his birth mother had been a heroin addict and turned to prostitution to feed her habit. Social services had intervened and took Colin away. He had been adopted by a kindly middle-aged couple, Reg and Marjorie Crane. They had seemed a nice couple. That was until when he was 6 or 7 years old and Reg Crane used to visit him in his bedroom at night and make him do disgusting things to him and tell him to keep it their little secret.

This had made Colin become an introverted child. At school, he became the victim of bullying and ridicule.

He hated school and left at sixteen years of age with no real career prospects, so he decided to run away. Away from the abuse of Reg Crane and away from his unhappy life. Before he left his home city of Bristol, he went back to the Crane's house. He knew they both loved their stupid cat Timmy. He found him in the front garden easily enough and enticed him over with a piece of fish. When he got close enough, he rammed a knife into its body and gutted it open. He then left the bloody remains on the Crane's doorstep. Served the fucker right.

Colin had drifted in and out of jobs pretty much since then. He had moved to Gloucester for a while and then up Oxford and Banbury.

He just didn't seem to mix with people and never kept a job very long.

The scars of his boyhood abuse were still raw.

When he was 25 years old, he decided to return to Bristol.

He visited the Crane's house once again and saw that his stepparents still lived there. They were now older and seemed more vulnerable. He had never forgotten the terror that he had endured in that house.

He came back over the course of a few weeks and realised that Reg Crane still went to skittles every Wednesday night down at his local.

Colin waited one night until the old boy came staggering home after a good night out. He remembered that Wednesday night had been one of the nights he had been visited in his bed. He could recall the smell of beer and whiskey on the bastard's breath as he removed Colin's pyjama bottoms.

Just as Reg Crane reached his front garden gate, Colin had stepped out of the shadows of the conifer trees that lined the street and smashed a coal hammer over his head a couple of times and then ran away. He thought he had killed him.

Two days later, he read that Reg Crane had survived the wounds but was in a critical condition in hospital. If the bastard survived, Colin hoped that he would carry the scars for life as a penance for the rest of his days.

Colin had got away with it. Nobody saw him or suspected him. That was the problem with him. Nobody ever noticed him. But that was all about to change.

Very soon, people would take notice. People would know the name of Colin Crane. They would not forget the name in a hurry. That was a fucking promise. Especially that bitch of a manager at the *Alpha*.

He threw back the bedclothes and headed for the shower. Suddenly, he felt a whole deal better and he had a clearer vision of what he needed to do. He needed to call his one and only friend that he knew back from his school days. There was business to be done.

CHAPTER ELEVEN

Present

The day was still grey, and the rain was relentless. Tony shut the newspaper, glanced at the time and then checked his phone for the umpteenth time. No message. He sat back down and looked out of the window in the hope that he would see her coming.

He felt that something wasn't right, but he felt powerless at this moment to do anything about it. He decided to give it another half an hour.

The clientele was forever changing in the shop. Now, to his left were a couple of school kids around 14 years of age or so. They were eating some type of breakfast muffins and playing on their phones.

To the right was a smartly dressed elderly gentleman. He was reading the *Times* newspaper whilst he sipped on his tea.

At the counter was a young woman clad in running gear. She was ordering an espresso. Ready to kickstart the morning, no doubt, Tony mused.

He liked people watching. He found it fascinating. You could learn so much by doing it. This, of course, stemmed back to his time in the army. Awareness was the key to survival.

Even here in the coffee shop, he was tactically seated in the corner facing the door. He could survey the whole room from here and be ready to move if need be.

His situational awareness and tactical positioning had saved his live on more than one occasion.

* * *

Past

He vividly recalled a time in Northern Ireland when he was in a bar for a night out with the lads. This pub, *The Shamrock,* was known as a safe environment for soldiers to have a drink in. They drank there regularly without incident or trouble.

As Tony wasn't much of a drinker at the time, he had become the lad's unofficial driver and lookout whilst the rest of them got pissed.

This Friday evening, Tony sat with a pint casually scanning the room. The pub was packed to the rafters.

His eyes came to rest on two thickset men sat at a table by the toilets. Both were huddled in conversation over their pints of Guinness. By their dress, they both looked like they had just finished a gruelling day's work on a building site.

Occasionally, they would look up from their conversation and glance around and a couple of times, they caught Tony watching them.

Not particularly unusual in this pub. Tony couldn't put his finger on it, but they began to make him feel uneasy.

After some time, the men drained their glasses and got up from the table. They both lifted tool bags onto their shoulders. One of the men gestured that he was going to the toilets. The other man headed for the exit.

Tony watched the man disappear into the toilets. A few minutes later, he came back out and left the pub.

Tony immediately sensed something was wrong, as the man was leaving without the tool bag which he had gone into the toilets with.

He got up and pushed his way through the crowd and entered the toilets. A few guys were stood at the urinals. There were four cubicles in total. The doors were open on three of them. The door was shut on the fourth one in line.

Tony moved towards it, dropped onto his knees and looked under the gap at the bottom of the door to see if anybody was in there. It appeared empty.

He knocked on the door and asked, "Is anybody in there?"

Nobody answered, so Tony went into the cubicle next door and pulled himself up the wall to look over into the locked one. He immediately saw the tool bag shoved down behind the toilet's soil pipe. He also spied a small red light blinking on and off.

He jumped down in a flash and ran out into the bar. He headed over towards the landlord, Kieran Moran.

Kieran, who had just finished pulling a pint for a customer, regarded Tony heading towards him purposely.

"Is everything alright, Tony?"

"I think you have a problem. There is a suspect device in the gents' toilet and I suggest you get everybody out of here as quickly and orderly as possible," Tony informed him.

Kieran's eyes widened in fear. "Shit, are you sure?"

Tony regarded the worried landlord, "99% sure, yes."

"Right, I will make an announcement now."

Tony clapped him on the shoulder. "Good man. Now, can I use the phone? I need to get the bomb disposal team here asap."

Within minutes, the place was cleared. These people were used to the atrocities that blighted their country. They were all switched on enough to know what to do in a crisis. Many calmly brought their drinks out with them.

The off-duty paras helped the elderly and infirm outside and to a safe distance from the pub.

Finally, Kieran, Tony and the two other bar staff left the premises.

Everybody gathered at the far end of the large gravel car park. Luckily, *The Shamrock* stood detached and away from any residential housing.

Tony informed the assembled group that the bomb disposal team and the emergency services were minutes away. Just stay well back and let them do their job.

"Sir, excuse me. But I can't find George. I thought he was here, but I can't see him."

Tony regarded a concerned looking elderly woman who was tugging nervously on his coat sleeve.

"Who is George, pet? Your husband?"

"God, no. My husband has been dead ten years or more. George is my dog. I think he has gone back into the pub."

Tony looked at her worried face and then glanced towards the pub.

"Wait here," he instructed and began heading back towards the building. Just then, a deafening explosion ripped through the night air. Concrete, wood and glass flew everywhere.

The crowd ran for cover, cowering and screaming. The pub was ablaze. Sirens could be heard coming closer.

Tony dived to the ground as the blast rang out and was showered with dust and debris, but he was unhurt. His eardrums were ringing and everything around him sounded muffled.

From his fallen position, he felt a damp tongue lick his face and he turned to see a Yorkshire terrier, which he presumed was George, the missing dog, looking mighty pleased to see him. He was all in one piece, as were the crowd. This had largely been down to Tony's awareness and quick thinking. It could have been a totally different story. This had been a deliberate and premeditated attack on the British army, without a doubt. They had been lucky this time.

Tony's training had been instrumental in averting a bigger scene of carnage. The OODA loop had been the key factor. Observation, orient, decide, act. The military, police and security all worked a form of this tried and tested formula. It was developed by a United States Air Force Colonel named John Boyd and it was rapidly being used as a major training strategy in warfare.

Tony had used the concept many times when he was 'working the doors'. It had saved his ass in this environment as well. It was a very valuable tool indeed.

For his bravery on that night at *The Shamrock* pub, Tony later received the Queen's gallantry medal.

* * *

Present

The rain was still coming down, but a little lighter, as the sun tried to push through the clouds. It was amazing how a bit of sun can change people's personas. Things always seemed better when the sun was shining. The trouble with living in the UK was that those sunny days were few and far between.

As a young boy, summer seemed to go on forever. Rarely did you get more than one or two days rain in a row. These days, though, the whole climate had changed.

How Tony longed to be in some sunny climate now. Away from all the turmoil, lying on a beach somewhere exotic with a cocktail in his hand and the woman of his dreams next to him.

He recalled the last time that he had gone abroad and got a bit of sun on his back. It had been a while now. It was when he had decided to go out to Lanzarote to seek out his old friend and mentor Ray Steele.

The Past

Tony was earning some decent money now, and apart from Rob and his erratic mood swings, things were going okay. He was coming around to the fact that he might just be able to stomach the job and take the cash for now. Maybe he did have a future after all.

He cleared the holiday with Robbins. He was told to be back in a week, as some important things were in the pipeline and he was needed there. Also, Robbins expressed concern over Rob. He informed Tony to keep an eye on him because if he became a problem, he was out. Robbins couldn't afford any passengers, especially if they were turning into a cokehead. He told Tony that he would leave the matter in his hands for now to make his friend shape up or ship out.

The night before leaving on holiday, Tony went around to Rob's flat and rang the doorbell persistently, but nobody answered. He could hear music through the door, but nothing else. He also tried phoning Rob, but with no luck. He left a voice message letting him know where he was going and when he would be back. He could do no more for now.

Tony grabbed an early morning flight out of Newcastle International Airport on a bleak grey Tyneside morning and headed for the sun of Lanzarote.

The third most populated of the Canary Islands, Lanzarote has a pleasant sunny climate all year around. Tony had never been there before, and he was looking forward to exploring some of it with Ray.

Tony landed at the airport in the island's capital Arrecife. He then took a taxi ride a short distance to the small seafront resort of Matagorda. It was at the quieter end of the island. Just the right sort of place to get a bit of peace and quiet.

Tony sat back and enjoyed the taxi ride. The warm air blew in through the open windows, so did the smell of the sea. The barren volcanic scenery sped by, as the driver put his foot down.

Some twenty minutes later, Tony stood outside the address that he had been given. *Ray's Seafront Bar and Grill.*

He hadn't phoned Ray to tell him that he was going to fly over to visit him. He wanted to surprise the old bugger.

The building was a typical Mediterranean style. White washed stucco with a red tiled roof. The bar's neon sign hung proudly above the door and strings of fairy lights adorned the external walls and the large patio area. Large cactus plants of various shapes and sizes adorned the outside area. The bar looked directly out to the sea. It was the perfect location.

For the first time in a while, Tony felt himself relax.

A small gathering of people sat outside eating brunch, drinking coffee or enjoying their first beer of the day in the beautiful sunshine.

Tony walked up the steps into the dark, cool interior. Inside, it resembled a pub back home. Obviously, it had been decorated this way to encourage the less adventurous British holidaymaker to feel at ease in surroundings in which they were comfortable.

There was Bass Bitter on tap, as well as San Miguel and other local brews. *The Sun* and *Daily Mirror* newspapers lay on the table tops alongside Heinz tomato ketchup and Coleman's mustard bottles.

Tony walked up to the bar where a young girl with long brown hair stylishly tied back in a ponytail with a yellow ribbon was busy cleaning glasses.

"Hello, I am looking for Ray, is he around?"

The girl ran appraising eyes over Tony and then asked, "Is he expecting you? He's busy out the back at present."

"No, he isn't. I'm here to surprise him. I'm an old friend from England. I haven't seen him for years."

"What's your name? I'll go and speak to him."

"Thank you. Tell him that Tony Slade has come all the way from England to kick his arse."

The girl didn't know how to take this. She just nodded and disappeared into the back room behind the bar.

Tony wandered around the bar whilst he waited.

The walls were adorned with a lot of British memorabilia. There were old football programmes, many of them Newcastle United. There were also film posters, boxing and Martial arts photographs, retro vinyl record sleeves and vintage tin advertising signs. It all added to the flavour of the place.

Tony smiled to himself when he spied an old black and white framed photograph of Ray and Terry Norris stood in the old gym in Durham. The date read August 1975. Both men stood shoulder to shoulder staring into the camera lens. They were tough, confident men. It brought memories flooding back.

From behind him, he heard a gruff Geordie accent.

"We were a fucking handful back then, I can tell you. Right hard bastards."

Tony immediately recognised the voice, even after all this time.

He turned around to gaze into the vivid grey eyes of Ray Steele. An older Ray, no doubt. The lines and scars of a tough life lined his features, but he was all there. He still looked in shape. He wore a bright coloured Bermudian shirt over a white vest that fitted him well. No sign of a belly or man boobs.

"Tony Slade. Well, I'll be fucked. The last time I saw you, you were in uniform. A slip of a kid. Just growing a wispy beard, I recall. I doubt your balls had dropped then. Where the fuck has the time gone? It's great to see you, son."

"It's great to see you too, Ray."

Both men embraced each other.

"Fuck me, lad. This is a surprise. When Lucy came back and told me, I thought it was some sort of joke."

Tony laughed. "No joke, my friend. I'm here for a while and looking for somewhere to stay."

"How the fuck did you find me?" asked the older man.

"I got your address from another old student of yours, Phil Glover. We just accidently bumped into each other when I was back in Newcastle."

"Christ, what a stroke of luck. A good man, Phil. He came out here last year to visit," remarked Ray.

"Yeah, so he told me. That's how I knew where you were."

"Come on. Let's get a beer and catch up." Ray guided Tony back towards the bar.

"Lucy, set us up a couple of bottles, will you, pet?"

The girl that Tony had spoken to at the bar smiled and said, "Right away, Boss."

"Tony, this is Lucy. She manages the establishment with her husband, Camilo. They keep my little investment ticking over for me and run it like clockwork. I couldn't live without them."

Lucy put two ice cool beers down on the bar in front of them.

"Lucy, this is Tony Slade, a good friend of mine back in the day and one of my top Jujutsu students."

Lucy extended a bronzed, slim hand. "Pleased to meet you, Tony. Sorry to be so cagey with you, but Ray is a bit particular with who he meets."

Tony shook her hand. It felt soft and cool. "Not a problem. Pleased to meet you. You must be special if you're getting praise from this man."

They all laughed.

"Come on, let's take the weight off our feet." Ray gestured to a quiet corner table. "Lucy, this may take a while. Bring us over another couple of bottles and a bottle of Johnnie Walker. Thanks, pet.

They both retired to the corner table and took a pull on their beers.

"God, lad, I can't believe you're here. The last I heard you were playing Rambo out in Africa someplace. Are you out of the army now?"

"Yeah, I've been out a long time now. I've been in and out of various jobs. I've even been back on the doors. I'm getting too old for all that shit though."

Ray nodded. He understood. He had worked the doors on the clubs well into his sixties. It was a different world to when he started back in the 60s. Now, drugs

were everywhere and that made the punters unpredictable and dangerous.

"So, what are you doing these days for work'?" he
asked.

Tony took another pull on his drink and shuffled a
little uncomfortably on his chair.

"I'm working for Kenny Robbins."

Ray nearly choked on his beer.

"What? THE Kenny Robbins, Tyneside gangster and
Mr fucking Big?"

Lucy approached the table with their beers, the
bottle of whiskey and a couple of shot glasses. Both men
fell silent. She placed them down without saying a
word, knowing she had gate-crashed a private conversation, and went back to the bar.

"Well, is it?"

Tony looked sheepishly at Ray. "Yes, the one and
same, I'm afraid to say."

Ray shook his head in amazement. "Fucking hell, my
son. Things must be tough. Robbins is a psychotic
bastard."

"I know all that Ray and I haven't come out here for a
lecture. He's paying good money. The best money I have
had for years, and when I earn enough, I'll be out of it."

Ray raised his eyebrows. "What just like that?
Robbins will let you walk off into the sunset after
knowing all his crooked deals? Come on, son. Wake up.
You don't just walk out on men like Robbins."

"You watch me, Ray. I'm not afraid of Robbins. I've
been fighting all my fucking life and have nothing to
show for it. No wife, no kids, no family, no house and,
up to now, no future. Violence and killing is all I know.
It's all that I am fucking good at. But I'm getting old and

it's time to get out and do what you've done and make a new life away from all that shit. You, of all people, can understand that, Ray, surely?"

Ray picked up his whiskey glass and swirled the amber liquid around with the ice and took a sip. "Yes, I can understand. I'm just asking you to be careful. I knew Robbins' old man from years back. We had a bit of a run in. Well, a bit of a Mexican stand-off really. We were both wary of our reputations at the time. Nothing came of it, but it wouldn't have surprised me if he had come looking for me with a shotgun. Like father like son. Both are dangerous fuckers. Just watch your back and if you ever need a place to keep your head down, it's here for you, okay?"

Tony raised his glass and touched it to Ray's. "Thanks, my friend. I appreciate that. Now, tell me how you got this place?"

Ray went on to explain that he had got fed up with the gym. He had found people gravitating towards the shiny big chain gyms. The old spit and sawdust ones were dying.

When he took the gym over from Terry, it had been struggling, and it just went from bad to worse. He had been struggling to pay the bills and then, this fitness franchise came calling and asked if he would sell up. It was a godsend and Ray went with it. They had asked him if he had wanted to be part of the new set-up, but Ray knew he was too old in the tooth to change. These days, fitness was all about qualifications, courses and exams. Ray couldn't be doing with all that bollocks.

In his day, he and Terry had trained many a champion without a qualification between them, only their real world fighting experience. In Ray's mind, fitness was simple. It wasn't rocket science. There had been no fancy machines, no expensive supplements and no fucking Zumba classes. They had all been fit, super strong monsters without all of today's fitness industry mumbo jumbo.

He told Tony how he recalled winning a gold medal in Judo at Crystal Palace back in the 60s, and he had been training on pie and mash, Guinness and ten cigarettes a day. Fuck it, what did those fitness gurus know?

He informed Tony that he was 75 years old and still ran on the beach most mornings and he had a punch bag rigged up in the back garden that he used. That was it. Fuck the rest of it. His Jujutsu days were over after having a knee replacement and a couple of his neck's cervical vertebrae shaved down. But, in his own words, he could still do a bit if needed. Tony believed him.

Ray went on to say how he sold the gym and moved out here. He bought the bar and then met a lady. Ellen was her name. She was English and a widower. She and her late husband had lived out in Lanzarote since the 80s and had bought and sold property.

Ray and Ellen had hit it off immediately and after a whirlwind romance, they married. She invested in the bar and they extended it into a grill. The punters loved it and it had become a very successful business. Ray had never been happier.

Then, one-day, sad news arrived. Ellen had been diagnosed with cancer. It was a particularly aggressive form and it had got into her bones. Within a year, she had died.

Ray had been devastated. The business began to suffer, until two of his customers came to him and said that they could manage the place for him if he wished.

They were both university graduates in business studies and had owned their own bar for a while in Tenerife, the largest of the Canary Islands. That had been Lucy and her husband Camilo.

Camilo had been born here and Lucy, who was British, had moved out here after a holiday romance that had ended in marriage for them both.

Ray had readily taken them up on the offer and that was it.

They had become like a son and daughter to him and great company

Gradually, Ray learnt to live with his grief and had put all his energies into the business. He also became landlord for a few holiday villas that his wife Ellen had owned.

Tony was impressed how Ray had coped with a sad tragedy and had gone on to make a comfortable life for himself.

As more drinks flowed, Tony spoke to Ray about his army experiences and adventures. They then reminisced about the *Top Dog* and the characters that had been there.

Both men later took a stroll along the seafront and Ray showed him his home before returning to the bar for evening dinner.

Then, finally, as the skies darkened outside, and the whiskey bottle was drained, Tony told Ray that Terry Norris had been his real dad.

As the sun went down, Ray showed Tony to a spare room in his villa behind the bar and grill and bid him goodnight.

Tony clambered into bed a little worse for wear himself and was asleep before his head touched the pillow.

CHAPTER TWELVE

Tony woke up with a fuzzy head and the taste of stale whiskey in his mouth. He rolled over in bed and saw the morning sun streaming brightly through the curtains. It hurt his eyes.

He sat up, threw back the sheets and swung his feet down to the cool tiled floor.

He rubbed his hands through his hair and over his stubbly chin.

How much did he end up drinking last night? He just remembered falling into bed eventually. That Ray Steele was a bad influence, the old bugger.

Tony rose gingerly, stretched his stiff muscles and headed for the shower.

Twenty minutes later, Tony walked into the bar where he was greeted by a mug of black coffee handed to him by Lucy.

"Good morning, Tony. I thought you might need this."

"Lucy, you are a lifesaver. Thank you."

Tony took a sip from the mug. It tasted like nectar. Pure nectar.

"Heavy night, I guess?"

Tony smiled. "Yeah, you could say that. I drunk way too much."

Lucy laughed. "I take it you won't be wanting the *Gutbuster* breakfast we offer then."

Tony shook his head. "You guessed right, pet. Coffee is just fine. Thanks."

He looked around the bar. "Where's Ray? Is he up yet?"

Lucy nodded towards the front door.

"Oh yes, he's up alright. He's been out running on the beach and he's swimming in the ocean as we speak."

Tony walked towards the open door and looked out across the road to the sea. He spotted Ray just coming out of the waves and beginning to walk up the beach.

Tony shook his head in amazement. "That man is a machine. I swear he's not human. He drank as much as I did last night."

Lucy came and stood by him. "He is certainly one special man. He's been like a father to me since I came to work here."

Tony regarded her and saw the caring look in her eyes as she watched Ray getting closer. Ray was a true warrior. He was a man that could be brutal when needed but also, he could be gentle. He didn't need to carry his fighting ability around with him like a cross. That is what Tony had loved about him when they had first met and in the times that they had trained and worked together.

Ray crossed the road and walked up onto the sandy boardwalk of the bar.

"Well, well, well. Sleeping Beauty has arisen at last. How are you feeling?"

Tony raised his mug in a salute. "I'll be a lot better after a few of these."

"Good stuff. We've got a busy day ahead of us."

"We do?"

"We do. I'm going to show you a bit of this lovely island, if you are up for it."

"Sounds good, Ray," Tony answered.

"Okay. That's sound. I'll grab a shower and be with you in fifteen minutes or so."

* * *

The rest of the day, Ray drove Tony around the island in a 1967 Ford Thunderbird convertible which he had bought and shipped over from the States. It was a deep red colour and went like a dream. The climate was perfect for a convertible.

They drove up into the Fire Mountains and visited Timanfaya National Park.

Ray told Tony that this part of the island was a must for any visitor because of its unique 'lunar' landscape and rare plant species. The volcanic landscape was awe-inspiring as were the many geysers.

Both men watched several demonstrations of how hot the area is. Ray informed Tony that temperatures just a few metres below the surface can reach between 400°C and 600°C. They watched as dry brush thrown into a hole in the ground caught fire immediately, while water poured into a bore hole erupted seconds later in the form of a stream-like mini-geyser.

They ate a late lunch at the famed *El Diablo* restaurant that provides an impressive backdrop to the national park and serves Canarian food, which is cooked by placing a cast-iron grill over a large hole in the ground using geothermal heat.

Tony loved the experience and found Ray knowledgeable about the island, quoting facts and figures about the history of the place with ease.

They drove back through the picturesque village of Yaiza, then down to the bustling seafront streets of Puerto del Carmen before heading back to Matagorda.

Tony could see why Ray had fallen in love with the island and part of him envied his friend.

Maybe he might just consider moving out here. Ray had already suggested it. He had told Tony that if he ever did, he could stay with him at the bar until he found his feet. He also told him that he could do with a trustworthy person to help him manage his property letting business. The idea was appealing, but Tony needed more money behind him.

This made him think about Kenny Robbins and the job back home. A small black cloud descended on his mood by the time they arrived back at Ray's place and he told his friend that he was going to take a little stroll and would see him later.

Tony arrived back at the bar around 8.00pm and as he walked up to the entrance, he noticed three men in heated conversation with Ray.

The walk had cleared Tony's head and he felt in a better place and was looking forward to dinner with his old pal. Now, alarm bells sounded as he surveyed the scene ahead of him.

He had worked enough club and pub doors to know what was occurring. He knew Ray had worked a damn sight more of them than him and as tough as the old bugger was, he was facing off on his own against three large, drunken young men.

As he got in hearing distance, the saga began to unfold. The ringleader of the three was a big blonde lad who looked like he had stayed out in the sun too much that day, as his skin was the colour of a tomato. Too much sun and too much beer was a dangerous combination.

Tony had seen it all before. A different face but the same old game. The signs were all there. The posturing of the body. Splayed arms and puffed out chest. The pacing up and down. Weight shifting from foot to foot. The look of indignation and hate on the face.

"What do you mean we can't come in?" the blonde man asked.

Ray stood straight and firm in front of the door.

"Like I said lads, you have had enough. Move on to somewhere else. We don't need you in here. We have families in here with children. They are enjoying their meals in peace. There are other bars to drink in further down the road. Grab a taxi to Puerto del Carmen. They have a great nightlife there."

'Blondie' looked around him for the support of his mates. "Did you hear what this old fellow said, lads?"

The other two men, who were also as sunburnt as lobsters, nodded and stupidly grinned.

'Blondie' turned back to Ray. ''Well, Granddad. What about if we just walk right on in?"

Tony noticed Ray subtlety shift his weight and blade his body slightly. It was a pre-cursor to violence.

"I wouldn't do that, son. That wouldn't be a smart move on your part."

'Blondie's' face broke into a sickly smile.

"Well is that so, Granddad."

He moved to push past Ray.

As soon as his hand landed on Ray's chest, the older man cranked on a vicious wrist lock that took 'Blondie' to his knees in pain and surprise. The follow-up edge of the hand chop to the side of his neck put him down.

Tony moved forward fast and clamped a hard strangle on one of the other guy's neck. He turned his hips into him and stretched him over his back as he pulled him out of the entrance and dumped him onto the pavement.

The man made to get back up, but Tony kicked him in the face sending him sprawling again minus a few teeth. "Stay down, you prick," he ordered.

The last guy took a swing at Ray, but the veteran fighter ducked under it with ease and smashed a side kick into the man's knee. He cried out in pain as he collapsed to the ground.

Camilo arrived from behind the bar with a steel Louisville slugger baseball bat and joined Tony and Ray.

They watched as eventually, two of the three men staggered to their feet and helped their fallen buddy with knee ligament trouble off the premises. They wandered off into the evening mumbling half-heated threats and licking their considerable wounds.

"The police are on their way, so don't bother trying to come back," Ray shouted.

He then turned to his customers. "I apologise for the need for violence. Hope you will stay and continue your meals."

The assembled crowd in the holiday mood gave him a rousing round of applause and then, went back to eating and drinking. The show was over.

Ray regarded Tony. "Thanks for the help, son, but I had it under control."

Tony's face broke into a grin. "I know you did. I just couldn't resist it. Just like old times."

Ray slapped Tony on the back. "Come on. All this exercise has made me hungry. Let's eat."

The remainder of the holiday went without incident. They spent their mornings running on the beach and swimming in the sea. In the afternoons, Ray drove Tony around to more sightseeing locations, including the stunning beaches and scenery of Papagayo and a cruise across to Fuerteventura. Their evenings were spent dining outside, drinking good wine and fine whiskey and talking about the past. Tony hadn't felt so relaxed in a long while.

When Ray dropped Tony off at the airport for his flight back to the UK, he told him not to forget his offer of work and a place to stay. He just had to call.

Tony embraced his old friend and told him that he would keep in touch. Ray's final words to Tony before they departed were to watch his back with Kenny Robbins, do not underestimate him and be smart. Tony acknowledged what Ray had said.

CHAPTER THIRTEEN

The plane landed at Newcastle International just after midnight. It was nearly 1.00am by the time Tony had retrieved his baggage and picked up his car.

Before he drove off, he switched his mobile phone back on and noticed three miscalls from Rob. Then, his phone suddenly rang. He looked at the screen and saw that it was Rob now. What the hell was he ringing for this late at night?

Tony had tried to ring him a few times in Lanzarote but with no success. He had been worried. Although he was now glad to see his buddy calling him, he was also concerned.

He pressed answer, but before he could speak, Rob cut in.

"Tony. Thank Christ. I've got to see you, mate. I wasn't sure exactly when you would be back. Can you come around now?"

"Whoa. It's nice to hear from you too, old pal. What's the urgency? I've just got off a flight. Can we catch up tomorrow? I need some sleep."

Rob raised his voice as he cut in again.

"Sorry to be rude, Tony, but I've got to fucking see you now. I haven't much time. I'm in deep shit and Robbins is coming down on me."

Tony could hear the desperation in his friend's voice. He could also sense fear.

"Okay, Rob. It's cool. I'll be there within half an hour. What's going on?"

"I'll explain when you get here. Please be quick."

"Alright, sit tight. I'll get there as fast as I can."

"Listen, Tony. I'm at another flat. I moved out of the dockside one. Nobody knows where I am. I'll give you the address now."

Tony wrote it down.

"Ok, I'll be there as soon as I can."

"Thanks, man. I'll be waiting. Hurry up. Please." The line went dead.

Tony closed the phone and frowned. Something was up, and he had a bad feeling about it.

Whatever Rob had been up to had now seemed to have caught up with him. Rob had always been reckless and had rode his luck many times. Had it now run out?

He pulled out into the night traffic and headed towards Rob's new flat on Northumberland Road.

Tony knocked on the door of Rob's flat. It had taken him fifteen minutes to get here. The traffic had been reasonably sparse due to the late hour. On the journey, he had puzzled what trouble Rob had gotten into. He knew in his heart that it wasn't good.

He went to knock again, but the door opened quickly. Rob stood there. He looked tired and dishevelled. He was unshaven, and he had heavy black bags under his eyes. He looked a forlorn sight in a stained white t-shirt and baggy grey tracksuit bottoms. He was a far cry from the soldier Tony once knew.

"Come in, man. Christ, it's good to see you." Rob stood back to let Tony through. Tony noticed that before the younger man shut the door, he had looked furtively down the corridor towards the lifts.

As Tony walked into the living area, he immediately noticed that it looked like a tip. Disregarded foil takeaway dishes, newspapers and dirty clothes were strewn around, along with empty lager cans and spirit bottles. The remnants of white powder stained the glass coffee table.

Rob didn't seem to notice the mess. "Sit down, Tony." Rob gestured to an armchair. Tony moved towards it and before sitting down, lifted a half-eaten Chinese takeaway meal that looked a few days old off the seat.

"Want a drink?" Rob reached for a half empty bottle of Johnnie Walker black label.

Tony shook his head. "No thanks. Now, what is this all about? Spit it out."

Rob half-filled a crystal tumbler with whiskey and flopped down onto the sofa.

He took a large gulp of his drink. It burnt a trail down into his stomach. He regarded Tony. "I am in deep shit. I've been a greedy prick and now it's all coming down on me big time. I thought I was being clever, but the coke and the booze fucked with my brain."

Tony lent forward in his seat. "What are you talking about, Rob?"

He took another mouthful of whiskey and reached for the bottle again. "Okay. I'll start at the beginning."

Rob told Tony that after working a while for Robbins, he had been trusted enough to move into his close inner circle. This meant he was closer to the real illegal action behind the business front.

He had been entrusted with going around and collecting the weekly takings from the many different businesses that Robbins ran. He began to handle a lot of cash. More than he had ever seen in his life. The temptation had been too much, and he had started skimming a little off the top for himself.

At first, he had been sensible. With so many businesses and plenty of cash transactions, it had been easy to pocket money here and there. It just wasn't traceable. Nobody seemed to notice. But as time went on, and his little enterprise had not been rumbled, he took more.

He stashed some away, but he was now living a life way above his means. He was being seen out in the clubs splashing money around like water. He had begun visiting casinos and was losing on the tables, which only made him take more money. It was becoming a downward spiral. Booze and coke gave him temporary solace, but he knew deep down that it was getting out of hand.

It all came to a head last week when Tony was away. He had gone to one of Robbins' clubs. It was a little lapdancing place called the *Pussycat* in Collingwood Street.

He collected a briefcase of cash takings as usual and went back to his car. He had done a few lines of coke before the visit and was in a reckless frame of mind.

He started pulling money out of the case and stuffing it into the glove compartment. He was so engrossed in what he was doing that he didn't see Billy Sherwood, the manager, come up to his car to return Rob's mobile phone that he had carelessly left on his desk.

He had seen what Rob was up too. Billy had worked for Kenny Robbins for ten years or more and he had worked for his father before that. He was old school and furiously loyal to his boss.

Before Billy could question him, Rob drove off.

He knew that Billy would go to Robbins and with a bit of investigation, the allegations would be proven right. Robbins would then come looking for him.

Rob explained that he had moved out of his flat straight away and found this one from a mate in the letting business. He hadn't been answering his phone either. He needed to get out of Newcastle, but he was frightened to leave the flat. He knew Robbins had eyes and ears everywhere, but he also knew that it wouldn't be long before he found him here.

Tony listened to his friend. Rob was a broken man and a desperate one. They had both faced danger many times in the past, but he had never seen Rob as scared as this.

"You mentioned that you had stashed some money away. Where is it? Here?" Tony asked.

Rob drained his glass. "I may be a prick, but I haven't totally lost it. No, it's not here. It's in a safe place."

"Where is it then?"

Rob regarded Tony. He seemed to be weighing up the decision to tell him or not.

Tony also sensed this. "For fuck's sake, Rob. If you want my help, then tell me or I'm out of here."

Rob panicked. "Okay, Tony. I'm sorry. I'm just fucking paranoid. The money is in a lock-up down by the docks. The lock-up belongs to an ex-girlfriend of mine. She inherited it from her old man. It used to be a garage for car repairs."

"How much money are we talking about here?" asked Tony.

Rob averted his glaze towards the window. "Around £250,000."

Tony whistled. "Fucking hell. You have been a busy boy."

Rob looked sheepish. "Like I said, I got a bit carried away."

He continued.

"The ex-girlfriend is called Emma Snow. She runs a little sandwich shop near the central train station. It's called *Emma's Tasty Bites*. She has the key to the lock-up there. She doesn't know anything about what I've been up to. In the lock-up is a silver Audi Quattro. The money is in the boot, plus a Glock 9mm with a few spare clips. Just in case of emergencies. I keep the two sets of car keys here."

Tony listened and said nothing.

Rob abruptly stood up and walked to the window. It looked like he had come to a decision. He turned to Tony.

"If you can give me a lift to the lock-up, I'll give Emma a call and ask her to meet me there with the key. I'll pack my gear and passport and be out of here. I'd rather take my chances than stay around here waiting for Robbins and his goons to turn up. Will you help me?"

Tony also stood up. "If you're sure you want to do this. There'll be no coming back."

"I know. But I've burnt all my bridges here. I fucked up. I need to disappear."

"You do know that Robbins will come hunting for you."

Rob nodded grimly. "Will you help me, Tony?"

Tony held his friend tightly by the shoulders.

"Yes, I will help you. But we need to plan this right. You need to sober up. Get a shower and shave and a change of clothes. Then, we will get a couple of cups of coffee in you to get you straight. Next, you pack and don't leave anything to trace you to this flat."

Rob nodded.

"Right, you hit the shower and I'll get the coffee on."

"Thanks, man. I owe you big time." Rob headed to the bathroom.

"Yes, you do. You are one stupid bastard," Tony answered.

Tony went into the small kitchen. It was in the same state as the rest of the flat. He managed to rescue two mugs from the sink that looked half decent. He then searched high and low for coffee. There was none.

Tony walked to the bedroom door and called out, "Rob, you've run out of coffee. I noticed a 24-hour Tesco not too far away from here on the journey in. I'm going out to get some. I won't be long."

Rob opened the door clad in just his tracksuit bottoms. Tony couldn't help noticing how thin he had gotten.

"No worries, man. I'll have a shave first, so I'll be here to let you in again."

"Okay. I'll be ten minutes tops."

Rob heard the front door shut. He went back to the bathroom and lathered his face with shaving cream. He regarded his face in the mirror and smiled for the first time in days. Good old Tony. He knew his old buddy would come through for him.

If he could get a head start tonight out of the city, he would go down to Dover. He had a contact down there that owned a fishing boat. A few quid should get him a ride over to France and then, he would get a plane to foreign parts. He had many friends around the world due to his army connections.

Suddenly, things didn't seem so bad. Maybe he could turn this around.

He began to rub shaving gel onto his chin. It must be a week since he had last shaved. He began to put the razor to work. Soon, his face was clean and smooth.

He began to run the shower. His thoughts were more positive now. Just then, he heard a knock at the door. Was that Tony back already?

He moved into the living area. "That was quick. The kettle has just boiled?" he called as he opened the door.

As he done this, he instantly regretted it. In his moment of euphoria, he didn't think that it couldn't be Tony. He had only been gone five minutes or so.

When he opened the door, he was staring at the huge figures of Errol and Rudi. Before he could shut the door again, it was forcibly pushed inward, and he found himself being shoved back into the living room.

Rob sprawled onto the carpet as the two big men loomed over him like an eclipse. Then they moved aside to let Kenny Robbins take centre stage.

Rob felt his world cave in. He tried to get to his feet, but his legs felt rubbery.

He then felt the toecap of Robbins's highly polished leather Italian shoe catch him full in the face and he once again fell back to the carpet with the coppery taste of blood in his mouth.

"I thought I would pay you a little house visit and bring you a moving in gift." Robbins looked around the room. "Slumming it here, son. Has all my fucking money run out?"

Rob stayed silent.

"It didn't take me long to put two and two together after Billy came and seen me."

Robbins moved closer.

"Rob, you've been ignoring my phone calls, son. Not ill, are you?"

Robbins signalled Errol and Rudi to pick up Rob from the floor. The two men hoisted him up like a rag doll and held his arms. Rob was still stunned from the kick and offered little resistance.

Robbins got right up in his face. "You have disappointed me, Rob. I let you into my trusted inner circle and how do you repay me? You try to fuck me over. You had it pretty good, my son. Money in your pocket, car, flat. But it wasn't enough, was it?"

Rob went to speak, but was cut short when Robbins drove a knee up into his groin. Rob groaned in pain and his body went slack. He only remained standing because of the two men holding him up.

"Don't even try to make excuses. There are none. Your lifestyle of drugs and gambling just spiralled out of control and you got reckless and you got fucking desperate. Nobody, and I mean nobody, steals from me."

Robbins moved in again and drove a swift punch into his stomach.

This time, Errol and Rudi let him drop to the carpet.

Rob knew he was finished. His head was swimming with pain and his body felt weak. If he didn't try something fast, he was going to die.

As Errol reached down to pull him up, Rob summoned the last of his energy to smash a punch on to the big man's jaw. Errol was taken by surprise and staggered backwards in pain.

Rob scrambled unsteadily to his feet and then ran at Rudi. He drove his head into his abdomen, but it was like hitting concrete.

Rudi reached down and wrapped his powerful arms around Rob's waist, lifted him clear of the ground and then slammed him down hard onto the coffee table. It exploded in a shower of wood and glass on the impact.

Rob slipped in and out of unconsciousness.

That had been his last effort.

He lay on the carpet trying to shake off the pain that seemed to be spreading all over his body. His head felt numb.

The three men were talking, but it all sounded muffled.

Rob shook his head and it cleared slightly.

He then heard Robbins say, "Check the flat over, boys. Make sure there isn't anybody else hiding in here."

He saw Rudi and Errol lumber off towards the bedroom.

Robbins moved across to the window and looked out down to the street below.

This gave Rob a moment to get his phone out of his pocket, switch it on and then slide it under the armchair near to him.

He then heard Rudi and Errol return.

"All clear, Boss," Errol said. The big man was dabbing at his bloodied lip with a piece of kitchen towelling. He regarded Rob and came across the room and drove a hard kick into the prone man's body.

Rob was once more dragged to his feet. He heard Robbins' voice, but it was fading in and out like a bad radio signal.

"Where is my money?"

Rob spat blood from his bruised lips.

"Fuck you, Kenny. I have nothing to say."

Robbins shook his head.

"Wrong answer, son." He sighed wearily. "Ok, Rob. You and the boys here are going for a drive to a nice little spot in the woods. When you get there, you will tell them where my money is. I guarantee it. Unfortunately for you, this outing in the woods isn't for a picnic, but you may get a chance to dig your own grave if you're lucky."

As Rob's vision cleared a little, he noticed the two big men were holding Browning 9mm semi-automatic handguns. He knew the game was well and truly up. He had survived countless fire fights in his army days, but now he was going out to these fucking clowns.

As if reading his thoughts, Robbins smiled, "Ironic, isn't it? No way for a war hero to die, is it? You shouldn't have fucked with me, Rob. I did like you, but I've got to make an example of you. Otherwise, every little fucking toe rag will think that he can have a piece of me, and that isn't happening. Have you told anybody else about this?"

Rob remained silent.

Robbins moved in and grabbed him by the cheeks and squeezed tightly.

"Well, have you? What about Tony?"

This made Rob think. He knew Tony would be back soon. He had to get out of the flat quickly.

Through bloodied lips, he replied, "No. I haven't told anybody. I didn't want anyone to know. Not even Tony. Anyway, as far as I know, he is out of the country."

"So, who were you calling to as you opened the door then?"

Rob thought quickly. "It was some tart I had phoned to come over. She told me she might be able to get away when her old man went to sleep."

Kenny Robbins studied the face of Rob for a glimmer of a lie, but seemed to be satisfied. He then straightened his tie and nodded to Errol and Rudi.

"Right, let's get moving just in case she does turn up. Take him outside discreetly. Let me know when it's done." With that, he turned and left the flat without a second glance.

Rob felt a strange sense of calm come over him. It was a feeling of acceptance for his impending fate.

He looked at Errol and Rudi and smiled ruefully. "Suppose I haven't got time for a piss?"

CHAPTER FOURTEEN

Tony returned to the flat. It had taken him longer than anticipated, as there had been a burst water pipe on the road to the supermarket and he had to be diverted by an emergency crew. It had put an extra fifteen minutes onto the journey.

He arrived back and knocked on the door and, to his surprise and alarm, it swung open on its own.

Immediately, his army training instincts clicked in. He stood by the wall outside the door until his eyes grew accustomed to the dark. Moonlight was filtering in through the window, casting pale silvery light into the flat.

He strained his ears for any noise. He could hear the shower running faintly.

"Rob, are you in there, mate?" Tony shouted. He received no reply.

He repeated it again, but still there was no answer.

Tony reached around the corner of the door and found the light switch. He flicked it on and the room was bathed in bright light.

He silently moved in and let his eyes survey the living room. He immediately saw the broken coffee table and blood stains on the cream coloured carpet.

He moved through the rest of the flat quickly, knowing in his heart that Rob was not there.

The bathroom was steamed up with condensation from the running shower.

Tony ripped back the closed shower curtain, but the bath was empty. He turned off the water.

He noticed a half-filled sink of soapy water and a razor on the side by the taps. It looked like Rob had got interrupted. It had to have been Robbins.

The lock of the flat door hadn't been broken, so he must have mistakenly opened it. Robbins couldn't have arrived long after he had left. Had Robbins seen him?

Tony's mind was working overtime as he made his way back into the living room.

If Robbins had got to Rob, the chances of him staying alive were slim.

Suddenly, Tony felt sadness wash over him when he thought of his friend.

There was nothing he could do. He needed to carry on as normal, so Robbins wouldn't suspect that he knew anything. He just had to keep his head down and see how this all panned out. To do anything else would spell suicide.

Confronting Robbins wasn't going to help. If he knew that Rob had confided in him, then Tony would be next.

He needed to get out of the flat and home and make sure there was no trace of him there. He was sure that one of Robbins's goons would be back to give the flat a good going over to check that there wasn't anything incriminating left behind. Tony didn't want to be there when that happened.

He was just going to leave when his eye caught sight of an object under the armchair. He dropped to his knees and fished it out. It was Rob's mobile.

He presumed that, in whatever struggle had ensued in the flat, it must have fallen out of his pocket. He pressed the button and the phone lit up. It was unlocked. Had Rob done this?

Tony slipped the phone into his pocket and left quickly.

* * *

Tony had a restless night. He tossed and turned in his bed with visions of Rob and Kenny Robbins running through his mind. Somewhere in the early hours of dawn, he drifted off wearily to sleep.

He awoke at 8.00am to his phone ringing. He reached out to the bedside table and grabbed it. He looked at the screen. It was Robbins calling.

He sat up in bed and took the call. "Good morning, Kenny."

A bright and breezy Kenny spoke back. "Good morning to you, Tony. Good trip?"

Too fucking chirpy, thought Tony. "Yes, all good thanks," he replied.

"Great. That is good news. Can you get over to the office now? I have a little job for you. That waste of space Rob has gone AWOL and I need a driver. Thirty minutes or so, okay?"

It wasn't really a question; it was a statement.

"Alright, Kenny. I'll be there."

The phone went dead.

Tony got out of bed and hit the shower. His mind was racing. Robbins was going to spin the tale that Rob had gone off without a word and left him inconvenienced. *The crafty bastard*. Tony was going to have to play this very carefully. Robbins knew that Rob was his best buddy and that Tony might be more than a little suspicious that Rob had done a runner.

* * *

"Coffee?" asked Robbins.

"Yes, thanks. Black, one sugar," replied Tony. He was sat in a plush leather chair in Robbins' office.

Kenny Robbins was seated behind his desk. Today, he was wearing a casual polo shirt, not his usual suit. Tony could detect a powerful physique beneath it.

To his left, Rudi and Errol sat on the large sofa fiddling with their mobile phones.

Kenny called over to them. "Can one of you boys sort some coffee, please?" He told them what they wanted, and Rudi was the one who left the office to sort it out. Errol sat grinning to himself as if he had won some personal bet.

Once the coffee was served, Kenny got down to business. "As I mentioned earlier, that prick, Rob, hasn't turned in for work. I know he is a mate of yours, but he has been a fucking liability of late. He's developed a dangerous cocaine habit and it seems to be out of control. He's just not reliable anymore. You haven't seen him since you got back, have you?"

His eyes bored into Tony's, trying to read his thoughts.

Tony took a sip of his coffee. "No, I haven't. I didn't land until midnight last night, so I went straight home to bed. I haven't spoken to Rob since before I went on holiday."

Robbins stared at him for another moment, then broke his gaze to sip at his coffee.

"He's not answering his phone and his flat is empty. He's just disappeared."

Tony played it cool. "As I said, Kenny. I have no idea where he is."

Robbins nodded.

"Okay. Well, never mind for now. You see, he normally does this job, but seeing as he is indisposed, so to speak, I think you'll be the perfect man for it."

Tony said nothing. He just carried on drinking his coffee.

"I have to leave the country for a short while on business and I need somebody to chauffeur the missus around and see that she's okay. Not very exciting, I grant you, but she's like gold dust to me and I need somebody that I can trust to do a decent job. Are you up for that Tony?"

Tony nodded. "Yes, no problem. How long are you away for?"

"Probably four days. Five tops. Just take her wherever she wants to go and keep an eye on things. Make sure she's safe."

"Is she likely to be in danger?" Tony asked.

"Not any immediate danger that I know of, but I have a big deal going down soon and there are some jealous people out there. Desperate people. And desperate people get ruthless. It's just a precaution."

Tony acknowledged this. "Okay, so where is she now?"

Robbins opened a desk drawer, took out a large piece of white card and handed it to Tony.

"She's coming in on a flight at midday from Italy."

Tony regarded the card. Written on it in black marker pen was the name Annette Rossi.

"You can pick her up at arrivals. Okay?"

Tony looked puzzled at the name.

Robbins noticed. "She is Mrs Robbins, all but by name. We've been together for five years. I tend to think of her as mine. Is there any special person in your life, Tony?"

Tony drained his cup. "Nope."

Robbins smiled. "Married to the army, eh?"

Tony forced a return smile. "Yeah, something like that."

Robbins reached back into the drawer and came out with a thick envelope and some car keys.

"Down in the parking lot is a blue Mercedes. You can borrow that for the job. Chauffeur her around in a bit of comfort. In the glove compartment is a card for fuel that you can use. In the envelope is your wages. If all goes well, when I get back, I will give you a little bonus on top."

Tony picked up the keys. "Anything else I need to know?"

Robbins reached for a cigar. "There is just one thing, Tony. Make sure no harm comes to her. I wouldn't like that. She can be a little highly strung at times. I need to know that she will be safe while I'm gone. You understand?"

Tony got up from his seat and nodded that he understood and left the office.

Rosie looked up from her computer as he came out.

"Where is that pain in the ass Rob today?" she asked.

Tony thought on his feet. "Apparently, he took off on a little holiday."

Rosie smiled. "Ibiza would be my guess. Sea, sand and... well, you know Rob."

Tony played along as he left the room. "I heard it was a caravan in Skegness with his mum."

As Tony went down in the elevator to the parking lot, he knew that Rob was dead. He wouldn't have given up the whereabouts of the money. If by some miracle he had done a runner, he would have headed for his girlfriend and the lock-up.

Suddenly, he remembered Rob's mobile phone and fished it out of his pocket. He went into his address book and scrolled down the names to find Emma Snow. As he found it, to his surprise, the phone went off, causing him to nearly drop it. He looked at the screen and he saw that it was Robbins calling. Why would he call Rob's phone if he knew he was dead? Maybe he realised that the phone was missing, and they needed it for a possible clue to the money? Maybe he thought Tony had it and would answer out of habit? Or could it be that they knew about Emma and the lock up?

Tony knew that Rob wouldn't have spilled his guts and told them. He was sure his old friend had dropped his phone and left it open for him to find.

The phone stopped ringing, but he was a little concerned that somebody might have heard Rob's distinctive ringtone, which was the theme tune to Star Wars.

Tony turned the phone to vibrate and put it back in his pocket. Ringing Emma would have to wait for a moment. He needed to get to the airport.

* * *

The airport was surprisingly quiet compared to its usual hustle and bustle. Tony thought to himself how ironic it was that he hadn't been to this airport for years; now, here he was twice in a matter of days.

He made his way to arrivals and looked on the screen for Naples. The plane had landed ten minutes ago, so he guessed that it wouldn't be long before the passengers came through after retrieving their luggage.

He wondered how Annette Rossi had become 'Mrs Robbins'? Where had they met? Obviously, she was Italian or of Italian descent. Had Naples been her home?

The arrivals door slid open and a small stream of people walked through. Many of them were looking out for a familiar face in the gathered crowd to meet them. Others purposely were striding towards the exit and the taxi rank.

Tony held the white card with Annette's name on it up at chest height and waited. He scanned the faces. He had no idea what she looked like. He was sure though that if she was Robbins' woman, she was going to be nothing less than a bit special.

Coming through the door now was a stunning dark-haired, olive skinned woman, who Tony estimated must have been in her early forties. He appraised her. He knew even before she made eye contact with him that this was Annette Rossi.

She was around 5ft 9 inches, slim build and her skin was flawless. Her long dark hair was pulled back into a ponytail with a red ribbon. She wore a stylish 2-piece blue suit with a white blouse under the jacket. Her legs were shapely in a pair of black high heels. She walked with the coolness of a catwalk model.

Tony thought she was the most beautiful woman he had ever laid eyes on. He held the card up high so that she would notice it.

He hoped his mouth wasn't gaping wide open as she walked towards him.

As she neared him, he noticed a small frown play on her face. Obviously, she had expected Rob to be there and not a stranger. Tony walked forward and introduced himself. "Hello Miss Rossi. My name is Tony Slade. I work for Kenny and he has assigned me to pick you up and look after you for a few days."

Annette eyed Tony warily. "I have not seen you before. I was expecting my usual driver. Would you please excuse me? I will have to make a phone call to confirm this."

"That's fine. I understand," Tony replied.

He watched her walk a short distance away and begin speaking into her phone. She returned a few moments later and her face broke into a smile revealing an even set of white teeth.

"Sorry about that. It is all fine now."

She extended her hand. "I am Annette. Sorry, I didn't catch your name."

Tony took her small soft hand in his. He was beguiled. "Tony Slade. It's a pleasure to meet you."

He was lost in her brown eyes and suddenly, realised that he had been holding on to her hand a little longer than he should have. He released it and coughed awkwardly.

"Let me take your suitcase and I'll show you to your car."

"Thank you," Annette said.

They started walking towards the exit and the car park.

Tony took a deep breath. *Get a grip*, he told himself. He was acting like a love-struck teenager. This was Robbins' woman and don't fucking forget it... Still, she was drop dead gorgeous.

Driving back through the city, Annette asked Tony how long he had been working for Kenny and she also wanted to know why Rob wasn't driving her today.

Tony answered her questions the best he could without raising any suspicion. Annette seemed to be happy with this.

Surprisingly, she had chosen to sit in the front passenger seat and not the back.

She told Tony that she was not royalty and didn't want to be treated in that manner.

Annette was very down to earth and not what Tony had envisaged before meeting her. He thought that she would be aloof and all business, but nothing could be further from the truth.

As they sped on towards the Quayside, Tony couldn't resist the occasional glance at her. Her skirt had ridden slightly above the knee. Her legs were bare and tanned. Tony swallowed hard. *Keep focused,* he told himself.

He also regarded her red painted finger nails. There was no ring on her left hand.

She was quiet now looking out the window. A slightly sad look was playing upon her face. She then broke the silence with another question, "Have you ever been to Italy, Mr. Slade?"

Tony glanced at her briefly. The sad faraway look was still in her eye. "No, I haven't. I've seen a lot of the world but never Italy. I would like to go there."

She slowly nodded. "You should. It is very beautiful."

"I've heard. Do you come from Naples?"

"Yes, I was born there."

"You must tell me about it."

Annette regarded him, "One day maybe. So, where have you travelled to, Mr. Slade?"

"Call me Tony, please. Mr, Slade doesn't sit too well with me."

A small smile played on her lips. "Okay, Tony. So, where have you been in this world?"

"I did a lot of travelling when I was in the forces. I was a paratrooper and I was stationed here, there and everywhere."

"What was your favourite place, Tony?"

Tony indicated and pulled out around a heavy truck parked up unloading before answering.

"I didn't have one. I wasn't there for sightseeing; I was there to do a job."

He was suddenly aware of the hard edge to his voice. "I'm sorry. I didn't mean to sound so harsh. I apologise."

Annette smiled again. "It's okay, Tony. I shouldn't have asked. It is none of my business. Kenny is always telling me I talk too much."

Tony looked at her momentarily. He drank in her beauty and the subtle scent of her perfume.

"No, it's nothing to do with you. It's me. Maybe you just made me realise that I've been too many places in my life, but only in times of war. I never really thought beyond that until now."

"I think I understand what you are saying. We all have regrets in our life."

Annette went back to staring out of the window and Tony finally switched on the radio. The sounds of Rod Stewart singing about Maggie May came over the airwaves.

A brief time later, they pulled into the parking garage at the Tyneside Luxury Apartments complex. They were recently built million-pound apartments overlooking the Docklands. It was prime territory of the rich and famous. Rumour had it that Geordie musician and singer Sting owned one.

Tony marvelled how Robbins lived here. Then, that was Robbins. He was friend to the stars and a highly successful businessman on the surface, but a vicious crook underneath.

He was clever and powerful with half of the Tyne and Wear police force and crown prosecution in his pocket. Tony couldn't help but take his hat off to the bastard.

Kenny was no fool. He had done his time grafting and getting his hands dirty. He started at the bottom and worked his way up. There were no privileges just because he was Joe Robbin's boy.

When he came out of the Navy, he had worked in the shipyards for a while and then on a barrow in the markets. He then worked on the 'doors' and had a reputation for being a dangerous fucker. He went on to 'mind' a few big celebrity names.

He worked security for the likes of the Rolling Stones, The Who and David Bowie amongst others.

In the backstage world of rock and roll, he found out about people's excesses. Mainly, it was drugs. He didn't touch them himself. He was too busy into his fitness and Martial arts, but it planted seeds for the future. Supply and demand.

He put a guy's eye out in a fight in a nightclub in which he was working and did some time inside for GBH. When he came out of prison, he started work for his old man, and the rest is history, so to speak.

He took over the reins eventually and by then, had his finger in about every pie going. He invested his dirty money and laundered it wisely in bars, nightclubs, casinos and gyms. All of them were a legitimate front for his shadier dealings.

Kenny Robbins had done well for himself. He had also hurt some people along the way.

Tony escorted Annette to the elevators which would take her up to her apartment on the sixth floor. He couldn't help but wonder how a woman like this had got mixed up with Robbins.

As they both stood in the small space, he was aware how close he was standing to her. Again, he could smell her perfume. He looked at the sleek curve of her neck and the small emerald pendant on a fine gold chain that she wore around it. She was a class act. A woman way out of his league.

Well, in fact, most women of any substance had been out of his league for as long as he could recall. He hadn't had a serious or lasting relationship since the days of Katy.

The army had been his life. A visit to a local brothel occasionally had been it. He hadn't time for a meaningful relationship. In his mind, women just brought problems.

Annette seemed to sense he was watching her and turned to face him.

"You seem a little uneasy, Tony. Are you ok?"

"Everything is fine. I just want to make a good impression on my first day. This type of work is a little new to me. I have not 'minded' a female client before."

"Don't worry, Tony. I don't bite."

Her face broke into another wonderful smile.

Tony felt a flutter in his stomach. Christ, this woman was beautiful.

They both seemed to regard each other for an eternity, but in truth, it was just seconds. Then, the bell tinged as the elevator reached its destination.

"Here we are. This is me," Annette said.

She stepped towards the opening door. Tony moved forward first.

"Wait. I'll go first. It's just a precaution."

He exited the lift. All seemed quiet. He regarded the numbers on the wall indicating the apartments.

"What's your apartment number?" he asked.

Annette stepped out to join him. "218. It's this way to the left."

They walked a short distance until they came to apartment 218.

"Do you want me to check inside for you?" asked Tony.

Annette produced the door keys from her black leather Gucci handbag.

"No, Tony. I will be fine. Kenny is far too overprotective of me. I don't wish to be treated as a high-flying business tycoon or pop star. I am just an ordinary person. Nobody has special interest in me."

You are far from ordinary, thought Tony.

"I understand, Annette, but Kenny gave me a job to do and I feel..."

His words were cut off by a cool, slim finger touching his lips. "Enough now, Tony. You have done an excellent job. Now, please don't worry."

He stared into her brown eyes and felt a slight heat rise to his face. Then, they both broke into laughter. Tony couldn't remember the last time he had laughed with a female. She then handed Tony a small white business card.

"This is my number. Ring it when you get home, so I will have your number too. Plus, you can check I have not been murdered in my bed."

Tony took the card from her.

"So, Tony I will ring you tomorrow in the morning. I have some things to do and would be grateful for you to drive me again."

She inserted the key into the lock of the door. She turned back once more and smiled. "Goodbye, Tony, and thank you for everything."

With that, she slipped into the apartment and shut the door.

Tony stood there for a moment regarding the door and then, the card she gave him. This woman was something special. Well, the job turned out to have a few perks after all.

CHAPTER FIFTEEN

Tony returned to his car, his thoughts still on Annette. He reached in his pocket for the car keys and that was when he felt the mobile phone. His thoughts now turned to Rob.

He got into the car and scrolled down the phone to Emma Snow. He needed to talk to her.

Tony dialled the number and after half a dozen rings, it was picked up. He immediately heard the concerned voice of Emma.

"God, Rob. Where have you been? I have been out of my mind with worry, you bastard. Where are you?"

Tony interrupted her. "Emma, this isn't Rob. This is his friend, Tony Slade."

There was a moment's silence and then she asked, "Why have you got Rob's phone? Who are you again?"

Tony explained who he was and went on to tell her that Rob was in serious trouble. He heard a gasp on the end of the line. Then, silence once more.

"Emma, are you still there? I need to ask you some things, private things, that Rob told me."

When she spoke, Tony could hear the emotion in her voice, but she also had a defiance.

"Rob mentioned a friend named Tony Slade to me about a week ago and he told me that if a man phoned me saying he was that person, I needed to ask him two questions that only he would know."

"Okay," said Tony. "Fire away. Ask the questions."

Emma sniffed a few times and composed herself. "Hold on a moment. I have the questions written down here somewhere."

Tony waited. He could hear the rustling of paper at the other end of the phone. Then, Emma was back.

"Right, here we are. This is the first question. Where were you both when Rob tripped down a flight of stairs and broke his left ankle?"

"We were both coming out of a bar in Berlin on a little R&R break shortly after the Falkland's conflict. The bar was called the *Zum Nussbaum* and it was his right ankle that he broke."

"Okay, and the second question is what happened to the pet snake he owned when he was a boy?"

Tony broke into a laugh. "He had a corn snake which he let out one day to play with and a cat came in through the open back door and picked it up in his mouth and ran off with it. He never saw the snake or cat again."

"What was the snake's name?"

Tony smiled as he remembered it. "The snake was Sid."

"Alright, Tony Slade. I believe it's you. What can I do to help you?" asked Emma.

"Emma, Rob told me that you hold a key to a lock-up garage down by the docks. The garage used to be your father's business. Rob keeps a motor in there. Is that right?"

"Yes, that's right. It's a silver Audi Quattro. It's his pride and joy. I have the key to the garage on my business premises. Rob told me to keep it safe."

"Do you also have a spare set of the car keys?"

"No, Rob kept them separate."

Smart move, thought Tony. Rob must have been thinking clearly at one stage.

"Okay, Emma. I want you to listen to me carefully. Did he ever mention to you where he kept them?"

"No. He never told me, and I never asked. It was his business."

"Okay. Thanks for your help. I'll be in touch with you again soon, but first, I must find the car keys. Also, this is a dangerous situation. I don't believe anybody will be looking for you; otherwise, they would have already paid you a visit. But don't talk to any strangers and certainly don't mention the lock-up or me. I aim to get to the bottom of all this, Emma. I promise that I'll sort things. So, just sit tight. If I call you again, it'll be on Rob's phone. You will know it will be me, okay?"

When she answered, her voice sounded scared. "Okay, Tony. Rob told me if anything ever happened to him, then I could trust you completely. I believe that. I will wait for your call."

"Good girl. Just to confirm, *Tasty Bites* is the name of your business and that's on Dean Street just off Mosley Street. Is that right?"

"Yes, that's right. I live in a flat above the shop. I am there most hours."

"Alright, Emma. We'll speak soon."

He was just about to hang up when he caught her voice ask.

"Is he dead? We weren't exactly star-crossed romantics, but I did love him."

"I can't answer that honestly now. But it doesn't seem good. I'm sorry."

Emma sobbed again.

"I knew all about his dodgy deals, but I didn't realise the extent of trouble he had got himself into. He was taking coke and it made him a little crazy... Maybe if I had tried harder, I could have stopped him?"

"Don't blame yourself, pet. He only came to me as a last resort. I knew nothing myself until recently."

There was only silence at the other end of the phone.

"Take care, Emma. I'll call you soon. Bye."

Tony closed the phone and pocketed it. He would now wait until it was dark and then head over to Rob's flat and see where the car keys were hidden.

* * *

At 10.30pm, Tony parked his car some distance from Rob's flat. He wasn't sure if the place was still being watched. He walked the rest on foot. He surveyed the street. It all seemed quiet. He then entered the building and made his way up in the lift unchallenged.

Outside the door of the flat, he checked around him again. He rang the bell a few times as a precaution. He didn't really expect anybody to answer. He then extracted a small leather wallet from his pocket. When opened, it revealed a set of lockpicks.

Tony grinned to himself. Another little skill he had picked up courtesy of HM Forces. God bless them.

He was inside the flat in under a minute. He closed the door and scanned the room. He immediately noticed that it had been tidied up. The broken coffee table was gone and so were the blood stains on the carpet. Robbins' boys were certainly thorough.

He moved through the rooms silently searching cupboards and drawers. But he could not find the car keys.

He was anxious to get out of the flat as soon as possible. This was taking longer than he anticipated.

He grew increasingly frustrated as his continued search proved fruitless.

Tony went back into the living room and momentarily sat down on the sofa and scanned the room. Where the hell would Rob hide those keys?

Rob, in his haste to leave his other flat, hadn't taken that much with him. So, there wasn't exactly a lot of places he could have hidden the keys.

What he had brought with him was his large music collection. Ever since Tony had knew him, they had both shared the same passion for music and loved to quiz each other on the subject in the spare time that they had in the army.

The collection that Rob had amassed was the one thing Tony knew his friend truly treasured.

Tony glanced over at the stereo system and the huge music selection there. Rob had been an avid collector of all genres of music. Not just CDs but also vinyl. He was super protective about his vinyl and wouldn't let anybody touch it. It would have gutted him to leave this all behind.

He had to have hid the keys there somewhere.

Tony moved across the room and scanned the shelves of records looking for anything that might prove a clue. Then he saw something. His eyes were drawn for some reason to an album by a late 70's rock band from the US called *The Cars*. Rob loved this band who had had a big top five hit in the British charts in 1978 with a song entitled *My Best Friend's Girl*.

The Cars, could it be?

Tony pulled the album off the shelf and looked inside the sleeve and bingo, there was two sets of car keys. The fobs carried the Audi emblem. He pocketed the keys and returned the album to the shelf. He mused with the fact that this band had had another major hit with a song called *Drive*. You clever bastard, Rob.

He was just getting ready to leave when he heard a key turning in the front door. Shit, somebody was coming in.

Tony ran to the bedroom. He could hear two voices speaking. He waited by the door and listened.

"Mr. Robbins told me to keep an eye out in case anybody came around to the flat. About half an hour ago, I saw a man enter it. That's when I rang. Being the caretaker, I have a spare key to all the flats."

"You did well, Granddad. Here's a little something for your trouble. I'll have a look around and return the key to you after."

Tony recognised the Scottish tones. It was another of Robbins' boys. His name was Don Frasier. He ran one of Kenny Robbins' gyms *Body Power,* which was situated down by the Monument metro station.

Tony had been there a few times with Rob to work out. Frasier was an ex-Marine and when he found out that Tony was an ex-Para, the banter had begun about who was tougher. It had got a bit heated and Tony decided not to use the gym again. The word was that Frasier was a steroid head and a bit of a psychopath. He had at one time been the Marines' middleweight boxing champion and he was itching to goad Tony into a fight. Maybe he was going to get that opportunity quicker than he had anticipated.

"Thanks, Mr, Frasier. I will leave you to it then."

"Granddad, before you go, what did this bloke look like?"

"I only saw the back of him. He was about 6ft, broad, black leather jacket and short dark hair flecked with grey."

There was a moment's pause, then Tony heard Frasier thank the man again. He then heard the front door shut and the bolt slip across.

Tony ran to the bedroom window and opened it. He looked out onto a long winding fire escape. He thought about using it, but knew he wouldn't have time.

He heard Frasier's footsteps in the hall a short way from the bathroom and bedroom.

Tony shot a glance at the wardrobe and he decided that had to be his hiding place.

He ducked in amongst the clothes and slid the door shut moments before Frasier entered the room.

He heard a mobile go off and then, Frasier was talking into it. "Hello, Kenny. Yes, I am in the flat now checking it out." There was a pause, then talking began again. "Looks like whoever was here has left by the fire escape. The window leading to it is wide open. No, the old boy didn't get a good look at him. I will check the rest of the place and then call you back. Yes, I will have a check around again for the mobile phone, but when I cleared up the place the other day with Errol and Rudi, we didn't see it. Anyway, don't worry, Kenny. Enjoy your trip. I'll call you back if I find anything."

Through the slates in the wardrobe door, Tony could make out Frasier. He was looking out the window again. He hoped that he would be satisfied and leave.

Frasier suddenly turned around and glanced in the direction of the wardrobe and started walking towards it.

Tony braced himself the best he could. When Frasier opened the door, Tony would have to hit him as hard as he could and knock the bastard out. He couldn't risk being recognised and secondly, he wasn't in the mood for a down and dirty scrap with this lunatic.

Frasier got closer and Tony held his breath ready to pounce. He then saw Frasier looking at the door. He began smoothing his hair down and flexing his biceps through his tight white sweatshirt.

At first Tony couldn't figure out what he was doing and then, the penny dropped. There was a large mirror on one of the wardrobe's doors and Frasier, the vein bastard, was preening himself in it.

Frasier's mobile phone sounded again and with one final look at himself, he answered. "Fucking hell, Jean. I told you not to phone me while I'm working. I'll be around in an hour or so. Okay, okay, calm down. I'm sorry for shouting, baby. Alright. I'll be there soon and get those sexy undies on that I bought you for your birthday. I'm going to give you a good seeing to. Bye."

Class act, thought Tony from his hiding place.

Frasier snapped his phone shut and glanced once more in the mirror suggestively grabbing his crotch and smiling to himself.

Tony breathed a sigh of relief as he saw Frasier leave the bedroom. Five minutes later, he heard the front door slam shut.

Although Tony was uncomfortably cramped in the wardrobe space, he waited another five minutes before exiting his hiding place and then leaving the flat.

That had been a close call, but he had got the keys.

He decided to use the stairs and not the lift.

As he headed towards them, the door of Bob Wager, the caretaker, opened slightly and the old man watched the figure leave by the stairwell.

CHAPTER SIXTEEN

The next morning Tony got a call from Annette. She asked him to pick her up at ten o'clock. She was going to the *Crystal Spa and Health Club*. The club was situated at the Gateshead Metrocentre. Tony said that he would be there.

The Gateshead Metrocentre was the biggest indoor shopping and leisure complex in Europe. If you couldn't find what you were looking for inside there, you probably wouldn't find it anywhere.

Tony had never been there before, so he went online to familiarise himself with the directions and what the complex housed. He had been taught in the forces to always be prepared and think ahead. This line of thinking had served him well in the past.

Tony had never been in a spa and health club and didn't particularly want to. In his world, people pedalling stationary bikes whilst reading a book wasn't his idea of exercise. Also, hanging around by the pool and the potted artificial palms with a latte in your hand and paying £500 a year for the privilege was off his radar. Give him a spit and sawdust gym with a punch bag anytime.

As promised, he picked Annette up on time. She was dressed to exercise in a tight pink sleeveless training top, which showed off her tanned and toned arms. She also wore black lycra knee-length leggings and expensive looking Nike trainers. Her hair was held back off her face by a stretchy pink hairband. She wore little make-up but still managed to look stunning.

As they drove, the sun shone through the clouds and brightened up the city. Annette slipped on a pair of sleek black Jimmy Choo sunglasses. She looked every inch a woman of class and elegance. Tony was mesmerised.

"So, how come you're not using one of Kenny's gyms to train at instead of this health club?"

Annette's face broke into that lovely smile again. "I'm not a snob, Tony, but can you really see me down at the *Power Gym* with Don Frasier and all the other meat-heads there checking out my ass every five minutes?"

Tony laughed. "Yeah, okay. Stupid question."

He felt a little self-conscious after what she had said because he realised he would have probably been one of those guys doing the checking out. Hell, a man is only human. He decided to move the conversation along swiftly.

"So, what are you going to do at *Crystal* today? If you don't mind me asking, that is," enquired Tony.

Annette turned to face him. "Well, I am going to have a facial and a massage later, but first, I am going to do a spin class."

"A what class?"

Annette regarded Tony as if he had just landed from the planet Mars. "A spin class. You do know what that is, don't you?" She mimicked cycling with her arms and legs.

Tony smiled. "Oh yeah, that bike thing, isn't it?"

"Yes, Tony, that bike thing. Are you teasing me?"

"What? Me? No. I am just not up to speed with these new fancy fitness workouts."

Now, it was Annette's turn to smile. "Spin is hardly new. It has been around since the early 90s, but for a man of your background, I don't expect that it is high on the list of your training regimes. Am I right?"

"Spot on. Besides, I can't see myself wearing those tight cycle shorts."

"Oh, I don't know, Tony. You look like you keep yourself in shape."

They both laughed and looked at each other. There was an embarrassing moment of silence between them.

"Anyway, in the early 90s, I was probably crawling around in some jungle somewhere, if my memory serves me right."

Annette looked confused.

"A long story," Tony answered.

"You've intrigued me, Tony. Maybe you can tell me more later?"

Tony tried to make light of it. "Shit, pet. I wouldn't want to bore you with my war stories."

They were pulling up outside the complex.

"Something tells me you are far from boring."

Annette regarded Tony. He felt that her big brown eyes could penetrate his soul.

Tony broke the silence by asking, "So, how long will you be?"

Annette looked at her watch. Tony couldn't help noticing that it was a Vivienne Westwood model. He made a mental note to stop reading those female magazines in the dentist or doctor's waiting rooms.

"My class is at 11.15am. My treatments are at 12.30pm. I am then having lunch with my friend, Helen. It will probably be 2.30 to 3.00pm."

"Do you want me to wait around for you?"

Annette laughed again. "What, and put you through the hell of hanging around a health club? No, it is fine.

You go off, do what you wish, and I will ring you. Don't panic."

"Okay. Fine," replied Tony.

She unbuckled her seatbelt and opened the door. She hesitated, then turned back to him.

"Look, Tony. As I mentioned before, if I had my way, I would really like to drive myself around. No disrespect to you. I do not want or need a babysitter." She sighed deeply. "But it is what Kenny wants and insists upon. What Kenny Robbins wants, he gets."

Tony didn't know what to say, so he remained quiet.

She looked at him sat silently. "I am sorry, Tony. I should not have said that. I was wrong to take it out on you. It is nothing personal to you and I am grateful that you are taking care of me. Please will you accept my apologies."

As she said this, she momentarily reached over and touched Tony's hand. It felt like electricity shot through his body. He was taken aback. Then, her hand was gone, and she slipped out of the car.

"I will call you later. Have a good day."

Tony watched her walk away and finally, she disappeared into the crowd.

A car horn beeping behind him brought him back to reality. He indicated and pulled the car away into the traffic.

He must be crazy. He couldn't do anything with this woman. It would be suicide. The rational part of Tony's brain knew this, but he was also thinking with another part of his anatomy that had been redundant for a while.

He pushed the on button on the radio and it came to life. He smiled to himself as the song playing at that moment was *It Must Be Love* by Madness.

* * *

With time to kill, Tony rang Emma Snow and asked her if it would be convenient to come over and see her and go to the lock-up garage. She said that it would be fine. He arranged to meet her outside *Tasty Bites* within half an hour.

When he pulled out outside the café, he saw a blonde-haired woman waiting by the pavement's edge. He estimated her to be in her late 30s. She had a pretty face, although at present, it was strained with worry. She was dressed simply in blue jeans, a white sweatshirt and trainers.

She saw the car pull up and hurriedly dropped the remains of her cigarette into the gutter and came closer to the side window which Tony lowered.

"I'm Tony Slade. You must be Emma."

The girl nodded.

"Have you got the lock-up keys?" asked Tony.

"Yes, I have," she replied.

"Okay. Jump in and show me where it is."

Emma got into the car and fastened her seat belt. She smiled nervously at Tony.

Tony lightly touched her arm. "It's all going to be ok, I promise."

She nodded.

"Okay, which way?" said Tony.

They drove down to the west Quayside area. Much of this had been renovated and modernised, but there were still some industrial units in the area. Many were for heavy plant machinery and car repairs. They were small businesses still trying to survive in an unstable economic climate.

They pulled up outside a large shuttered lock-up at the end of a row of six similar ones. The unit next door looked to be a wholesale paint business. A small forklift picked up pallets of paint and brought them in and out of the entrance. Apart from that, it was quiet.

"This is it," Emma said, "Welcome to what used to be *Snow Auto Repairs*. My father owned it most of his adult life. He died about a year ago. I'm an only child, so when he died, he left it to me. My mother died of cancer a long time ago. I didn't really know what to do with it, so I sold all the garage equipment off. I just hung onto the lock-up. Maybe it kept a part of my dad with me. Then, I met Rob and he suggested that I hung on to it for the present, as he could store his car there. That was fine by me. He told me that it was his pride and joy and he didn't like leaving it on the street. Funny, he hardly ever drove it. I didn't mind though. I was happy for him to use it."

Tony regarded the weathered shuttered front and the red and yellow rusted sign above the doors, barely readable now.

They both got out of the car.

Emma continued to talk. "I knew deep down that Rob was a dodgy bugger, but he was lovely to me and I was lonely. I had recently come out of a troubled relationship and he treated me like a princess. He was a right Jack the lad, no doubt, and I also knew about his other women, but when he was with me, it was like it was just us two that existed."

Her words trailed off as she seemed lost in her own thoughts.

She then regarded Tony. "what did he get involved with Tony? Was it that bad?"

Tony looked at her concerned features. He could see the black rings around her eyes from lack of sleep. Worry was etched on her pretty face.

"He got involved with some bad people and did some stupid stuff himself. He knew the risks. In the end, those bad people caught up with him."

He saw tears form in her eyes.

"Emma, the less you know, the better, just in case these people come sniffing around, you understand?"

He now saw fear flicker in those same eyes. She nodded.

Tony held out his hand. "Right, give me the key and we'll open up."

The large shutter doors had a smaller door built inside it, which the key opened without much trouble. Tony noted that it had been recently oiled.

Once inside, Emma found the lights as Tony locked the door again from the inside.

The fluorescent lights brightly lit up the gloom and Tony regarded the large space, now mainly empty. It smelt of petrol and engine oil. The once whitewashed block work walls were a dull grey with numerous splashes of oil and grime over them.

Along one wall was a long work bench still littered with small car parts and tools. On the opposite wall were a few filthy looking sinks and a small toilet cubicle.

Tony spied a page three girlie calendar on the wall above the work bench. It was dated 2001.

At the back of the lock-up was a small office area.

The only other thing in the lock-up dominated the centre floor under a large white dust sheet. Tony walked towards it and pulled back the sheet. Underneath it was the gleaming unblemished body of the Audi.

He pulled the sheet completely clear and took the car keys out of his pocket and pressed the electronic fob to pop the locks open.

Inside the car, it was spotlessly clean and smelt of strawberry air freshener. There was nothing of note in the glove compartment. He knew what he was looking for was in the boot, but he didn't want Emma to see.

"Emma, can you do me a favour whilst I finish checking the car. Go and have a rummage in the office and see if Rob has left anything of importance in there."

"Okay," she replied, "Is there anything that I should be looking for?"

Tony headed for the boot. "I don't know. Look for some paperwork perhaps or maybe a note?"

Once Emma had headed off in the direction of the office, Tony opened the boot.

Inside, he saw a large holdall. He unzipped it and his eyes were greeted with a huge amount of cash, all in different numerations.

Rob wouldn't have left this behind if he had done a runner. Tony pushed down a cold knot of hate for Robbins, which was slowly rising in his stomach.

He quickly glanced towards the office. There was no sign of Emma.

He looked further into the bag and found something else. It was a small oblong black leather case.

Tony unzipped it and inside was a sleek black Glock 17 model 117 handgun with two full ammo clips of 9x19 parabellum cartridges.

He weighed the gun up in his hand. It had been a while since he had held a firearm, but it felt good. He quickly returned it to its case.

He smiled to himself. Good old Rob. He was obviously thinking ahead of the game before getting involved with the cocaine.

He heard Emma's footsteps on the concrete floor. Then, he heard her voice. "There's nothing in there, Tony."

Tony straightened up and shut the boot quietly.

"What exactly are you looking for anyway?" She was now stood by his side.

Tony looked at her questioning features. "I don't know. I thought Rob may have left a note or message for me."

Tony covered the car over once more. He moved towards the shuttered door.

Just then, they heard a noise and they both flinched and turned quickly, just in time to see a pigeon fly out of a hole in the sky light.

Tony looked at Emma and his face broke into a grin.

"Come on. Let's lock this place back up and you keep the key safe. I'll be back again soon. Don't come here again or mention this place to anybody. It must remain our secret. Do you understand?"

She stared into Tony's eyes, searching for something. Hope maybe?

She then nodded. "Okay, Tony. I'll do whatever you say. I trust you and you are..." She hesitated, then continued, "You were Rob's friend."

"Good girl. Now, let's get out of here. I don't want too much attention drawn to this place. I'll drop you back home."

Tony dropped Emma back at her cafe with the promise that he would keep in touch.

"Take these spare set of keys, Emma, and keep them safe for now. When I'm ready, I'll call you again, but don't call me. Okay?"

"Okay, Tony. I'll wait for your call. If I can help in anyway, I will."

He looked at his watch. It was nearly time to pick Annette up. He said goodbye to Emma and headed the car towards the Millennium Bridge.

* * *

Tony picked Annette up from the reception area of the spa. When he walked in to the spacious area, he spied her sat on a white sofa, flicking her way through a glossy magazine. She looked glowing. She had now changed into a light floral print dress, a small black leather jacket and matching ankle length boots.

Tony drank in her beauty as he walked towards her. "Your carriage awaits, Madame," he said in his best upper crust accent.

Annette looked up from her reading and smiled broadly. "Hello, Tony. I hope the wait wasn't too long for you. This babysitting job can be a bit boring. Not very James Bond like."

Tony laughed. "I've seen enough action to last me a life time. Believe me, I'm enjoying this job. It's a pleasant change."

He wanted to tell her that he was enjoying it more than you will ever know, Miss Annette Rossi. But he kept his thoughts to himself.

Instead, he asked, "So, where would you like to go now?"

They started walking towards the exit.

"If you can drop me back at the apartment please, Tony. That would be great."

"No problem," Tony replied.

As he opened the door for Annette, he smelt the fresh scent of lemons on her. Was it her shampoo or shower gel maybe? God, he had the urge to reach out and touch her. She was so close.

He let her pass and her body lightly brushed against him. That same feeling of electricity shot through him.

Tony knew that the next few days were going to be tough for him being in this woman's company. Every ounce of his discipline would have to come into play to stop him making a fool of himself.

CHAPTER SEVENTEEN

Once Tony had dropped Annette off, he decided to go to the gym himself and work off some of the tension he felt in his body. It would do him good to have some distraction.

He decided to head for Kenny Robbins' *Power Gym* as it was close by. The gym itself wasn't too bad it was just that it was managed by that prick Frasier.

He had first bumped into him a few times at Robbin's offices and he had always been a surly bastard.

He was an ex-marine and knew Tony was an ex-para. That had been the start of the bad blood between them. Frasier hated all paras.

Maybe if he was lucky, he wouldn't be on duty in the gym today.

As he walked into the gym reception, his hopes were dashed. There was Frasier behind the counter. *Large as life and twice as ugly*. He was chatting to a couple of big men. They looked Eastern European to Tony.

When he saw Tony, he broke off the conversation. "Well, well, well. If it isn't Tony, the para. How is it going, my man? Come to find out how the real men train?"

Frasier laughed at his own joke.

Without breaking stride as he headed for the changing rooms, Tony retorted, "Yeah, that's right, Frasier. I'll let you know when I see one."

The smile faded from Frasier's face. "I'm surprised you have time to train. I heard you were babysitting the lovely Annette. Is that right?"

"That's right, not that it's any of your business."

Tony saw Frasier flex his muscles under his tight Reebok vest. He was built like a truck. It wasn't natural though. He was on the 'gear'. A steroid monster. A lot of the lads were on steroids in this gym. Health spa, it was not. Tony knew that this made Frasier unpredictable and dangerous.

"I'm just letting you know that Kenny worships her. I hope you are looking after her right and not getting any wrong ideas."

Tony stopped and turned back in Frasier's direction. "And what sort of wrong ideas would that be?"

The sickly grin was back on Frasier's face again. "Like I said, she's a beautiful woman. She's a bit neurotic though in my book and a little overfriendly at times. I guess that's the Italian blood in her. Just wouldn't want you getting the wrong idea."

"Well, thanks for your concern. But it's none of your business. I don't need your opinion. Now, fuck off before you overload that dumb Marine brain with too much overthinking. You know that you guys have got a job to organise your shit into the pan, let alone think for yourself."

Frasier made to move from behind the counter and so did the two big men with him. Tony was ready for it to kick off, but just then, three young lads came in through the door and Frasier had to serve them.

As Tony headed to the changing rooms, he heard Frasier shout after him, "I'll catch you later, old man. If you fancy settling that age-old question about who is tougher, a Paratrooper or a Marine, let me know and we can get up in the ring."

Tony ignored it and disappeared into the changing rooms.

When he emerged from the changing rooms five minutes later, Fraser was nowhere to be seen. The two Eastern European lads were up in the ring sparring with boxing gloves and shin pads on. They looked fit and handy. Obviously, they knew their way around the roped arena.

Tony went to the far end of the gym and did twenty minutes on a rowing machine and then headed to the pull up bar before ending with half a dozen rounds on the heavy bag.

He sensed the two men in the ring watching him, so he brought it up a notch, hitting the bag with a steady tattoo of punches and elbows with a few knees and kicks thrown in, plus an odd spinning back fist for good measure. When he was done, he sat down on a bench to towel his face and drink some water.

He suddenly felt a shadow loom over him and he looked up to see the two big men in front of him.

"You hit the bag pretty good. Don tells us you are a fighter. A boxer and a Jujutsu man. Is this correct?"

Tony looked up into the man's face. He had short blonde hair and a broken nose. He had been in a few wars, he guessed.

"I was back in the day. Not now though."

The blonde man looked at his friend. He was about the same height and age. Mid-twenties. He had a shaven head and a small goatee beard. Tony noticed scar tissue around the eyes.

'You are being too modest, my friend. His face broke into a grin. My name is Alexandros, and this is my friend, Borys. We are from Poland. We are both K1 fighters. You know of this sport?"

Tony didn't bother to introduce himself. "Yes, I know of it."

He got up off the bench to move.

Alexandros spoke again, "Would you like to spar a few rounds with us?"

Tony regarded both men. He didn't like where this was heading, and he suspected that Don Frasier had put them up to it.

"No thanks, boys. Not today. Besides, I am old enough to be your father."

The shaven-headed man named Borys intervened, "I think you would be okay up in the ring. You are in decent shape. Come on, just a couple of rounds."

"No thanks, boys. I am too old for that shit now."

As Tony made to move off, both men causally blocked his way.

"Maybe you are right. Don mentioned that most Paras are... how did he put it? Chicken shit cowards. Maybe you should just stick to hitting the bag," said Alexandros.

Tony knew it was an out and out insult and a challenge. He swallowed hard and looked them both in the eyes. "Can you move out the way, please? I think the conversation is done here."

There was a moment's standoff and then, the two men moved aside to let Tony past.

"Watch how you go, Granddad," called Borys. Both men sniggered as they walked back towards the ring.

Tony ignored the comment and walked away, but his adrenaline had been spiked and he sensed this confrontation was not yet over.

Once Tony had entered the changing rooms, Don Frasier appeared from his office and approached the two men. He pressed a couple of small plastic bags full of pills into their hands. "Here you are, boys. There's a little present for you."

The man called Alexandros said, "He didn't go for it."

"No sweat. How about giving the prick a little surprise visit in the changing rooms instead and give him his present? Know what I mean? Make it good as well. Don't spare the fucker.

Both men nodded and grinned. They had seen a lot of violence in their homeland. They were good at it. They liked it and had no reservation about who they hurt. That's why Don Frasier liked them around the gym as a little extra insurance against anybody walking in there thinking they were 'King of the Hill'.

He watched both the big men stroll towards the changing room entrance. He grinned to himself as he headed to lock the gym door for a while. Poor old Slade. He almost felt sorry for him. He had seen these boys in action before and they were fucking monsters.

Alexandros told Borys to wait by the door and not let anyone inside. He then walked into the changing rooms and surveyed them. They were empty, except for the last of the six shower cubicles. The curtain was pulled shut. Outside, he saw a towel hanging on a hook. He heard running water and saw steam rising over the curtain top.

The big man smiled to himself as he crept towards the curtain. This was going to be easy. He positioned himself outside. This stupid prick called Slade wouldn't know what hit him, and Frasier had told them he was dangerous. What a joke.

In one swift movement, he ripped the curtains back. It took him a few seconds to realise that the cubicle was empty. A few seconds were all that Tony Slade coming up behind him needed.

Tony slammed the brass knuckles he was wearing into the back of Alexandros' neck. The man fell forward into the shower cubicle. Tony was on him quickly, firing three more rapid punches into the kidneys and one more under the left ear. It was all over. Alexandros slid in a heap to the tiled floor. The water jetting out of the shower was mixing with his blood.

Tony pulled the shower curtain back over and ran silently across the room to hide behind the lockers. He watched Borys come in, obviously looking to see what damage his friend had inflicted. He saw the blood streaked shower curtains and grinned.

As he drew level with the edge of the lockers, Tony launched a big right cross into his jaw. Borys crumpled to the floor in pain and surprise. Tony hit him with another two shots in the head, which probably were not needed, and the man was now joining his mate in 'Sleepsville'.

Tony moved to the hand basins and washed his hands and arms along with the brass knuckles. He returned them to his kit along with his towel. Handy little tool to have. It had been a habit of his to carry them from his days on the 'doors'. Stroke of luck that he had them in his bag today.

Tony regarded his two sleeping opponents. They had made a big mistake. This hadn't been a fight. This had been combat. A fucking assassination, if you like. A totally different world to sport fighting, and they had been out of their depth.

He hated having to tap into his dark side, but these lads had taken him there and now, they paid the price.

* * *

Don Frasier looked up from his computer screen and nearly choked on the sandwich he was eating.

"Your changing rooms need a bit of a clean-up, Frasier. They are a right fucking mess. Shit all over the floor."

Frasier was speechless as Tony drew near the reception counter.

"By the way, you good for nothing sack of shit. If you pull a stunt like that again, I will gladly come back in here and break every bone in your body. You understand?"

Whilst Frasier still stood there open-mouthed, Tony flipped the catch on the main doors and exited the gym.

Tony got back to his car and sat in it. His hands had a slight tremor to them, but that was okay. It was the aftermath of adrenaline. The shaking would subside soon. He flopped his head back on the headrest and closed his eyes. He breathed deeply and began to feel himself relax. The tremors in his hands stopped.

The effects of adrenaline were old friends of his. The feelings never went away in situations of stress, but the more you were exposed to them, the more manageable they became.

Tony had been in more situations of high stress and violent confrontation than he cared to remember. He knew adrenaline could be a friend or a foe. You just needed to know how to manage it.

As ex-heavyweight boxing champion Mike Tyson's old trainer and mentor, Cus D'Amato would say, "The difference between the hero and the coward is that the hero has learnt how to control his fear where a coward hasn't." Wise words from a wise man.

Tony felt better. He started up the car and headed home for a soak in a warm bath.

CHAPTER EIGHTEEN

Tony awoke the next morning after a surprisingly good night's sleep. The previous evening after the long soak in the bath he had made some dinner and then sat down with a couple of fingers of Johnnie Walker black label and listened to some music. It had been a while since he had done this. He had listened to some early Rod Stewart from the *Gasoline Alley* and *Every Picture Tells a Story* era and then some Bad Company and Thunder, in his opinion two of Britain's best rock bands ever. He had a varied musical taste. The tracks always reminded him of some place or time in his life.

He had retired to bed around 11.30pm and spent half an hour reading a Michael Connelly novel, *The Wrong Side of Goodbye*, featuring the ex-cop and legend, Harry Bosch. He was one of his favourite fictional characters. Due to the late hours he had kept in the past through his door work, he always found it hard to sleep, so he read.

It was 8.30am when his phone rang. He was in the kitchen preparing a breakfast of scrambled eggs and bacon. He was sipping on a black coffee.

He picked it up and answered, "Hello."

He was immediately happy to hear the voice of Annette on the other end.

"Good morning, Tony. I hope I am not disturbing you."

"No, not at all. I'm just making some breakfast."

Tony eyed the toaster waiting for his toast to pop up without burning. He hated burnt toast.

"I wonder, can you pick me up about ten o'clock. I have some errands to run in the city centre."

Tony took another sip of his coffee and expertly caught his toast with his free hand as it popped up suddenly.

"No problem. I'll be there. See you then."

* * *

Ten o'clock sharp saw Tony pick up Annette and drop her at the Metrocentre. She told him that she should have everything done by midday and she would ring him.

Tony decided to stay in town. He had a little browse around a few shops and then bought a newspaper and headed for *Costa* to read it leisurely over an Americano coffee.

On the stroke of midday, Annette rang him, and he picked her up where he had originally dropped her.

It was a beautifully sunny day for October and Annette said she would love to have a stroll around Leazes Park and would he join her. Tony was only too happy to oblige.

Opened in 1873, Leazes Park was the oldest park on Tyneside. Being close to the city centre, Leazes Park was a haven for people and wildlife away from the harshness of the built-up environment. With its lake full of ducks and swans, it really was a little piece of tranquil magic amongst the bustling city around it.

When they arrived, Tony parked up and they walked. The watery Autumn sun filtered through the trees above them and a carpet of yellow and brown leaves were underfoot.

As they walked, Tony marvelled at how relaxed he felt in this woman's company.

Yesterday's trouble at the gym seemed a million miles away. At this moment, he felt a different person. The violence yesterday had come easily to him. Maybe the men got more than they deserved, but in the murky world that he had travelled for so long, you learnt that if you showed any weakness, you were a dead man.

Sometimes, extreme violence negates violence. For people living outside of this world, it may be hard to understand or justify. But the world of violence was a place far removed from the normal.

There was an unwritten code to follow. It was the law of the jungle and you needed to abide by it, however unpleasant it may be sometimes to survive.

That was why Tony Slade had survived for so long. If you could imagine the worst atrocity one human being could inflict on another, then Tony had seen it and some-times, had to do it himself. It could change a man forever.

You became cold hearted and almost devoid of emotion. You can live a lonely existence, unless you are lucky enough to get a tiny light come into your life. Tony felt that he just had. He was suddenly ashamed of the violent nature of his life and yearned to break free of its bonds. If that wasn't possible at this present time, he would settle for this idyllic moment with Annette and be damned with tomorrow.

Annette told Tony whenever she needed time to think that she would come here. It was a sanctuary for her. She referred to it as her walking meditation. Tony could see why.

"So, Tony. You mentioned yesterday that you were an ex-military man," said Annette, "I suspected you were when I first met you."

Tony regarded her, "Does it show that much?"

Annette smiled, "I know Kenny likes to hire ex-forces. So, I was guessing you would be no different."

"Parachute regiment and some mercenary work. That was where I did my crawling around in the jungle, by the way. My whole life has been the forces," replied Tony.

She nodded, "You have seen a lot of conflict then?"

"More than my share, I suppose. Northern Ireland, Falklands, Africa."

"Are you a violent man, Tony?"

The question caught him slightly off guard. He thought for a moment. "Let's say that I am a man of violence, but not a violent man."

Annette raised an eyebrow. "A very cryptic answer indeed," she replied, "So, how come you have ended up working for Kenny?"

"Just lucky, I guess."

Annette punched him lightly on his arm. "I am being serious. Why?"

"Okay. As I said, since I was 18 years old, my life has mainly been the army. I had a role and a purpose. It was like one big family. When you leave, a lot of your skills are not required or wanted. It is tough when you go back to Civvy street."

"Back to where?" asked Annette.

Tony suddenly realised that a girl born in Italy may not be up to speed with all the British sayings.

"Sorry. It's a saying. It means back in the world outside of the army or any institution. When you have been shoulder to shoulder with a brother in a fire fight, working with million-pound equipment and jumping out of planes, coming back to drive a delivery van or work in a super-market isn't exactly appealing. I don't fit in anywhere."

Annette saw the sadness in Tony's eyes. "So, I guess you still need a buzz and to live on the edge. Am I right? So, that is why you work for Kenny."

Tony regarded Annette. "To be honest with you, no, that's not the reason. This job is a means to an end. It pays good money and when I have enough of it, then I will walk. I need to find a purpose in life. I have had enough of violence and I am far too old to be chasing around like *Rambo* these days."

Annette smiled, "Rambo is getting far too old to be chasing around like Rambo these days."

They both broke into laughter.

Tony was amazed how easy he was finding it to talk to this lovely lady. He was so relaxed in her presence. He could not remember the last time that he had talked to anybody about how he felt. It was something in his world that you learned to bottle up and not reveal.

"Have you ever been married, Tony?"

Tony watched Annette stoop down and pick a tiny purple flower as she asked the question and brought it to her nose to smell its scent.

"No. I've never been married." He went silent.

It made Tony think of Katy. He had often wondered what would have become of him if they had married? Would he have joined the army, or would he have been content with an 8 to 5 job? He couldn't see it himself.

No, she was happy in the States with her husband and her child. *His child?*

He went silent. He had more than once wondered. The timing from when they fell back into bed together that

Saturday evening long ago was about right to when she told him that she was expecting a baby. Christ, she would be a grown woman now, probably with her own children.

Tony couldn't cope with these speculations, so he had put the thoughts out of his head, realising that Katy had chosen her life's path and so had he. So, he had let it go. Funny how it had all just crept back into his thoughts. His thoughts were interrupted by Annette's voice.

"I am sorry, Tony, if I am prying. As I said before, I talk too much. I shouldn't have asked."

Tony shook his head. "Please don't apologise. I just don't talk about these things and it can be difficult. But I know I need to open up sometimes."

Annette gazed into the distance and it was now her turn to look sad, 'I understand, Tony. Truly I do."

Something in her voice made Tony look at her.

"Are you okay?" he asked.

She seemed to suddenly come back to the present and smiled that beautiful smile that Tony couldn't help but find irresistible. "Yes, I am fine."

They walked on for a few moments in silence. The warm sun felt good on their faces. It was such a peaceful a spot that you wouldn't believe a big sprawling city was just outside of the gates.

Annette suddenly stopped and looked at Tony, "Do you know what I would really like right now?"

"No idea," replied Tony.

"A large mug of hot chocolate. And there just happens to be a cafe around this next bend."

"In that case, we better get you one. I could murder a coffee myself."

Annette looked confused. "Murder?"

Tony laughed, "I will explain. It's another of our very strange British sayings."

They sat in the shade of the trees at a small wooden table. There were a handful of people sat at similar tables eating and drinking. Parents watched their children play on the grass as they chatted. It was an idyllic scene.

Tony ordered a hot chocolate and an Americano coffee, black with no sugar.

"Do you like living in Newcastle?" Tony asked Annette.

She took a sip of her drink. "It is okay, I guess. But it is not home. Don't get me wrong, it is a wonderful city but just different."

"Tell me about home. It's obvious you love it. I would like to know more. As I said, I have never set foot in Italy."

"You wish to know? Honestly?"

She seemed surprised that somebody had the time or inclination to want to listen to her. It was obvious to Tony that Kenny Robbins didn't and probably was more concerned with parading her around on his arm like some trophy in his social circles.

Tony nodded. "Yes. I would like to know very much."

Annette smiled, "Okay, I will tell you."

She told him how she was born and grew up in Naples on the beautiful Amalfi coastline of southern Italy. It was a place where the temperatures in the summer soared to 35 degrees. This coastline was now a major holiday destination for sunseekers coming to Italy.

Annette explained how the city of Naples was founded by the Greeks 2800 years ago and was called Neapolis, or New City.

Her father had been a fisherman, working in the clam and oyster business. Clam shelling and oyster processing had been Naples' primary business, so much so that part of the city was nicknamed 'Tin City' in the 1920s. Annette spoke of how when she was a little girl she would sometimes go out on the boat with him and help.

She told Tony how her family lived a simple but happy life. Her father had died some ten years ago, but her mother was still alive and worked as a cleaner at the Grand Medina Hotel on the bay front.

Annette seemed reluctant to go on with her story. It seemed difficult for her to talk about this part of her life, but Tony sensed that she needed to open up just as much as he did.

He gently coaxed her to continue. He wanted to know everything about this woman.

She continued to tell him that she had got married at 18 to her childhood sweetheart, Paolo. They were happily married for five years and she then fell pregnant. They were both overjoyed and life looked good until tragedy struck.

Paolo had also been a fisherman. One day whilst out fishing, an unexpected storm hit. The boat that he was in capsized and Paolo had drowned. His body, along with three others, were never found.

On hearing this, Annette went into shock and miscarried their baby.

After eventually getting over the tragedy, she threw herself into work and pursued her passion for singing. She never really had a meaningful relationship again until Kenny Robbins.

She said that she had worked in the same hotel as her mother in the day and at night, she had been a cabaret singer in local clubs and this was where she had met Kenny.

She had been singing regularly at the *Azzurro Delfino,* a well know nightclub in the city. Kenny Robbins and some of his business associates had visited it one evening and stayed to hear her sing. He then came back another couple of nights on his own.

On the second night, he had approached her when she had finished her set and asked if he could buy her a drink. She said yes.

Over the drink, he told Annette how he had been captivated by her voice. He carried on telling her that he had big music contacts in the UK and he reckoned that he could get her a recording deal.

At her own admission, she had been star struck. She was flattered that this man had shown an interest in her singing. For her, this could be the big break that she craved. It was her last hope of making it in the music business and here was this charming man telling her that he could make it happen. She was sold on the idea and although she loved Italy, she knew that she would have to go to the UK to seek her fortune.

That was that really. She was a stranger to the UK, so Kenny looked after her and soon, the business arrangement became an affair.

"Have you found your fame and fortune?" asked Tony.

Annette took another sip of her drink and stared out across the grass for a moment.

She then let out a small chuckle. "I am still waiting. The picture Kenny painted wasn't quite true. He told me that he had fallen out with the music business contact but he might be able to get me some work in the nightclubs. But I already had that. It wasn't what I wanted. He called me ungrateful and the work never materialised."

Tony saw tears appear in her eyes and he wanted to desperately reach out and comfort her. but that wouldn't be appropriate. *Would it?*

He took a mouthful of his coffee, giving her a moment to compose herself, then he asked.

"Did you know what sort of business Kenny was into?"

Annette took out a tissue from her handbag and dabbed at her eyes. "Not at first. I thought he was just a legitimate businessman. Then, I heard and saw stuff that changed my mine. Then, one night, Kenny laid it out for me and told me that I needed to keep my mouth shut. We argued, and I told him that I wanted to go back home to Italy and he told me that this was my home now and that he would never let me leave him."

Tony could feel this beautiful woman's pain, but he felt helpless.

Suddenly, Annette got up from her chair. "I am sorry, Tony. I have said too much. Please forget what we talked about. You are here to do a job for Kenny. He pays your wages. You are not employed to listen to the rantings of his woman. Let's head back."

Tony got up and moved closer to Annette. The urge to take her in his arms was overpowering, but somehow, he resisted. Instead he said, "I'm sorry for the way things have turned out for you. I truly am."

Annette sadly began to walk back the way they had come. "As I said before, it is not your problem, Tony. I have said too much. But thank you."

The journey back was a little subdued. Tony dropped Annette back to her flat.

Before she entered, she told Tony that she was going to a concert at the O2 Academy that evening with her best friend, Claire. It was Simply Red in one of their comeback shows. She asked if he could pick them both up at 6.30pm from her flat and take them there. He said he would be there and then she was gone.

Tony drove back to his flat in silence. He was deep in thought. He knew whatever Annette said, her problems were now becoming his business. He felt the familiar tingle of adrenaline in his belly.

No woman had ever affected him in this way. He had always kept his emotions well under check, but now, something was happening to him and he was frightened to acknowledge what it might be.

CHAPTER NINETEEN

Tony returned to his flat. His head was full of thoughts about the conversation that he and Annette had had earlier.

It was obvious that she wasn't happy. Was it crazy for him to feel that he could offer her a way out? Would she want it? Was it any of his business? Even if he made it his business, what then? It would mean going up against Kenny Robbins.

Most people would think that he had a death wish, the fact that he was even considering it.

His thoughts were interrupted by his mobile going off. It was Annette.

"Hello, Tony. My friend Claire has let me down for this evening. Her child has a stomach bug so she cannot make the concert. I would really like to go, but I do not want to go alone. Would you accept the spare ticket and accompany me?"

Tony needed a millisecond to say yes. He would love too.

When she hung up, Tony went straight to the bathroom, and showered and shaved. He then pulled his best blue suit out of the wardrobe and ironed a crisp white shirt. His army days had taught him how to look after himself. Sewing, cooking and ironing were no problem to him.

As he dressed, he played Bon Jovi's acoustic album, *This Left Seems Right.* It was one of his favourites that he hadn't heard for a while. He found himself singing and humming along to it. It had been a long time since he had done that.

At 6.30pm sharp, Tony rang the doorbell to Annette's apartment. He waited as he heard her footsteps approaching from the other side of the door. He felt a pleasant sensation of anticipation in his stomach.

All the traumas that he had been through in his life and here he was with jelly legs waiting for a beautiful woman to open the door.

The door opened, and Annette stood there. She looked stunning. Tony had a job to stop his mouth dropping open. She was now wearing her hair was up. She wore a tight-fitting knee length black dress; which Tony could only presume that she had sprayed on. A short stylish leather jacket was worn over the top of it. On her feet, she wore a pair of gold high-heeled sandals. He glimpsed her red painted toenails through them. She had matching gold earrings, necklace and small handbag.

Tony couldn't help himself and found himself saying, "Wow, you look amazing."

She smiled, "Why thank you. You don't look so bad yourself. Shall we go?"

Tony regathered his composure, "Yes, of course."

They walked out to the car and Tony held the passenger door open for Annette to get in and then went around to the driver's side.

Unknown to him, across the road sat in a black 4x4 Land Rover Discovery was Don Frasier. He was snapping away photographs of them from a long-lensed camera.

As Tony pulled away, Frasier followed at a distance.

* * *

The concert was first class. In Tony's opinion, Mick Hucknall, the main man of Simply Red, still had one of the best white soul voices in the world. It hadn't faded with the years. The performance was slick and professional.

After the show, they made their way to a little restaurant that Annette knew called *Carlo's*, which served some of the best Italian cuisine in the North West.

It was a quiet little spot just off Collingwood Street, which was referred to as the 'Diamond Strip' due to its concentration of high-end bars and eateries.

Annette didn't get to go there too often as Kenny wasn't a great lover of Italian food, so she thought that she would treat herself this evening.

They sat by the window and over a dinner chosen by Annette of Pappa al pomodoro soup, followed by Rose pesto prawn pasta and finishing with Tiramisu, they chatted generally about everything and anything. Tony felt incredibly relaxed.

Over the years, his army training had made him introverted. You learnt to keep the horrors of war inside. You tried not to let anybody see the effects that it left on a person. Many of his friends who returned from war had suffered badly with post-traumatic stress disorder. It could manifest itself in many ways and at any time.

Tony had been lucky to a certain extent. He hadn't really suffered with it, but he did still find sleep difficult and woke many a night even now from a nightmare. that would have him gasping for breath and bathed in sweat. He saw the faces of so many friends. Friends that were no longer alive.

One nightmare visited him often.

It was whilst working as a British mercenary with a Ugandan paramilitary unit during the bloodiest human rights abuses in the East African country's civil war. His unit had come upon a village who had been holding out against the government's army. They had all been brutally and mercilessly slaughtered. Men, women, children and livestock. Most had been shot down like dogs; others had been hacked to pieces with machetes.

Tony saw himself walking through the carnage. Blood was everywhere and the smell of decomposing flesh. It was a smell like no other and one you never got used to, no matter how much you dealt with death.

He had been passing a hut when he had heard a noise inside. He went to investigate.

He treaded his way over the two corpses of an elderly man and woman and entered the dark, cool interior. All was silent, except for the incessant buzzing of flies.

His senses were on red alert and he gripped his M16 tightly. As his eyes became accustomed to the light, he found a young boy of ten or twelve crawling slowly across the floor. His eyes showed terrible pain. They were also pleading.

Tony noticed that both the boy's legs had been hacked off below the knees. It was a pitiful sight. The boy was beyond any medical help and no doubt would die soon, but he was in extreme pain and was suffering badly waiting for the blessed release from life.

Tony couldn't walk away from him and had made the decision to mercifully put a bullet through the boy's head to put him out of his misery. It had been the right decision but still a tough one. You don't just walk away from shit like that as they do in the movies.

The memory haunted him continually. Tony would wake some nights with a start after seeing the young boy's face in his dream.

This type of trauma made you harden your heart. It became extremely difficult to let anybody into your life, as you were terrified of getting too close to them and then losing them also.

Being with Annette was like having somebody pull a heavy curtain open and let in the sunlight for the first time in many years. Even if it was only briefly. Tony needed this type of healing.

As he looked across the table in the cosy candlelight at this beautiful woman that he had only known a brief time, he realised that he was falling in love with her.

He knew it was crazy, but he couldn't help himself. He thought this sort of stuff was only for Mills and Boon books. Not in real life.

He had wondered at times if he would experience the feelings of true love ever again after Katy all those years ago.

As Annette delicately sipped her red wine, she caught Tony staring at her. "Is everything alright?"

Tony snapped out of his thoughts. "It couldn't be better," he replied.

He raised his one solitary glass of Pinot Noir that he had allowed himself in a salute.

Across the street from *Carlo's*, Don Frasier watched them.

He sat in the black 4x4 firing off a dozen or more shots from his Nikon 35mm SLR camera.

He smiled to himself. Very cosy. Very cosy indeed. Far too intimate for just a bodyguarding job, surely? This was beginning to turn out interesting.

After the meal, Tony drove Annette back to her apartment.

At the door, she turned to him and asked. "Would you like to come in for a coffee?"

The sensible option for Tony would have been to politely decline and head off home. but he was in too far. He felt a current dragging him further and further out into deeper water.

Just don't let it go over your head, a little internal voice whispered.

Tony heard himself say, "I would love to come in."

They entered the flat and Annette flicked on the lights as Tony closed the door behind him. He appraised the space. It was no more than he would have expected from Robbins. Highly polished wood floors with expensive rugs covering them. There was a huge cream coloured leather sofa and two reclining armchairs dominating the sitting room in front of an ornate fireplace above which hung a JMW Turner watercolour of Venice. A big picture window to his left opened, as patio doors onto a small balcony overlooked the mighty Tyne river.

It was all impressive.

Annette slipped off her sandals and walked barefooted towards the kitchen beyond the sitting room.

"Sit down and make yourself at home. I will put the coffee machine on. Black with no sugar?"

Tony smiled that she had remembered. "I'm impressed. Yes, that would be great."

He watched her sensuous figure disappear into the kitchen.

"Put on some music if you wish. The hi-fi is over in the corner," she shouted as she busied herself with coffee cups.

Tony wandered over to the hi-fi. It was a monstrous music system with about a million different buttons.

"How the hell does this thing work? It looks like something from outer space."

Annette padded into the room. Smiling, she came up close to him, reached over and pressed a little red button marked 'on'.

"There you are. Easy." She gave him a cheeky wink and went back to the kitchen.

Tony looked at the massive collection of CDs. Some, he deduced, were Robbins. The Rolling Stones, The Who, The Doors, Deep Purple. All classic stuff.

There was more modern stuff, such as Whitney Houston and Celine Dion up to Adele and Ed Sheeran, and then there was a sprinkling of classical stuff and some Italian artists that he didn't recognise. He thought he would keep the mood of the evening and selected the classic Simply Red CD *Stars*.

Soon, the soulful vocals of Mick Hucknall filled the room.

Annette appeared with two cups of coffee. "I think that under your hard exterior, Mr. Tony Slade is an old romantic. Am I right?"

Tony took the offered coffee and sat down on one of the chairs. "Maybe I am, but don't go mentioning it. It will ruin my street cred."

Annette sat in the other chair opposite him and curled her legs up under herself.

They sipped their coffee.

"This is some place you have here," Tony said.

Annetta just nodded in response.

"You don't seem overly keen."

She smiled ruefully. "It is a lovely flat."

"I feel a 'but' coming here," replied Tony.

"Yes, there is. I miss Naples. I miss home."

"So, how often do you get to go back there?"

Annette looked sad. "Not as often as I would like."

Tony noticed a tear slowly run down her cheek. "Hey Annette, are you okay? I'm sorry if I upset you by talking about this."

She wiped the tear away. "No, Tony. It is not you."

She hesitated a moment as if deciding to continue with the subject.

Annette got up from her chair and sat on the rug in front of Tony. Almost as if she were afraid that somebody might overhear her.

"You asked me earlier why I haven't left here and gone back home."

Tony nodded and waited for her to continue.

"I can't. Believe me, I have tried. Kenny keeps my passport. He monitors my every move. He told me once when we had an argument that he would never let me leave him and if I tried, he would find me and kill me. He owns me Tony. The life he promised me hasn't materialised and now I feel I am just a prisoner. He allows me twice a year to go home for a week. But I must always check in with him and let him know my comings and goings. Therefore, he has me bodyguarded when he is not around. He pretends it is because he loves me, but really, he is just a control freak and madly jealous. You don't leave men like Kenny ever. Yes, I have all this," she gestured with her hand around the room, "But inside I have nothing. I am trapped."

Tears began to stream down her face.

Tony got to his feet and gently pulled Annette up from the floor into his arms and held her.

"Okay. It's okay."

She sobbed into his shoulder as he soothingly stroked her hair. His head was swimming. Thoughts of hatred for Robbins and thoughts of love for this woman in his arms.

His heart thumped in his chest. This was madness, but he knew that he was too far gone to care anymore about the consequences.

He gently raised her face so that he could look in her eyes. He wiped a tear from her soft skin.

This beautiful woman was so unhappy, and he wanted to make things better for her.

The next thing he knew, they were kissing. It all felt right. He could feel Annette responding to him. The kiss became more urgent. The need in both was too strong.

She then broke away from him and said, "I don't want to be alone tonight. Please will you stay with me?"

Tony gazed into her eyes, "Are you sure you want this? If we do this, there is no turning back."

She answered him with another kiss.

* * *

Outside on the street, Don Frasier saw the light from the flat go out and surmised that there was no sign of Slade leaving. It looked like he was staying the night and not on the sofa, he bet. *Kenny will have to know about this. Then, we will see how fucking tough Tony Slade is,* he thought to himself.

CHAPTER TWENTY

Tony awoke from his sleep. It took him a moment to recollect where he was. It felt strange not to be in his own bed and even stranger not to be alone.

He glanced at the illuminated numerals of his wristwatch. They read 3.15am. The moonlight streamed through the window and cast a pale light on the sleeping form of Annette next to him.

Her dark hair was spread out on the pillow like a halo. He could hear her shallow breathing. He watched the gentle rise and fall of her chest.

He slipped back the covers and padded to the bathroom. Tony flicked on the light and shut the door. He went to the sink, turned on the taps and splashed water onto his face and then sucked a few handfuls into his mouth.

He regarded himself in the mirror on the wall above the sink. *Well, you've done it now boy. Up to your neck in it*, he thought.

Tony went back into the bedroom and stood at the window. He looked out at the twinkling lights on the river below, deep in thought.

He thought back to earlier and their love making. The first time had been frenzied. The need in both urgent and animalistic. Next time, it had been slower and gentler. He had kissed and caressed every inch of her. Her skin had felt like velvet.

After, he had held her close as she slept. It hadn't been long until Tony fell into a comfortable sleep too. The first one in some time.

His thoughts then went to what Annette had told him earlier. She was practically a prisoner and a slave to Robbins. Yes, it all looked rosy on the surface, but just like Robbins himself, the relationship was rotten to the core.

She was living with a control freak and a dangerous one at that. He wouldn't give up Annette without a fight and in that moment, Tony knew that it was also going to be him that he would be fighting.

He was in no doubt that he was in love with Annette. He could only hope that she felt the same about him.

He heard a rustle of sheets behind him and turned to see Annette approaching him, her naked body glowing in the moonlight. Tony felt something stir again inside him.

"Are you okay, Tony?" she asked. Her voice was heavy with sleep.

He wrapped his arms around her and pulled her tight towards him.

"Yes, everything is fine."

They kissed long and deep.

"Let's go back to bed," she whispered and led him by the hand back into the warmth of the sheets.

She nuzzled down into Tony's chest and was soon asleep once more. This time, though, sleep didn't come easily for him. His mind was too active. It was already planning.

Tony knew his life was about to change once again.

* * *

Tony awoke in the morning to the delicious aroma of freshly brewed coffee. He opened his eyes to a vision of Annette stood over the bed. She was wearing a very short towelling bath robe. She offered him a cup of black coffee.

He thought that he had died and gone to heaven.

Tony pushed himself up to a seated position. "Good morning and thank you. I must say, this hotel has first-class service."

Annette laughed and sat on the bed next to him. They kissed.

Her hair was damp, and her skin smelt of lemons again. She was fresh out of the shower.

"How did you sleep?" she asked.

Tony put on his best Groucho Marx accent, "I don't remember much sleeping, sweetheart!"

She playfully punched him on the shoulder.

"Hey, watch my coffee. You might spill it on my delicate bits."

He put his mug down on the bedside table and then grabbed Annette and rolled her onto her back. She looked so beautiful. He stared into her brown eyes. He felt re-born and re-energised.

The dark thoughts of last night evaporated as she touched his hardness. He undid the belt on her robe and slipped it open. They made love once more.

Later, they lay naked together, just savouring the feel of each other's closeness.

Annette ran her hands over the numerous scars on Tony's body and the fading tattoo on his right shoulder of the British parachute cap badge wings. Underneath it read the words *Death from above*. He remembered having it done as soon as he had received his beret. He had been proud to wear the tattoo and still was.

She touched a pink scar on his torso that looked very much like a bullet wound.

"Battle scars?" she asked.

He nodded, "Those are just the ones you can see, pet."

Annette didn't push the conversation any further.

Then, it was Tony's turn. He traced his fingertips down Annette's bare back and stopped at a series of small white scars at the base of her spine.

"Hey, never mind me. Where did you get these scars from?" he asked.

He felt her body become tense, "It's not important now."

He turned her to face him. He saw tears forming in her eyes.

"Was it that bastard Robbins? It was him, wasn't it?"

"Please, Tony. Let it go. It was a long time ago now."

Tony stroked her cheek. "Tell me, please. I need to know."

Annette seemed to be deciding what to say. Then, she spoke.

"Kenny can get violent sometimes. But he is clever. He never marks me where it can be seen."

"Those marks look like cigar burns to me. Is that what they are?" asked Tony.

Annette relented. "Yes. This is what he does to me if I do not please him or do what he wants."

Tony felt his pulse rate raise. This re-ignited memories of his mother and what she had suffered for years at the hands of a man who was supposed to love her. He felt his emotions come to a head.

"You have got to leave this monster, Annette, and I'll help you to do it, if you let me."

Annette got up out of bed. "I know all this Tony, but I can't. He will find me, and God knows what he will do. I am scared. Anyway, why would you want to get involved with me?"

Tony rushed to her side and held her in his arms. "Annette, I am involved."

He took a deep breath and continued before she could reply.

"Christ, I have fallen in love with you. I know I have only known you a matter of days, but I have never felt this way about anybody, ever. I want to help you. I can get you away from here and give you a new life. I promise. Please say yes."

Through her tears, she smiled. "Tony, I think I have also fallen for you. I was frightened to even think it, but now I know it is true. You make me feel safe. I want to be with you too. But this is madness, isn't it?"

Tony kissed her. "Maybe it is, but I want you. I need you. Last night wasn't just a one-off thing."

She held him close. "I need you too."

"Then that settles it. I will come up with a plan. You must trust me on this. It won't be easy, and it will most certainly be dangerous. But I have been dealing with danger all my life. We will succeed. I promise. Just trust me and do whatever I say. It won't happen overnight, and we must do nothing to raise suspicion. Do you understand?"

Annette nodded. "Yes, I understand. I will do what I must to escape this nightmare and be with you. But you must also understand what getting involved with me entails. Do you really love me, Tony? Are you sure?"

"Annette, I have never been more certain of anything in my life. Now, get dressed and we'll go out and get some air. Let's spend as much time together as we can before Kenny returns. It may be a while until we can meet again."

CHAPTER TWENTY ONE

They decided to pack a picnic. The day was theirs. The late October sun was still surprisingly warm.

They hit the A1 out of the city looking for some peace and tranquillity in the countryside. For the moment, they put their worries and concerns on hold and concentrated on getting to know each other better and enjoy their time together.

Tony turned on the radio and the velvety voice of Radio Two's Ken Bruce could be heard introducing the classic track by 10cc entitled *I'm Not in Love.*

The radio seemed to be playing out his life these days.

As the countryside began to flash by, the *Angel of the North* came into view on the southern edge of low fell, overlooking the A1 and the A167. No matter how many times Tony saw the sculpture, it never failed to impress him. Designed by Anthony Gormley and finished in 1998 at the cost of one million pounds, the iconic structure had become the symbol of the gateway to the North East.

The landmark figure stood 20 metres tall with a wingspan of 54 metres. Gormley designed the wings so that they were angled 3.5 degrees forward to create a sense of embrace. Due to its exposed location, the sculpture was built to withstand winds of over a 100 mph, its foundations containing 600 tonnes of concrete to anchor it to the 70 feet of rock below.

"There it is then. The Gateshead flasher," remarked Tony.

"The what?" replied Annette.

Tony grinned. "Well, that's the unofficial name for it due to its location and appearance."

"I am not familiar with the term flasher. What does it mean?"

"I'll explain that one later. Anyway, in 1998, Newcastle United fans decorated it in a huge team shirt in tribute to local hero Alan Shearer."

Annette regarded Tony. "Alan who? Is he famous?"

Tony rolled his eyes in mock disbelief. "I do love you Annette, but I am going to have to educate you about local social history."

"You guys are crazy about football up here. I am afraid I know little about it, only that most Italian teams are better." She gave Tony a coy smile.

"Is that right now, is it?" Tony replied, poking her in the ribs. "I will have you know that Newcastle United are the greatest underachievers in the football league. Stick with me, pet, and I will introduce you to the weird ways of the 'Toon Army'."

They both laughed enjoying the simple banter. If only life could always be this good.

They drove on and eventually ended up at Derwent Walk Country Park. It was amazing that in a short journey you could leave the hustle and bustle of the city and find open space and greenery.

Half of Gateshead was comprised of mature woodland, riverbanks, ponds and wildflower meadows.

They strolled along a quiet country path which brought them to a secluded lake, complete with lily pads and moorhens. They spread out a picnic blanket on the grass and enjoyed a simple lunch of bread, cheese, ham and salad.

After they had eaten, they both lay out on the blanket and watched the clouds shift and move in the sky. The sun shone warmly down on them. It really was a perfect day in every way.

Annette finally broke the silence. "How will we go about it? How will we get away?" She leant up on her elbow to face Tony. Concern showed in her dark eyes.

Tony regarded her. God, she was beautiful, even when she was serious.

"When are you next planning to go to Naples?" he asked

"I have gone twice this year. Kenny will not let me go again until next year. When he returns from his business trip, he will take my passport and lock it away."

"He really is a fucking piece of work," said Tony, shaking his head.

"Can you make an excuse to go. A special case. Tell him your mum is ill and you need to go back to be with her?"

Annette bit her lower lip, considering the question. "Yes, maybe that would work."

Tony sat up and pulled her to him. "That's it then. That is what we'll do. Give it a week or so and then tell him that she rung you and needs your support. This will give me time to organise other stuff. I have a good friend in Lanzarote named Ray. He is solid and trustworthy. I am sure he would look after us and help us disappear when the time is right."

"That will take money, Tony. Everything I have is Kenny's. I do have a small savings account of my own, but Kenny can monitor it. He would certainly be suspicious if I suddenly removed a considerable sum of money."

"Don't worry. You won't need to do that until the last moment. Same with any jewellery. In the meanwhile, I have money to take care of things."

Tony thought of the money in the boot of the Audi in the lock-up. It was perfect for their needs and would help them make a new life far away.

"Once you fly to Naples, you can then make arrangements to travel to Lanzarote. You can stay with Ray and then, as soon as I can, I will join you. Hopefully it will give us enough time before Robbins realises something isn't right."

"I am scared, Tony. Scared of what Kenny might do, but also scared that we might actually be able to do this."

Tony hugged her tightly and stroked her hair. "That is what Winston Churchill called the 'Black Dog'. It's a fear of failure but also a fear of success. You have lived in misery for so long that you can't allow yourself to imagine that there is a better life for you. To be honest, neither can I. My life has been dark for so long, I can hardly believe what has happened over these last few days. But one thing I do know is that my need for a life with you is overriding any fears that I have about how I am going to get it. You must also be brave and weather the storm and I promise you that we will come out of the other side. Is that what you want, Annette?"

"Yes, it is Tony. More than anything."

They kissed deeply and held each other lost in their thoughts.

* * *

Don Frasier snapped off a few more shots, then slipped back through the trees and headed for his vehicle. He could hardly contain his excitement. The evidence was there for all to see. He had that bastard, Slade, nailed. Fucking banged to rites. Robbins would have his liver on a skewer for this. *Serves him right for sticking his fucking nose in where it wasn't needed.*

Before Slade had crept up the ladder of Robbins' empire, Don Frasier had been in line to join his inner circle. This would have meant more money, a bigger car, more women, more coke and more responsibility. Plus, ultimately, more respect.

He didn't want to be running a gym forever. He had been a Marine and a fucking good one at that. He had commanded men. Commanded respect. He craved that level of power again and he would get it. He wasn't going to let a wanker like Slade destroy his dream.

These photos would be the nail in the coffin for Slade and then, Frasier would be back in favour and back at a shot of the big time.

Frasier pulled away unnoticed. He glanced at the camera on the seat next to him. He was old school and didn't trust modern technology. Too much could go wrong with digital shit and computers. Things could get deleted or experience some technical blip. He wasn't going to fall foul of the 'gremlins' of the hi-tech age.

He settled for a 35mm film on a roll. Archaic to some maybe, but solid and dependable to him. You knew where you stood with good old colour film.

He wasn't going to wander into *Boots* either to develop them. He wanted no trace back to him. Also, he didn't want something on a memory stick that could get easily lost.

He was going to get hard copies of these images, so he could hand them to Robbins personally, and he had a friend that ran a little photography business down by Newcastle central station that would develop them with no questions asked. Game on.

* * *

Tony dropped Annette back at her flat in the early evening. She had asked him in, but he declined. Robbins would be back tomorrow, so he asked her to clean the flat and make sure that there was no evidence of him being there.

He told her that they had to start acting professional towards each other again. It was essential that nobody got a sniff of anything going on between them. He said that he would keep in touch by mobile discreetly. They had to stay apart unless the job dictated otherwise.

She held him tightly and he could feel the tension in her body. He desperately wanted to make love and then, after holding her tight, reassure her that everything was going to be alright. But he couldn't afford to be distracted. The old army training had kicked in and he was going into combat mode. Hopefully, it would be for the last time. He had one more mission to accomplish before he could purge his soul for good.

He drove home and hit the shower. The warm water soothed the tension in his own body. He felt his muscles loosen and the anxiety ease.

Afterwards, dressed in a white cotton t-shirt and black tracksuit bottoms, he sank into the armchair with a single *Jura* malt whiskey.

Over the last few years, he had become a bit of an expert on whiskeys. This came about after he had visited Edinburgh and went to the *Whisky Experience*. It was a tour taking you through the history of the 'water of life', a museum with one of the world's biggest whiskey collections and a tasting.

Since then, Tony had read a lot about the subject and regularly treated himself to a different bottle. He had built up quite a little collection from standard blended stuff to expensive single malts.

A CD played in the background. It was one of his favourite classic albums. *Madman across the Water* by Elton John, a 1971 recording containing the brilliant *Tiny Dancer, Levon* and the epic *Indian Sunset.*

He closed his eyes and let the smoky taste of the whiskey hit the back of his mouth as Elton sung. *Blue jean baby, L.A lady, seamstress for the band...*

He knew in his heart that things were going to get worse before they got better. Planning was the key. That's what his army training had taught him. Pay attention to detail. He couldn't afford any mistakes. Robbins was a wily and dangerous adversary.

Something, though, niggled at the back of his mind. In the last few days, he had let his guard slip when he was with Annette and it troubled him. He had taken a few risks, but he was sure that nobody had seen them act inappropriately, had they? He needed another whiskey to contemplate that question.

He drained his glass and headed for the sideboard where the half empty bottle of *Jura* sat.

He turned up the stereo a little. *Hold me closer, tiny dancer, count the headlights on the highway...*

As he refilled his glass and dropped in a few ice cubes, he still couldn't shake off that feeling of unease.

CHAPTER TWENTY TWO

"So, Tony, how did my little babysitting job suit you? Annette told me that you took good care of her."

Tony was sitting in Kenny Robbins' office as he had done on numerous occasions recently. Rudi and Errol were ever present, lurking in the background.

"It went fine, Kenny. As instructed. But I was hoping you might have something a little bit more exciting for me than waiting outside hair salons, health spas and boutiques."

Tony had to play the game. He had to keep as much distance from himself and Annette and not show what she really meant to him.

Robbins broke into laughter. "Not enough action for you, eh? Well, you seem to have done an excellent job and looked after my women. I'm glad I can trust somebody to do that for me without trying to get in her knickers."

Robbins looked for any reaction on Tony's face, but it remained emotionless.

"You know what I'm saying? Too many wankers out there looking for a crack at the title, so to speak. I value loyalty, Tony. I look after people that look after me. You understand?"

Tony nodded.

"So, there were no problems. Nothing I should know about?"

Tony remained poker faced. "Not that I recall. Why do you ask?"

"Maybe it's just me, but Annette seemed a bit edgy last night when I got back."

Robbins left the statement hanging in the air.

"Probably just missing you, Kenny. You know what women are like. That's why I'm single."

Robbins smiled, "Yeah, maybe you're right. Sensible man. Women, eh? Can't live with them, can't live with them."

Everybody broke into laughter and the tension in the room evaporated.

"Anyway, on to other matters. This fiasco at the gym with Don. You said he set you up for a beating. Why would he do that?"

"It's simple. He was a Marine and I was a Para. It's a military thing. He wants to prove that he is the better man. Just macho bullshit that has got out of hand."

Tony paused a second. Robbins remained silent, so he continued.

"In my opinion, he is a waste of space and a liability. I didn't want to end up doing what I had to do in your gym, but Frasier forced the issue. It couldn't be avoided. It was them or me."

Robbins lit up a cigar and slowly drew on it.

"You are more than capable with those hands of yours Tony for a man... let's say, of advancing years. You are indeed in a minority of middle-aged men who can still cut it. I like that. No, I respect it. So, if I kick Don out, do you want to organise the gym? I don't want you there 24/7, as I have other things for a man of your skills to do. But you can organise a manager and keep an eye on the running of things. I need a firm hand. For instance, I don't want any freelancers dealing steroids or any other pharmaceutical shit in my gyms. What they do outside is their own business, but not on my premises. Is that clear? if anybody wants.....how should I put it. Anything in the physical enhancing department, they come through me or in this case, you. I don't use the stuff myself, but if there is a lucrative market out there and in this city, it's fucking mine. This is all under the counter, so to speak, Tony. On the surface, the gym is open to everyone and anyone and is squeaky clean. That also means that the changing rooms will be devoid of broken and bloodied bodies."

He paused and looked Tony in the eye with a small grin playing on his lips. Tony thought that he looked like a great white shark moving in for the kill.

"So, what do you say? Do we have a deal?"

Tony hadn't expected this turn of events, but it would keep Robbins happy and it gave him solid cover until it was time to play his hand.

"That's a very generous offer and I'd like to take you up on it. Can I ask something though?"

"Ask away, Tony."

"Can I personally deliver the good news to Frasier myself?"

Robbins took another draw on his cigar and blew a cloud of smoke towards the ceiling. He then shook his head and his face broke into a huge grin.

"What the fuck. Be my guest."

Tony got to his feet. "Thank you, Kenny." They both shook hands. "I think there's no time like the present."

Tony walked towards the door.

"Oh, Tony," called Robbins.

Tony turned on his heel.

"Be gentle with him, eh?"

"I will Kenny. I will even wear a condom."

Robbins broke into a huge belly laugh that echoed around the office as Tony left.

Once Tony had left, Kenny Robbins gestured to Rudi and Errol.

"Look, lads. Knowing Don Frasier, he isn't going to go easily. I think you should follow Tony to the gym in case things get messy. We can't afford to have the law sniffing around at this stage. If this deal with Amsterdam I have been working on comes off, we need to keep a low and respectable profile. If our mutual friend Marco wants to invest in a piece of my business and have our own little 'Euro deal', then we need to be careful and present a professionally run business. I don't want him thinking that we are a bunch of Geordie clowns."

Both men nodded.

"Understood, Boss. We'll check it out," said Rudi.

"Okay. Get after him and whatever happens, try and be discreet, boys."

The two big men left and when they had, Robbins pulled out his mobile and pressed a button. He waited for a connection.

"Hello Annette, sweetheart. It's me. Look, I know I 've neglected you recently being away so much. I've decided that I'm going to make it up to you tonight. I'll book a table at your favourite restaurant *Carlo's* and we can spend some quality time together and you can tell me about all the things that you have been up to recently. How's that sound?"

On the other end of the phone, Annette steadied herself. *Carlo's* was the last place she wanted to go. She had been there with Tony a couple of nights ago. Would somebody mention it to Kenny? She knew how jealous he could get and then how violent. But she couldn't refuse. She knew that would also cause trouble and possible suspicion, as she was always asking to go the restaurant and Kenny rarely agreed. She heard herself saying that would be lovely and how she would look forward to it.

When she hung up the call, she headed for the kitchen for a coffee and a couple of Panadol. She felt a headache coming on. She needed a lie down.

* * *

Don Frasier had just finished a workout with a private client and as it was Sunday, he was ready to shut up the gym at lunch time. He was in a good mood.

He had left the roll of film the previous evening at a shop named *Ruddy Fast Photos*. It was owned by a mate of his, Malcolm Ruddy.

Malcolm had liked the play on words for his business. In his eyes, it spelt professionalism with a sense of humour. He had told Don that they would be ready the next morning.

Don always used Malcolm for his 'special' little jobs. He didn't ask questions and knew better to do so when it came to Don Frasier.

Malcolm always needed money. Any sort to fuel his gambling habit. He was a sucker for poker, especially now that you could gamble so easily online. He was like a kid in a sweet shop.

Owning a photo developing shop wasn't going to give him enough income to feed his habit, so he didn't mind getting it any way he could. Legal or not.

He dreamed of going to Las Vegas to play with the high rollers in Caesar's Palace or the Bellagio. But unfortunately, his poker skills were not in that league.

This, he would put down to bad luck or maybe too much *Jack Daniels*. Either way, he always needed cash and Don paid well.

Malcolm stayed up late to develop the photos and was interested to see the subject matter. He didn't recognise the man and women in the photographs, but they must be important to Don because of the money he was paying him.

* * *

That morning at 9.00am Frasier had picked up the photos from Malcolm. He was now savouring the moment when he would give Kenny Robbins a ring and let him know he had something for him. But he didn't want to rush it. He needed to get his demands right. He needed to know what he wanted in exchange for the photos.

This had occupied his thoughts all morning and was still occupying them when Tony Slade walked into the gym.

Frasier immediately went on the offence.

"Well, well, well. Look what the cat has dragged in. If it isn't the babysitter. Hope you've been a good boy. I hear Kenny is back."

Tony ignored the barbed comments. "I am here as the bearer of unwelcome news. For you, that is."

Frasier's face turned into a sneer. "Is that right? Don't tell me you have a terminal illness and only have days to fucking live."

"My, Frasier, you are on form today. Actually, I'm here to deliver a message from Kenny himself."

"Are you now. Well, what is it? I have things to do."

"Well, it's like this. You're out of the gym and I'm taking your job. As from now. What do you think of that? You've fucked up once too often Frasier, with the stunt you pulled the other day with the Polish lads. Kenny wasn't impressed, so he wants you gone. You've become a fucking liability."

"You what? What the fuck are you talking about, Slade?"

Tony walked closer. "You heard or are all the steroids you're taking making you deaf as well as shrivelling your dick? Robbins wants you out now."

Frasier's eyes narrowed. "Think you got all the aces, do you? The fucking big man? Well, I'm about to drop a bomb shell on you, arsehole."

Tony broke into a smile. "Save, it numb nuts. You are out, any way you want to cut it."

It was now time for Don Frasier to smile. There was something about the smile that Tony didn't like.

"Let me tell you a little story. When you were doing your babysitting, duties looking after the lovely Annette, I took it on myself to follow you around and take some photos. My, what interesting photos I've got."

Tony felt an explosion of adrenaline course through his body like a speeding bullet, but he kept a rein on it.

"Don't know what you're talking about."

The malevolent smile remained on Frasier's face. "Is that, right? Well, let me jog your memory. The cosy meal at *Carlo's*. The romantic picnic at Derwent and the overnight stop at the flat. Shall I go on?"

Tony felt the fear and anger well up in him and he lunged towards Frasier. "You bastard."

Frasier moved back behind the counter and waved a large brown envelope in Tony's face, taunting him.

"It's all here. All the evidence that will soon be winging its way to Kenny."

Frasier stood his ground smiling triumphantly.

Tony realised that Frasier had him. The niggling unease he had felt the previous night had now manifested itself into this mess. Tony knew that he had been cavalier when he had been with Annette and now he was about to pay the price if he didn't do something fast.

"Okay, Frasier. What do you want?"

"Want? I don't want fuck all from you. I have all I need here," said Frasier waving the envelope. "Kenny will be indebted to me for this one. Instead of leaving, I think I will be due a little promotion in the ranks of the firm."

Tony had to think fast. "I have a proposition for you."

"Forget it, Slade. I'm not interested. Now, get the fuck out of my gym."

Tony edged closer to the counter. "Look, hear me out. You always wanted to know who was the hardest. Para or Marine, right?"

Frasier eyed Tony suspiciously. "Yeah. And..."

"Well, let's do it now. A straightener in the ring. Winner takes all. You win, then do what you must do. I win, I have the photos, but I will disappear and never come back. It's a no brainer for you. What do you say?"

Tony could see Frasier considering it. "Why should I bother when I can hurt you more with these photos?"

Tony had to now go for the final throw of the dice. He had to hope that he could press Frasier's machismo button one more time.

"Because you need to know. Personally, I think you are a pussy and I could hand you your arse with one hand behind my back, but if you want to live with the fact that you turned down the challenge, that is up to you. But I didn't think a Marine would back down. Although I can see your scared."

Frasier licked his lips. It was a sign of the effects of adrenaline. Dry mouth. The saliva glands closing as they knew that they wouldn't be required when the fighting started.

Tony turned the screw. "Come on, you're a big gay pussy. Let's do it now and fucking get the answer that I already know: that you couldn't fight sleep."

"Alright, Slade. You got it. I've been itching for this. Winner takes all."

Frasier put the envelope on the counter.

Tony eyed it.

"Is there any more?"

"That's it. Two sets and the negatives."

"What about where you developed them? Anything there?"

Frasier smiled his sickly grin again. "Not that I know of. But I can't be sure. If you beat me, you'll find a business card in my wallet in my jeans pocket. It has the details of where they were developed."

"How do I know you're telling me the truth?"

"You don't. But I think you're out of options, don't you?" answered Frasier.

Tony knew that he was right, and he hated the bastard for it.

"Right," said Tony, "I'm changing into my training gear. What's it to be a straightener or all in?"

"All in. I'm going to fuck you up badly, Slade. See you in the ring, wanker."

Tony headed for the changing rooms whilst Frasier locked the gym doors.

* * *

In the changing rooms, Tony went to his locker and got out his training kit. He saw the slight tremor in his hands. It was adrenaline beginning to course through his veins once more. It was the pre-fight build-up which he was aware of. Understanding how the body and mind reacted to the adrenal response normally determined the outcome of the situation.

As a young man, he had tried his damnedest to get rid of these unpleasant feelings until one of his drill sergeants had informed him that these feelings would never go in times of adversity. The key was to accept them, control them and make them work for you.

When Tony did his first parachute jump as an eighteen-year-old kid, those words came back to him big time.

Tony breathed deeply and got a rein on his heartrate. He brought it under control as he changed into tracksuit bottoms and a vest top. He felt the slight tremble once again as he laced up his wrestling boots.

Part of him wanted to smash Frasier, but another part of him was tugging him away from violence. He felt like a small boat tied to the harbourside being pulled by the current of the tide. The rope was doing its best to hold him in the place whilst the waters beckoned him towards the far horizon.

As he walked out into the gym, he knew that this time he had no choice. If Robbins ever got to see the photographs, it was all over for him and Annette.

Frasier was in the ring already shadow sparring. He was stripped to the waist. Tony took in his heavily tattooed and muscled body. He was built like a bull and a fucking raging one.

For all Tony's bravado, he knew that this was going to be a fucking war. The man was younger and stronger. He hoped that his own fighting experience would be the difference. It had to be.

Tony climbed into the ring. He looked across at Frasier and estimated that the man was about four inches shorter than him but at least a stone heavier. He decided to try and move around and keep the mad fucker at bay until he could set him up for a finish.

"Are you ready for a lesson, soldier boy?" snarled Frasier.

Tony stared him down. "Enough talk, fatso. Let's do this."

As predicted, Frasier roared forward and winged a big overhand right at Tony's head. Tony moved out of the way as Frasier almost went crashing through the ropes.

Frasier charged again, and Tony shot out a stiff jab into his face and then another. He moved off line and planted a low roundhouse kick into his opponent's thigh and hit him with another jab that this time drew blood from Frasier's nose.

It didn't seem to faze him, and he came back with a sharp left hook which gazed Tony's jaw.

Fighting bare-knuckled was a different ball game to gloved fighting. Although more damage could be inflicted to your opponent, more damage could also be inflicted on your own hands.

As Tony landed a good right cross on Frasier's jaw, he felt pain shoot down his arm and into his hand.

He moved away and tried to buy a bit of time, but Frasier bored forward again and fired a kick into Tony's stomach. He followed it with a good uppercut under the chin.

Tony staggered back into the ropes, slightly dazed. He felt the coppery taste of blood in his mouth.

Fraser grinned and moved in for the kill, the scent of blood in his nostrils.

Tony moved off the ropes and smashed the heel of his hand into Frasier's face. His hand was still painful, and he didn't want to chance another punch. He moved in and fired a follow-up elbow, but Frasier blocked it and grabbed Tony in a tight bear hug, driving his head into his face. Tony was once again driven backwards into the corner post.

Frasier attempted to bite into Tony's ear, but he countered it by pushing a thumb into his eye. Frasier released his grip.

The man's face was a mask of blood that was dripping off the end of his chin. A look of psychotic hate was in his eyes. He spat a mouthful of blood onto the canvas.

Tony waited for him to close in again. They clinched in a wrestle and Tony could feel Frasier's power. He didn't want to be this close to the mad fucker.

Frasier ground his head once more into Tony's face and grabbed him by the testicles. Pain raked through Tony's body. Fighting against it, he clutched the younger man by the ears and headbutted him full in the face. He then pulled his head down into a rising knee. He heard the satisfying crack of Frasier's nose breaking. He fired another big knee into his opponent's solar plexus and heard the air whooshing out of Frasier's body. His resistance weakened.

Tony then wrapped the man's head into a front guillotine choke, joined his hands and squeezed his forearm against the windpipe.

Frasier was struggling for breath, but he was still game. He attempted to lift Tony from the floor, but Tony changed his grip and brought a sharp downward elbow onto the base of Frasier's skull. The man sunk to his knees and Tony was on his back in a flash, wrapping his arm once more around the windpipe in a rear chokehold and squeezing as he flattened Frasier to his stomach.

Frasier struggled valiantly, but Tony was in his favourite position and he knew it was over for his opponent. He sunk the choke in deeper and he felt Frasier's body go limp. He was asleep.

Tony turned the man onto his side. He would recover unconsciousness soon enough. Time to get a move on.

Once out of the ring, Tony grabbed the envelope of photographs and then went into the changing rooms and found Frasier's jeans lying on a bench. He searched the pockets until he found his wallet and then he checked it for the business card.

It took him longer than he would have liked, as his hands were once again shaking badly and blood and sweat stung his eyes. He also felt nauseous. The come down after a fight always followed.

Finally, he found the card and breathed a sigh of relief. Now to get out of here.

Just then he felt the cold touch of steel on the back of his head and the voice of Frasier. "You should have finished me off properly. If it had been me, I would have finished you. Now, put your fucking hands up and walk over towards the far shower cubicle."

"Is that a gun you got, Frasier?"

"Well, it isn't my fucking finger, Slade. Now, fucking move."

Tony walked slowly towards the shower. The situation had escalated badly, and Tony knew that he was in trouble. Frasier seemed hellbent on getting rid of him. Tony had badly underestimated the man.

He needed to buy time. In his Jujutsu training, he had learnt gun disarms and practised them many times.

He had even taught them in the forces, but it had been a while. He was rusty, and it wasn't the sort of thing that you wanted to fuck up on.

"Frasier, think about what you're doing. It's crazy. You won't get away with it. Think of the consequences. You aren't suddenly going to endear yourself to Robbins by killing me."

"Once he sees the photographs, he will understand. It will save him the job of killing you himself. Now move."

Tony knew that Frasier was right. He held all the aces. He needed to buy some time. He reached the shower and stopped.

"Right, get in and turn the water on and stay facing the wall. I don't want to see your ugly mug when I blow brains all over the place," instructed Frasier.

Tony thought quickly. This was his last chance. "Can't kill me face to face, can you, Frasier? A fucking coward to the end. I might have known."

Frasier snorted, "Fuck you, Slade. I know your game. You want me to turn you around, so it will give you a chance to try some of that Jujutsu shit. Well, it isn't going to happen."

Tony suddenly felt a searing pain in his kidneys as Frasier punched him hard in the lower back. Another blow in the same area dropped him to his knees.

The water of the shower crashed down on Tony. It muffled Frasier's voice, but he knew what was coming. Tony Slade, war hero, was going to end his days shot in the back of the head in a fucking shower. All his sins had finally come to bear. Maybe it was Karma.

An image of Annette drifted into his mind. Sweet, beautiful Annette. He had failed her.

With one last surge of effort, Tony tried to get to his feet, but he received a blow from the gun to the back of his neck. It stunned him badly. He drifted in and out of consciousness and waited for the shot.

Time seemed to slow down, but the shot didn't come, or had it? Tony couldn't tell. He was disconnected from the real world, just like he was drowning.

Then, came the warm spray of blood. It had happened, yet he felt no pain. He could still move, and he found himself turning on his knees and facing Frasier.

The man's face was in panic. He was clutching at his neck. His body twitching. Tony could now see as his brain began to come back into real time that there was a knife in the man's neck. The blood spurting everywhere was Frasier's.

As Tony's vision cleared more, he saw the huge frame of Errol, who was responsible for driving the knife into Frasier's neck.

Then, Rudi appeared and pulled Tony to his feet and dragged him out of the shower, as Frasier's dead body now took his place.

* * *

Thirty minutes later, Tony was sat in the gym reception with a cup of coffee as Rudi sat opposite him.

"You back in the land of the living?"

Tony nodded, still not quite sure what had just happened.

"How did you know?" he asked.

"Mr. Robbins asked Errol and myself to follow you down here. He half expected some shit to go down and fuck me, he was right. When we got here, the gym was locked, but we had spare keys. We came in and heard voices in the changing rooms and came across the little scene. Frasier was about to blow your fucking brains out, so Errol dealt with it."

Tony sipped his coffee. "Well, I thank you, boys."

Rudi stood up. "Don't thank us. We did it for Mr. Robbins, not you. Frasier was a prick, but the jury, in my opinion, is still out on you as well. Mr. Robbins has got a big deal in the pipeline and can do without any distractions. You know this?"

Tony nodded and sipped his coffee.

Rudi continued. "Frasier must have really hated you to attempt to kill you for taking his job. A bit extreme to me, don't you think?"

Tony remained silent.

Errol appeared from the changing rooms.

"It's all clean in there and Frasier is wrapped up and ready to roll."

"Okay. I'll back the car up to the rear entrance," said Rudi.

Errol regarded Tony. "You are a lucky man, Slade. If we hadn't come in when we did, it would have been curtains for you."

"Yeah." Tony managed a weak smile. "Shower curtains, I think."

Errol didn't laugh at the attempt at black humour. "Is this yours? I found it on the changing room floor."

Tony saw that Errol was holding the envelope of photographs.

He got to his feet, heart again pounding, trying not to appear to eager. "Yes, it is. Thanks." He took the envelope from Errol's offered hand.

"Clean yourself up and then go home, Slade," said Rudi, "We'll wrap things up here."

Tony got to his feet. "Okay, I'll just get my bag."

* * *

In the changing rooms, the strong smell of bleach and disinfectant filled his nose.

The place was spotless, including the shower where Frasier had come to his end. There was not a sign of the carnage that happened in it earlier.

In the corner, wrapped up in heavy duty black plastic, was the body of Frasier.

Errol and Rudi certainly were handy men. No wonder Robbins liked them both around. Obviously, this wasn't the first time that they had done this type of work. Neither seemed particularly bothered by it.

It looked to Tony like they were just taking out the daily rubbish for refuge collection.

In the world that these men and Tony travelled, death was a constant companion.

He shook his head at the thought that he himself wasn't fazed by what had happened here either. He realised that he had been desensitised to killing a long time ago.

He wasn't proud of this fact now, but the damage had been done and the battle scars had been left behind forever.

Tony changed out of his gym kit, which was splattered with blood, and washed his face and hands in the sink. He picked up his bag and put the photographs inside. He checked his coat pocket. The business card was still there.

As he left the changing rooms, he glanced back at the packaged body of Frasier and wondered if that was how Rob also left this world. He swallowed down his anger as he walked back out into the gym.

Rudi and Errol were waiting at the door to let him out. They both nodded at him as he walked by.

He was finished here, but there were still things to be taken care of elsewhere. He was grateful that he was still alive to do it. He had been careless and that couldn't happen again if he wanted his plan to succeed.

CHAPTER TWENTY THREE

"What's the matter, darling? You've hardly touched your food. Are you not feeling well?"

Annette put down her fork and stopped playing with her food. "Sorry, Kenny. I think I have a migraine coming on."

They were both sat at their usual table in *Carlo's*. It had been a tense evening for Annette. Luckily for her, the staff working this evening were different to the ones on duty when she ate here previously with Tony.

Carlo the owner had been busy due to a shortage in the kitchen, so he hadn't really had time to talk to them, which Annette was grateful about. Now, she just wanted to get home without incident.

Kenny finished his glass of Chablis. "In that case, let's get you home. You don't look well."

Annette inwardly breathed a sigh of relief. "Thank you, Kenny. I am sorry to spoil the evening."

Robbins smiled. "No matter."

"I will just use the bathroom," said Annette pushing back her chair.

Kenny gently touched her hand. "I'll pay the bill and get our coats. I'll have you home in no time.'

* * *

Once in the bathroom, Annette went to the toilet and then checked her face in the mirror. She looked tired. She had not been looking forward to Kenny's return. All she could think about was Tony and their plans. But she knew she had to keep it together and not make Kenny suspicious.

She re-applied her lip gloss and ran a brush through her hair.

She regarded her reflection one more time and then re-entered the restaurant.

Immediately, her heart sank. Carlo was at the table talking to Tony. She swallowed hard. She momentarily felt lightheaded and dizzy. She steadied herself against the bar and breathed deeply. She then saw both men looking in her direction, concern etched on their faces.

Annette composed herself and walked towards the table. Her legs felt like jelly.

Carlo assisted her to a seat. "Signora, you don't look so good."

Annette managed a weak smile. "I will be okay. I just need to get some sleep. Can we go now, Kenny?"

Kenny nodded. "Carlo, may we have our coats please."

Carlo nodded politely. "Of course, Mr. Robbins."

He clapped his hands and gestured for a young waiter to retrieve the coats.

He returned a few moments later with them.

Kenny helped Annette into her coat.

Carlo fussed around getting the table cleared and reset.

"Please, both of you, come back soon when all is well and have a meal on the house."

"That is very generous of you. Thank you."

Kenny shook Carlo's hand.

"Good night Carlo."

Robbins put his arm around Annette and led her out of the restaurant.

* * *

The chilly air felt good on Annette's face. She still felt a little unsteady on her feet as they walked to their car. What had Kenny and Carlo been talking about? Had he mentioned that she had been in the restaurant the other evening with Tony?

She felt panic rising but tried to rationalise that if he had mentioned it, Kenny would already have approached the subject. She was becoming paranoid. Kenny and Carlo always talked. It was probably something and nothing.

Annette wasn't convincing herself though. How she wished she could talk to Tony. He would rationalise it all and convince her that everything was going to be okay.

Once in the car, Kenny clicked in his seat belt and glanced at Annette. "Buckle up, sweetheart."

Annette was jolted back from her thoughts. "Oh yes. Of course. Sorry."

She fumbled with the belt until Robbins reached across and did it for her. He looked her in the eyes.

"There's nothing else bothering you, is there? You've been a little distance since my return. Nothing happened when I was away. Did it?"

He was so close that she could smell his aftershave and the aroma of wine.

"No. Everything is fine, just the migraine. Honestly."

Robbins held her gaze a few moments longer. Annette felt as if he was searching her soul for an answer. Finally, he broke off his gaze and started the car.

"Let's get you home then."

* * *

it was midnight when Tony parked his car up some distance down the road from Malcolm Ruddy's shop.

He quietly got out and scanned the street. It was empty. Tony was dressed head to toe in black. He blended in with the shadows as he silently walked towards the shop. He noticed a light burning in the upstairs window. He deduced that Ruddy must live in a flat over the premises. As he neared the shop front, he glanced around, but all was quiet.

The shop stood on the end of a small rank of other businesses. A hairdresser, newsagent, mobile phone shop and a couple of charity shops. They were all well set back off the busy main streets. Ideal for Tony.

With one more look just to make sure that he wasn't being watched, Tony walked down the side alley by the photo shop and scaled the wall into the backyard of the premises.

Stealthily, he moved like a big cat to the back door. He produced a small Maglite torch from his pocket and inspected the door. It wasn't alarmed. As he suspected, Ruddy wasn't running a big business concern here.

He reached in his pocket once again and produced the small wallet which contained his tools to pick a lock. Within a few minutes, the door was open, and Tony was inside.

He was guessing that Ruddy would have decided it was a clever idea to get some copies of the photos, seeing that Frasier was so desperate for them. He also guessed that he wouldn't know what he had but hoped that he might be able to somehow make a quick buck out of them somewhere down the line.

Tony knew that just going into the shop and asking for them wasn't going to work, and he had learnt his lesson from Frasier. It was no more Mr Nice Guy until the job was well and truly done. He couldn't afford anymore slip-ups.

He had to surprise Ruddy. Put the fear of God into him and get the photos.

Tony crept through a small kitchen which smelled of a recently cooked curry. Then, he went through a stock room, which led through to the main shop. To the left was a staircase that led up to the flat above.

He silently made his way upwards praying that the stair treads didn't creak.

At the top of the stairs was the door to the flat. He pressed his ear to it and faintly heard a television.

Tony thought about picking the lock but, because he didn't know the setup of the room, he wasn't sure if Ruddy would hear him or not.

He decided that he was going to have to burst in hard and fast and hope that the element of surprise would work. It was a sure-fire military tactic. He pulled his balaclava down over his face.

From his belt, he drew an expandable steel baton and readied himself.

He knew that kicking just above the lock would open this door, which was old, and the lock was outdated.

He took a deep breath, steadied himself and then smashed a hard kick into the door with his boot. It splintered and swung wide open with the first contact.

Tony entered fast and scanned the room. The lights were on and he immediately spotted Ruddy. He was sat in an armchair with his trousers and pants around his ankles pleasuring himself whilst watching a late-night adult TV channel.

Ruddy nearly had a heart attack. He tried valiantly to pull up his trousers and stand.

"Don't you fucking move, or I'll hurt you," shouted Tony.

Ruddy slumped back into the chair, his erection rapidly deflating along with his bravado. Fear was in his eyes.

He watched Tony as he scanned the room again to see if anybody else was present.

"Are you alone here?"

Ruddy nodded dumbly, still in shock.

"Right then. Now if you co-operate with me, I will be out of here in no time and you can go back to whatever you were doing. You understand?"

Ruddy suddenly found his voice. "What do you want? If you're looking for money, you've come to the wrong place, man."

"I don't want money; I want the copies you made of Frasier's photographs from earlier on. Now, let's have them and don't fuck me about."

"I don't know what you're talking about. I don't know anybody called Frasier or anything about photographs," retorted Ruddy.

Tony moved menacingly closer. "Oh, dear Malcolm. I really hoped we could do this painlessly."

He brought the baton down with speed and power across Ruddy's right knee.

The man squealed in pain and clutched frantically at his busted kneecap.

"Now, Malcolm, I am going to ask you again and please don't disappoint me."

* * *

Tony got back into his car twenty minutes later. He had the photos. It had taken the other kneecap to be shattered, two fingers and a wrist before Ruddy had coughed up the whereabouts of them.

Tony didn't particularly like what he had done but he was in too deep to turn back now. He had to make sure all evidence was destroyed.

When he left Ruddy with the threat of burning down his shop with him in it, he was sure that he had got what he wanted and that Ruddy would keep his mouth shut.

Suddenly, he was overcome with tiredness. His body was sore from the earlier fight and the following incident. His right hand still hurt from hitting Frasier's skull. He really was too old for this *Die-Hard* shit.

It had been a close call earlier and it had shaken him up badly. He had seen conflict all his life one way or another and survived it in the far-flung corners of the world, but today, he nearly 'bought it' on home soil from a man such as Frasier. There was a lesson to be learnt. It wouldn't happen again.

He now had a reason to live and he wasn't about to lose it, even if it meant digging down   into his dark side one more time.

Today, inadvertently, had starting the ball rolling and he knew he had to see it through to the end no matter what.

But right now, all he needed was to get some sleep. He started the car and headed for home.

* * *

Tony awoke from another bad dream in the early hours of the morning. The dream had been vivid. He had seen Don Frasier's grinning face looking down at him. There was a gaping hole in his neck but somehow, he was still alive and waving the photographs in his face taunting him. Tony couldn't understand how the man was still breathing. He then saw the faces of Rudi and Errol staring grimly at him and finally, Kenny Robbins coming into view with a gun in his hand. It was at this point that he had awoken.

Tony threw back the bed clothes and got up. His aching muscles protested. He walked to the kitchen and poured himself a glass of water. He took it through to the living room and flopped down into the armchair.

Shit, the dream had been so real. Another horrific image to add to the catalogue of others in Tony's head. He wondered if he would ever sleep peacefully again.

He swallowed a large gulp of water that did little to sooth his parched throat.

When he had arrived back at his flat earlier, he had jumped straight into a warm shower in the hope of easing his aching body and relaxing him for sleep. It had worked temporally with the help of a couple of double malt whiskeys. But the respite had been short-lived.

He now felt wide awake. His thoughts drifted once again to Annette and wondered if she was sleeping.

He thought of the earlier violence that he had witnessed and was again party too. It had been part of him for as long as he could recall. He didn't feel anything. Just dumb. That wasn't a good thing. And he also began to wonder if he could walk away from it and renounce violence or would it follow him to his grave. Fuck, it nearly had.

He glanced over at the freshly opened bottle of *Jura* on the sideboard and contemplated another shot, but decided against it.

No doubt in the morning Kenny Robbins would be demanding his version of events at the gym, so he needed to be alert and not nursing a hangover.

On the way back to his flat, Tony had disposed of the photographs. He had burnt them on a little patch of wasteland beyond the railway. Nobody had been around. All the evidence destroyed. Thank God.

Today, he would have to put his own plans into action.

Firstly, he would contact Ray in Lanzarote and start laying down plans for Annette.

He finished his water and decided to make some coffee. Sleep would not be coming back now.

* * *

A week after the incident.

Colin Crane stood in the empty car park of the *Golden Lion* public house in the Bedminster area of south Bristol. He glanced at his watch. It read 3.30am.

A fine drizzle was falling. The night sky was overcast. No moon was visible. That suited Colin Crane just fine.

The weather would keep any late-night revellers from suddenly stumbling past unexpectedly. Also, the darkness concealed him.

He took a drag on his roll up and scanned the road outside.

He was meeting Ronnie. Ronnie Patterson. They had been mates since school days.

Ronnie had saved him on more than one occasion from being beaten up by the school yard bullies in secondary school when he was 12 years old. He had sort of become Colin's bodyguard.

Ronnie had been slightly older than Colin. He had been big for his 14 years and strong. He was in the school rugby team. He was also a bit of a fighter.

Colin had felt safe with Ronnie around. He always had a story to tell or a cigarette or bubble gum to borrow.

Ronnie had been his only real friend.

With no real home life Ronnie became an important person in Colin's life.

He didn't mind if he had him steal the odd thing out of Mr. Patel's corner shop or the local Tesco for him. He didn't even mind when Ronnie touched him up behind the bike sheds or got Colin to do naughty things to him in the toilets. It was a sign of being special friends Ronnie had told him.

Colin had kept quiet about this. He had needed a friend but also, he needed the protection from the seemingly endless stream of bullies lining up to kick the shit out of him.

Over the years, they kept in touch on and off.

Ronnie was now into bodybuilding in a big way and had won some important competitions.

He trained here in Bristol at the renowned *Raw Power* gym. The gym was noted for its bodybuilding and strongman champions.

Ronnie also worked on the 'doors' in the city centre where he was a well-known face. He had a big reputation as a hard man. He kept his secret of being gay well hidden. It wouldn't have sat well with the image he had cultivated, even in these liberated times.

Ronnie had been surprised when Colin had turned up at the door of the *Jungle Hut* nightclub that he was presently working at. He had been more surprised when he found out what Colin wanted, but Ronnie was a man with contacts and told Colin that he would consider it.

Earlier that evening, Ronnie had called Colin and told him that he had what he wanted and the price. When the deal was agreed, Ronnie told Colin where they would meet up. This resulted in Colin going to the pub car park in which he now stood.

He watched the main road from the shadows of two large dumpsters in the car park corner. The area smelt of food waste, beer and stale urine.

He lit another cigarette and zipped his jacket up tighter from a chilly blast of wind. He then saw the bright headlights of a car cut through the darkness. It indicated and pulled into the carpark.

The car was a black BMW. It was Ronnie's.

Colin stepped out of the shadows into the headlights and raised a hand.

The car turned and reversed up towards the dumpsters out of sight of the main road.

The driver's side door opened and out jumped Ronnie.

Colin thought that he looked bigger than ever. He was dressed in blue jeans, a black t-shirt and a black leather jacket over it. His bald head gleamed in the light from the car interior.

"Alright, Colin, my old mate. What are you doing in the shadows? Playing with yourself?" Ronnie broke into a snigger at his own joke.

Colin ignored the quip. "Hello Ronnie, you got it?"

"Hey, ease up there, cowboy, and let's see the colour of your money first."

Colin reached in his overcoat pocket, produced an envelope and handed it to Ronnie.

Ronnie opened it and thumbed through the wade of notes. "Fuck me, rob a bank, did you? Okay, Rambo, we're in business. Come around to the boot."

Ronnie pressed a button under the dashboard and the boot lid sprung up.

Both men moved to the back of the car. Ronnie lifted the floor covering and the spare tire out to reveal the space below. A tartan blanket was lying there concealing something.

He grinned at Colin. "I suppose you aren't going to tell me what the fuck you want this for, Colin? Are you planning on starting World War 3?"

Colin said nothing, so Ronnie shrugged and revealed an ink black 9mm Uzi sub-machine gun pistol and two ammunition clips. "There it is, my son. What a fucking beauty."

Colin leant into the boot and picked up the weapon. It felt good in his hands.

"Steady, Col, my old friend. Let's keep it out of sight. Can't be too careful, okay?"

Colin nodded.

"Right, I will show you how it works and how to load it."

Ronnie moved to take the gun from Colin's grip, but he held onto it tightly.

"No need, Ronnie. I already know how it works."

Ronnie saw a strange look in Colin's eyes.

"Alright. That's cool. Well, here are two magazine clips. Each fire twenty-two rounds."

Colin smiled as he took them from Ronnie.

"It looks like we are all done here then," said Ronnie. The look on Colin's face had unnerved him. He replaced the tyre and floor cover, then slammed the boot down.

"It's unmarked and can't be traced back to me or to the bloke I got it from. Eastern Europeans are bringing this shit in by the sack load. They ask no questions and just want the money. It's a sweet deal, so don't fuck it up for me."

Colin sneered. "Don't fucking sweat, Ronnie. I am not going to fuck it up for you. You know you can trust me. Like always."

Ronnie didn't like the vibe that he was getting here.

"You're all on your own now, so be fucking careful. I have no more to do with it."

Colin was still gazing absentmindedly at the gun. He then turned it towards Ronnie.

"Remember schooldays, Ronnie. Remember all the fucking bullies. How they tormented me. The little shits wouldn't be so fucking brave now if they saw me. Would they? Little spotty, four eyed Colin Crane, the little fucking weasel. They would be shitting themselves now. What do you think Ronnie?"

Colin pointed the Uzi in Ronnie's direction. Ronnie's feeling of unease grew. He moved back to the welcoming light of the car. "They certainly would, Colin. You are the fucking man now. But remember, I sorted those bullies for you, didn't I?"

Colin just stood there with a lopsided grin on his face.

Ronnie was glad when he got back into the car and shut the door. He slid the window down a couple of inches. "Take care of yourself, Colin. Whatever you are up to. I think it's best that we don't contact each other for a while, okay?"

"No worries, Ronnie. You won't be seeing me again any time soon."

Ronnie pulled away. As he left the car park, he looked in his rear-view mirror and saw Colin still standing there.

Crazy fucker. What the fuck was he going to do with that gun? Ronnie thought. The less he knew about it, the better.

CHAPTER TWENTY FOUR

Annette sipped her coffee and regarded Kenny across the breakfast table. He was busy forking scrambled eggs into his mouth whilst he read the *Daily Telegraph* and the *Daily Mirror* newspapers at the same time.

It was a habit that Annette couldn't understand, even when Kenny explained that he liked to keep his finger on the pulse of the business world, but also liked to keep things real by not forgetting his roots. By reading the two contrasting newspapers, he felt that he achieved this balance.

When they had awoken earlier, Kenny had asked her how she was feeling. She had answered much better. He seemed pleased. He told her that last night at the restaurant, poor old Carlo had thought it was his food that had made her feel ill and that was why he had been so concerned.

Annette was relieved to hear this and it would explain why both men had been in close conversation when she had come back from the bathroom.

Carlo hadn't mentioned anything else. Thank God, she was in the clear. Now, she had to pluck up the courage to execute the next part of the plan.

"More coffee, Kenny?" she asked.

Still engrossed in his papers, he absentmindedly offered out his empty cup towards her for a refill.

She did this and he grunted a thank you as he carried on reading.

Annette got up from the table and started clearing the dishes into the dishwasher.

"I think I will give Mamma a ring and see how she is keeping."

Kenny took a gulp of his coffee and without looking up from his reading, said, "Yeah, great idea, pet. You do that. Send her my regards."

* * *

Annette wandered into the bedroom and shut the door. She picked up the phone and dialled her mother's number. After three rings, it was picked up.

"Hello, Mamma. Yes, I am fine. Look listen to me, Mamma. I haven't got long. I am finally going to leave Kenny, but I need your help. Please, Mamma. No questions. Just listen to me. This is what I need you to do."

She returned to the kitchen ten minutes later. Kenny was talking on his mobile. He didn't look particularly happy.

She busied herself wiping down the work surfaces and listened in on the conversation.

"Listen, Rudi. Are you sure that the gym is 100% clean? No traces? Nothing out of place?"

Kenny was nodding and walking around the kitchen in circles like a caged tiger.

"This is getting like a bad day in fucking Bosnia. I can't afford any more of this shit going on. I guessed Frasier might be a bit pissed off, but fucking shooters at dawn. I am not having any more of this." He drained his coffee cup and put it down with a bang on the table. "Okay. Call Tony and we'll all meet down the gym in an hour, okay?" He snapped his phone shut and walked off into the bedroom.

Annette carried on pretending to clean. Her stomach was churning inside. She knew better than to say anything when Kenny was wound up. Her heart had skipped a beat when she had heard Tony's name mentioned. She missed him so much and longed to hear his voice. But what was this about guns. Was Tony alright? What had happened yesterday?

Annette suddenly flinched as two strong arms enveloped her waist. She hadn't been aware of Kenny sneaking up behind her. He planted a kiss on her neck. "Sorry for the shouting, pet. Got to be going. Business to attend too."

She turned to face him. "Problems?"

Kenny shook his head. "Nothing I can't handle, pet. This Tony character I took on is proving to be challenging work. Trouble seems to follow him wherever he goes. I'm surprised he behaved himself when he was minding you. He did, I take it?"

Anette stepped back from his grip and reached for her coffee cup. "Yes, I told you. Everything was fine."

Kenny nodded and reached for his jacket on the back of the chair. "So, what are your plans today? Hairdressers? Gym? I can drop you somewhere if you like."

Annette took a deep breath. It was now or never. Inside, she was shaking. "I am not sure. Mamma is not well. Some sort of virus. She is in bed. I am worried for her, Kenny. She is all alone at home."

Kenny straightened his tie in the mirror. "So, what's on your mind?"

"I was thinking of maybe flying back out to help her for a few days."

Kenny's face darkened. "Fucking hell, Annette. You've just come back from there. She was okay then, wasn't she?"

"Yes, she was. But you know what a virus is like. They just come on overnight."

"Isn't there anybody out there that can pop in and see the old girl? A friend or neighbour? We've hardly seen one another the last few weeks."

"That has not all been my fault, Kenny."

As she said this, she instantly regretted it. She was meant to be trying to get on his good side. Annette walked towards Kenny and put her slim arms around his neck. "I am sorry, Kenny. I know business is business. But she is my Mamma. She needs me. You would not like any old, how do you say, Tom, Dick or Barry attend to your mum, would you now?"

The tension in Kenny's face broke into a grin. "It's Tom, Dick and Harry."

Annette laughed. "You know what I mean. Don't tease me."

"You are right. I wouldn't want just anybody looking after my old mum. The only difference is she is in a care home in Gateshead, not living in Italy."

Annette gazed into his eyes. "It will only be a few days, a week at the most. Until I know she is alright. I promise I will make it up to you."

Kenny kissed her lips and then grabbed her face with a powerful grip and squeezed her cheeks until it drew tears to her eyes.

"Okay, you can go. But keep me in touch. Things are going to get busy by the end of the week. You know the deal with the Dutch is as good as done. We have a big event this weekend to close it. I want you by my side Saturday night, okay?"

Annette shivered inside, but she kept her composure. "Of course, I will be back for you. I promise Kenny."

Kenny held her gaze. "Good. After the deal is done, we have some making up to do and you can show me just how much you have missed me."

As he said this, he let his hands glide over Annette's breasts. She held her breath, praying he would stop. His touch repulsed her.

Kenny's mobile phone rang again. He broke away from her, reaching out for it.

"Okay. Your passport is in my sock drawer in the bedroom. Book the flight I'll drive you to the airport myself. I must go now. I will speak to you later. 'he told her.

He left the flat talking once more into this phone.

* * *

When he had left, Annette sat down. She was shaking. She had done it. She was surprised by how easy it had been to lie to Kenny. There was no turning back now. The wheels were in motion.

She called Tony's mobile phone. It went to voicemail. She tried three more times, all without success.

Frustrated that she couldn't get through, she threw the phone down on the table and wandered into the bedroom. She saw that Kenny had indeed left her passport on the bed and a credit card.

Normally, he would have booked the flight, but because he was busy with other things at present, he had uncharacteristically left it to her. The credit card wasn't of much use to her beyond booking the flight to Naples. If used after that, it would leave a paper trail.

She would use it to get to Italy to buy herself some time before then flying on to Lanzarote.

She went back to the kitchen carrying the credit card and phoned the airport. Fifteen minutes later, she had booked a return flight to Naples.

She suddenly had a feeling of nausea sweep over her, as the reality of the situation hit her. There would be no return flight this time. She was never coming back here to Kenny Robbins. She had dreamt of this moment many times. Dreamt of escaping his controlling clutches. To get her life back.

Tears welled up in her eyes. Kenny had been charm itself when they first met. He still could be when the mood took him. But when the mask slipped, and he showed his dark side, it terrified her.

In the early days of their relationship when she had nagged him about her stuttering musical career, he had promised her that it was all in hand. But nothing had ever transpired.

Once when she questioned him about it for what seemed the umpteenth time. He had turned on her and slapped her hard around the face.

This was the beginning of the physical abuse. The odd slap became a punch. But always to the body, never the face again. The cigar burns were always strategically placed.

Annette realised that his sadistic streak knew no bounds when he was in a rage, so she learnt to keep her mouth shut for fear of what he would do to her.

One evening, he told her that her music career was not going to happen.

At first, she had cried bitterly and then, in a moment of frustration and anger, she had told Kenny that he had used her and had ruined her life.

Kenny had grabbed her by the hair and threw her into the wall. He had told her that he owned her. That she was an ungrateful bitch for all that he had given her. Her life had been nothing before he met her.

Defiantly, she had told him that she longed for that life back and she was going to leave him.

As Kenny Robbins began to slowly unbuckle his expensive leather belt and wrap it around his fist, he had informed her that no women ever left him, not until he decided.

The pain that followed his final words convinced Annette that she was trapped forever.

* * *

Tears flowed freely now as she began to pack a suitcase. The designer dresses, handbags and shoes were no longer of any interest to her. She packed the essentials that she would need and then, collected any money or jewellery that was in the flat.

Any credit cards that she owned would be stopped straight away when Kenny found out what she was up to, but as she had already acknowledged, credit cards would trace her whereabouts and she could never risk that.

She would now go to her bank and close her account and withdraw her savings.

Her flight was scheduled for 6 o'clock that evening. She shivered in anticipation.

As she left the bedroom, her mobile phone went off. She picked it up and recognised Tony's number. She had been careful not to list his name in her phone and made sure that all messages from him had been deleted. She knew that Kenny checked her phone when he thought she didn't know.

She had watched him more than once in the middle of the night slip out of bed and take her phone from the night stand and go out into the lounge to look at it. He knew her password. No secrets from Kenny. After ten minutes or so, he would return it to the nightstand and slip back into bed. This had made her paranoid about leaving anything remotely suspicious on it that Kenny would question her about.

"Hello, Tony. Thank God. I have been trying to contact you. I have missed you so much."

"I have missed you too sweetheart. Sorry I missed your calls. I had a late night last night and overslept. Is everything okay?"

Annette told him that the flight to Naples was booked and she would be on the 6.00pm plane that evening.

Tony congratulated her on being so brave and assured her that soon they would be together and starting a new life.

He then told her about the previous evening and what had transpired at the gym. He thought it best to leave out what had gone down at Malcolm Ruddy's shop.

She was horrified to hear what had happened with Frasier, but was glad that Tony was alright.

Tony said that he desperately wanted to meet up with her before she went, but they would have to be mega careful. There could be no more slip-ups.

Annette informed him that Kenny was going to drive her to the airport himself, so she guessed that they would be leaving around 4.00pm.

Tony promised that he would try to ring her later and see what he could arrange. He then told her that he had to go, as he had another call coming in and it was from Errol.

"Morning, Errol. What can I do for you?" asked Tony.

"Tony, man I have been ringing for ages. Mr. Robbins wants you down the gym. He's there now and I wouldn't keep him waiting."

Tony detected the threat in Errol's voice.

"Okay, Errol. I'm on my way. I 'll be fifteen minutes or so. Send him my apologies."

The phone went dead.

Tony quickly dressed and grabbed his keys. It wouldn't do to piss Robbins off at this point.

He reached for the front door handle and winced in pain. His hand still hurt. He hoped that he hadn't done any permanent damage. He grimaced. *I'll just have to live with it*, he thought.

On the journey to the gym, Tony went over in his head the phone conversation with Annette. It was really going to happen. There were still some dangerous twists and turns to navigate, but if it all went to plan, then a new life beckoned. He had to pinch himself to realise what had happened in such a short space of time with Annette. He just couldn't believe it was happening to him. But it was happening to Tony Slade. The soldier, the fighter and the drifter was finally going to settle down with a beautiful woman who loved him and he loved her.

Whatever lay ahead over the next few days, he was ready for it. One more battle to win.

CHAPTER TWENTY FIVE

By the time Tony reached the gym, he was running well behind time. The traffic had been hell in the city centre. Major roadworks also hadn't helped the matter.

When he entered the gym, Kenny, Rudi and Errol were all waiting. It looked like they were just finishing a workout.

Kenny Robbins was sat on a weight bench sipping on a bottle of water. His grey Nike Pro t-shirt was stained dark with sweat.

Rudi and Errol were still curling some impossible weight on a set of dumbbells. Stripped down to muscle vests, Tony realised just how big these men were. They certainly would have given Arnold Schwarzenegger a run for his money back in the day.

Kenny looked up as Tony approached them.

"Ah, nice of you to join us, Tony. I was about to send out a search party." He took another long swig on his water.

Tony held up his hands in defence. "I'm sorry, Kenny. I overslept and then the traffic was a bastard. What can I tell you?"

Robbins rose from the bench and approached Tony. "I'm not surprised you needed a lie-in with all the fucking action that went down in here yesterday. I'm more than a little pissed off that I had to clean up your mess again."

"Hey, Kenny. It was that bastard, Frasier. I didn't know it was going to get that heavy. Honestly."

Tony sensed trouble in the air and began to position himself for a possible physical response.

Robbins also sensed it and smiled ruefully. "Don't panic, Tony. You're alright here. If I wanted you sorted, the boys would have already been on you like a pair of fucking silverback gorillas. But I don't want any more bloodshed if it can be avoided. I just need to give you one more final warning that I cannot afford any more trouble at present. There have been more bodies strewn around here in the last few weeks than in a fucking *Die-Hard* movie. It has got to stop. If you want to run this place, it will be run the right way. I don't need any heat coming down on me or my businesses. I am on the brink of something big and I am not about to lose it. Do you understand me, Tony?"

Tony nodded.

"Okay. Let's move on to other matters then," said Robbins.

The tension in the air evaporated.

"Come, take a seat and talk." He gestured towards the leather chairs in the reception area. They sat down facing each other.

Tony noticed a blonde-haired girl working behind the reception desk. He estimated that she was in her mid-twenties. She was wearing a red polo shirt and black leggings. The shirt bore the logo *Power Gym*.

Robbins saw Tony looking at the girl.

"That is Karen Smart. The relief manager. Smart by name and smart by nature. Nice ass as well." Robbins' face broke into a leering grin. "Anyway, I brought her in from one of my other gym's in Gateshead, seeing that Frasier... how should we put it, has gone AWOL. She will show you the ropes. How the gym runs day to day. Karen has worked here before when Frasier was on holiday. She will stay until you're happy."

"Fine," replied Tony, "As I said, I can do a decent job here."

Robbins regarded him. "I hope so, Tony. I really do."

He leaned in closer. "I am going to let you in on a little secret before the rest of the team show up for a briefing. I am about to pull off a big deal with a Dutch business man who wants to invest in my businesses with a view to eventually buying me out. Hopefully, it will be my ticket to sail off into the sunset with Annette."

The mention of her name made Tony's stomach churn, but he kept his poker face. Robbins planned to sell up and fuck off. How ironic.

"The man, Marc Bergkamp is coming over Friday night for the weekend. We are going to wine and dine him. Show him around and give him a VIP table at the cage fight promotion, *Gladiator Wars*, this Saturday evening at my nightclub *Jesters*. It's a black-tie event. Special invite. Champagne dinner and then six quality fights. 250 quid a ticket. The local hierarchy love it. Police, lawyers, politicians, TV stars, footballers. Under all their pomp. they love a bit of blood and some bubbles. Nice little money spinner. His son Edwin is going to be fighting top of the bill against our own local boy done good Alex 'the real' McCoy. That is going to be a tear up. Heard of him?"

"Can't say l have," replied Tony.

Robbins carried on. "There's talk of the winner possibly going to America to fight in the UFC."

Tony was impressed. To fight on *The Ultimate Fighting Championships* was every cage fighter's dream.

"So, everybody in the firm needs to behave like fucking boy scouts and put on a professional face. I will need you to chauffeur the Bergkamps around and be on hand if I need you. You understand?"

Tony knew that if he was going to organise a getaway, then he had to get a move on, as he was going to be busy and be at Robbins beck and call at the weekend. Come Saturday evening, he needed to be ready to go. Annette had told him that Robbins wanted her back at his side for the fight and when she didn't show, the blue touch paper would be lit. He needed to be as far away from the fallout as possible.

"Did you hear me, Tony?"

Tony realised that he had been wrapped up in his own thoughts so much that he hadn't acknowledged Robbins.

"Yes, I fully understand. You can count on me."

Robbins rose to his feet gingerly. "I am going to hit the shower before I stiffen up for good. I don't know if working out these days is good for me or not."

Before he walked away, he addressed Tony again. "So, Tony, your first job is to get this gym ship shape and running like clockwork. I am sure the Bergkamps will visit it. You will work with Karen to make sure it is.

He glanced towards the girl who was busy stacking tubs of protein powder on the shelves. "Karen, pet. Leave that a moment. Come over here and let me introduce you to the new gym manager. This is Tony Slade."

Karen was a likable girl and seemed to know what she was doing. Tony felt sorry for her because as she went through the running of the gym in detail for him, his thoughts were a million miles away from the place. All he could do was think of Annette.

When Karen had finished the orientation tour, he thanked her for her time and said that he would welcome her help for the time being. She smiled and walked away seemingly happy.

Tony afforded himself a small ironic grin. No doubt she would be promoted to full-time manager very soon in his permanent and sudden absence.

As he helped himself to a black coffee from the vending machine in reception, he saw Robbins appear from the changing rooms. He was dressed in an immaculate charcoal grey suit and a black silk shirt. He once again looked every inch the successful businessman.

He was talking into his mobile and looking slightly stressed. He was nodding and seemed animated. Tony tried to catch some the conversation, but was distracted as Errol and Rudi lumbered over towards the vending machine. They both nodded at him. Tony nodded back. Things were looking up. It would be Christmas cards next.

Robbins snapped his phone shut and walked over to join them.

"Black coffee please, Errol."

The big man obligingly gave him the untouched one that he had just got for himself.

He took a sip and grimaced. "That tastes like fucking tar. We need to get some better stuff in than this shit."

He glanced in Tony's direction. "Make a note of that, will you, Tony? Anyway, that was my solicitor on the phone, Charles Gibson. He has informed me that Bergkamp is flying in tomorrow instead of Friday, so we need get everything good to go today. He will be landing tomorrow at midday. Tony, you will pick them up."

Tony nodded.

"Right then, boys. Let's go. There's a lot of work to do before the Dutch get here."

Robbins turned to go and then exclaimed, "Shit. I forgot that I told Annette that I would take her to the airport later. Her dear old mum isn't well." As he said this, he rolled his eyes sarcastically, "But there's no way I will have time to do that now."

He thought for a second and then said, "Tony, you can do that, can't you?"

Tony's heart leap inside, but on the outside, he remained cool. "Sure, I can do it. No problem. You carry on with whatever you need to do and leave that with me."

He couldn't believe that he was being handed a golden opportunity to see Annette before she flew out.

"You have her number, don't you, Tony?"

Tony regarded Robbins. Was he playing games here? Maybe Tony was just being paranoid, as he remembered that Robbins had given him Annette's mobile phone number when he had asked him previously to look after her.

"Yes, I have it in my phone as instructed."

"Good man. Well, I'll leave that to you. I'll ring her and let her know the situation and tell her that you'll contact her."

With that, he threw his still full coffee cup in the waste bin and signalled to Rudi and Errol and they all left the gym.

* * *

Once they had gone, Tony went outside to a quiet spot and called Annette and put her in the picture about the change of travel arrangements. She was over the moon that she would have Tony drive her to the airport and they could share a few precious moments together.

He also filled her in on the deal that Robbins had going with Bergkamp. He explained how it couldn't have worked out better for them because the next few days, Robbins would be busy and too preoccupied to think of much else. This made it easier for their plans to work.

She agreed and told him that she was surprised that Kenny hadn't changed her plans and demanded that she should be by his side for Bergkamp's arrival.

This did slightly concern Tony that Robbins indeed still had time to do this, but just hoped that he would be too tied up with his own greedy and selfish plans to give Annette too much thought.

He also asked Annette if she had any spare passport photos, as he would need them for new documents. She told him that she would have them ready for him later.

When he finished the call, he wandered back into the gym. He had to give Karen the impression over the next few days that he was surveying his new domain and was keen to take up the post of manager as soon as possible.

Robbins would expect to find him here working and ready to deal with any problems that might arise.

The gym was now reasonably busy, as it was lunchtime and many of the local office workers had popped in to train.

Tony had been in and out of gyms for the majority of his life. He no longer had the same fire in his belly for long arduous workouts like he had as a younger man. When you were a young buck, you could train every day and think nothing of it. You took your fitness and health for granted.

Tony now understood at his age that recovery time took longer and longer. In your younger years, you woke up and jumped out of bed as a God given right. Now, he realised that it was a God given gift.

With age comes wisdom, they say. Maybe that was right.

He regarded the middle-aged beer-bellied men huffing and puffing on treadmills and rowing machines. Housewives and young mothers sat on stationary bikes clocking up the miles but going nowhere. Young lads crowded around the free weights, flexing their muscles in the mirrors, each jostling for Alpha male superiority.

He remembered the days when he was like this, but luckily for him, he had Terry Norris and Ray Steele and his Jujutsu black belts, Gordon Phelps, Pete 'Pitbull' Reilly and Arthur Stiles to knock him back into reality and know his place.

God bless them all. A different breed and a different era.

The thought of Ray Steele jolted him back to reality. He needed to phone Ray and put him in the picture about what was about to go down. He hoped that he would understand and be ready to help.

He found Karen in the back office on the computer. When he entered, she looked up from her work.

"I hope you don't mind me using the office for the moment."

Tony smiled, "Please use it and do what you need to do."

"Thank you. Don Frasier didn't like me to be in here."

"Well, you don't have to worry about that anymore. I think you'll find me a different person to Frasier."

Karen seemed to relax. "Thank you, Mr. Slade."

"Call me Tony, please."

She flashed him a coy smile, "Okay. Thank you, Tony."

Karen then went on to tell him that all the financial records would be up to speed and everything in place by tomorrow. Tony thanked her. She then went on to say that she was looking forward to working with him and was glad Frasier had been sacked.

Inwardly, Tony mused what she would really think if she knew the truth about Frasier's departure. Ignorance is bliss, so they say.

He said his goodbyes to Karen and told her that she was doing an excellent job and to hold the fort for the present until Bergkamp was gone.

* * *

Once Tony was in his car, he dialled Ray Steele's number and after two rings, he heard a familiar gruff voice answer.

"Hello, Tony. How are you, lad?"

"I'm good, Ray. Look, I'll come straight to the point. I need to run something by you."

"Okay, son. Fire away. This sounds serious."

"It is," replied Tony.

Tony went on to tell Ray the full story and his plans. The older man listened silently and when Tony had finished, he spoke. "You need to be careful, Tony. Robbins is a fucking nutcase. You stealing his women is going to cause a shit storm and he will do everything he can to hunt you down and kill you."

He paused for a second and then added, "But you know all this already, don't you?"

Tony felt the familiar tingle of adrenaline in his belly. "Yes, I do, Ray, but I have a real chance of happiness, maybe my last chance, and I have got to take it, no matter the danger. I understand if I'm asking a lot of you."

Tony heard a chuckle on the other line of the line.

"Son, you have always been a bit of a maverick, even from the early days in Terry's gym. Then again, so have I. You know I'll help you, Tony. It goes without saying."

Tony breathed a sigh of relief.

"Once I get out to Lanzarote and get Annette, we'll disappear far away. I know where I'll go but I won't tell you, Ray, just in case that bastard comes asking questions. You understand?"

"Aye, son. I understand. I respect your decision. Give the girl my number. I'll pick her up at the airport once she's in Lanzarote. I have a good friend who manages some villas for me on the quieter side of the island. She'll be safe there for now. He has a couple of handy lads that work for him. They'll keep an eye on her. Once you make your move, you'll need to be fast, as Robbins will be all over this like a rash. He's no fool. No matter how careful you are, he'll find your trail eventually."

"I know, my friend. I'll be careful. Thank you. I'll be in touch again soon." Tony went to hang up but added, "Be careful yourself."

Ray chuckled again. "I'll be fine. At my time of life, I welcome a little excitement. See you, son."

When Ray Steele ended the call, he pocketed his phone and walked into the cool of his stockroom at the rear of his bar. He weaved his way between the boxes of assorted products that he had stored there.

He moved a large barrel of beer away from the back wall and fiddled with a couple of the stones. They came away to reveal an aperture. He reached into the space and bought out an oily yellow rag.

He unwrapped it to reveal an old colt service revolver. It had been his since the 40s. His older brother Tom had brought it back with him from Burma in World War Two.

Ray felt the weight of it in his hands. He cleaned it regularly and he knew that it was in good working order. He would be ready if need be.

CHAPTER TWENTY SIX

Tony pulled his car up outside Annette's apartment block. His heart was racing. The wheels were well and truly in motion and moving quickly. There was no turning back now. Today's decisions were going to be life-changing.

He regarded himself in the rear-view mirror. His face bore the lines and scars of many battles. In fact, his whole life up to now had been a battle, one way or another. He was tired of that life. He never in a thousand years would have believed that there was another way of life for him. But now he could almost taste it.

So much had happened in such a short space of time since Rob had got him the job with Robbins.

Tony felt a pang of sadness as he thought of his old friend. The feeling then turned to anger, as he remembered that Robbins had been responsible for his death. He breathed deeply and let the feeling subside. He had to stay focused.

Thinking of Rob also made him think of the car and money in the garage lock-up. He would be heading for it very soon. But one step at a time.

As he exited the car, he glanced at his watch. He was in ample time to get Annette to the airport. Once he had done that, then he needed to work on the next part of the plan.

* * *

When Annette opened the door, Tony gently eased her back into the apartment and took her in his arms and they kissed passionately. He kicked the door shut with his heel.

Eventually, when they broke contact, they both laughed.

"God, it's so good to see you," Tony said.

Annette hugged him again. "It is so good to see you too."

Tony let her go and looked her in the eyes. "Are you all ready?"

She nodded. Concern etched her beautiful face. "I am scared, Tony."

He held her hands. "I know. So am I. But we need to make the fear we feel work for us and spur us on. You must be brave. We're nearly there. You do still want this, don't you?"

She gently cupped his face and kissed his lips softly. "More than anything, Tony. I want to spend the rest of my life with you far away from here."

Tony smiled. "Good. Then let's get you on that plane. When you get to Naples, ring me and we'll discuss how you get to Lanzarote next. Ray is ready and waiting there. I'll give you his number. He'll pick you up when you land."

Annette nodded and moved to pick up her suitcase.

"I've got that," said Tony, "Have one final look around and make sure you haven't left anything. You won't be returning here ever again."

Annette felt a shiver run up her spine. This was well and truly it. She was leaving Kenny for good.

She glanced quickly around at what had been her home. She felt no regrets. There were too many unhappy memories here. It was time to go.

She quickly ran over to the CD collection and pulled out a disc.

"*Stars*, Simply Red." She held up the CD. "Good memories to take with me."

* * *

At the airport, they kept everything professional. Robbins had many eyes and ears across the city. They needed to be careful.

Once Annette went through to departures, Tony went and bought himself a coffee and the newspaper. He found a seat and read the newspaper whilst he waited for Annette's plane to take off.

Once it was airborne, he phoned Robbins to tell him. It went to voicemail. A few minutes later, he received a text from him. It just read 'thanks'.

Tony got up and left the airport. The man was all heart, he thought.

---

10 days after the incident.
Colin Crane watched the *Alpha* coffee house from across the street. He stood in the bus shelter for partial concealment. He pulled the blue baseball cap that he was wearing further down on his head. He didn't want to be recognised.

This was the third day in a row that he had come here. The other two days he had made sure to dress differently so as not to stand out. Old Colin was fucking smart. People only saw a geeky looking misfit when they looked at him, but they were fools. They didn't know the real Colin Crane.

He now watched Kim the manager working around the tables. She was chatting happily to the customers and tidying away mugs and trays. He surveyed her every move with hatred burning in his eyes.

He had followed the bitch home two evenings in a row. She had no idea that he had been behind her in the shadows. He had observed her entering her flat, oblivious to his presence.

He had seen her light go on and watched her pull the curtains shut. Snug as a bug in a rug.

He knew her routines and habits. He could get to her anytime he liked. Dead easy. But not just yet.

He felt a tingle of anticipation run through his body. He closed his eyes and played the scenario through in his mind.

He felt the excitement of anticipation rising. It ached for release but not now.

He was suddenly startled when a hand tapped him on the shoulder. His eyes snapped open and he flinched.

He heard a voice say, "Sorry to startle you, young man, but do you want this bus?"

Colin turned to see an old man with two Asda carrier bags in his hands gesturing towards the bus which had arrived at the stop.

He hadn't heard it pull up. He had been lost in his fantasy.

He moved to one side to let the old man by and said politely, "No, sir. I don't want this one. Please go ahead."

The old man moved past Colin. "Thank you, young man."

Colin Crane smiled, "No problem. Watch your step now."

A moment later, the bus pulled away and he regarded the coffee house once more. He saw Kim by the front window now sticking up a poster.

He looked at her lithe body. She was stretching up to place the poster a little higher. Her t-shirt rode up a little, revealing her smooth flat belly. Colin could see that she had a piercing in her navel. He could also see her breasts straining against the fabric of her top. He felt a stirring in his loins.

Girls like her just stared through Colin. They weren't interested in him, especially sexually. No, they wanted to be fucked by some rugby type or cage fighter.

He thought back to the last time that he had been with a girl. It had been some time. It had been Mandy Willis. She had worked on the checkout at Tesco. Colin used to shop in there regularly and had somehow plucked up the courage to ask her out. She wasn't any oil painting. A bit of a fat cow really. But Colin needed sex and he wasn't bothered how he got it or with whom.

It had been a disaster. They had gone back to her flat and when he stripped off, the fat bitch just laughed at his body and pointed out that the size of his dick wasn't too impressive.

Colin had hated her for that. The fat bitch soon changed her tune when he got his hands around her throat and threatened to strangle her.

He had held her down on the bed with a bit of a struggle and fucked her. He had been rough, and she didn't like it.

That was the end of that relationship. She had threatened him with the police but never followed it up. He never went back to that Tesco store ever again.

Two weeks later, he had followed Mandy from her flat one evening and as she crossed the play park nearby, he had also run up behind her and hit her over the head with a hammer.

He didn't kill her, just put her in hospital for a few weeks. Served her right for laughing at him.

She never knew who did it. He had got away with it. Colin was too clever. He just wasn't too good around women. He didn't seem to gel with them. They all treated him like shit. Either they were taking the piss out of him or talking down to him like he was some sort of retard. Just like Kim.

He looked once more towards the shop window. Kim was no longer there.

"I will be coming for you soon, fucking whore," he whispered.

With that, he turned and melted away into the shadows and joined the rush hour crowds on their way home.

He was anonymous to them. A nobody. But soon, they would know the name of Colin Crane.

CHAPTER TWENTY SEVEN

Tony returned to his flat. He looked around the place. He had no real personal belongings in it. When Robbins had found it for him, it came fully furnished, white goods and all.

He had always travelled light. He had never been able to lay down roots. He had gone where the army had sent him. He never really had anywhere that he could truly call home.

Tony went to the bedroom and found the one large suitcase that he owned on top of the wardrobe. He got it down in preparation. When it was time to go, he knew that he would have to do it quickly.

He moved through to the kitchen and pulled out the bottom drawer of a unit and rooted around until he found a plastic carrier bag. Inside it was the money that he had been saving from the wages Robbin's was paying him.

He counted it. He had saved a lot and it would help with a few payments that were going to be needed before he left the country. He transferred the money into a small holdall and brought it into the bedroom and sat it by the suitcase.

Tony began to fill the case with the belongings that he would need over the next few days.

He felt the flicker of anticipation flutter in his belly as he thought of what he was doing. He breathed deeply and the feeling subsided.

He would soon ring Emma Snow and arrange with her to get the key to the lock-up to drive the Audi away and its contents.

The money in the boot would give Annette and him a good cushion.

He also needed to phone an old army buddy, Doug Jacobs. He had been in Northern Ireland with him and they had remained in contact.

Doug had been pensioned out of the regiment after losing his left leg in a bomb explosion. It should have, in all intents and purposes, killed him, but miraculously, he had survived it.

When he had visited Doug in hospital after the incident, Tony had been surprised how upbeat he was about the whole thing.

He told Tony that he had been given a decent pay out and he was glad that his life had been spared. He was in no doubt that he had been given another chance and he was going to take full advantage of it.

Tony admired the tough bastard. Lesser men would have gone under in his circumstances, but not Doug. He went and got himself a business degree and opened an import/export business, which became hugely successful. The word was if you wanted something, Doug was the man to go to. He was Mr 'Fix-it' and he didn't mind bending the rules either.

Tony knew that Robbins would not rest until he hunted him down, so he needed a new passport, papers and credit cards, and so would Annette.

He knew that Doug would do this, but there was just one slight problem: he lived in Bristol down in the West country. Tony was going to have to make a trip down there before he could leave the country. He really didn't want to, but it was necessary to his plans.

The plan in his head was to wait for the cage fight event to start on Saturday and then travel down to Bristol to pick up the documents and fly out of Bristol airport to Lanzarote where he would meet up with Annette. Then, they would fly to Morocco for a while and decide on their future. This would hopefully buy them enough time to disappear for good.

Tony searched his mobile phone for Doug's number. It had been a while since they last spoke, and he hoped that the number he had him listed under was current.

He rang the number and it went to voicemail, but he recognised the voice on the personalised message as Doug's. There was no mistaking his broad West country accent.

When they had both served together in Belfast, the standing joke between them was that neither could understand each other and everybody else couldn't understand either of them with their distinct accents.

Tony left a short message asking Doug to get back to him as soon as possible, as it was an urgent matter.

As he hung up, his phone rang, and he saw the name of Kenny Robbins flash up on the screen.

He answered it. "Hello, Kenny."

"Tony, how goes it? Sorry about the short text earlier on. I was a bit preoccupied. I take it that Annette got away without any problems?"

"Yes. It was all fine. No problem."

"Good. It's probably best that she's gone for a few days with Bergkamp visiting. I'm sure he would have admired her beauty, but that won't clinch the deal. Sometimes, women can be a help or a hindrance. You know what I mean?"

"Yes, I do," replied Tony, "As I said before, that's why I'm single."

Robbins laughed loudly down the phone, "Sensible fucking man."

There were a few moments' pause and then, Robbin's voice took on a more serious note.

"Look, Tony. Karen at the gym is a great girl, but I would like your presence down there the next few days. I want everything in place when our Dutch friends arrive."

"I understand, Kenny. Leave it to me. It'll all be good to go when they visit."

"Good man, Tony. I stand to make a lot of money if this deal goes through and I won't forget the people who are loyal to me. The Dutch fly in tomorrow morning at 10.00am. It'll be Bergkemp and his son, plus his lawyer. Now, Muhammad doesn't go to the mountain, so to speak, so I want you to pick them up and bring them to my offices. I'll be there with some of the firm. We'll soften them up with some buck's fizz and croissants. These foreigners like all that fancy bollocks. You okay with all that, Tony?"

"I'll be at arrivals for 10.00am, Kenny."

"Alright. I can't afford any more fuck-ups."

"I promise it'll all be fine, Kenny."

Robbins laughed again. "Okay, Tony. I guess I am a bit uptight. I need a good shot of whiskey to unwind me, I think. I'll leave you to it. I'll see you tomorrow morning."

The phone went dead and Tony put it back in his pocket. He truly hoped that it would all go smoothly. It was going to be a busy few days.

Tony decided that he would drive down to the gym and get some more background from Karen on its daily running, as he wanted to be on the ball tomorrow if the Dutch threw any questions his way. He wanted to be as professional as he could.

* * *

When Tony entered the gym, it was nearly 8.30pm but it was still heaving with customers.

He spied Karen cleaning the large mirrors that ran the length of a wall where the treadmills were situated.

The flat-screened wall-mounted television were all tuned in to a music channel. He looked at what was on. He briefly watched a scantily clad young woman who he didn't recognise surrounded by a bunch of male dancers. She was singing about something that Tony couldn't understand or didn't particularly want to.

Karen looked up from her cleaning and regarded the expression on his face. "Not your cup of tea I take it, Boss?"

Tony looked in her direction. "Not my cup of anything. Who listens to that crap?"

Karen laughed, "You'll be surprised."

"Give me some real music like the Stones or Elton John every time."

"It's just a different generation, that's all."

Tony raised his eyebrows. "Is that right? You know, I went to the Doctor's the other day and he asked me if I was allergic to anything. I told him, yes, R&B music."

Karen rolled her eyes. "Coffee to settle your nerves? I have a new blend."

"You're a lifesaver. Thank you."

As Karen headed to the vending machine, Tony told her that he was going to the office and could she bring it to him there.

She threw him a mock salute in acknowledgement.

He headed towards the door at the back of the gym which had a small sign on it which read 'Manager'. This had been Frasier's domain. Tony wondered what he might find in there. He yet hadn't had the place to himself.

Once inside the office, Tony closed the door and surveyed the room. It was a decent size. A large desk commanded the centre of the room. It had a black leather swivel chair behind it. Tony could imagine Frasier sat in it. The King of the Castle. Well, like many Kings throughout history, this one had been well and truly toppled.

There was a CCTV screen on the wall to the left of the desk which projected images of the gym.

If there were tapes made of the recordings, Tony would hope that Robbins or Rudi or maybe Errol had erased any images of the violence that had recently happened here. He was sure that Robbins was smart enough to have dealt with that matter swiftly.

The rest of the office contained a few filing cabinets and a tall metal locker. There was also a small two-seater sofa facing the desk. There was a window behind the desk with half-open dusty venetian blinds hanging from it. The window overlooked the carpark, which was rammed full of cars at present.

The gym certainly seemed a lucrative business and, in another world, maybe Tony would have enjoyed the challenge of running it. But he needed to remember that beyond the seemingly innocuous workings of the gym was also the dark underbelly of Kenny Robbins' business empire built on intimidation, violence and illegal activities.

Tony pulled open the locker door. Inside the door hung a calendar of female bodybuilders. The current page was on *Miss September*, although the year was well into the month of October. She must have been a favourite of Frasier. It did nothing for Tony. Give him some curvy womanly shapes any day. This lady named Mona looked like she could wrestle grizzly bears for fun.

Inside the locker was a pair of *Twins* boxing gloves. Excellent quality gloves. They seemed almost brand new. There was also a jar of Vitamin D tablets, a half empty tub of protein powder and a couple of body building magazines. Nothing very exciting.

He closed the door and sat down behind the desk. Just then, there was a knock on the office door and Karen came in with a cup of coffee.

"Sorry about the wait. I had a few things to deal with on reception." She came in and placed the cup down on the desk.

"No worries. Thank you," replied Tony.

Karen eyed him sat behind the desk in the big leather chair. "Suits you, if you don't mind me saying."

"You think so?"

"Oh definitely. It could have been made for you."

Tony took a sip of coffee. "Yes, I think I could get used to sitting here being waited on by my staff every day. Do you also do massage?"

Karen laughed, "In your dreams, Boss. I'm afraid my duties don't run to that."

Tony smiled, "Well, in that case, I will make do with this wonderful coffee. Strong and black."

Karen walked towards the door and called over her shoulder, "Just the way I like my men." She paused at the door and turned around. "Seriously though, Boss. The chair suits you more than that arsehole, Frasier."

Tony raised his cup. "Why thank you very much, young lady."

Once Karen had left, Tony pulled open the top two drawers of the desk. Again, he found that there was nothing of great note in them. Just the usual office stationary, printer paper, jiffy bags and envelopes.

The bottom drawer was, however, locked.

Tony reached for a silver-plated letter opener, which was in a jar of various pens and pencils on the desk top. He worked it into the top of the drawer and moved it around until it sprung open the lock.

It was a deep drawer and the first thing that Tony saw in there was an expensive Nikon Camera. No doubt the one with which Frasier had taking his incriminating photographs.

There was also a small holdall.

Tony lifted it out and opened the zipper. Inside was a stash of light green coloured tablets in small plastic bags. They looked like steroids. There were also some vials of a colourless liquid, plus some fresh syringes. At the bottom of the bag was half a dozen rolls of fifty-pound notes held together with elastic bands. Obviously, Frasier had a thriving little business going on off the record.

Tony decided that he would certainly take the cash and the camera. The money would go a long way to paying Doug Jacobs off once he came up with the goods.

That reminded him that Doug had yet to call him back.

He drank down his coffee and popped the cash and camera into a black dustbin liner that he found in the locker.

He put the tablets and the rest of the gear into another dustbin liner. He would bin this. It wouldn't do for Bergkamp to come across any of this shit tomorrow.

He went out into the gym and saw that Karen was again busy on the reception. He slipped out the entrance and found the large plastic dumpster around the corner of the gym and threw Frasier's stash into it. He then put the bag with the money and camera in the boot of his car.

When he came back in, Karen was just getting off the phone.

"What time does the gym shut?" he asked her.

"Everybody out at 10.00pm," replied Karen.

"Then I will wait around, and you can show me how to lock up. Plus, I can escort you safely to your car."

"Are you sure?" asked Karen.

"Definitely. It's no problem," said Tony.

"That's great. Normally one of the personal trainers are here and they stay until I've locked up, but none of them are in tonight."

"Then it's just as well I came down. Come on. Let's start to gently ease a few people out, shall we?"

* * *

After Tony watched Karen drive off safely, he got into his own car. He clicked his belt in place and was ready to head for home when his mobile phone rang.

He pulled it out of his pocket and saw the name of Doug Jacobs on the screen.

Great, he thought to himself as he pressed the answer button.

"Hello, Doug. Long time, my friend."

"Tony Slade. How are you, you old bastard?"

"All the better for hearing your voice. Still making millions, are you?"

There was a laugh from the other end of the phone. "Oh yeah. I'm a regular Bill Gates, don't you know?"

"So, how are things?" asked Tony.

"All good. I've recently been fitted with one of those hi-tech, bionic legs. I go to the gym these days and run on the treadmill. Can you fucking believe that? I'm also getting married next year. You better be there."

"Wow. Married. Who is the unlucky women?"

"Hey, cheeky fucker. She's the love of my life and her name is Sarah. She's a physiotherapist that helped me with my rehabilitation. We became good friends and things just blossomed from there. Life is good, my friend."

"Well, I'm pleased for you, Doug, and I wish you all the best."

"Thank you, Tony. Now, down to more pressing matters, what can I do for you? The phone call was a bit cryptic."

Tony explained what he needed but would not tell Doug why. He didn't want him to be dragged into any trouble that would inevitably follow.

Doug accepted this and told Tony that he could sort everything out and gave him a price. He also informed him that it might take a week or two.

Tony asked if it could be quicker, but Doug told him that was being quick, so Tony had little choice but to agree. He asked Doug to ring him as soon as things were ready.

Doug gave Tony a post office box number and address to forward all the documentation to that he would need. He promised to keep in touch.

It made Tony uneasy that he wouldn't be able to make a clean break straight away. The longer he was in the country, the riskier it became. But things had moved a lot more quickly than he had anticipated. He would just have to bite the bullet and wait. He would feel a lot better when he could put some miles between Robbins and himself.

When Tony got back to his flat, he realised that he hadn't eaten for a while, so he made himself a ham sandwich and got himself a cold bottle of Budweiser from the fridge.

He switched on the television, kicked off his shoes and flopped down onto the sofa. He took a long pull on his beer. It tasted good. He chewed on his sandwich as he absentmindedly watched the TV screen. He flicked through the channels, but nothing seemed to catch his interest. Finally, he started to watch the film, *Heat*, for the umpteenth time. Even though it was already halfway through, he still got drawn into the classic dialogue between the two screen giants that were De Niro and Pacino.

When the film ended, it was well past midnight. He decided to see if he could get some sleep. Just then his phone rang. He saw on the screen that it was Annette calling. He immediately answered. "Hello, darling. Are you okay?"

"Hello, Tony. Yes, I am fine. I arrived safely, and I am with Mamma."

"Good. Now, enjoy a few days with her. I'll contact you on Saturday and then, you'll start to put the travel arrangements we discussed into play. You must not leave a trail to where you are heading. Robbins will be straight on your scent when he eventually realises that you're not coming back. Have you spoken to him yet?"

Annette told him that she hadn't.

"Right. Well, ring him when we hang up. Tell him that your mother isn't too good, and you will keep him up to speed. If it comes to Saturday and you haven't returned and he contacts, you, just tell him that she has taken a turn for the worst and you can't leave her. He won't like it, but it'll buy us both time. After that, just don't answer your phone to him."

"Okay, Tony. I miss you so much. I need you with me to give me strength."

"I understand, darling and I miss you too, but you must find the strength. I know you have it and we will be together soon, I promise. I love you and will speak to you again when I can."

"I love you too, Tony. Please be careful."

Tony hung up. Tiredness seemed to have suddenly left his body. The phone conversation had triggered his mind to fresh thoughts. The plans ran through his head. Every detail had to be right.

For Annette, she would fly out of Italy to mainland Spain. This was unavoidable and could be traced, but time was a factor. Then, from there, she would travel on the train from Madrid to Cádiz in Southern Spain.

There was a weekly ferry from Cádiz that went to Lanzarote. It sailed to Las Palmas de Gran Canaria and then, on from there, to Arrecife, Lanzarote. This is where Ray would meet her and look after her until Tony arrived.

It would take Annette a full three days or more of travel, but she would be difficult to trace, and that was worth it.

Tony would eventually fly out to Lanzarote himself and hope that it would take some while before Robbins realised that he had done a runner and tried to trace him.

If it all went to plan, they had a great chance. Tony just prayed that there would be no slip-ups.

He knew now that sleep would not be coming, so he unpacked his tracksuit and left the flat for a run to burn off the anticipatory adrenaline that had just flooded his body.

CHAPTER TWENTY EIGHT

The next morning at 8.00am, Tony was showered, shaved and reading the morning newspaper over a cup of black coffee. He felt surprisingly fresh considering that it was well past 3.00am when he had got to bed after his run.

After breakfast, he dressed in a sharp grey suit and blue shirt, one of the few items that he had left unpacked. He looked every inch the dedicated chauffeur and minder to the Kenny Robbins' empire.

He went into the bathroom and brushed his teeth. He then checked his hair in the mirror and put a light dusting of *Boss* aftershave on his face. He noticed the small scar at the corner of his left eye. It looked vividly red in the harsh glow of the fluorescent light, even though it was decades old. It sparked the memory of the incident that had nearly claimed his sight.

It was way back in his early days of working on the doors with Ray Steele. They had been asked to work the door of a particularly rough public house named the *White Stag* in Durham not far from the University way before it had become a fashionable place to hang out.

Everything had been going well until a shout went up from the bar that trouble was brewing.

Tony arrived at the bar first to see a large guy in a heated argument with an attractive blonde-haired girl. He gathered quickly from the bar staff that this guy was kicking off because his advances towards his young lady had been rejected. He was obviously hyped up on alcohol and wasn't taking the knock back to well.

When Tony approached him, the man was posturing and swearing at the girl.

"You are a fucking stuck-up bitch. I know you Brenda Hughes. You think you're too good for the likes of me. Well, fuck you."

Tony noted that the man was dangerously close to this girl and making her and her friends extremely uncomfortable. Tony also noted the empty pint glass in his hand.

He approached from the side and at distance before he spoke. "Okay, pal. That's enough. I think it's better for everybody here that you leave before you do something that you'll regret."

The man turned to face Tony and regarded him like a piece of rubbish. "Fuck off out of my face. This isn't nothing to do with you."

Tony had seen and heard this all before. He took a deep breath and pushed down the rising adrenaline.

"Well, that's where you're wrong. It's my job to keep order here, so I'm asking you to leave."

The man turned fully towards Tony.

Tony looked him up and down. He was a burly fucker. Probably in his late 20s. He had a bit of a beer gut hanging over his trousers but was obviously up for a fight.

"I'm not going anywhere. Are you going to make me, boy?"

Well, there it was. The gauntlet was thrown down.

"If I must, yes. I'll also let you know that I was prepared to let you walk, but now I'm going to fucking hurt you badly you fat turd."

The blue touch paper had been lit. Tony had deliberately done it. The man had to now save face and make his move.

Tony would be prepared for it. That is what he trained for. That said, when the man moved, it was faster than Tony anticipated.

The pint glass came flying towards his face.

Tony moved his head, but the edge of the glass caught the corner of his eye and broke on impact.

By now, though, Tony had gone into warrior mode.

He grabbed the man's glassing arm by the wrist and slammed his forearm up into the extended elbow joint. It snapped like a carrot and the glass dropped harmlessly to the carpet.

Tony drove his knee into the man's balls and then grabbed his greasy hair and slammed his head off the edge of the bar. It was over.

Ray Steele and another doorman, Greg Stones, arrived on the scene and dragged the man's unconscious form from the premises.

Tony retreated to the toilets and surveyed his facial wound. Blood seeped from a deep gash by his left eye. It had been close, and he certainly could have lost the sight from the eye. It was going to need stitches.

Some thirty plus years on from the incident, as Tony looked in the mirror, the memory seemed just like yesterday. It was another example of the legacy of the violent life he had led.

Tony left the bathroom and the memory and grabbed his car keys. It was time to pick up Bergkamp and crew from the airport.

* * *

Tony recognised Marc Bergkamp immediately as he walked through the arrivals gate.

He was a small man, around 5ft 7 inches. He looked in his early 60s. His grey hair was combed back smartly, and his beard neatly trimmed. He wore gold framed designer glasses, and the cream suit and powder blue shirt he was wearing looked expensive and handmade. The leather shoes were *Gucci*. He looked cool and assured.

Walking beside him was an older man about six inches taller. He was balding and sported a full grey beard. He wore a conservative grey suit. Tony had him pinned as the lawyer.

Finally, close behind them pushing a luggage trolley laden with expensive looking leather suitcases, was who Tony presumed was Bergkamp's son, Edwin.

He was around 6ft plus and athletic looking. The cauliflower ears gave away his fighting pedigree. He walked easily with an air of confidence. He had close cropped blonde hair and a deep suntan. He wore a blue suit stylishly over a tight white t-shirt.

As the men drew closer, Tony stepped out of the sea of people waiting to pick up new arrivals coming in to Newcastle.

"Excuse me. Mr. Bergkamp? Mr. Robbins sent me to pick you and your party up. My name is Tony Slade." Tony extended his hand towards the Dutchman.

Within a blink of the eye, the younger blonde man had stepped in front of Bergkamp and put up a barrier between him and Tony. He stared at Tony. Tony returned the stare. His eyes never wavered.

Marc Bergkamp spoke, "It's okay, Edwin. The man is who he said he is."

Edwin looked at Tony a moment longer and then stepped back.

Marc Bergkamp reached for Tony's hand and shook it. "Pleased to meet you. Apologises for Edwin. He is my son but also my minder. Kenny sent me an image of you from his phone. I recognised your face as I came through the doors."

Very clever, mused Tony.

"No problem. I understand," replied Tony.

"As I said, this is my son, Edwin, and my lawyer, Frank Koeman."

Tony shook hands with both men and noted that Edwin liked to squeeze a little too tightly. It was just another subtle show of machismo.

"Okay, now we have all met, please lead the way, Mr. Slade," said Marco.

The car journey was uneventful. Surprisingly, just like Annette had done when first meeting Tony, Marc Bergkamp sat up the front next to him and chatted pleasantly about Newcastle and some of the sites on the way to Kenny Robbins' offices.

He told Tony that it was his first visit to the North East. He had been to London many times but never Newcastle. He said he didn't know much about the city, other than the fact that it had a lot of bridges and an underachieving football team.

Tony laughed and said that he couldn't argue with either of the statements, although this year, Newcastle United would be back in the big time of the Premier League once again. For how long was anybody's guess.

"I seem to remember one of Newcastle's famous managers, Bobby Robson, doing an excellent job at my home team PSV Eindhoven."

"Indeed, he did. It was a pity that he never got the time to do the same at Newcastle," replied Tony.

"Yes, it was a sad loss to the football world," answered Bergkamp. After a pause, he changed the subject. "So, Tony, have you worked for Kenny for long?"

"Not really. A few months or so."

"Is he a good boss? Does he look after you?"

Tony sensed that the Dutchman was trying to find out a little more about Robbins from the people close to him.

"He pays well, so I guess that makes him a good boss."

Bergkamp laughed. "Ah, so money is your motivation, Tony?"

"Isn't it most people's?" he replied.

Bergkamp laughed. "I guess so and I also guess it means that you are prepared to do anything to get it."

"I have my limits," answered Tony.

Bergkamp nodded. "I have found in my experience over the years that every man has his price. If he wants something bad enough, usually, nothing will stop him trying to get it at any price."

Tony thought of Annette and couldn't argue with the statement.

The rest of the journey lapsed into silence. Tony couldn't help but like Bergkamp. He seemed chilled out. But when you looked behind his steely grey eyes, he could see a man not to be underestimated. What if Robbins had?

Tony showed the men into Kenny's office. He was there all smiles and charm to welcome them. Buck's fizz, coffee and croissants were offered.

Tony saw Errol and Rudi in their usual place. There were a few more of Kenny's top boys present. Andy Roth, an old-school enforcer and trusted friend. Roth was boarding on being a psychopath. His reputation for his love of torturing people was well known. He was ferociously loyal to Robbins and would make a very dangerous enemy.

Then there was Joe Walsh and Danny Ewan, who both ran the illegal underbelly of his operations, and Charles Gibson, lawyer and dodgy bastard extraordinaire. There were a few other faces that Tony didn't recognise.

"Are you staying for a spot of breakfast, Tony?" asked Robbins.

Tony didn't fancy croissants and bullshit. "No thank you, Kenny. I will head off down the gym and check on things."

"Okay, suit yourself," replied Kenny.

As Tony reached for the door handle, Kenny called his name. "Just a quick minute of your time."

Robbins came closer to Tony, out of the ear shot of the others.

"Thank you for getting Annette away yesterday and picking up Bergkamp this morning. How is he?"

Tony regarded the Dutchman across the room sipping his coffee and chatting to Charlie Gibson.

"He seemed pretty chilled, Kenny, but then again, he's foreign. I'm probably not the best person to ask, as anybody foreign in my past, I shot."

Kenny Robbins' face broke into a huge grin. "You're a crazy fucker. I can't help but like you, Tony. You sure you won't stay?"

"No thanks, Kenny. I'm afraid if I start eating croissants, the next thing I know, I'll be wearing pink and baking quiche."

Robbins rolled his eyes in mock disbelief. "Get the fuck out of here. Oh Tony, have this."

Tony looked down as Robbins pressed a wade of twenty-pound notes into his hand.

"Like I said, I appreciate what you've done."

Tony nodded in acknowledgement and left. Fucking hell, he almost felt a flicker of feeling for the bastard.

When Tony left the offices, he felt his stomach rumble. He hadn't felt like breakfast earlier but now he did. He would swing by *Oscar's* coffee shop. They served up great pancakes and didn't make bad coffee either. His stomach growled once more as he thought about them.

* * *

As Tony walked in through the doors of the gym, he was pleasantly full, but suddenly, he felt the food churn in his stomach, as he was instantly drawn to a commotion at the reception. His awareness antenna went up. He felt a tingle of anticipation course through his body. That didn't sit well with the three pancakes and syrup he had just eaten.

As he drew nearer, he saw Karen at the desk along with one of the personal trainers that worked out of the place. He was a young dark-haired lad named Carl.

Both were trying to reason with a guy who was posturing and remonstrating loudly. He had two other men with him. Both were joining in to add their opinion.

As Tony got closer, he studied the man doing the shouting. He stood around 5ft 9 inches. He looked mid-twenties, solidly built and was sporting a red mohawk haircut. His muscular arms were covered in tattoos. He wore a tight sports rash guard and shorts. His two buddies were dressed in similar attire. Both sported baseball caps.

Tony could hear that 'Mohawk' was not happy about Karen refusing him entry into the gym. Karen was looking concerned and so was Carl the young personal trainer.

Tony knew it was time to step in. His years on the doors ensured that he knew how to deal with irate people.

"What seems to be the problem here, guys? Can I help?" he asked.

'Mohawk' looked Tony up and down. "Who the fuck is asking?" he snarled.

Tony knew that the situation probably wasn't going to end well judging by this guy's aggressive response.

"I'm Tony Slade, gym manager, and you are?"

"I'm Alex McCoy," 'Mohawk' answered.

"Yeah, the 'Real' McCoy," chimed in his two cronies as if it meant something to Tony.

When Tony didn't respond, they continued.

"The 'Real' McCoy. North East middleweight MMA champion of *Cage Chaos*."

"Okay," replied Tony without looking impressed, "So, like I asked, what's the problem?"

McCoy regarded Tony as if he had just been beamed down from the moon.

"As far as I know, Don Frasier manages this place and he lets me use it for free. I don't know you, pal. I don't have a membership or need one, as I was trying to explain to this dumb bitch here."

As he said this, he pointed an accusing finger in Karen's direction. This made his cronies burst out in a fit of giggling.

Tony stared them down unsmiling.

"Well, Frasier no longer manages the gym. I do. So, here's the deal. Firstly, you will apologize to my staff and then, I'll honour your previous arrangement with the former manager today. But as from tomorrow, you'll sign up for a monthly membership. How does that sound?"

McCoy's breathing became heavy.

"You can fuck right off. I can walk into any gym in Newcastle and train for free, so you can stick your offer up your ass."

Tony felt the old familiar feeling of adrenaline rise. He knew the situation was heading south. You try and be nice, but there are just some pondlife who won't play ball.

McCoy was just another in an extensive line of inflated egos. A young buck with a bit of a reputation. Eager to flex his fledgling muscles in the big pond of life. Well, in this pond, he was just about to encounter a great white shark in the form of Tony Slade.

He had been there, done it and got the t-shirt, whilst McCoy had been a promise in his dad's ball bag.

At this moment, Tony recalled a poster that he had seen recently on the internet. It was of an old and wise looking Clint Eastwood. Under his iconic image read the words *Too many assholes and not enough bullets.* How true.

Tony regarded the three men in front of him all standing defiantly, smug in their over-confidence. This was going to be their downfall. He had seen it a hundred times before.

"Okay, guys. I think I've been fair. As you just said, you can walk into any gym in Newcastle for free, so I suggest you go find one."

"You clever cunt. Fancy your chances of making me leave. Well?" snarled McCoy.

Tony steadied himself and pulled in a breath of air to take the slight tremor from his voice as he prepared for physical confrontation.

"So, is there anything I can do here to get you to leave quietly?"

"No there isn't, Granddad. We aren't going any-where," said McCoy.

"Shall I call the police, Tony?" asked Karen.

Tony never took his eyes off the three men as he answered her. "No, I don't think that will be necessary."

"You said your name was McCoy, is that right?"

"Yeah, so?" replied 'Mohawk'.

"Aren't you fighting this weekend on Kenny Robbins show, *Gladiator Wars*?"

"That's right. Top of the bill. What about it?"

"Well, the thing is, if you don't go now, the only thing that you'll be fighting for is your fucking breath, and I'm sure that Kenny will be well-pissed to hear that you had to pull out of your big chance to crack the *UFC*."

Without taking his eyes off the three men, Tony called over his shoulder. "Karen, no police but you can call the paramedics though and tell them to make sure that they have room in their vehicle for three sorry looking assholes."

Karen wasn't sure what to make of that statement and stood with the phone poised at her ear.

McCoy's face broke into a grin. "You've got some balls, I will give you that. Do you really think that you can take the three of us out? You are fucking deluded old man."

Tony smiled back. "Are you really that good, McCoy. You don't look much."

He knew that this would offend McCoy's giant ego.

"Yeah, I am fucking good, pal," retorted McCoy.

Tony nodded and held up his hands as if in compliance and then, with speed that belied his years, he punched his fore knuckles into the throat of the tallest of McCoy's cronies who dropped to his knees gasping for breath. He then pivoted, and power slapped the other one in the side of the head. He crumpled like a cheap suit. Next, Tony grabbed McCoy by the testicles in an iron grip and ran him backwards towards the gym entrance.

He spat out his words vehemently as he went. "You dumb little fucker. The only reason I don't bury you like your mates is that my boss Kenny Robbins would go ape shit if I put you in hospital and he had to cancel his show, so I'm doing you a fucking favour here."

Tony drove McCoy out of the door and onto the pavement before he let go of his grip.

McCoy was bent over holding his testicles in considerable pain. He couldn't speak. Tony stood in front of him far enough out of the ear shot of the people in the gym.

"Now, son, you might be King of the cage or whatever, but out of it, you are fuck all to me. I have spent a big part of my life dodging bullets and bombs and I have taken many a life. I am fucking good at it. Now, get your mates and fuck off out of my gym and don't come back unless you are bringing an apologize with you and a big bunch of flowers. Do you understand?"

For a second, he saw defiance in the younger man's eyes. Then he nodded, and Tony felt his body relax.

McCoy walked towards the door.

The cage fighter looked back and regarded Tony warily for a moment. He gingerly rubbed his groin and stared at Tony as if seeing him for the first time. He was looking beyond the smart suit and polite demeanour and realised that he had crossed paths with an old lion.

He helped pick up his fallen cronies and they all moved unsteadily towards the exit.

At the door, McCoy stopped, and Tony thought that he was going to come back, but he decided against it and walked on out.

A huge cheer went up from the clients of the gym and Tony took a theatrical bow.

Karen came over to him. "Jesus, Tony. You were like the bloody Terminator."

"You better believe it, sweetheart." He gave her a sly wink as he headed towards the toilets.

***

In the toilets, Tony ran icy water over his face from the sink. He noticed the slight tremor in his hands. It was the aftermath of violence, ever present.

He studied his face in the mirror. He looked at the lines and scars that etched his features. How many times had he done this over the years? His face was older, but he was still examining himself after some act of violence whether it was justified or not.

Was violence ever justified?

He began to question that lately, but with that said, he still found violence easy.

Maybe he should have just let McCoy into the gym?

What if Robbins and Bergkamp had walked in as he was administering his own brand of justice out to the three lads?

That would have blown everything.

He was old enough to know better.

He was no longer the 'fastest gun in town' and soon, his luck would run out.

He knew he had to remove himself from the volatile environments and the circle of people that inhabited them to truly be released and to start afresh. He was so close to it now that he could practically taste it.

Just a few more days. He had to keep it all together. Just a few more days.

When he came back out into the gym, he wore the mask again and went about his business, showing no emotions to what had just happened.

He noticed some of the gym clientele now looking at him with newfound respect. Others looked at him with a sense of fear.

He went into the office to get away from their gazes.

Tony sat down at the desk, got out his phone and checked it. Nothing from Doug Jacobs. That wasn't good news.

He sat in silence with his thoughts. Then, a tap on the door brought him back to reality.

"Come in," he said.

The door opened, and Karen came in carrying a mug of coffee.

"I thought you might need one of these."

Tony smiled. "Thank you, Karen. That would be great." He took the offered mug from her. "All quiet out there now?" he asked.

Karen nodded. "Yes. Thank you for helping Tony. Those guys were scary. I can handle most things, but that was beginning to get out of hand. I'm sorry I couldn't deal with it better."

Tony took a sip of his coffee. "Don't worry. I'm just as sorry that I didn't deal with it better."

Karen raised her eyebrows. "Really? I thought you were bloody amazing with all that Kung Fu shit. Are you a black belt or something?"

Tony looked down at his trousers and said, "No, this belt is sort of tan looking, don't you think?"

"Ha, ha. You know what I mean. You took those three guys out like they weren't even there."

"Just got lucky, I guess," replied Tony.

"You were as good as Chuck Norris."

Tony smiled. "Hey, nobody is as good as Chuck Norris."

Karen regarded him for a few seconds longer, but Tony didn't say anymore.

"Well, you are a bit of a mystery man, aren't you?"

Tony took another sip of his coffee. "Me? No. What you see is what you get."

Karen shook her head and smiled as she left the office.

When Karen left, Tony checked his phone and found that he had a miscall from Doug Jacobs. In all the earlier excitement, his phone must have gone on to silent in his pocket. He rang the number back.

Doug answered it on the tenth ring, just as Tony was thinking of hanging up.

"Hi, Tony. Sorry about that. I was seeing a client out and I am still getting used to the old bionic leg."

"No worries, mate. What news have you got for me?"

There was a moment's pause and then Doug spoke.

"Not good, my friend. The old guy I deal with that sorts out the passports has been rushed into hospital with pneumonia. He is stable, but it's going to be a little longer than anticipated until he's well enough to do the business."

Tony cursed under his breath. This was not what he wanted to hear. Now that the plan was in action, he couldn't afford any fuck-ups and now, here was a major one.

"Shit. How long are we talking here, Doug?"

"Three to four weeks, depending on the situation."

"Fuck. Isn't there anybody else that can do it?"

"With respect, my old friend, you aren't looking for a plumber here. This is specialised and not exactly legal. Plus, I don't expect my contact wants to be in a hospital."

Tony breathed out deeply. "Sorry, Doug. You're right, but I'm desperate here."

"What the fuck have you got yourself into, Tony? This sounds like heavy shit."

"Doug, I can't tell you. I really can't. Just keep me in touch and see if you can get it done sooner rather than later."

"Okay, Tony. I'll do what I can. Are you sure I can't help?"

"Only by getting those passports asap."

"Okay. Like I said. I'm on it. You be careful, do you hear me?"

"Yeah, I hear you. Thanks."

Tony hung up.

This delay would mean that Annette would be in Lanzarote longer than he wanted. He knew that sooner or later Robbins would find out where she had gone and then put two and two together. But he had no choice. He had to go Saturday whilst the show was on and Robbins was preoccupied. At least it would give him a head start.

Tony knew that it was going to go down to the wire, but he was in it to the end. He was used to being in the heat of battle and this was just another one. But he knew that that wasn't strictly true. This time, it was the most important battle of his life and one he had to win.

He needed a drink, so he decided to head off into town to find a quiet bar. Somewhere to chill out and release the knot of tension he felt in his belly.

He knew a little piano bar on Collingwood Street. The pianist there played a great mix of his sort of music. Elton John. Billy Joel, Bruce Hornsby, Steven Bishop, amongst many others.

He hoped that a couple of malt whiskeys and a few chilled tunes would lighten his mood.

CHAPTER TWENTY NINE

Tony crouched in readiness, his muscles taut and coiled like a spring. He saw his buddies one by one jump out into the darkness.

Then, it was his turn. He sat on the edge of the plane's open doors ready to give the thumbs up signal. He got the nod and then, he was gone out into the vast wilderness of the open air, plummeting fast. This never failed to give him a rush of exhilaration. It was a special feeling.

The chilled air current was cold against his face as his body picked up more and more speed. He counted in his head until he knew it was time to open his parachute.

NOW. He pulled on the cord... nothing.

No panic. Try it again. Go... nothing.

He tugged again and again, but the chute didn't open.

In his head, he could hear a strange buzzing sound. He couldn't figure out what it was.

The reserve chute. Go for that. Hurry.

He pulled it, but got the same result. Nothing.

He was falling fast now, and he began to make out the twinkling lights of the town below. Those lights were getting closer by the second.

Frantically, he tugged on both chutes, but his efforts were futile. They would not open.

How could this be? He had checked, and triple checked the parachute as he always did. So had a buddy. So how?

Suddenly, realisation hit him. He was about to die.

He became strangely calm.

He saw the face of his mother smiling kindly in front of him. She looked peaceful and radiant. Then, the beautiful face of Annette. At first, she was smiling, but now, the smile faded and was replaced with concern and fear.

He then saw the grinning features of Robbins nodding knowingly. Beside him were Errol and Rudi, both men shaking their heads in disgust.

The ground was coming up fast now and Tony braced himself for the inevitable impact.

There was that buzzing sound again. It was getting louder. It just kept repeating itself over and over.

Tony awoke from his nightmare and sat bolt upright in bed. His body was covered in a thin sheen of sweat. His sheets were also soaked.

As the realisation that he had been dreaming dawned on him, he breathed a huge sigh of relieve.

He glanced at the bedside clock. Fuck, it was 10.00am.

He then noted the buzzing sound that he kept hearing was the sound of his front doorbell.

He threw back the bed covers and quickly slipped on a pair of grey jogging bottoms and a white t-shirt bearing the statement 'You're going to need a bigger boat' across the chest. It was a homage to one of his favourite films, the 1975 summer blockbuster, *Jaws*.

The immortal line, uttered by the late, great Roy Scheider, had gone down in film history.

He rubbed his hands through his hair and ran his tongue around the inside of his mouth. It felt as dry as sandpaper. That was down to the fact, no doubt, of the three very nice double whiskeys he had sank last night courtesy of *Glenfiddich*.

He had enjoyed a good evening in *Monroe's Piano Bar*. The atmosphere had been chilled and the scotch on the rocks had gone down far too easily.

He remembered finally leaving the place around 11.30pm after Joe the piano player had banged out the full-length 8 minutes 33 seconds of the classic *American Pie* by Don Mclean.

Tony remembered when the song was first released way back in 1971. It had become a favourite of his.

When he left the bar, he walked home, as he wouldn't ever chance drinking and driving. Especially when his current job relied on it.

It wasn't like the old days back in the 70s where you would drive home half cut, park up by crashing into your dustbin whilst your next-door neighbour was doing the same thing. It seems unthinkable now.

Tony remembered on many occasions being in the back of an army truck bumping and weaving its way down some dark country road in Ireland heading back from town after a night out 'on the piss' with the lads. Crazy days.

From *Monroe's*, he had walked along the length of Collingwood Street soaking up the atmosphere on the pavements outside the bars and restaurants. He took in the sounds, the smells and the colour. He knew that it was going to be a long time, if ever, that he would see Newcastle again.

Although he had spent a big part of his life away from the North East, it would always have a special place in his heart.

The doorbell sounded again. Whoever was outside was getting more impatient.

"Okay, I'm coming," shouted Tony.

He opened the door and was shocked to see Kenny Robbins stood there. He was alone.

Robbins walked straight into the flat. "We need to talk," he said as he pushed past Tony.

Tony felt the bubble of unease in his stomach again. What the fuck did Robbins want with him now?

He quickly glanced towards the bedroom door. It was shut. Just as well, as he didn't want Robbins to discover that his bags were packed and ready to go.

He tried to compose himself. "Morning to you too, Kenny. Can I get you a coffee?"

Robbins shook his head.

"Do you mind if I get one?" asked Tony as he headed towards the kitchen.

Robbins followed him. "I've been ringing your mobile for the last hour without success, so I've had to come all the way here. I'm more than slightly pissed off."

Tony flipped the switch on the kettle and spooned some coffee into a mug.

"Sorry about that. I had a late night. So, what's so urgent, Kenny?"

Robbins pulled out a dining room chair and sat down. "I took the Bergkamps out for a meal last night. We went to *Carlo's*. You know it, don't you, Tony?'

Tony eyed Robbins. "Yes, I know it."

"Of course, you do. You took Annette there for a cosy little meal whilst I was away. Carlo mentioned it to me in conversation. Well, is that true? In my absence, you were getting cosy wining and dining my lady."

Tony heard the kettle click off. He reached out for the handle and kept his hand on it. "What are you trying to imply here, Kenny?"

Robbins got up from the chair and moved across to the work surface opposite Tony. He reached out, and his left hand idly brushed along the wooden knife block that sat on it.

"Why don't you tell me what you were up to, eh?"

"Kenny, I can't believe you are standing here suggesting that I was up to something with Annette. She had tickets to a Simply Red concert at the O2 with a friend. They also had reservations to have a meal in *Carlo's* afterwards. She asked me to drive them both, but her friend cried off at the last-minute due to her kid being ill."

"What was her friend's name?" asked Robbins.

"What?" replied Tony.

"Her friend, what was her name?"

"Fucking hell. I can't remember."

Tony thought a moment. "Maybe it was Carly or Claire. Yes, I think it was Claire."

Robbins said nothing but that tied up. Claire Reed was her best friend and she did have a two-year-old child.

Tony continued. "Annette said she really wanted to go and asked if I would accompany her and make sure she got home safely. That was it. I was doing the job you asked. Nothing more, nothing less."

Tony filled up his mug but kept hold of the kettle. He noted that Robbins was still toying with the handles of the knives.

"Was that all, Tony? No shoulder to cry on?"

"Why does she need one?" retorted Tony

Robbins hand tightened its grip on the handle of the largest knife in the block. Tony noted it.

"Look, Kenny. Nothing happened." He paused a moment and then cautiously carried on. "Why? Did Carlo say otherwise?"

Robbins regarded Tony and his lips broke into a thin grin. "No, he didn't. Just that you shared a table together."

"That's because she asked me to sit with her. She didn't want to dine alone. The reservation was for two. That was it. Fucking hell, Kenny. I even paid for my own meal, if that's what's bothering you and I didn't have a dessert either. I can't be doing with all this 'Rocky death by chocolate shit'. I am a cheese and biscuits man myself, but most places don't do them now."

Robbins shook his head in disbelief. "You are one cool bastard, Tony. I give you that. Others would have been shitting themselves by now."

"It's only because I'm telling you the truth, Kenny."

Robbins moved away from the worktop and the knives and walked towards Tony.

Tony never took his eyes off him.

Robbins then extended his hand.

"Okay, I believe you. Sorry about that. I'm a little uptight with all that is going on and maybe I'm getting fucking paranoid as far as Annette is concerned and with good reason. I'm crazy about that woman. She's mine and I need her in my life. She's good for me, even though sometimes I might not deserve her."

Robbins seemed to be lost in his thoughts for a moment and then, he continued. "You did right. I asked you to keep an eye out for her and you did. I was wrong, okay? The woman drives me fucking crazy. Sometimes I get all fucked up."

Tony nodded.

Robbins smiled. "Good. Now we are straight, you can let go of the kettle, Tony."

Tony released his grip on the kettle as Robbins walked back into the living room. Tony breathed a sigh of relief and followed him.

"Did Annette talk about me, Tony?"

Tony looked puzzled. "How do you mean?"

"Well, as lovely a lady as she is, she can be prone to fantasy and making up stories. I know she misses home and she blames me for not fulfilling her ambitions when I brought her to the UK. She has gone over to Italy this time telling me that her mother is ill, but my guess is that she just wants to get away from her life here. I do care for her, but my business is demanding and I'm not always around. A woman like her can get lonely and vulnerable. She can start imagining things. Creating situations that aren't there. Some of my former drivers have mentioned that she sometimes talked about these things behind my back. Did she talk to you?"

Tony swallowed a mouthful of coffee. "We kept things on a business level. She didn't really say anything about her private life. She asked me a few things about my travels in the army, she seemed interested in that, and she told me that she was born in Italy and spoke a little about her home town, but that was it really."

"No talk of running back to Naples?"

Tony swallowed hard but kept his poker face. "No. None."

Kenny nodded. He seemed to be satisfied. "Once this deal goes through, I'll be as good as retired and then I'll whisk her off to foreign parts and live a life of luxury. She'll want for nothing."

Tony forced a smile to his face and raised his coffee mug. "Well, here's to you both." He hoped his voice sounded genuine.

"I'll ring her and ask her to get back here for Saturday evening. I decided that I want her on my arm at the show. I'll convince her that this is where she belongs."

Tony's face kept impassive, but inside, he cursed the fact that Robbins was going to fuck up his plans if he wasn't careful.

Tony thought that Robbins was about to leave, but instead, he sat down on the sofa.

"Sit down a moment, will you, Tony."

Tony sat down on the armchair opposite Robbins. He sensed the subject wasn't finished just yet.

Robbins seemed to be thinking about what he wanted to say or maybe if he should say it. Finally, he spoke.

"Look, Tony, I've decided to come clean and tell you something and I'm hoping that we know each other well enough now to understand what I'm going to disclose to you and that we can keep it secret between us."

Tony was intrigued and a little uneasy. "Alright, Kenny. What's on your mind?"

Robbins regarded his hands for a moment and fiddled with the large gold ring on his left little finger. He then looked up. This stare was intense.

"As I just said, Annette and myself haven't been getting on too well lately. She's getting increasingly more homesick. She wants for nothing, but that doesn't seem to be enough for her. I know that she was recently telling your mate Rob Green about this as he was driving her around for a while."

Tony bristled at the mention of Rob. Robbins didn't seem to sense this.

"Rob began to take a bit of an unhealthy interest in her because she confided in him. It was brought to my attention. I confronted Rob about this and put him in his place that Annette was going nowhere and that she was my women. Prone to flights of fantasy and nothing more. I told him that the only help she may need is of a psychiatric nature. Rob didn't drive her again and I had a quiet word with Annette about telling tales."

Tony said nothing, but he could guess what sort of quiet word it was that Robbins had with Annette.

"Can I ask, Kenny? Is that why Rob went AWOL?"

Kenny Robbins leant forward. "I am going to be honest with you. Rob was a good man. He became a trusted employee. He became my collector. He would go around my various businesses and bring me back the money from the more illegal side of the operations. It was always hard cash. Substantial amounts. The bars, betting shop, snooker hall, clubs. He was the man in charge of it, but he got greedy and started helping himself to a dip here and there. It was difficult for me to know what money was missing, as it is hard to track, but I began to get more and more suspicious. At first, I thought it was one of the employees at the businesses themselves, but after sending Errol and Rudi around for a word, that proved not to be the case. The ironic thing was that I was also sending Rob around to the businesses for a word whilst all the time, he was the one responsible."

Robbins shook his head in dismay.

"Then, I was being told by Joe Walsh and Danny Ewan that Rob was being seen regularly around the clubs in town drinking champagne, snorting coke and buying everybody drinks. Acting the big man. He was also dropping considerable amounts of money at the casinos. Not the sort of money that he would have got just by working for me. This was serious amounts. Way above his station. It all began to click into place. Finally, Billy Sherwood saw Rob stuffing money in his pockets out of the collected stash and came and told me. I now had the evidence. I confronted him."

Kenny breathed in deeply and a flash of anger flickered in his eyes and his voice.

"I trusted that fucker, Tony. I let him in and paid him well, but it wasn't enough for the greedy bastard. I will not and cannot tolerate that behaviour. Nobody can get away with it. Before I know it, every little fish in the sea wants a nibble and then it all goes tits up. I had to make an example of him. Nobody takes Kenny Robbins for a mug and gets away with it."

Tony listened quietly. He knew what was coming next. He had known all along. "So you killed him, is that, right?" he asked.

Robbins nodded. "Yes. I liked Rob, but he fucked me over and he had to go. I know he was a friend of yours, but there is no fucking sentiment in this business. Its dog eat dog and I had bigger teeth than him and anybody else in this city. Tony, you must understand where I'm coming from. It was nothing personal. You, of all people, should know that. You were a mercenary, for Christ's sake. You killed for money, not Queen and Country."

Tony contained his raising anger and swallowed it back down. This was not the time and place to push this. There was too much at stake. "So, why tell me now?" Tony asked.

"Because, Tony, I need to know that I can trust you. I wanted to sweep the board clean and be up front. I can be a violent man. That I can't deny. Needs must. But I am also a fair man. This deal now on the table with Bergkamp will hopefully pave the way for a more legitimate way of life. I will look after the people who have looked after me. The next few days are essential, and I need my team to watch my back. I've tried to keep this deal under wraps, but I know that the word may have leaked out, and I also know that there are people out there that would like to see me fuck it up. So I needed to come here and make 100% sure that, as part of the team, you are on board with me."

Tony took all this information in without a flicker of emotion, but part of him wanted to lunge across to the sofa and rip out Robbins' throat for what he had done to Rob and the pain he had caused Annette. But he knew that he couldn't. If he wanted to really hurt Robbins, he knew that he had to stick to the plan.

Robbins spoke again. "So, do we understand each other, Tony?"

Tony nodded, "We understand each other perfectly, Kenny. Let's get through these next few days, shall we?"

Robbins stood and his face broke into a grin. "Good man. I usually trust my instincts and they told me that you were a loyal character, but I needed to know face to face. Right, I will leave you to sort yourself out. I plan to show the Bergkamps around the gym this afternoon around 2.00pm after lunch. I'll see you then."

He then flipped open his phone and pressed a button. "Rudi. Bring the car around to the front. I'm leaving."

Tony heard the muffled reply.

Robbins answered, "Yes, everything is fine. It's all sorted out."

So, Robbins had the heavy mob at hand ready to come in and do what? What they had done to Rob, no doubt, if this conversation had gone the wrong way, mused Tony.

Robbins walked towards the door.

"Kenny, you didn't have to tell me about Rob. I would have been none the wiser," said Tony.

Robbins stopped and turned around. "Really? You didn't suspect anything, even after searching Rob's flat. The old boy, Bob Wager, who's the caretaker there is my eyes and ears. Somebody fitting your description was seen going in and out of the place right after Rob's disappearance on a few occasions. Was that you? You must also have his mobile phone, I'm sure."

Tony said nothing.

Robbins continued. "No matter. Like I said, it's best that people do not underestimate me. I'll see myself out. Thanks for the chat."

He opened the door and was gone.

Tony sank back into the armchair. He blew out his cheeks in relief.

Well, there it all was out in the open. The death of Rob, the problems with Annette, the deal that was going down and Tony being seen in the flat. It was all coming to a head for Robbins and he was getting twitchy.

The whole episode had unnerved Tony, but now, it made him more determined than ever to get Annette and himself as far away from Robbins as possible. He was one dangerous and unpredictable man at this moment in time. His up and down moods suggested a man on the brink. That was not good news.

* * *

When Robbins turned up at the gym later with Charles Gibson, his lawyer, and the Dutch party, it was all smiles and business as usual. The earlier conversation seemed forgotten.

The Bergkamps and Koeman where shown around the premises by Tony and then Karen said that she would show them the books, and they retired to the office. Tony left that side of things to her. Karen was a whiz with computers and figures.

Tony stayed on the gym floor and chatted with Edwin who chose to stay with him.

"So, you're topping the bill Saturday night against the local champ?"

Edwin nodded. "Yes, that is true. I am looking forward to it. Do you know of this McCoy?"

A smile played on Tony's lips. "Not really, but our paths crossed once, I believe."

Edwin went on to tell Tony that he had been a successful K1 kickboxer in Holland for many years and had then moved into MMA. He had a 12-0 record in the cage. He was ambitious and saw this fight as another stepping stone to bigger things.

Tony knew that Edwin had impressive credentials and he hoped that Alex McCoy would live up to his big reputation come fight night. He was slightly gutted that he wouldn't be around to see it.

"I wish you all the best, Edwin."

Edwin regarded him. "You will not be there to watch?"

Tony realised his slip up. "Yes, of course I'll be there, but I'll be working and never quite know where I might be."

This seemed to satisfy the Dutchman. "You look in decent shape, Tony. Were you a fighter?"

Tony smiled. "Maybe not in the sense you mean, my friend. I did box for a while and train in Jujutsu and I have had many fights working on the doors of pubs and clubs, but I did most of my fighting in the military."

"Ah, I see. I figured that you were a tough man when I first laid eyes on you at the airport. I was right, yes?"

"Back in the day I suppose I was."

Edwin laughed. "I think maybe you still are now."

Tony walked towards the vending machine. "I fancy a coffee. What about you, Edwin?"

"Water please, Tony. Thank you."

Tony liked Edwin. He secretly hoped that he would smash McCoy or choke his ass out.

As they both sat down to enjoy their drinks, the office door opened, and everybody came out. Once again, it was all smiles and handshakes. It looked like it had all gone well.

Robbins came over to Tony and Edwin. "Excuse me, Edwin. I just need a quick word in private with Tony."

Edwin stood up. "Of course, no problem."

He turned to Tony and offered his hand. "Thank you, Tony, and I will see you soon."

Both men shook hands and Edwin wandered off towards his father who was talking to Charles Gibson and Karen.

When he was out of earshot, Kenny told Tony that it had all gone well. Bergkamp and Koeman liked how the business was running.

"We're off to the snooker hall and massage parlour next to show them the set up there and the offer of a free massage if wanted," said Robbins with a wink. "We're having dinner tonight at 8.00pm down at the quay in *Whites*. Come and join us, Tony. I think it might well be a celebration. I'll leave your name at the door. Why not bring a lady friend if you want?"

Robbins raised an eyebrow expectantly.

"I tell you what. Why don't I bring Karen? I think she deserves a night out, don't you?"

Robbins glanced in her direction. She was now showing Edwin the new Stairmaster step mill that the gym had recently acquired.

"Are you and Karen an item then?"

Tony shook his head. "Christ, no, Kenny. I'm old enough to be her dad. I just thought that she deserved it after all the work she has done."

Kenny nodded in agreement. "Yes, that is a great idea, if you haven't got a special lady to bring yourself?"

"Unfortunately not, Kenny. My mother died a long time ago."

Robbins broke out into a laugh and shook his head. "Okay, Tony. I'll catch you later."

Tony watched him walk back towards Bergkamp.

CHAPTER THIRTY

The meal that evening went well. Everybody seemed relaxed and Tony sensed no tension in the air.

They all sat around a large circular table in the middle of the busy restaurant. There was Robbins, Charles Gibson, Marc and Edwin Bergkamp, Frank Koeman, Tony and Karen.

Tony was surprised to be sitting in their company. There were other men in the firm that deserved the right to be where he was, but for some reason, Robbins wanted him. That said, the topics of conversation stayed on an informal level, so there was not going to be any major secrets spilled in front of Karen and himself.

He glanced at Kenny Robbins every now and then. He played the genial host well. He hid the fact that he was a ruthless bastard. It was admirable really, but Tony wouldn't forget it.

He tried to relax and enjoy the meal and not think about what Robbins had disclosed earlier.

He also noticed that Rudi and Errol sat at a table nearby. They gave him the evil eye every now and then. No doubt pissed off by the fact that he was sitting at Robbin's table and not them.

Tony raised a glass in their direction but just received icy glares in exchange.

"They don't seem too happy. Are they pissed off with you for some reason?" mentioned Karen.

Tony took a sip of his wine. "No, I think they are a little peeved because there was only one bread roll with their soup. I mean those big fuckers need some feeding."

Karen smiled. "Somehow, I don't think that's true. But I think it's best that I don't know."

"Yeah, you're probably right. Let's not let them spoil the meal."

The food was excellent. Scallops, steak, chocolate and strawberry cheesecake plus champagne, followed by vintage port and the cheeseboard.

By the time it was finished, Tony was stuffed and everybody else seemed in good spirits.

The bill was paid and they all made to leave.

Errol and Rudi had cars at the ready to take Robbins and the rest of his party home. It looked like they weren't going to find any extra space for any hangers on.

Errol strolled over to Tony and gave him a big toothy grin. It reminded him of a great white shark moving in for the kill.

"Hope you enjoyed your meal at the top table, Tony. You can burn the calories off by walking home. Now, fuck off, asshole."

Errol strolled back to Rudi and both men broke into laughter.

Tony and Karen decided to share a taxi home. Tony bid them all goodnight and cheekily blew Errol and Rudi a kiss as the two Mercedes slid away into the night traffic.

"You like to live dangerously, don't you, Tony?" asked Karen.

Tony smiled at her. "What? Me? Hell no. I'm a choir boy at heart."

It was a lovely evening, so Tony and Karen decided to walk a while to take in the night air and clear their heads a little.

As they crossed the road and walked towards the Millennium bridge, Karen linked her arm into Tony's.

"I feel safe with you, Mr. Slade. I like you," she said and then added quickly, "But in a fatherly daughterly sort of way... I mean, you are my boss and... shit, I must stop talking. It's that bloody champagne."

Tony laughed. "It's okay, Karen. Don't worry. I'm not going to jump on you. It's fine. I like you too. We're cool, yes?"

Karen looked up at him coyly and hugged his arm tighter. "Yes, Boss. Shall we find that taxi before I put my foot in it again?"

Tony nodded in agreement.

Karen was a lovely kid and he did feel a protectiveness towards her, even in the brief time that he had known her. He guessed that he was just a sucker for a damsel in distress. He thought that this must be what it would be like if he had a daughter. Walking, talking and enjoying each other's company. Simple pleasures.

They walked past the Millennium bridge towards a taxi rank. Suddenly, Karen tightened her grip on Tony's arm and groaned. "What is it?" he asked.

"Oh shit. It's Liam," Karen answered.

"Liam?" Tony was puzzled.

"Liam Bradley, my ex-boyfriend. We split up a few months ago, and not on the best of terms. I haven't seen him since, and I don't want to now. Just keep walking and he might not notice us."

They passed two young men, obviously out for a night on the town. Both were chatting animatedly and staggering along the pavement.

Karen was just going to breathe a sigh of relief when she heard a shout. "Karen! Karen! Hey, wait up!"

"Bollocks," Karen muttered under her breath.

Tony saw a guy approaching them. He estimated that he was in his mid-twenties and stood around 6 feet tall. He was smartly dressed. He had short black hair gelled back and he sported designer stubble on his face. He looked the worst for wear from drinking alcohol. He had a ginger-haired mate with him, an Ed Sheeran lookalike that also look completely pissed.

Liam's face broke into a leering grin. "Well, well, well. Fancy bumping into Little Miss Perfect. What are you doing out after 10 o'clock?"

Karen let out a sigh. "Let's not cause a scene, shall we, Liam? Just walk on. I have nothing to say to you."

Liam blocked her way. He swayed unsteadily on his feet. "Hey. I'm not going to make a scene. Anyway, you're the fucking drama queen, not me."

Karen made to move on. "Okay. Whatever. Goodbye, Liam."

Liam grabbed her arm.

Tony stepped forward.

"I suggest you let her go, son."

Liam regarded Tony through blurry eyes as if noticing him for the first time. He ballooned his body and sprayed his arms in a threat display.

Tony had seen this on more occasions than he cared to remember whilst working in the pubs and clubs. False bravado gained from the effects of drinking.

"Who is this wanker, Karen? Your bodyguard or granddad? Hang on. Not a new boyfriend? Fuck me, you must be getting desperate."

He broke into laughter and so did his mate.

"Leave it, Liam, and go home."

Tony stepped forward. "That's good advice. I should take it."

The menace in his voice seemed to seep through into Liam's drunken head.

"Is that right" 'he answered, but his voice didn't now carry as much bravado as it had a moment or two ago.

Suddenly, the yapping poodle had met a pit bull.

Tony recognised that this lad was no fighter and no threat, but he needed to turn the screw one more notch.

"Yes, it is right. You asked who I was. Well, I will tell you. I am your worst fucking nightmare."

Liam nervously laughed, stepping back and out of the way. So, did 'Ed Sheeran'.

"What do you do for a living son?" asked Tony.

Liam looked confused.

Tony repeated his question.

"I'm an estate agent. Why?"

"Are you good at your job?"

'Well, yes, I am good." Liam began to look nervous.

"Well, I'm good at my job too and have been for a long time. My job is to hurt people and do horrible things to them that you could only imagine in your worst nightmares. Now, unless you want a demonstration of my skills, I suggest you leave Karen alone and piss off home. Understand?"

Tony now saw the fear in both men's eyes. They had suddenly sobered up a little. Funny how the fear of violence does that.

They both backed off and without another word, melted away into the people walking in the opposite direction.

Karen breathed a sigh of relief. "I am so sorry, Tony. It seems that every time you are with me, there is trouble."

Tony linked her arm and directed her towards a waiting taxi. "Maybe it's the other way around, Karen."

* * *

The taxi dropped Karen home safely and then brought Tony back to his flat. Once inside, he rang Annette. He was glad to hear her voice and know that she was well.

He told her of the latest developments and that Robbins was going to want her back for Saturday. He assured her to just keep to the same plan.

Once she was in Lanzarote, she was to ring him. Tony also told her that she may have to stay out there a few weeks longer than anticipated until the passports were sorted, and then, he would come for her. She would be safe with Ray for now.

Her voice sounded strained and fearful, but she told him that she would do whatever she had to do to get away.

When Tony hung up, he rang Ray in Lanzarote and put him in the picture. Ray assured Tony that all was good at his end and he would look after Annette for as long as necessary and not to worry.

This put Tony's mind at rest. Ray was a diamond and he would someday make it up to his old friend.

It was now past midnight, but Tony needed to make one more call. This would be to Emma Snow. He used Rob's mobile.

Tony was surprised that she picked up after the second ring.

"Hello. Is that you, Tony?"

"Yes, Emma. I'm sorry that I am ringing so late, but things are on the move and I need your help."

"Have you heard anything about Rob?"

Tony decided that it would be prudent not to disclose what Robbins had told him. It was better at this moment in time that Emma didn't know.

"Not yet," he replied.

"Oh. I thought maybe…" Her voice trailed off. It sounded disappointed.

Tony moved the conversation on. "Emma, I need you to do me a huge favour. Remember the car in the lock-up?"

"Yes, I do."

"I need you to get it and drive it for me on Saturday evening. Can you do that?"

Emma agreed.

He filled her in with the details of Robbins' fight event. He told her to get a taxi to somewhere close to the lock-up and make sure that nobody saw her. Then, she was to drive the car to the club.

Across the road from Robbins' club was a pay and display car park. She was to drive the car into it at 11.00pm sharp and wait for him. He would be there as soon as he could.

Emma told him that she understood and would do it.

Before Tony hung up, he told Emma that he would check in again with her early Saturday evening.

In the morning, he would contact Doug Jacobs and find out the latest. Whatever happened, he was going to have to drive down to Bristol on Saturday night and hide out there until he had the passports. He couldn't risk being in Newcastle any longer.

Tony poured himself two fingers of malt whiskey and went out onto the small balcony.

He breathed in the cool night air. It was late, but once again, he knew that sleep would elude him. His mind kept churning over the finer points of the plan.

He was troubled about how long he would have to spend in Bristol. He hoped that Doug would bring him some positive news come the morning.

He sipped his drink and let the subtle flavours play on his tongue before swallowing the amber liquid. It tasted good.

Tony knew that he had been drinking too much of late. He would have to curb his habits in his new life.

He did surmise, though, that with all he had been through in his life, whiskey had become his only vice.

Some of his colleagues hadn't been as fortunate. Drugs, prescription and non-prescription, had become their metaphorical crutch to cope with life. Others had found themselves in need of professional help to come to terms with the horrors of war.

They walked around like zombies. Medicated up to the eyeballs. Poor lost souls. Shells of the brave men they had once been. Many forgotten heroes. Thrown on the scrapheap after their use was served. More than a few decided that this life was too much for them and they checked out altogether.

Yes, he had been one of the lucky ones.

Tony took another drink and watched an aeroplane high in the night sky. He imagined himself on it. Flying away from his troubles.

Tony had travelled the world in planes to foreign parts before, but the next time, it would be with the women he loved.

He watched the plane become a distant dot. He drained his glass and decided to see if sleep would claim him.

* * *

Tony Slade of One Parachute regiment was on checkpoint on a lonely country road that led into Londonderry.

It was a bitterly cold November evening in 1977. There was drizzly rain falling that made visibility difficult.

On the checkpoint with him was Sergeant Barry Stokes, a London cockney and Private Gary Philips, a good Welsh lad from the Valleys. Then there was Rob Green, the youngster but a tough dependable soldier. The four of them made a solid team. They knew each other well.

It had been reasonably quiet that evening. It was nearly midnight and the men were looking forward to ending their watch. Only another half an hour before Sergeant Bob Heyward and his team took over.

"I'm thinking of taking that little Irish barmaid Sheila to the cinema on Saturday," said Barry Stokes.

"Oh yeah. Back row job is it, Serge?" asked Gary Philips.

Stokes grinned, "Maybe, if I'm lucky. She's a sexy piece of skirt. But being a Catholic girl, I don't know what she's willing to give out. Know what I mean?"

"You're a fucking romantic at heart, aren't you, Serge." commented Rob Green as he took a drag on his cigarette.

Stokes ignored the jibe. "Thinking of going to see that new Spielberg film *Close Encounters of the Third Kind*."

"That's what he's hoping for in the backrow," replied Rob.

They all laughed.

"Alright, Green. Button your fucking lip."

"Have you seen that film, Tony?" asked Stokes.

"Fucking hell, the last time Tony was at the cinema, they had a bloke playing the organ at the front," commented Philips.

They all laughed again.

Slade stood by the Land Rover next to the Sergeant sipping on a mug of tea, but his eyes never left the road, even during the banter.

"Bollocks, smart ass. The last time I went to the cinema on a date was to see the *Exorcist* way back. Never bothered since."

"Fuck me, Tony. It wasn't that scary," chided Rob.

Tony Slade grinned good naturedly. "Do me a favour and fuck off."

Rob was about to answer when headlights cut through the night gloom.

Tony Slade put his mug down.

"Eyes front, lads. Somebody's coming our way," ordered Stokes.

All the men tightened their grips on their weapons and walked forward to the checkpoint. As the vehicles drew nearer, Tony could make out that one was a Granada and the other a Jaguar.

Both cars slowed down and pulled over to the checkpoint.

Stokes signalled to the driver of the lead car, which was the Granada, to wind down his window.

"Evening, sir. Do you mind your passengers and yourself stepping out of the vehicle? Just a routine search."

The driver got out without fuss and so did his two passengers. They were all middle-aged males. Pretty non-descript.

Tony went to the Jaguar and made the same request.

The driver and his passenger got out. They were both big men. One white and one black. They seemed vaguely familiar.

The black man asked, "Does the boss have to also get out?"

"Yes, everybody in the vehicle, please."

The back window of the Jaguar slid down with a purring sound.

Tony couldn't see who was in the back seat, but he did see the chunky barrel of a Browning automatic pointing at him.

He tried to level his weapon, but he was a fraction too late.

The bullet from the gun hit Tony squarely in his chest blowing him clean off his feet.

The flak jacket he was wearing wasn't designed to stop a bullet at close range, especially the calibre of a Browning automatic.

As he lay on the cold tarmac, he heard more gunfire around him.

All the men in the vehicle had been armed and they had swiftly and mercilessly cut down the whole team.

Tony couldn't move. He began to shiver, and his breathing became shallow.

Then, he became aware of a shadow looming over him.

He looked up into the grinning features of Kenny Robbins. But what was he doing here?

Behind him, he now recognised the two big men as Rudi and Errol. They all pointed guns at him.

"I trusted you, Tony. But like all the others, you thought you could fuck me over. Did you really think that you could walk away with Annette?"

Tony tried to speak but could only cough up blood.

"Goodbye, Tony, and good riddance."

Tony closed his eyes waiting for the next shot.

* * *

Tony suddenly jolted himself awake and found himself laying on the sofa in his living room.

At first, he was confused, but then remembered that he had migrated to it after an hour of tossing and turning in his bed.

He rubbed his eyes, that were still blurry with sleep, and sat up. He saw the early morning sun beginning to filter through the curtains.

Christ, that nightmare had been too real for comfort. Recently, they had been coming thick and fast. Most nights. There seemed no end to them. Each night brought another terrible vision. They were gradually becoming more vivid and detailed.

If he didn't sort himself out soon, he would start going crazy.

When he had left the forces, he had nightmares regularly, but over the course of time, they faded. But now, they were back again with a vengeance.

No doubt a shrink would say that these bad dreams were a way of telling him something. A premonition, maybe?

Tony noticed that the television was still on. He vaguely remembered watching a documentary way past midnight about the American rock band Kiss and that was it. Now he was staring at the smug features of Piers Morgan on *Good Morning Britain*. That was a more frightening prospect than Gene Simmons in full make-up.

Tony clicked the image off with the remote, rose wearily and headed towards the shower.

Once he was in the shower cubicle, he turned on the water faucet. He noticed that his hands were still trembling.

He stood under the shower and let the hot water ease his aching muscles. It also helped erase the memories of the grinning features of Robbins pointing the Browning at him.

Fifteen minutes later, he was dressed and waiting for the kettle to boil.

At 8.00am, he rang Doug Jacobs. He hoped he would pick up. He couldn't wait any longer.

He was in luck. Doug answered.

"Morning, Tony. How are you doing?"

"Morning, Doug. I think my answer will probably depend on what you're going to tell me next."

Tony heard a sigh on the end of the line.

"Okay, Tony. I have some good news and I have some bad."

Tony rolled his eyes in frustration. "Let's have the good news first then, Doug."

"Well, my contact, old Lennie Morrison, is stable and will be coming out of hospital on Monday." He paused.

"So, what is the bad?" asked Tony.

Doug continued. "He needs a few more weeks of recuperation at home, so I don't know how soon he will be well enough to resume his work, so to speak."

Before Tony could answer, Doug cut in.

"I suggest you get down here to Bristol as soon as possible. I have a little flat you can bed down in. You'll be right on hand for when Lennie does get well and then, you can get the passports first hand and away you can go. How does that sound?"

"This Lennie is the only option, is he?" asked Tony.

At the other end of the line, Doug rolled his eyes in frustration before answering. "No, he's not the only option. You can contact some of those fucking clowns advertising on the net or you can wait for the best and somebody you can trust. If you want to succeed in whatever it is you are up to, then you better learn to be patient, my friend."

Tony knew he had no choice.

"Okay, Doug. I'm sorry, man. I'm grateful for your help. I'll drive down tonight. It will be late, but I'll give you a call when I'm there."

"No problem. I'll get a spare key cut and it's yours for as long as you need it. You'll be safe. I'm sorry I can't do more, but nobody could have foreseen Lennie getting ill. But look, he is a tough old dog. He'll get it done as soon as he can."

Tony resigned himself that he would have to wait. But he would rather do it in Bristol than here under the watchful eye of Robbins and his crew.

He thanked Doug, hung up the call and poured himself another cup of coffee.

Today was the day. Saturday. It was finally here.

He walked into the bedroom and regarded his packed bags. He would put them in the boot of his car ready to switch with Emma that evening. He had the money safely stashed in the luggage. That was it.

Once more he felt the familiar tingle of adrenaline run through his body. He breathed deeply and got a rein on it. Now, he had to see the day out and keep Robbins happy.

He would head down to the gym for a while to kill some time and keep everything normal. Later he would head to *Jesters* for the show and then, make his move.

As he drained his cup, he looked around the flat. He wouldn't miss it. It had just been another roof over his head. He picked up his bags and headed for the door. He found himself whistling the song *Wherever I Lay my Hat, That's my Home*. Now, who the fuck sang that?

CHAPTER THIRTY ONE

As Tony pulled up outside the gym, he was surprised to see Robbins' Mercedes parked there.

Now what? he thought as he got out of his car and entered the gym.

He saw Karen on the reception talking to a young couple and she acknowledged him with a wave.

He scanned the gym and spied Errol and Rudi at the far end in the free weights section, bench pressing some impossible weight again that made Tony tired just looking at it.

There was no sign of Robbins. Maybe they had got permission to use the Merc? He began to relax a little. He was beginning to get a little paranoid.

Tony then saw Errol catch his eye and gesture to him to join them. The knot of tightness returned to his belly as he walked in their direction. He put a brave face on his feelings.

"Glad you came in, Tony. I was just about to ring you," announced Errol.

"Morning, boys. Going a bit light, aren't you?"

With a grunt, Rudi re-racked his barbell with the guidance of Errol.

"Very funny, Tony. You should be on the stage."

"Yeah, fucking sweeping it," added Errol.

"It's only because the boss thinks you are flavour of the month that I don't shut that smart mouth of yours up. So, watch it, because there will be a time that you will fall out of favour."

Tony smiled. "What can I do for you? I didn't think you would have time for a workout with all that is going down at present."

"Well, that's why you look like you do, and we look like this. We never miss a workout, even if World War 3 was declared," Rudi informed him.

Tony said nothing.

"Anyway, enough banter. Mr. Robbins just rang. He wants to see you at the office."

"Okay. Thanks, I have a few things to finish up here first."

"No, he insisted you come now," said Rudi. "Kenny is in a hurry and wants to run something by you. He says it's urgent. He is then planning to take Bergkamp Senior somewhere out of the city to do some clay pigeon shooting. Show him the country life."

"Fucking hell. What's Robbins going to be using? A sawn off?" Tony joked.

Rudi and Errol didn't react. They stared at him stonily.

Tony felt a cold shiver trail down his spine but hid the feeling.

"So, what is it about?"

Both the big men picked up their water bottles. "Who knows? I suggest you get going and find out."

* * *

Thirty minutes later, Tony was sat in Robbins office in front of his desk. He was sipping a cup of black coffee whilst Robbins himself spoke venomously into his mobile phone.

"Listen, Barry. That cage will be up and ready by 2.00pm. I don't want to hear any of your fucking excuses. Do you understand me?"

Tony couldn't hear the reply, but could tell by the expression on Robbins' face that he didn't like it.

"Look here, you prick. I am going to send Errol and Rudi over to the club now to tear you a new fucking arsehole unless you get busy. Now, get on with it, you muppet."

Robbins slammed his phone shut and threw it onto his desk.

"Fucking wankers. You just can't get the staff these days, Tony. They're all whinging little bastards afraid to do a good day's graft. I can do without it. I want this show to go like clockwork and anybody fucking me about will be sorry. Fuck, I used to be up at 4.00am as a younger man and down the fruit markets freezing my bollocks off in amongst the spuds and apples trying to earn a crust. These soft bastards today don't know they're born."

Tony sat silently whilst Robbins poured himself a scotch and downed it in one huge gulp.

"Right, anyway. Sorry about all that shit. I'm having a difficult day so far. I only hope it can get better. Right, let's get down to business."

"What did you want me for, Kenny?" asked Tony.

Kenny Robbins sat down into his chair. "I haven't got much time to fuck about here. I have a hundred and one things to do, plus Annette phoned me earlier telling me that she won't be back for the show. Her old lady has taken a turn for the worst and she can't leave her.

Personally, I'll be glad when the old cow snuffs it. Annette spends more time with her these days than me. So that has fucked up my plans to have her on my arm tonight to soft soap Bergkamp. I'll be having words with her when she gets back. I suppose I'll have to find some other bimbo to come with me, so she can flash her tits at the Dutchman."

Tony sipped his coffee. He didn't think that it was his place to comment. Inside, he was glad that Annette wasn't coming back to the bastard.

Robbins lit up a cigar and seemed deep in thought.

Tony broke the silence.

"So, what can I do for you?"

Robbins seemed to come back to the present. "Right, yes. Talking of not being able to get the staff, my head doorman at the club, Norman Parsons, has gone down with some sort of food poisoning. According to him, he is shitting through the eye of a needle. It was probably eating in that dodgy curry house on Grey Street, the *Spice Palace*. Fuck knows what goes into their chicken tikka, but it isn't chicken. That's for sure. Anyway, the silly bastard can't mind the door tonight for the show, so I would like you to do it. You have plenty of experience in that field, so I think you would be the ideal man for the job. There will be some good coin in it for you. You up for that?"

What could Tony say? Robbins wasn't really asking him; he was telling him. He would do it. It would keep the peace and keep Robbins off his back.

"Yeah. No problem, Kenny. I can handle that. For one moment, I thought you were going to ask me to wear a dress and escort you to the show."

Robbins nearly choked on his cigar.

"Fuck me, Tony. I wish I was as calm as you. How do you do it?"

"Meditation."

"Really?" asked Robbins.

"Or did I mean medication?"

Robbins grinned. "So, all is good for tonight? I can leave that in your capable hands?"

Tony nodded.

"Good man. Be at the club for around 5.00pm and I will have other door staff who are also working *Jesters* to show you the set-up."

Suddenly, Robbins phone rang. He picked it up and regarded the name. He looked at Tony. "It's that fucking plank, Barry, again. I might be some while. We're done here. See you later at the club."

Tony nodded. He put down his empty cup and got up and headed for the door.

As he left, he heard Robbins ripping into the hapless Barry once again.

＊ ＊ ＊

"So, how did Robbins take the fact that you weren't coming back today?"

Tony was driving, talking on speaker phone to Annette.

"Not good, Tony. He was angry. He wanted me back, but in the end, I persuaded him that I couldn't come. He wasn't happy and told me that if I didn't get back by next week, he would come out here and get me."

"Well, that isn't going to happen. It's done now, so it's time to get on your way to Lanzarote. Give me a call when you get there and take care. This'll all be over soon and then we have the rest of our lives together, okay?"

Annette's voice sounded small on the end of the phone. "I know, Tony. Please take care of yourself and get to me as soon as possible."

"I will. Just hold tight with Ray. I won't be able to contact you until I'm in Bristol, as the rest of the day is going to be hectic. I love you. I promise that I'll see you soon."

Tony heard her voice shake a little. She was holding back the tears. "I love you too."

Tony hung up and headed back to his flat. The clock was ticking.

* * *

2 days ago.

Colin Crane walked through the Cabot Circus shopping complex in the centre of Bristol. It was heaving with people, which was not unusual for a Saturday afternoon.

He had been into some of the shops in vain hope, asking about work, but he could tell by the expressions on the faces of the management that he wasn't what they were looking for. They all gave out lame excuses that there was nothing available at present and told him to leave his details. He wasn't about to do that. He knew that they would end up in the bin.

As he left the shops, he could sense other employees sniggering behind his back and thinking who wants that dick working here. Fucking weirdo.

Colin was used to this. He had put up with it forever, it seemed. He wasn't cool or hip enough for their dumb shop. He didn't have pink hair, or his fucking nose or lip pierced. Well, fuck them all.

As he walked, he regarded all the young girls scantily clad in short skirts and tight tops. Some of them were only school age, putting it out there. The fucking slags. He imagined what he would like to do to them.

He visualised holding them at gunpoint and making them drop to their knees and take his hardness in their mouths. This excited him.

He then thought of Kim at the *Alpha* coffee house. Now that would be something special. He knew her time was coming very soon. He felt a rush of energy rush up inside.

He could feel the hardness in his jeans but also the hardness of the gun inside his coat.

As he walked through the crowds, he knew that at any time he could pull out the weapon and cause mayhem. That made him feel good. He liked the feeling of superiority it gave him.

Colin was so wrapped up in his thoughts as he rounded a corner that he nearly collided with a group of teenagers.

"Hey, watch it, dude. You want to sort those fucking glasses of yours out," exclaimed a big lad of around 16 or 17 years old. He had a spotty face with a wispy little beard on the end of his chin. He sported a baseball cap on his head back to front.

He was with another lad and two girls. They all broke into laughter at his quip.

Colin Crane just stopped and stared at them.

The youth saw his silence as an entry to have another go at him.

"Well, get the fuck out the way, you weirdo."

Colin continued to stand there as still as a statue.

The youth now got up in his face.

"Were you just looking at my girlfriend's tits, you fucking pervert?"

A blonde girl suddenly joined in. "You weirdo. Turning you on, is it? Look, I think he's got a hard-on in his pants."

They all looked at Colin. He now stepped back to try and hide his embarrassment.

He turned to walk away, but the main youth shoved him into a doorway of an empty shop front.

"Keep an eye out," he shouted to his friends

"What you going to do, Josh?" asked the group.

The lad called Josh got right up in Colin's face.

"Right, you pervert. You owe me £20 for eyeing my girl up. So, let's have it and you can go on your way."

Colin said nothing.

"Well, in that case, I will have to take it. Where's your wallet? Don't fuck me about. I'm carrying a knife."

The youth patted Colin's jean pocket with no success and was about to try his coat when Colin spoke.

"I'll get it for you. it's in my inside jacket pocket."

Josh smiled, "Right. Well, get the fuck on with it then and I won't have to cut you."

As he said this, he looked over his shoulder grinning at his mates.

By the time he turned back to Colin, he was staring at the barrel of an Uzi.

The lad's eyes grew wide with fear. Suddenly, all his swagger was gone.

Colin smiled at him and when he spoke, his voice was a whisper. "I could blow your brains out, you little fucking weasel, and then, I could do the same to your dumb fuck mates. You are fucking lucky that I am going to let you live. Now, say sorry to me for being an asshole."

It was the youth's turn to stare dumbly.

Colin pushed the gun closer to him. "Say sorry."

The lad looked like he was about to piss himself. He stammered sorry and moved back out of the doorway.

"What happened, Josh? Did you get any money off the creep?" asked the group.

The youth kept backing away as Colin returned the gun to his jacket and stood watching him.

"Let's go," said Josh, "He hasn't got anything. Come on. Let's get out of here."

He moved off into the crowd and the rest of the group followed, puzzled at the sudden turn of events.

Colin watched them go and then, moved off in the other direction. He felt elated. The look on that little shit's face was priceless. He couldn't wait to see more. Colin Crane wasn't going to be fucked over ever again. No way.

Wasn't it Andy Warhol who said that everybody will get their fifteen minutes of fame? Well, Colin was overdue his.

CHAPTER THIRTY TWO

The Past

6.00pm found Tony stood on the door of *Jesters* night club. He wore a full tuxedo. It was an age since he had been suited and booted and he felt uncomfortable. Obviously, working on the door of this nightclub was a big step-up from some of the dives he had worked in the past. When Kenny Robbins threw a show or a party, it was always going to be upmarket, and this special fight night event certainly was all that.

Cars pulled up constantly to the venue. Mercedes, Bentleys and Jaguars seemed to be the normal mode of transport for the glamourous people who got out of them.

Tony spied page three models, television personalities and sports stars among the crowd entering the nightclub. He could almost smell the money in the air.

"Another fucking world, isn't it?"

Tony turned to regard the man stood next to him. He had met him earlier. His name was Scott Hurst. He was half Tony's age but a good solid doorman. He had shown him around the club and given him the lowdown on how it all worked.

Tony found him to be a likeable guy. He reminded him a lot of Rob. Fun to be around. Always chatting. But his affable personality shouldn't be mistaken for softness. Nobody worked the door of a Kenny Robbin's establishment if they were a pussy.

"Yes. You are right there," replied Tony.

Scott grinned. "Cass fucking hates them. That's why she stays inside. She tells me it's darker in there so, she can't see their stupid smug faces."

Tony laughed.

He had met Cass Fordham earlier. She was one of a very small minority of female door personnel. But she was tough as nails. A Geordie father and a Jamaican mother made for a tough upbringing in the North, but she survived. She had just embarked on a professional career as a boxer. All the early signs said that she was going to be good.

It felt strange being back on the doors. Tony knew that he had to see the night through, but he was glad that this was no longer his means of income, no disrespect to Scott, Cass and the rest of the team working there tonight.

He had been the young lion once, just like these guys. Hungry, enthusiastic and up for anything.

Back then, Ray Steele had been the wise old head. Now it was his turn.

For a moment, he thought of Ray and how he had gone out of his way to help him and accommodate the arrival of Annette. He looked forward to sharing a beer with him in the sun again soon. He was brought back to reality again by Scott jabbering on.

"Here. Isn't that the bird who won the celebrity in the jungle thing?"

Tony regarded a glamorous looking lady slipping out of a taxi as gracefully as she could in the ridiculously short skirt that she was wearing.

"I couldn't tell you. I've never seen it."

Scott regarded him as if he was some sort of alien. "What? Never, like?"

"Nope."

"Fucking hell. Amazing," replied Scott shaking his head. He continued, "Well, I think that's her. Geordie girl. She certainly looks hot. I would if she let me."

It was Tony's turn to shake his head. "Put your tongue away. She's heading this way."

"Look, if she had a Kangaroo penis in her mouth, I must stand some sort of chance," Scott whispered.

Tony wondered what the hell he was going on about.

Scott straightened his bowtie and drew himself up to his full 6 feet 2 inches.

As the girl passed him, he winked at her and said, "Alright, darling."

She carried on walking without engaging eye contact but said, "Fuck off, loser."

Scott looked mortified. "Yeah, that's her. The moody bitch."

* * *

The show was due to start at 9.00pm after a five-course champagne meal. Robbins reckoned the top of the bill fight between McCoy and Bergkamp would start around 10.30pm.

This worked in nicely with Tony's plans. By the time the show was done, and the final stragglers had left, he would be well gone.

He breathed in deeply the cool night air as he felt the tingle of anticipation run through his body. He was ready, and now the moment was nearly on him, he felt good, just as he always had when the moment of truth came knocking. He had learnt over a lengthy career that to conquer your fears, you had to face them down.

As he peered at a sea of faces heading towards the club, he suddenly saw Alex McCoy emerging from the throng. He had a small entourage following him.

He was stopping to sign a few autographs and have photos with various people. He seemed to be loving the attention.

When his eyes met Tony's, the smile left his face rapidly. Tony's body tensed, waiting in anticipation for the comeback that McCoy had promised.

Scott seemed to sense the change in his colleague's body language.

"Everything okay, Tony?"

"Maybe," Tony replied, his eyes never leaving McCoy's, who was heading his way.

"See this guy approaching us?"

Scott looked forward. "Yeah. Fuck, it's Alex McCoy. You know him?"

"Let's say that we're acquainted. Last time we met, it didn't turn out too good. You know what I'm saying?"

Scott regarded Tony and nodded, "Okay. Understood. How do you want to handle this?"

"I'll do the talking and you just watch my back."

Scott nodded. "You got it."

McCoy stopped in front of Tony and looked him in the eye. "Well, this is a surprise. We meet again. Not managing the gym tonight?"

Tony coolly eyed McCoy. "Not tonight. I have other duties to fulfil. Making sure everybody has a nice evening and that they enjoy your fight."

McCoy nodded. He then extended his hand to Tony.

"I want to apologise for the other day. I was a prick in the gym. It's this weight cutting and lack of food. It makes me edgy and aggressive. I shouldn't have taken it out on your staff or you. I'm sorry about that. I sent flowers and an apology to the girl. Are we straight?"

Tony regarded the extended hand, then reached and shook it.

"Apology accepted. It's forgotten. I wish you all the best for tonight."

McCoy nodded and headed to go inside the club.

He then stopped and turned. "I knew you couldn't be just some bog-standard gym manager. Not with the skills you possess. My bollocks still bear the bruises. Respect, man."

He disappeared inside.

Tony breathed out heavily. "Well, that was unexpected. Maybe my luck is changing. A problem resolved without violence."

Scott smiled. "I'm glad too, my friend. I can tell you, my ass cheeks were so tight that you wouldn't have got a playing card between them."

They both broke into laughter and the tension that had hung in the air a few moments ago evaporated.

* * *

The show started on time and Tony and the rest of his team kept a low but concentrated presence inside the club, but, with this clientele, the likelihood of any serious trouble going down was low.

Tony could remember that when he boxed, there used to be more fights in the crowd than in the ring at some of the venues. This was certainly a step up and he could see Robbins' logic.

At 10.00pm, he stepped outside for a breath of air and phoned Emma Snow. He wanted to check that there were no last-minute hitches. She confirmed once again that all was good and that she would be there at 11.00am as promised in the car park.

He was relieved that all was going to plan. His car, or really speaking, Robbins' car, was in the car park and in the boot, were all his worldly possessions. Once he swapped cars, it could stay there. He wouldn't need it again.

Tony calculated that it would take him around five hours to get to Bristol. He would take the A1 and then the A46 before finally joining the M5 to Bristol.

He had spoken briefly to Doug Jacobs earlier in the day and he had told him that he had a flat sorted for him in an area named Clifton. He had texted Tony the address and told him that he would find a key under the large ornamental flowerpot in the front garden.

According to Doug, Clifton, apparently, was a crime-free zone.

He was also told that the fridge was well-stocked. Tony was to make himself at home and Doug would contact him the next morning to meet.

Tony was suddenly aware that somebody had stepped out the door of the club beside him. He glanced to his left and saw that it was Robbins.

Kenny Robbins lit up a cigar.

"Taking a breath of air, eh, Tony? The show is going well. There's going to be an interval before the main event. Give the bastards a bit more time to hit the bar."

Tony nodded. "I guess I better get back in."

Robbins touched his arm lightly. "You're alright a moment. I'm sure they'll yell if all hell breaks loose."

Tony hesitated. "Yeah, I guess you're right," he conceded.

Robbins walked down the steps and stood looking up at the stars. He drew on his cigar and thoughtfully said, "You know what, Tony. I've been a lucky man. I truly have. Don't get me wrong, I've worked my bollocks off to get to where I am, but I've had a good slice of luck. I did a spell in prison when I was younger, and I knew that when I got out, I was never going back in again. I've survived two attempted knifings and a shooting. I've fought off some hard bastards who wanted a piece of the action. But I was too smart for them. Muscle will get you so far, but brains will take you further. You hear me, Tony?"

Tony said nothing.

Robbins turned and regarded Tony. "But you know that, Tony. You are one of life's survivors. You wouldn't be stood here if you didn't have the intelligence to back up your physical skills. But I realised, the same as you, that physical skills erode. Soon, every jumped-up would-be gangster on the block will come gunning for you. That's why you've got to keep one step ahead. That takes brains. Either that or a fucking big gun. Hence, the deal with the Dutch."

He laughed loudly, "You ever wish you lived your life differently, Tony?"

Tony walked down the steps to join Robbins looking up into the night sky.

"I think my life was already planned out for me at an early age. You could say that it was written in the stars."

Robbins nodded. "Yes, I can understand that. I don't think either of us were going to be a 9 to 5 pencil pusher. Do you?"

"No, I don't think so."

"So, what are your plans, Tony?"

Tony regarded Robbins. "What do you mean?"

Robbins smiled. "Come on, Tony. Men like you always have a plan. I know that you're not the typical man that I have working for me. I know you didn't want to come work for me in the first place."

Tony raised an eyebrow.

Robbins continued. "You look surprised. Rob told me, but he also told me that you needed money. Now that you have earned good money, I want to know what keeps you here? Especially working for a man that you don't really like. Is it just the money?"

Tony tried to read Robbins' face, but it was now in the shadows.

"What other reason could it be? Sometimes, you have got to do things that you don't necessary like."

"Like in the forces?" asked Robbins.

"Sometimes, yes."

Robbins dropped his cigar and crushed it under his foot. "Maybe that's your reason. Who knows? But I didn't get where I am by not realising a dangerous man. Did you enjoying killing, Tony?"

Tony didn't answer.

"Once a killer, always a killer. That's what I believe. We can't change, no matter how much we think we can."

He began to head back up the steps. "Why not join me after the show for a few drinks? Maybe we can discuss your future, especially if Bergkamp wants to run the show now. I'm sure that he could do with a good right-hand man. Come and find me in the blue lounge later, okay?"

Robbins disappeared back inside leaving Tony alone.

That had been a strange conversation. Robbins had also been strange. Did he suspect something after all this time or was he just curious about why Tony was still in his employment after what had happened to Rob? Whatever the reasons, he knew he would not be joining Robbins for that drink.

"Tony, are you out here? Tony?"

It was Scott calling him.

"Yeah, I'm here. What's up?"

"A small group of McCoy's supporters are getting a bit rowdy. Could do with your presence in here to try and cool them down before their boy comes on."

Tony skipped up the steps. "Okay, Scott. I'm coming."

CHAPTER THIRTY THREE

McCoy threw a big right cross, but Edwin Bergkamp countered it with a front thrust kick into the advancing man's stomach. It knocked McCoy back, but he just grinned and walked in again, throwing a left hook and a low round kick to the Dutchman's thigh. They clinched and exchanged knee strikes, both wrestling for dominance, attempting to drive each other up against the cage wall where it would be easier to get the takedown.

The bell sounded for the end of round four and both fighters broke and went to their respective corners.

The fight was even. Neither fighter had really got the better of the other.

Bergkamp was a little sharper on his feet due to his K1 kickboxing experience and McCoy was stronger on the ground seeing as he was a Brazilian Jujutsu black belt.

The fight was evenly poised for the final round.

Tony watched from the back of the club. He had one eye on the fight and one on the clock.

As soon as the fight was done, he was going to make his exit.

Due to the trouble with McCoy's fans earlier, the fight had been delayed whilst the security had asked for calm.

Most had abided to this, but a few assholes had to be ejected by Tony, Scott, Cas and the team.

It was now 11.35am. The last round, if it went the distance, would be five minutes long.

He had managed to ring Emma from a cubicle in the toilets and reschedule the meet for midnight.

If it went all the way, he planned to slip away before the result and miss the crowds exiting.

He glanced towards Robbins' cage side table. Tony saw him downing a scotch and talking to Marc Bergkamp. He began gesturing towards the fighters and mimicking throwing punches. He seemed to be relaxed and happy.

Tony thought again about their earlier conversation. He wondered what Robbins would be thinking when he finally figured out why Tony had stayed in his employment. To steal his woman. That's why. *As you said, Kenny, you have got to stay one step ahead of the game.*

The bell sounded and both fighters moved to the centre of the cage. Bergkamp threw a right, but McCoy shot under it and took him to the floor.

Bergkamp wrapped his long legs around his opponent and pulled him close, denying McCoy any leverage to punch.

Both men battled for an opening and then, McCoy was past the Dutchman's legs, straddled his chest and began to rain punches and elbows down onto his opponent's head. It was classic MMA ground and pound.

Tony noticed blood on Edwin's face as a cut opened over his eye. McCoy, sensing victory, carried on the onslaught, but got careless with his balance and Bergkamp bridged him off his body and turned him over. The Dutchman immediately got to his feet.

McCoy reluctantly got to his. He knew that he had missed a good chance of finishing the fight.

He moved forward and Bergkamp hit him with a low kick to the leg and then, fired a high round kick that caught McCoy flush on the jaw. The impact could be heard at the back of the club.

The Englishman's legs turned to jelly and Bergkamp closed quickly, his face a grim mask of blood. He grabbed McCoy by the neck and brought his knee up with a sickening crunch under his chin. He followed it with another.

Tony saw Robbins and Bergkamp Senior on their feet, urging Marc to finish it.

Tony had to admit that McCoy was a tough bastard because he was throwing punches back, even though he was standing on wobbly legs.

Both men looked tired. Both were now bleeding from facial wounds.

McCoy shot in again for the takedown but caught Bergkamp's knee in his face. He fell to his hands and knees and Bergkamp seized the chance to get onto his back and wrap his arm around his neck for a strangle.

McCoy bravely defended it, although he was badly dazed.

The bell sounded, and the referee rushed in to break both men apart.

Bergkamp got to his feet and raised his arms as his corner team rushed into the cage to stem the flow of blood from his cut. McCoy staggered to his feet and managed to also raise his arm.

It had been a terrific fight and a close one.

The assembled crowd showed their appreciation as they now waited for the result.

Tony glanced around. Everybody's attention was on the cage.

He headed towards the exit door.

As he moved past the cheering crowd, he felt an arm grab his and then a voice shout.

"Hey, remember me, asshole?"

Tony turned to face a young man who was obviously worse for drink. The face seemed vaguely familiar and then he realised that it was Karen's ex-boyfriend from the other evening that he had run into.

He was annoyed that this man should suddenly try to slow him down in his plans to move.

"Look, Lee, Luke, Liam or whatever your name is, I haven't got time for this shit, so sit the fuck down."

Tony pulled his arm away and made to move off, but Liam grabbed at him again.

"Don't fucking walk away from me, you prick. I want a word with you."

Now, Tony was angry. Without another word, he spun around and headbutted Liam squarely in the face. It was another favourite move of his that he had honed on the doors for as many years as he could remember.

He didn't even bother to look back at Liam. He knew that he was out of it and by the time he woke up, the cleaners would be in the club.

He headed for the door cursing under his breath that this idiot had once again brought him to the door of violence. He pushed open the front door of the club and felt a rush of cool air hit his face. It felt good. He stood on the top step of the club and breathed in deeply.

The door swung open behind him as a few other people exited.

Tony could hear the MC from the cage announcing the result of the fight. "And the winner by majority decision is…"

The door shut again, and the voice faded out.

Tony moved down the steps and headed down the road towards the car park.

He glanced at his watch. It read 11.55pm.

* * *

Tony sat in his car and watched the car park entrance. All was quiet. Not many people would be coming into it now at this hour, but he knew that very soon, when the club turned out, there would be plenty of people coming to get their cars to go home. He wanted to avoid this.

He tapped the steering wheel impatiently. *Come on, Emma. Don't let me down.*

He looked at his watch again. 12.04pm.

He felt a knot of tension in his belly. Had something gone wrong?

He checked his phone but there was no miscall or message.

Then, he saw it. The Silver Audi driving slowly through the entrance. It was Emma.

Tony jumped out of his car and signalled her to pull over by it. Emma did this and got out to meet him.

"Sorry I was late, but you wouldn't believe the amount of traffic on the roads. Saturday night, I suppose."

"No worries, Emma," replied Tony.

He glanced around the car park. All was quiet. He got his luggage out of his car.

Tony popped the boot of the Audi and put his bag in. He noticed the holdall that had been in there many weeks back when he had visited the lock-up. He unzipped it and saw the money and the gun were still there intact. Reaching in the holdall, he peeled off a wad of notes and shut the boot down.

He went over to Emma and handed her the money.

"Here, take this. It's not a lot and it won't bring Rob back, but it is something."

Emma stared at the offered money. Tears formed in her eyes. "He isn't coming back, is he?"

Tony said nothing.

"That bastard Robbins did something to him, didn't he?"

Tony thrust the money into her hand. "Take this, Emma. It's over. Get on with your life and forget Robbins. He doesn't know you exist, so let's keep it that way."

Emma took the money and then threw her arms around Tony and held him tight. "What about you, Tony?" she asked.

Tony gently eased her away. He gazed into her eyes. "You must forget about me as well. You never knew me. I don't expect anybody to come visiting you, but if they do, the less you know the better."

Rain began to fall heavily.

"Get in. I will drop you back home."

Emma got into the passenger seat with tears flowing freely down her face.

"Will I ever see you again?"

Tony let her go. "No, I don't think so. Forget about me. Enjoy the money and have a good life."

He pulled away and headed for the exit. The rain came down harder.

He flipped on the wipers and looked in the rear-view mirror

Tony eased out into the traffic. As he passed *Jesters*, the crowds were now spilling out onto the pavement.

He heard the chanting for local boy McCoy. The little bastard must have won the decision. He wondered if the next time he saw his face it be on a UFC fight event.

Scott and Cas came out of the door and took up positions either side of it, ushering people out. Their shift was nearly done. *I expect they wonder where I've got to*, thought Tony. *They were both good kids.*

He then saw Robbins come out of the club, stop on the top step and light up another cigar. Marc Bergkamp was with him and he did the same thing. Both men were smiling and chatting. Maybe Edwin had won, or was it that the deal was now done between them?

For a brief second, Tony thought that Robbins caught his eye as the car passed him, but maybe he just imagined it.

The rain was torrential, and people were running to get to their cars.

* * *

Ten minutes later, he had dropped Emma back outside *Tasty Bites*. As he drove away, he glanced in the rear mirror and just saw her standing staring at his car. She would survive. Time was a great healer.

With a tingle of excitement in his belly, he headed the Audi out of the city and towards the A1.

Within a short while, he left the city of Newcastle behind him for the last time.

He passed the *Angel of the North* and smiled at the memory of when he was explaining to Annette about its origins.

That moment seemed so long ago, yet it was only just a few weeks.

For a moment, a flicker of doubt ran through his mind.

Was he crazy? He was running away with a woman he had only known a matter of weeks.

But not just any women. The woman of Kenny Robbins. The North's very own Godfather.

Was Annette really in love with him or was he just a way out of her miserable life? No. He was sure that what they had was real.

He switched on the radio and the sound of Bryan Adams 90's chart topper *Everything I Do I Do It for You* was playing.

Poetic justice? Fuck it. Of course, he was doing the right thing. For the first time in a long time, he felt alive and he intended it to stay that way.

He glanced at the dashboard clock.12.50am.

The motorway was quiet.

Hopefully, he would be in Bristol for dawn.

CHAPTER THIRTY FOUR

Present

Tony leant back in his seat and stretched his stiff muscles. He glanced at the clock on the wall. She was now an hour late and no phone message. This concerned him and only reinforced the conversation that he had had with her a few days ago.

Annette had been in Lanzarote over three weeks and Tony had been stuck in England waiting for the passports that he was at last going to pick up tomorrow. Finally, Doug Jacobs had sorted it out and had rung him first thing this morning. It had been too late, though, to stop Annette flying over. The whole thing had been a nightmare.

Tony hadn't been able to do anything about it. He just had to wait, but he knew that by now Kenny Robbins would be going berserk and looking for them both.

So far, he felt that he had covered his tracks well, but he knew that Robbins would not give up until he had found them. He was uncomfortable still being in England and apart from Annette.

He had made sure that Ray Steele had been put in the picture and he had assured Tony that he would be extra vigilant.

Doug Jacobs had been good as his word, letting Tony use his flat during this time, and Tony really had grown fond of Bristol. It was a pity that he wasn't here under better circumstances to enjoy it more, but now, he was at the end of his patience.

A few nights ago, Annette had rung Tony and told him that she couldn't bear being apart from him any longer. Tony missed her just as much. She told him that she would get on a flight and come to Bristol to see him and then, they could both travel back together.

At first, Tony had said no. He had urged that it was just too risky, but Annette was insistent and finally, he relented because deep down, he needed to see her too.

They had decided that Tony wouldn't meet her from her flight, as they couldn't be sure that somebody might be watching the airport. Kenny Robbins might live in Newcastle, but his reach and influence stretched far.

Tony had given Annette the address of the coffee shop and told her to get a taxi straight there. She had promised to ring him as soon as she was in one.

Tony knew her flight had landed well over two hours ago. Every time he had rung her mobile, it had gone to answer phone. He had left three voice messages asking her to call him, but he had heard nothing. Something had to be wrong.

He knew he should leave the coffee shop, but what if she turned up? Maybe she had a problem with her phone?

He tried once again to stretch out the tension in his shoulders but to no avail. He then saw his phone vibrate on the table and he grabbed it quickly. He had a text message. It was from Annette. He breathed a sigh of relief as he read it. *On my way. Sorry for the delay. Will be there in 10 minutes x.*

Tony answered the message and allowed himself a small smile. She was coming. Although it had all been risky, now he couldn't wait to see her. He wanted to hold her in his arms, kiss her soft lips and smell her perfume.

Kim passed the table carrying a steaming pot of coffee, giving out free refills. She saw him smiling and looking at his phone.

"A woman, I would guess. Am I right?" she asked.

Tony looked up from his phone. "How do you know?"

"Us females just have the vibe for that sort of thing. So that is why you've been hanging around in here like a lost soul. There was me thinking that it was my excellent coffee that kept you sitting there."

Tony spread his hands wide. "I own up. You have me bang to rights. I can't deny it but, in all honesty, your coffee is still the best. May I have a refill, please?"

She obliged. Kim walked off faking annoyance. "Too late for charm, Mister. You are off my Christmas card list."

Tony let his head hang down towards the table. "I am deeply wounded."

Two minutes later, Kim came back with the refill. "On the house," she said as she placed it on the table in front of him.

"Thank you, Kim. That's really kind of you," Tony said.

"That's me. A big heart. A softie."

She returned to the counter.

Tony now glanced towards the door. Annette would be here any minute now. He felt strangely nervous. It seemed ages since they were last together. He realised just how much he had missed her. His anticipation was now building after all the earlier doubt. It would be like meeting for the first time again. They were nearly there.

* * *

Colin Crane parked the pushbike down a side alley. He had stolen it earlier on. He would now walk the short distance to the *Alpha* coffee house. He pulled the zip on his Parka coat up to his chin and dug his hands deep into his pockets.

Under the coat, the weight of the Uzi in the waistband of his trousers felt reassuringly good. Time to give that stuck up bitch, Kim, a present that she wouldn't forget.

He was a few minutes away from the *Alpha*.

* * *

The door of the *Alpha* swung open. Tony looked up and there she was, standing surveying the room. Tony had forgotten just how beautiful this woman was. Her dark eyes scanned around until she saw him. She smiled, but it was strained. Tony sensed something wasn't right.

He pushed his chair away from the table to stand up to greet Annette. As she approached him, the smile faded, and tears welled up in her eyes. She began to shake her head in distress.

As she came close, she whispered, "I am so sorry, Tony. I truly am."

Tony was confused. "I don't understand, Annette. What's happened?"

Annette held him and looked up into his eyes. "It's over, Tony. It's all over."

As she said this, she glanced over her shoulder towards the front entrance of the coffee house. The door opened and in stepped Kenny Robbins, closely followed by Rudi and Errol.

Now Tony understood.

The ground under him felt as if it had opened and he was going to drop into the bowels of hell.

He pushed Annette behind him and reached inside his jacket pocket, but the three men closed quickly. Errol and Rudi both shook their heads.

Robbins approached the table. He had a big smile on his face as if he was greeting a long-lost friend.

"Tony, how are you? It's been a while."

As he got closer, he lowered his voice and now, it was filled with menace.

"Sit the fuck down and don't do anything stupid. Let's not make a scene in here."

Tony hesitated. He looked around. There were too many innocent people present to start some crazy firefight.

He reluctantly sat back down into his seat.

Robbins gestured for Annette to also sit down and then, Rudi and Errol followed, before Robbins finally did the same, facing Tony.

"Well, isn't this cosy? I must hand it to you, Tony. You've got balls. I never fucking saw it coming. You played me good."

Tony sat quietly.

Robbins leaned in close. Close enough for Tony to smell his Armani aftershave and the faint aroma of scotch on his breath.

"You took a bit of tracking down. I had to rack my brains to think where you and my missus had gone to.

At first, I thought the fact that both of you were missing was just a coincidence, but then, I got to thinking about the weeks leading up to this. I didn't want to think that you were a fucking Judas and my women was a slag, but then, it dawned on me that it was true. I went to Italy to find out if she was still there or even if she ever went. There was nobody at Annette's mother's house. It was all locked up and a neighbour said that it had been that way for a week or so. So, where could you go? Hide in Italy? No, too obvious. Stay in the UK? Too fucking dangerous. So where then? Then, it came to me that you had recently come back from Lanzarote. I asked around a bit and found out that you had an old friend over there. Mr Ray Steele. The fucking legend that was."

Robbins saw Tony tense.

"I have got to hand it to the old bastard. He still had a bit of fire about him, but he was no match for Rudi and Errol. He spilt the beans in the end. Mind you, when you are nailed to the floor with six-inch nails driven into your hands, feet and then your bollocks, it usually does the trick."

Tony moved to get up, but Rudi and Errol pushed him back down.

"He told us finally where Annette was staying. The whole ordeal though was too much for his old ticker. Shame. I liked Ray. I think my old man worked on the doors with him back in the day. Never mind. We gave him a good burial at sea. He's probably washing up on the North African coast as we speak."

Tony lunged forward again. "You are a murdering fucker. You won't get away with this."

Once more, he was restrained.

Robbins carried on talking as if it was all perfectly normal.

"We found Annette at the villa. She wasn't best pleased to see me." He glanced in her direction. "But we had a little talk, didn't we, my love? And let's just say that with a bit of attitude adjusting, she told me it all. Every sordid detail."

Annette pleaded to Robbins through her tears. "Please, Kenny. Let him go. It was all my fault. I came on to him. You have got me back now. Just let him go."

Kenny Robbins regarded her with disgust. "You are soiled goods, pet. I don't fucking want you now. But then again, nobody else is going to have you either. You have a lesson to learn. When that face of yours doesn't look as beautiful anymore, no man will ever look at you again."

He then gestured at Tony. "As for this piece of scum, he is going to suffer before he dies. Nobody, and I mean nobody, fucks Kenny Robbins over and lives to tell the tale."

"Look, Robbins. Do what you have to do to me, but leave her be," said Tony.

"Very gallant of you, but you will both pay, so here is the plan. The boys and I are all armed. You are outnumbered and outgunned, so no fucking heroics. We are all going to get up and walk out to my car, which is just outside, and we are then going for a little drive together. Understand?"

Kim had seen the people enter the coffee shop and sit down with Tony. Something about their look and manner alerted her to the fact that they were not his friends. The woman with them looked petrified. There seemed to her a certain air of danger about the place.

She thought about calling the police. But what could she tell them? Kim regarded the phone on the wall and decided on her decision.

Tony knew that if he went out to the car, it would be all over. If he didn't do something right now, he was a dead man. Maybe he was anyway. There was no easy answer. There were too many innocent people in the line of fire in the coffee shop. He didn't know the best course of action, but his time had run out.

"Right. Let's get up nice and slowly," said Robbins.

Tony made to get up and then picked up his still-full coffee mug and threw the hot liquid into Robbins' face.

The man leaned away and grunted in pain as his hands threw up to protect his eyes.

Tony next targeted Errol, who was sat next to him, and smashed a reverse elbow into his nose. He heard a satisfying crunch as the big man slumped back into his seat. He then moved towards Rudi but stopped as he stared down the barrel of a chunky Desert eagle hand gun.

"Don't even fucking think about it," hissed Rudi.

Everybody in the coffee house was suddenly watching the scenario unfolding in front of them in disbelief.

At that moment, the front door burst open and Colin Crane stepped in. His coat flapped open wildly and, in his hands, he held the Uzi.

Kim, who was about to make the 999 call spotted him first and saw the wild-eyed look on his face and then the gun.

She instinctively reached for the phone on the wall behind the counter.

"Don't fucking move, bitch," screamed Crane.

Kim froze in her tracks. Time seemed to slow down.

Without another word, Colin Crane fired towards her and then started randomly spraying bullets everywhere.

Kim felt bullets whiz past her head and one glazed her earlobe. She dived to the floor behind the counter cowering waiting for Crane to appear and finish her off. Cups, plates and glass shattered and exploded as bullets ricocheted around. Staff and customers dived for cover screaming. Crane was now firing everywhere and anywhere.

Bullets ripped into Kenny Robbins as he tried to get to his feet. One of them pierced his heart and he died instantly, a look of total surprise on his face.

Errol was shot between the eyes. The back of his skull exploded all over the wall behind him.

Tony felt sudden pain rip through his shoulder and chest. He was flung backwards by the force. He instinctively reached out to shield Annette and saw red spreading across her white blouse. She stared at him helplessly. He grabbed for her as bullets ripped around them. They both went crashing head first into the edge of a table.

He then fell heavily to the ground. He managed somehow to turn over onto his back and through blurred vision, witnessed Rudi level the desert eagle at Crane and pull the trigger.

The retort of the big gun was deafening. The bullet caught Colin Crane full in the face and his whole head exploded in a mass of crimson, but not before he managed to fire three rounds into Rudi. Two hit his shoulder and one his chest. The big man dropped back into his chair but was still attempting to aim his gun in Tony's direction.

Crane's headless body stood teetering for a few seconds and collapsed to the ground next to a screaming woman who was clinging to a young child.

Tony had the Glock out and aimed at Rudi.

Both guns discharged simultaneously.

Suddenly, the noise stopped.

The smell of cordite hung heavy in the air. There was sobbing from the people still alive as they crawled out from their cover.

Shock and disbelief were etched on their faces.

Most had just come in for their usual daily cup of coffee or snack. Not in their wildest dreams would they have been expecting to be caught up in a massacre. This stuff just didn't happen in the UK.

Tony felt his breath becoming shallow. He felt numb. He could feel blood running into his eyes from a wound that he had sustained when his head had hit the edge of a table and more spreading from under his body from the bullet wounds. A coldness began to set into his bones.

Rudi was slumped back against the wall with a gaping hole in his neck. Blood was fountaining from the ruptured carotid artery.

His bullet had missed Tony but struck Annette. Tony turned his head to the right and saw Annette lying there staring at him. He knew in his heart she was dead.

He reached out and held her hand and squeezed it. There was no response.

Tony shut his eyes tightly. His dream was over.

He had courted violence all his life and it was inevitable that it would eventually catch up with him.

What was that old saying? *Live by the sword, die by the sword.*

He smiled ruefully.

He felt tired. So tired.

In the distance, he heard sirens.

He felt a darkness descending and thought he could sense somebody looking down at him and then nothing.

Epilogue

Andy Roth nearly dropped his mobile phone as he heard the gun fire from inside the coffee shop. What the fuck was going on?

He was sat in the driver's seat of Kenny Robbin's Mercedes just outside the *Alpha*. He had drove his Boss down from Newcastle to Bristol early that morning.

On the journey he had learned the story of Tony Slade and what he had been up to. He was now itching to have a piece of the bastard.

Moments previously he had seen Robbins, Rudi and Errol go inside with Annette to surprise that scum bag Slade.

He had to give the cheeky fucker some degree of respect to think he could walk off with the Boss's Mrs. He had some balls. But not for much longer.

Roth had been looking forward to making that piece of shit plead for his life before he died.

But now the circumstances looked like they had taking a turn for the worse.

Suddenly the shop door burst open and people began spilling out onto the pavement, some of them he noticed were covered in blood. Many were crying or screaming.

Something had gone terribly wrong.

He opened the car door to get out but then heard police sirens getting closer. He knew he had to go. He didn't want to be found here.

The Boss knew the score. If he wasn't coming out of the shop with Slade now, then he wasn't likely to.

Fuck this was a right mess. It was like the gunfight at the OK coral

Roth had no choice. It was now every man for himself. He couldn't afford to be arrested. He needed to get back up North.

He shut the door again and slipped the car into 'drive'. He pulled out into the traffic and disappeared up the road as two police cars passed him coming the other way.

Andy Roth grimaced as he looked in the rear-view mirror. He would find out what had happened in there. Make no mistake he wouldn't rest until he did. Some fucker would pay.

* * *

Doug Jacobs pulled his car up outside the flat that he had been letting Tony use. He had been ringing Tony Slade's mobile relentlessly for the last few hours without any answer, so he decided to go around and deliver the good news first hand.

On the passenger seat, next to him in a large brown envelope, was the passports and documents that Tony had been waiting for. Lennie had done a first-rate job as always. Here was the gateway for his old buddy to start a new life wherever he wished. Lennie hoped that he would finally find some happiness.

He walked up to the front door and rang the bell. No response came.

After four more rings, he produced a spare key and entered the flat.

He walked into the living room and saw a few magazines and books covering the coffee table and a half empty bottle of *Jura* stood like a lone sentinel in the middle of it.

"Hey, Tony, are you still in bed? Wake up you, lazy bastard. Uncle Dougie has only come to deliver the goods. Your stuff is here, my friend. Happy days."

There was no answer.

Doug went upstairs. The bedroom was empty, and the bed was made neatly. He checked the wardrobes and found Tony's clothes still in there. In the bathroom, he found a razor and wash kit.

He searched the whole place, but there was no sign of Tony. Maybe he had gone out for one of his morning runs?

He sighed and placed the envelope down on the coffee table. He didn't really want to leave it without seeing Tony, but he was due to fly out to the States today on business, so he couldn't hang on to the stuff any longer.

He moved to the sideboard and found a scrap of paper and a pen, scribbled a note and left it next to the envelope. It read, "Doug has delivered, as promised, my old friend."

He tried Tony's mobile once more. Again, it went to answer phone. Typical, the man had been phoning him non-stop for weeks and now that he finally had the documents for him, he couldn't get him to answer the phone.

He decided to leave a message.

"Hey, Tony. This is Doug. I've left what you needed in the flat. Enjoy your new life, buddy, and give me a bell sometime."

He left the flat quietly with one last glance back and then drove away.

www.ingramcontent.com/pod-product-compliance
Lightning Source LLC
Chambersburg PA
CBHW030806260626
47169CB00001B/211